PRAISE FOR *WHERE WE LIVE*

"Approaching middle age, Cleo, Mandalay, and Cliff go through a year of unsettling changes to their careers, families, homes, and hearts. As they each discover the future is not what they expected, they must re-imagine who they are and where they want to be. In deft, clear prose, author Karen Hofmann unveils the simple, miraculous transformations that are always at work, though seldom noticed, in everyday life. *Where We Live* is a fine and richly textured work of art, a story both brilliant and wise."
—CATHERINE HUNTER, author of *After Light* and *St. Boniface Elegies*

"With keen insight that is often astonishing, Karen Hofmann describes the fragility of human connections, with all their beauty and their pain. She adopts a clear-eyed, even unflinching focus while still managing to convey enormous empathy for her characters, despite – or perhaps because of – their flaws. The Lund siblings are very real, very human, and completely unforgettable. At the end of the book, I experienced the satisfaction of having come to know and care for these individuals and the regret in having to say goodbye."
—MARGIE TAYLOR, author of *Rose Addams* and *Harrow Road*

"Home is the resonant concept at the heart of this trilogy about the Lund siblings. Hofmann details their widely varied personal and professional lives with intelligence and compassion. As always, her writing is informed by an insightful ethos of socioeconomic and environmental sustainability. *Where We Live* is an absorbing and immensely satisfying finale."

—ALICE ZORN, author of *Five Roses* and *Arrhythmia*

"*Where We Live* is a deeply gratifying conclusion to the Lund family saga. Karen Hofmann is at her very best; her prose moves with remarkable grace, illuminating the complex inner lives of her characters, who reflect back to us profound truths about aging, parenthood, grief, betrayal, and desire. While each of the characters ultimately finds their own sense of home, they also come away transformed, on the precipice of something new and full of possibility. You'll leave this novel bursting with hope."

—CORINNA CHONG, author of *The Whole Animal* and *Belinda's Rings*

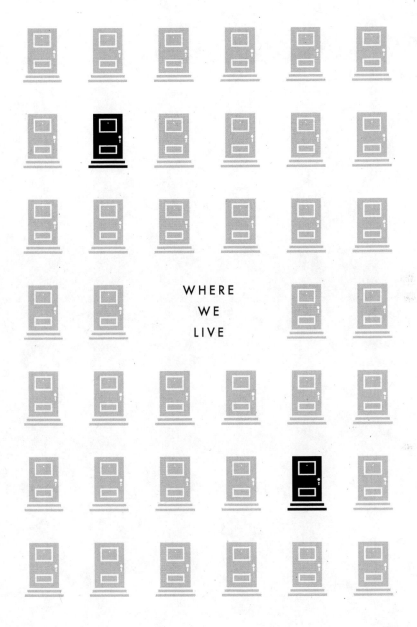

WHERE
WE
LIVE

WHERE WE LIVE

A NOVEL

KAREN HOFMANN

NeWest Press

Library and Archives Canada Cataloguing in Publication
Title: Where we live : a novel / Karen Hofmann.
Names: Hofmann, Karen (Author of Where we live), author.
Identifiers: Canadiana (print) 20230453910 | Canadiana (ebook) 20230453937 | ISBN 9781774390887 (softcover) | ISBN 9781774390894 (EPUB)
Classification: LCC PS8615.O365 W54 2024 | DDC C813/.6—DC23

NeWest Press wishes to acknowledge that the land on which we operate is Treaty 6 territory and a traditional meeting ground and home for many Indigenous Peoples, including Cree, Saulteaux, Niitsitapi (Blackfoot), Métis, and Nakota Sioux.

Editor for the Press: Anne Nothof
Cover and interior design: Natalie Olsen, Kisscut Design
Author photo: Julia Tomkins

NeWest Press acknowledges the support of the Canada Council for the Arts, the Alberta Foundation for the Arts, and the Edmonton Arts Council for support of our publishing program. We acknowledge the financial support of the Government of Canada through the Canada Book Fund for our publishing activities.

201, 8540 – 109 Street
Edmonton, AB T6G 1E6
780.432.9427
www.newestpress.com

NEWEST PRESS

No bison were harmed in the making of this book.
Printed and bound in Canada   1 2 3 4 5   26 25 24

*For my sister Katherine and my brothers Peter, Bernard, and William,
and for all siblings, who find in each other their first society.*

BEFORE

December, 2008

THE MESSAGE POPS UP in the airport in Managua, as soon as Ben's smartphone is picking up Wi-Fi again. In the main concourse, there is a highly polished granite floor, so smooth it seems like a mirror, showing everyone what they look like from below, and the usual row of clocks showing different times. Habana, La Paz, Londres, Los Angeles, as if anyone needed to know. As if it isn't always now, wherever you are. He almost doesn't read the message, which is only from his sister Cleo, until a word in the first line catches his eye. Hospital. He skims the message. Cliff, mudslide, spine, intensive care, surgery.

Bummer.

It's stopped him in his tracks and now Alison has noticed and turned around, stopped too. He clicks his phone off and slides it into the pocket of his shorts, takes a couple of longer strides to catch up with her.

Everything okay, dude? she asks.

Yeah, he says. Something minor.

Shit; he wishes he hadn't seen that message.

It won't take long to get through customs, Alison says. It's not a busy airport.

Through the glass front he can see a blue sky streaked with the kinds of clouds that say the wind and the water are alive. There are palm trees. And in the distance, far out there, a volcano.

He wants to stop and look at the scenery but Alison is leading him through the concourse, to the baggage carousels. The light and the siren go on just as they arrive, and luggage starts appearing on the belt. He sees his bag, first, an olive-green duffel, and then the long case with his board. He thinks he should look for Alison's and scoop it too, but he can't remember exactly which are hers, to be honest, and she grabs them herself before they look familiar. Slings a carrier over her shoulder, pops out the handle of her little wheeled hard case, begins leading the way out of the crowd.

God, she's well-made. There's so much efficiency in her movements. A kind of grace. And her frame is perfect: strong, spare, streamlined.

To the customs officials, she speaks Spanish. She actually gets one to crack a smile.

Alison has been here many times. Her family has a house here. They live in Vancouver, but they have a house in Nicaragua, where her father is involved in building hotels and her mom sources local jewellery – only fair trade, of course, Alison says – for import. Ben has never been to Nicaragua, or to Central America, before. His parents used to own a condo in Maui, and they always went there. Not nearly as interesting.

The surfing in Nicaragua is supposed to be spectacular.

In the lineup for customs his phone pings again, and he almost takes it out, automatic reflex, but then remembers. He doesn't want to see that. He doesn't want to know anything else.

Now back through the concourse to the exit, where, Alison says, checking her phone, a car will be waiting for them. They pass a grouping of eight heads on plinths. Women's heads.

They're meant to represent all of the cultures here, Alison says. Strong women from different cultures. I know one of the models.

The plinths are white marble, but the heads are black, the eyes featureless, without iris or pupil. Ben thinks that they are looking right through him. Judging him.

IT'S A THREE-HOUR DRIVE south and then west to the resort. They're in a four-wheel drive SUV, a heavy vehicle with tinted windows and a driver wearing a military-style uniform, dark aviator glasses, a mustache. You can nap if you want, Alison says. The first part is boring.

It is; they drive through endless farmland punctuated by small villages. Occasionally they skirt a town or city in which Ben can see neighbourhoods of low, red-roofed buildings crushed in among palms and dense dark tropical trees. Alison falls asleep almost instantly, but he is unable to, and the driver doesn't speak English, so he is forced to look at the miles of boring, and somewhat depressing, scenery.

What is he going to do about the message from Cleo? It had been sent while he was in flight, several hours before. He wants to ignore it; he's just starting out on a holiday, and it was stupid for it to arrive at that point. It's not like he can do anything about it.

It occurs to him that maybe he would have been expected to telephone, from the airport. Or even to get the first flight back. Would that be expected of him? He hadn't had time to process, to think. Alison had rushed him. No; that wasn't totally fair. He hadn't said anything to her. She had no reason not to move through the airport as swiftly as possible.

Is he going to have to say something, now? It will totally spoil the holiday, if he does. The news will cast a pall. And she might expect him to go back to Vancouver. Her parents might expect that. After the three-hour ride to the resort, they might expect him to go back to Managua and fly home. They will wonder why he drove out, even. Of course he could pretend that he just got the text, but Alison had seen him stop and react to a text in the airport. She had noticed something; she had commented on it. No way that she won't remember that and wonder if he got the text then, rather than later.

Dammit and dammit.

Better to just ignore it completely. Or not mention it. He can wait and not respond to the message, see what happens. Cleo will message him again, if there's a change. At that point he can make a decision.

Yes, for sure. That's what he must do. It's the only logical thing.

The driver says something and motions to a cooler on the front seat. Ben can see that it's plugged into the auxiliary outlet. He opens the case: it holds about a dozen bottles of drinks. There are some American brands and some local soft drinks, and a few bottles of beer. He wants the beer, but it might not look good to be drinking beer while Alison sleeps. He's thirsty, though. The vehicle is air-conditioned, but the heat devils coming off the pavement, on the road ahead tell him it's hot out. He grabs a bottle of the local pop, something clear as water. It has to be opened with a bottle opener – no screw-top – and it tastes like caramelized banana.

Okay, that was a surprise.

He hadn't even known that you could go to Nicaragua, till he met Alison. He'd assumed, maybe from his school classes or news on TV when he was a kid, that it was a totally Third World country, all jungle and guerilla fighters. Alison had thought that was funny. It's being developed, like everywhere else, she said.

She told him that it had some of the best surfing in the world.

She has listed sideways in her sleep so that she's leaning on him, and he lowers her gently onto his lap. She has the clearest skin, almost transparent. Her freckles are like flecks of mica or something just under the surface.

She's perfect.

The driver makes a sharp turn at a town called Barrio San Isidro and now they are heading west, through more farmland, but with scrubby hills to their right. On the hills, small puffs of smoke rise every few hundred metres. Peasants slash-burning the forest for more farmland, Ben guesses. Or do they have peasants, in Nicaragua?

Alison wakes up then. She wakes up like a Disney princess from a really old animated film, *Snow White* maybe. She opens her eyes and yawns a little pink-tongued yawn and smiles at him.

It is possibly at that point that he decides that he should try to stake some permanent claim to her. Well, semi-permanent. As permanent as people generally manage. A warmth spreads generally through him. Yes, it's a good idea. He's going to do it. He has the whole trip to do this.

That makes the issue of the message about Cliff even more inopportune. About Cliff's accident. How to handle that? Because he sees now that he has only been looking at it one way: as a bummer. What the hell was Cliff thinking, et cetera. News that would taint him with a sort of depressing aura, when his hosts were trying to celebrate Christmas. It would make him a sort of bleak drippy presence in the house, inhibiting them from celebrating properly. Every time one of them tried to tell a funny story, share a laugh, they'd think: *Oh but think about poor Ben. His brother.* And they'd sober up. And it would all stick to him: he'd be remembered forever as the dark cloud over the party.

But now that he's had a little time to think, he sees that there's a whole other way of progressing with this. It's the timing. That's what he needs to manage. Everything else should be very simple, very natural. He can set it up a bit, even. There's going to be those evenings, the family dinners, and the parents are going to be, like, so what do you do, Ben? Do you have siblings? And he'll tell them his story. Bit by bit he'll let them have it, how he was reunited with his family, because that's a beautiful story. Alison had teared up, when he'd told her. Actually, he'll let her tell it. She will enjoy that. She'll tell it better. And then he'll let it out reluctantly, his business partnership with Cliff, he'll let them winkle it out of him. The landscape company he and Cliff formed; how he took it on to help out his new-found bro. He won't have to say much. He won't have to say anything that's not true. He won't even have to say directly that Cliff's a bit slow.

He has been surprised by Alison, by some of her ideas. Of course she's very young, twenty-four to his thirty-one, and she hasn't seen so much of the world, so she is still kind of idealistic. Still kind of naïve. Example: she frowned at him and went stiff that time he made the joke about the autistic guy at the counter. He'd had to change course quickly. And the actors and characters in movies that she admires: girls his age — girls he knew when he was younger — he would have laughed at them, would have dismissed them as geeky losers. It's almost like Alison is from a different generation.

He can use that. If he's careful, if he gets the right detail, the right language. Alison's family will eat Cliff up, or at least Ben's version of him.

Then at the end of the holiday, maybe. The news. There might be more news, then, anyway. He'll just have to turn his phone off, until then, only look at his messages when he's alone, in case Cleo tries to contact him again. And then, maybe the last day they're here, he'll get the message and tell them. Yes.

My brother Cliff has been injured. I have to go back. But only at the end of the holiday.

He looks across at Alison. She's watching him. She really likes him; he can see that. She tries to hide it but she's not old enough to do it smoothly. She's into him. He looks at her perfect features and her clear skin, cleaner than anything he knows, and feels tears spring in the deep passages of his skull. He has to keep her. He just has to.

2016

1

ON HER FIFTIETH BIRTHDAY Mandalay Lund sleeps late, wakes to glittery February sunlight filtering through her muslin curtains, the house ticking with the movements of its other inhabitants, her not-quite-sixteen-year-old sons. For a few moments she gathers herself from the spaces into which her consciousness has travelled in sleep: the forests and sidewalks and studios. She identifies herself: a consciousness in a familiar room. She re-enters her roles: artist, teacher, mother. She relocates herself: a Vancouver morning; her house; her birthday. She re-assembles herself, consciously, as if she is re-entering her skin.

For a few moments she lies still, yawning, luxuriating. She's going to do very little, this day. It happens to be a non-teaching day for her. She's going to enjoy it. She imagines a leisurely walk, tea sipped while leafing through old issues of her collection of art and design magazines on the sofa. Some yoga. Maybe window shopping. Even the contemplation of simple pleasures is a luxury.

She remembers that she has also meetings with her department chair and with Duane, her sons' father, booked today. Unfortunately. But how to fit them in, otherwise?

She could lie here for hours, but a full bladder propels her, barefoot, along creaking floorboards to the bathroom, and although she gets back into bed, her footsteps and the sound of running water have set in motion a whole series of reactions from downstairs. She hears kitchen cupboards and drawers opening and shutting, utensils and crockery shifting. Feet on the stairs. And then here are her sons appearing in her bedroom doorway: Aidan, a little shorter and slighter, tousled, dressed in his usual school uniform, in front, and Owen, flushed and still damp from his early morning practice and shower, gap-toothed, in sweats, just behind. They have brought her coffee, orange juice, fresh-squeezed, gifts. They have got the coffee just right.

Happy birthday, Mother, they say.

You lovely children, she says.

Owen stretches out on the bed beside her and Aidan sits on the end.

We'll do your presents later, Aidan says. We have to get to school.

I don't need presents, Mandalay says, as always. It's their ritual. You two are everything I need. She means this, completely.

But we need to give you presents, Aidan says.

She leans forward to hug him, but Owen pulls her back, an arm around her shoulders.

How she loves her sons: her perfect, beautiful, kind, thoughtful boys. Her eyes moisten. In this moment, she has perfect happiness.

If she could preserve any moment in her life forever, it might be this one.

It's a day to give herself. A non-teaching day, and as a part-time instructor on a contract, she doesn't need to be in the studio, or her office, or attend meetings. She'll order supper in.

Her sons leave for school. The house in which they have all lived for over fifteen years is quiet; she hears only the white noise of the hum of the old refrigerator, the ticking of ancient plumbing, the creak of the floorboards as they jostle each other for growing room.

She rolls out her yoga mat. She could use a new one. (Maybe she could exchange some of Owen's spa voucher for a new yoga mat? Would the spa sell yoga mats?) This one, she has been using so long that it has chew marks along one edge, and the lilac-coloured foam has taken on a beige tinge, like smog over an evening sky. Should she wipe it down, at least, before she uses it?

No matter. She'll shower after. She lowers herself to the floor, maintaining consciousness through her torso and limbs. Her knees protest, a feeling like a sticky hinge. She observes her sit bones' position on the mat; she notes the slight tension in her shoulders. She reaches her upper body forward, stretching, rolling out her spine, creating space between her vertebrae. She settles into her body. Her body opens, speaks.

She had never imagined being fifty years old. But this is still her body, still strong, supple. She has a belly, now, where she used to have a flat waist; flesh spills over the containment of her bra; her bottom has lost some of its roundness. In the mirror, she sees a multiplicity of white threads in her hair, a translucency beneath her eyes, and pouches below her jaw. None of these things are welcome. They are signs, after all, of the body breaking down. They are signs that her estrogen has subsided. She no longer bleeds; she is past childbearing. But it is not as bad as she would have expected, at twenty, or thirty. It does not feel so bad. She can still see herself with pleasure, in her body.

She will weather middle age well, she thinks. She is not so identified with youthfulness. She has accepted that her fertile days are over. She has no regrets or unfulfilled girlish fantasies. She has kept up with current social ideas and with technology. She will be fine.

Later in the morning, she goes to her computer, set up as usual on the dining table, and begins to scroll through the online conversations she follows – on printmaking, which is her field, but also on consciousness, on mind-body awareness, on vegan cooking. She checks in to see what is happening in the worlds of master classes and retreats, residencies, galleries. Could she scrape together some grant money and go to this printmakers' colony in Baton Rouge for a month? Not this year: she needs more lead time. Grant applications are slow to assemble and be processed. As a contract instructor, she doesn't have PD funds. But maybe next year.

She imagines herself in the place she sees in the images: a site with weathered cabins, trees she doesn't recognize, red earth. She can imagine her hands on the equipment in the studios, pulling some new prints. Something earthy, wild, emphatic, in her work.

She opens a new window on her laptop, the government artists' grant site. The application process looks daunting, as usual. Statements of intent to write. Lists of recent shows to identify. Pages to be filled out by referees. Maybe next year. But the thought of the retreat, of spending a month at the artists' colony, walking barefoot through the warm dust, encountering new visions and personalities, soaking in a more vivid sunlight, warms her, creates a new space in her. A gift to herself.

As she's leaving the house later, her cell phone rings: her sister Cleo, with birthday greetings. Had Mandalay got the flowers Cleo had sent?

She has, and says thank you, belatedly. Also: Thank you for the gift card.

What will you do tonight? Cleo asks. Will you go out for dinner? Is someone throwing you a fiftieth birthday party?

Cleo never remembers Mandalay's friends' names.

Takeout with the boys, Mandalay says. A flick of sadness, now, like the brush of an animal's tail. Belinda would have thrown her a party, if she were well enough.

Cleo says: Have you talked to Crystal lately?

Crystal is their mother, from whom they were estranged since they were around twelve and thirteen to adulthood. She lives several hours' drive away, and seems to be declining, lately, though she has always been on the edge – of something. Of dysfunction, or complete dissolution, depending on your point of view. A minefield of a topic for conversation.

Depends on what Cleo means by *lately*. But anyway, she doesn't want to talk about Crystal today.

So I guess I've talked to her more recently than you have. I was wondering if you were finding her any different.

Different in what way?

More wandering. More forgetful.

Cleo is always very reactive to their mother's vagueness. She always wants to discuss Crystal with Mandalay. Or their brothers, Ben and Cliff, who are each struggling. Cleo takes too much on.

It's just who Crystal is, Mandalay says, firmly.

Cleo sighs and says, Have a happy one! We should get together soon!

Yes, we should, Mandalay murmurs. But they won't, she knows.

MANDALAY WALKS UP MAIN, over to Cambie, browsing shops. She's heading for a shop she likes – the one for which Cleo has given her a gift card. It's a new store, an upmarket home décor shop. It had previously been a rather funky five-and-dime, a shabby, small dollar store, more accurately – the kind that looks like it must be a front for drug dealing or illegal gambling, so unappealing and useless are its wares. She remembers how it had lured her sons with the garish plastic objects. Their noses pressed against the dirty glass.

The new shop is nearly empty, one wall bearing live-edge wood shelves sparsely lined with small pottery bowls and folded textiles, everything neutral, ironically negating, hip as can be. She spots a basket that she instantly desires, and enters the store to peep at its price tag. Tiny handwriting on a doll-sized tag, tied on with string. A hundred and fifty dollars. For a basket. Oh, my. But suddenly she wants a birthday present, something small even. Near the door, a bowl of small elegant wooden scoops. (What would one use them for? Coffee beans?) But they are over twenty dollars.

That must be what it costs for someone to make something like that. But who can afford that, twenty bucks for a tiny wooden scoop?

On the other hand, if everyone had fewer, and more beautiful objects, wouldn't the world be a better place?

AIDAN HANDS MANDALAY his birthday gift for her. He has handmade a card, which he does every year, and which she treasures as the real gift. He's done a linocut print on a piece of embossed wallpaper glued to cardstock. There's a pleasing overlay of texture and pattern. A motif of tiny teal-coloured whales is topped with an orange umbrella-shaped spout of tiny raindrops. It's witty and well-executed. There are five whales, each spouting ten raindrops.

No crits, Aidan says, teasing. She reads his message: I wanted to do a whale for every year, but the card stock isn't big enough! Ha ha! Thanks for being the best mom and supplier of art materials ever!

She leans forward again, catches Aidan this time in a quick squeeze before he presses her to open his gift, which he has also made himself. It's a heavy denim apron, the kind she wears in the studio. He has printed this item with a giant tentacled creature that emerges from the lower right corner and stretches its arms in a roiling, energetic fan across the fabric.

It's a giant squid? Octopus?

A kraken, he says. And I'll need to borrow it back to get my grade on it.

She laughs. Lovely, lovely, she says. I'll wear it always.

You could market those, Owen says with interest. It's very pro.

Maybe Circle Craft, on Granville Island, Mandalay says.

Those shops take too much commission, Owen says. Online.

He sounds just like Duane.

Aidan says: It's only fun to make one-offs.

Aidan, the artist. He gets it.

Owen's card is one from a stash Mandalay keeps above her desk, in the kitchen. She buys them at charity craft fairs: cards made by disabled artists, featuring foot or mouth painting, or colourful naïve motifs of birds and flowers. Owen has written *50 trips around the sun! Congratulations and you qualify for a free wash with fill-up!* and filled the rest of the space with xoxs. His gift is a spa card.

I'm not artsy like Aidan, he says.

It's perfect, she says. It's perfect.

Through long, long practice, she has learned to never show the slightest preference for one son over another. She thinks that she manages this, most of the time. They are, all three, happy, most of the time.

2

CLEO LUND LOVES HER HOUSE.

It is a fantastic house, built by a famous architect in the 1960s. Every room is like a sculpture of visually interesting planes and angles, light, texture, the subtle natural colours of wood and stone. The house flows, a creature of light and space. Every wall, every surface, surprises and delights and inspires. There is no wasted space, only golden means and perfect balance and sublime vistas. There are large windows, perfectly situated, and a handsome stone fireplace and a cleverly engineered staircase of fir treads that seem to float on their steel posts. The surfaces are polished concrete, fir, granite, glass, steel. Carefully curated furnishings of burnished ceramic tile, leather, organic fibres glow like art objects. There are no frills or flounces; nothing small or artificial looking. Not an extraneous detail. It is a beautiful, beautiful house.

Cleo is gratified that she still loves it, several years after buying it. She had worried that she might not. She had wanted it so much, had fought and worked for it so strenuously, that she had assumed that it would all backfire – that it wouldn't live up to her expectations, or that she'd burn out her passion for it. A house can't love you back, her sister Mandalay had said to her, once. But she is happy in her house, as Mandalay is, also, in hers.

At a brief low point in the real estate market, seven or eight years before, Cleo had found this house, through a conversation with a colleague she'd met at a conference, another engineer who shared her interest in architecture and had arranged through a contact to see it – although it wasn't on the market – and had fallen in love with its inspired lines, its credentials, of course, but also with its open concept design: flowing space, large windows, generous bedrooms and bathrooms, sleek, minimalist fittings.

Cleo's husband Trent had not loved the house. He had not wanted to buy it, and had to be persuaded. When they'd viewed the house, he'd only seen the orange tile countertops, the shag carpets, the faux-kitsch 70s light fixtures. He couldn't see, as she could, the house's great bones. He'd pointed out that she had always wanted to live in Metro Vancouver, and this house was still in the suburbs. Trent had worried that prices would fall further, that they should wait.

They had sold their house in anticipation of a market crash, in the aftermath of '08, and the market had gone down significantly, but not as much as Trent, an accountant, thought it would. But she could see the signs that the market was soon going to pick up by the increased number of calls the architecture firm she worked at was getting each week, and in her conversations with developers. Cleo knew it was the right thing. She, not Trent, understood houses, had access to the wind-shifts of the real estate market. For the first time in their married life, she had summoned up all of her resources, and had fought for the house. She had screwed her courage to the sticking point, and more or less bullied him into it, violating the terms of the unspoken treaty that her marriage (like most marriages) contained. She had cornered him, made him look at engineering reports and countertop samples. She had sat up in bed at night talking about glulam beams and in-floor heating and heat pumps and triple-pane argon filled windows, which had to be installed, since they had not existed, in the late 1960s, when the house was built. She had made Trent watch documentaries about the Modernist movement in architecture, its failure to convince. She had driven him around suburb after suburb and pointed out how house after house was simply a banal box, little changed from a cottage of three hundred years ago. She had explained how builders' houses were still put together using materials and techniques that hadn't changed in centuries: a length of timber a man could carry; a hammer and saw and nails; insulation and finishing wiring jobbed out, as they would have been in days of trade schools and guilds. She had brought him spreadsheets to show how this beautiful, rare house could not possibly lose them money.

The house had mattered to her more than anything else had for years: she knew both rationally and intuitively that it was the right house.

For bullying Trent, and for her passion for the house, she had expected to pay. Beyond Trent's snarling and threats – you'll have to get another job if the market falls; you'll be working until you're eighty; I'm not going to bail you out – she had thought she would have to pay. She had suspected at some level in herself that the unforeseen could arise, that the purchase could turn out to be a mistake, that she would be unable to derive pleasure from her win.

But she has not paid. She loves the house. It has turned out well. The house had needed no walls torn down, no beams or foundations augmented. The roof had been newer, hadn't needed replacing. She had known all of this would be so. Or not exactly known, but had made educated guesses. As a structural engineer, she knew what to look for.

She had put her heart and head into restoring it. She'd treated it as if it were a project for her most important client. She'd been on constant alert for good buys, for samples, for trends. She had used work hours (shamefully) to source materials. (But she often does work for her clients at home, in her own time – the boundaries are always blurred. Creative work happens when she is on the stationary bike, loading the dishwasher, driving to pick up kids.) She had used her connections with contractors to get various things done – the painting, the refinishing of the hardwood floors, the installation of new bathroom and kitchen fixtures.

It is the culmination of all of her skills and knowledge. It is perfect.

And it has functioned marvellously as a home. The big open kitchen and eating and living area have worked out fantastically. The children did their homework and played games and drew at the big table. They perched on stools at the kitchen work counters and talked to her while she cooked, and began helping her cook, and began to cook themselves. She and Trent began entertaining, having great parties. The children's friends came over; in the rec room, down-stairs, there were wrap-around bookcases built under the windows in which games and craft supplies and DVDs were stored. She'd bought foam mattresses and unbreakable dishes, and for several years, there had been sleepover parties almost every weekend.

Trent has a den, with a big-screen TV and a vibrating lounge chair and even a small fridge. He doesn't even need to come out.

And Cleo has a home office that is bright and efficient.

She had wanted the house, and she had worked hard for it, and achieved it. The house is a success. She had imagined it a success, and it is. And it's now worth double what they paid for it, according to recent sales in the neighbourhood, and of similar houses. Even factoring in the cost of the heat pump and new kitchen and bath-room fixtures, and especially the new windows, which they have just finished paying off, they have made money. Even Trent says that. Often.

Cleo loves the house, unconditionally.

ON THIS FRIDAY IN APRIL, Cleo moves around her house tidying, wiping things down, bringing it back to life with the movements of her hands. She has taken this day off, a vacation day, a catch-up day. The cleaning person has been there, within the last couple of days, so there is not so much heavy work, but details. She does laundry. She throws out the wilted vegetables and the leftovers. She wipes surfaces: the stainless steel of the appliances, the granite of the countertops, the porcelain of the bathroom sinks, the tile and glass and brushed nickel finishes of the house. She sweeps the breakfast crumbs; she finds a stray game piece under a bench and returns it to its box. She moves around her spacious, well-appointed, highly-functional kitchen. She lines up the ebonized wishbone chairs around the long maple table. She wipes a fingerprint from the surface of one chair back. She straightens pillows and magazines on the big sectional sofa and the coffee table. She opens a window, and can smell the rain that has just ended, the green April vegetation, and the sea. A house sparrow is singing, operatically, on the rhododendron. She opens blinds to let in the sunlight.

She moves to her daughter Olivia's room, to prepare it. Olivia will be home for a week, on a visit. Cleo hesitates before turning the door-knob. There is a long-standing agreement, or perhaps more an edict, as she does not agree to it: she may not enter Olivia's room without permission. A family therapist had decreed this, years ago, when Olivia was fifteen and acting out. Neither Cleo nor Trent was allowed to go into Olivia's room. This did not seem reasonable: Cleo and Trent *paid* for the house; it was *their* house. Olivia was a *child*: not contributing, economically; not able to make responsible decisions.

Cleo only wanted to enter to intervene in terms of decay and waste: to scoop up clothes; to empty the overflowing wastepaper baskets; to collect dirty dishes from under piles of discarded clothing. Cleo had been willing to agree to a compromise: Olivia would do her own laundry, and Cleo would not touch her clothes. Olivia was supposed to empty her garbage on a weekly basis and return dishes to the kitchen on a daily basis, if she didn't want Cleo to come into her room. But the therapist had said: No; absolutely no. You are not allowed in. That is Olivia's space.

Only because I cede it to her, Cleo had thought, but she had bitten her tongue. It had seemed more expedient at the time to appear cooperative, appear a reasonable person, willing to compromise.

But Olivia has been gone now for four years. She has almost finished her bachelor's degree; she would be finished, except that she changed her major. She has got a summer job in Toronto, where she has been studying; it's a research job, on campus. She hasn't come home for the summers for a couple of years now. This trip is only a visit.

The room still contains most of Olivia's things: her childhood books, the shelves of *Harry Potter* and Lemony Snicket and Laura Ingalls Wilder; the furniture, the framed art on the walls, a toy-store's worth of stuffed animals, tubs of artwork and dance-recital costumes. The room has been empty since the Christmas holidays. The cleaner doesn't go into it.

Olivia had eventually begun to return her dirty dishes, to take care of her laundry on her visits home but not until a couple of years ago. Cleo had dealt with the restrictions by buying more place settings of the dishes, by sometimes sneaking in, retrieving crusty cereal bowls, spaghetti-stained plates, yogurt-coated silverware, and smoothie-covered glasses when Olivia was out, carefully replacing any item she had to pick up to retrieve dishes. A burglar in her own house. It was not reasonable, but it was practical.

She had fired the therapist, of course. Eventually. The therapist had actually taught Cleo and Trent some useful techniques for communicating with Olivia. And Sam.

Cleo brings the vacuum cleaner into the deserted room; she dusts the surfaces; she strips the bed and washes the bedding. There is a lot of dust. A crazy amount of dust. Where does all of the dust come from?

It's satisfying, though, cleaning the room, making it spotless.

She spreads the fresh sheets on Olivia's abandoned bed; she smooths the duvet cover, plumps the pillows in their shams. She puts clean folded towels in Olivia's bathroom.

She would not want to do this every day. It's pleasant, as a one-off. She would be bored out of her mind if it was the sum total of her life. She wonders if she should even be doing it. There are a few voices in her head that are sneering, commenting that she is somehow wasting her time, squandering her mind on the mundane and frivolous, showing off, spoiling her daughter, or furthering traditional agendas, by taking half a day off to tidy and primp. *Pimp*, her children would say, a term that her children have picked up from reality TV, and that she especially dislikes. She feels conflicted: that she is doing something that is both necessary and disapproved of.

She doesn't clean Sam's room; Sam does it himself, and adequately. Sam is at school; he has an after-school job with the children's science camp run by the university. It's the same camp he went to when he was younger. Sam teaches some beginner coding and robotics to the kids. He's good with children: playful, gentle, extraordinarily patient. When he comes home at the end of the day, though, he's exhausted. He retreats to his room. He doesn't want dinner. He eats later, after she and Trent have gone to bed. Cleo leaves plated food for him to warm up. Trent says she is coddling him, but if Sam is rustling around in the kitchen, getting plates out of cupboards, he wakes her up. It's not that he's loud, but the sense that someone is moving around in the house, past midnight, disturbs her.

She's only being practical, leaving food plated for him.

Sam is no trouble. He's polite, respectful, if not tidy. He is dependable at his job. He does not come home drunk or smoke pot in his room, in the way many of Cleo's and Trent's friends and colleagues report their kids do. He does not go out much at all, but if he prefers solitude, what does it matter? Cleo has known the torment of being forced to socialize when she didn't feel like it. She won't inflict that on her children.

Of course, it's useful, learning to socialize: she has to interact with people all of the time, at work. But Sam, perhaps, will find a job in which this is not a requirement. She thinks, she hopes, that the world will be a more accommodating, a more flexible place for her children's generation.

She hopes that Olivia will not be too tired, in this week between the end of her classes and the beginning of her summer research job. Olivia had cried a lot on the phone this past year. Cleo had thought that Olivia would come home for the summer, take the summer off. But the job had been too good to turn down. Trent had said she should take it. It's a technically difficult job, Cleo thinks, for an undergraduate.

Olivia had cried on the phone that she was *so, so tired*. Cleo had tried not to jump in, to feel out first whether Olivia needed encouragement or a care package or a pep talk. But Trent had offered to fly her home for the week, if she could take it off. After the flight had been booked, Olivia had seemed less anxious to come back. I don't get any time off all summer, she had said. I don't know if I want to waste a whole week going home.

Perhaps she hadn't said *waste*. Perhaps she had just said *use up*.

Cleo puts a fresh bar of soap on the soap dish and fills the liquid soap dispenser. She knows they will not be the right kind of soaps. On her last trip home, at Christmas, Olivia had produced a fleet of little black-and-white tubes: soap and shampoo and moisturizer and toothpaste, with self-consciously semi-witty satiric names like Smear and Wipe and Ooze. Well, probably not *Ooze*. They looked like they had probably cost a lot. Things that look like they are being aggressively different than mainstream trends, especially in a kind of grungy way, usually are obscenely expensive, Cleo has noticed. Olivia had explained why they were so much better – environmentally, dermatologically, aesthetically – than the commercial brands that Cleo buys.

Cleo had thought of trying to find them, to stock the bathroom for Olivia's current visit. But she guesses, she knows, that Olivia will almost certainly have moved onto something else. It's completely possible that she will have disavowed boutique personal products entirely, and now be a fan of two-dollar bars from the grocery stores in Chinatown.

Why does she do this? (Why do you do that, Trent asks, finding her ironing pillow shams the night before Olivia arrives. Why do you do that? Sam asks, as she piles harissa-flavoured hummus and kale chips and vegan cashew-based pistachio ice cream into her grocery cart.)

Because she wants Olivia to feel fêted, pampered. Loved. She hardly sees Olivia, her first child, her only daughter. Which is normal, of course. She can't complain about Olivia going to school four thousand kilometres away, and returning only twice a year for short visits. That is normal. She misses Olivia, though. She cleans Olivia's room and prepares her bathroom with special soap and buys the food Olivia likes because she misses her. It's a ritual of welcome, of appreciation. Isn't it?

Because she does not know how else to say: I miss you terribly.

She had been disappointed that Olivia had chosen to go to university in Ontario, when she could have gone to a first-rate place while commuting from home. She and Trent had tried to talk Olivia out of it. She could live at home, commute. They'd pay her tuition, and she could work part-time in the summer, or take more classes, or work a bit and then travel. (They were both in agreement that she should have to work a little, contribute something, so she didn't get in the habit of being given everything, like some kids they knew about, the wrecks of offspring of some of Cleo's and Trent's wealthier clients.) Olivia would have to work. But living at home, everyone would save. And she could go somewhere else for her Master's, which would matter more. Trent had even offered to buy her a second-hand car, which Olivia certainly didn't need, in the satellite cities of greater Vancouver.

Olivia had been immovable. She had to go away. She couldn't stand living with them any longer. There had been shouting matches between her and Trent. Olivia's report cards had been invoked. They were fine report cards, A's and B's. All A's, for the last year, but not enough to get Olivia a full-ride scholarship. She had got a government voucher for a year's free tuition. She'd negotiated Trent's foolhardy offer of a second-hand car into a contribution of a few thousand more. If you could give it to me for a car, you can afford it, she had shouted, and Trent had caved in the face of her ranting, if not her logic.

They could afford to pay for her to go to university anywhere she wanted, really. Anywhere in Canada, at least. And at least she planned to do something practical, not a fine arts degree. It was just that it was an unnecessary expense, when she could live at home and go to a first-tier university.

In the end Cleo and Trent had given in, had decided to finance her. Four years, they had told her. But you have to keep your grades up. They had agreed between them, finally, to give in. Trent had said, one night as he and Cleo were going to bed, that it would be worth it to have a peaceful house. Olivia's screaming, all of the arguing, was going to kill him off early. His blood pressure was already dangerously high. He couldn't do it. He couldn't live with it.

And things *were* more peaceful, with Olivia gone. No more arguments, no sudden blow-ups over Olivia's messes, her spills of food on expensive furniture, her belongings strewn everywhere, her late-night noise, her refusal to get up, her wholesale appropriation of family belongings: Sam's hooded jackets; Trent's LPs, phone and laptop chargers. (Once she had unplugged Cleo's laptop, taking the charger, and Cleo had found it dead Monday morning when she needed it for a meeting.)

It was much more peaceful, once she moved out. Sam came out of his room more. The weekends and evenings were calm. Cleo and Trent had fewer fights.

Almost four years now. It has been successful. Olivia had switched majors, after her second year, so has lost some time, but she had been doing well. She had got summer research jobs on campus, had begun staying in Ontario. She'd won some small scholarships. They're still supporting her, and have paid for her flights back and forth, but they'd hardly noticed the money. On recent visits, Olivia and Trent have actually had some extended, civil conversations. Trent takes an interest in Olivia's field of study, economics. Olivia seems confident, able to marshal her facts, build an argument. Trent seems to listen to her ideas. It's much more amicable. The separation had done them all good, Trent says, and she has to agree.

It is only this feeling Cleo has, that her child is lost. It's not rational, so she doesn't pay it much attention, but it's the feeling that Olivia, so far away, seen so seldom, is lost, missing. It's like a hole in her viscera. Like a small animal, a fox or something, finding its pup gone, howling, in its incomprehension, the aching drive of its instinct: where is my pup? It's just a vestige of her lower brain function, Cleo knows that. But it's there, that aching: my child is lost. Just under the skin, sometimes, when she's not busy, when she slows down.

Cleo picks up the vacuum cleaner and dusters and glances around the room once more. It's a lovely room: large, beautifully proportioned, with a multitude of built-in fir shelves and drawers, a large built-in desk. She had replaced the worn-out carpeting, when they moved in, with authentic linoleum, lively with colour flecks; there's a good wool rug in an abstract design, a double bed. It's all clean and bright and harmonious.

It's a room so large that a whole family might occupy it, in a Third World country.

She hopes Olivia will be happy.

3

CLIFF LUND DESCENDS THE STAIRS in his two-story condo one at a time, gingerly, as if his spine were made of blown glass, as if he were balancing a platter of eggs on his crown. Grips the handrail, but not too tightly. He pulled it out of the wall, once – he can see the patchwork, still, rough and unpainted, where he reattached the supports. Some handrail, that pulls out of the wall when you need it!

Grip the handrail and bend the knee of the supporting leg and lower the pelvis. That's the hard part. There are some muscles in the back that work the pelvis. He can feel them seize up a little. But his back is better today. Quite a bit better. He can move around; he can go down stairs. He could probably go to work. He wouldn't be able to bend or lift but he could do up invoices or schedules or drive. He could mow. But he's not allowed to work, even on the good days, or he'll lose his insurance cheque.

Down the stairs is the garage, which is at present housing not his or Veronika's vehicles, but instead a small cityscape of boxes, bins, crates, cartons, cabinets. In them are clothing, paperwork, tools, files. Some of it is Veronika's, some his, but most of it seems like stuff generated by the house itself.

And some – the grey metal cabinets, the blue metal chests on casters – are the remains of his business, his former business. If he opens them, he'll see old invoices, old payroll printouts with the Lund Brothers logo. He'll see bumper stickers and logo-decorated hats. He'll see rusting clippers and edgers and pruning saws, chalk reels and tank sprayers and cartridge masks, all surplus when his business was bought out, on the verge of bankruptcy, and downsized. Some of the vehicles and larger equipment had been sold off, but he'd kept the extra tools.

He'd thought, maybe, that he'd be able to rebuild, to buy back the business. That he'd need this stuff again. He won't. That's all there is to it. It's all rusting away in his garage, which he needs because the strata council has come up with some new rule about how many parking spots everyone can have. He needs to clear it out. He's never going to need the files from his business again, and he's not going to give them to the new owners, who aren't even the ones who bought him out.

He's asked Veronika to move out her stuff, her boxes of clothes and broken irons and defunct remote controls, but she says she won't until he deals with his own stuff. Fair enough.

He ought to do it now, while he has some time on his hands. He knows that. Any good day, any day when he can get off the couch, he needs to get at this stuff. Cliff has never been a slacker. He knows how to put time to good use.

He's not very motivated to do it, he'll admit that. Go through all of this so that Veronika's car can be moved into the garage. There isn't anything to be achieved by it. It's not like he's building something. He's just being forced to do it.

He doesn't want to look at this stuff again. Also, it hurts his back, to bend over.

He finds a discarded office chair, releases the hydraulic lever so the seat is at its lowest setting. That's better. He can sit, knees good and high, and put boxes at lap level to sort through. At least look through.

He pulls closer a banker's box that's sitting on top of a stack. It's packed with printouts of customer accounts from oh-seven to oh-eight. He recognizes addresses, attaches them to properties in his mind's eye: Osler Street, Marine Drive, Marlow Place. He remembers a box hedge cut to razor-precision, a concourse of waterfalls, ponds stocked with a rainbow of water lilies, a slope forested in daphne and viburnum and flowering current and rhododendrons, each carefully placed so that they created a three-dimensional dance of light.

They'd lost those accounts, after the company re-formed and Cliff had been demoted from co-owner to employee. They were too expensive to keep going. So much skilled manpower involved. They haven't done much of the private landscaping and design work, the last several years – more public plantings, mass infill of juniper and begonias in waxy, unnatural reds, acres of lawn, which can be maintained by once-a-week mowing in summer.

He doesn't like to think of the design work, the finessing of rare plants and complicated plantings, these days. Something in the past.

He has no appetite for this chore.

What if he were to shred the lot? He has a paper shredder. He could do that: turn it all into paper spaghetti, bundle it in bags, stuff it in the recycling bin at the bottom of the strata parking lot. Not sort it; just shred the lot.

Would it be needed, though? At some point, would somebody come along wanting to see a document, and find it missing? In his horticulture program, he's had to take classes in bookkeeping, and the instructor had lectured them extensively on the legal ramifications of keeping records. So many small business owners, she had said, have lost everything because they couldn't produce the necessary document in a dispute.

That would have been the early 90s, maybe? They hadn't learned to use computers, in that course. Adding machines.

Nobody has asked for anything from these boxes for ten years, and that's the truth.

He'd had his own company. Well, he had owned it with his brother Ben. Lund Brothers, they'd called it. He'd inherited it from his previous employer, Mrs. Cookshaw. She had died, and, surprisingly, left him her company, the client list, the equipment, a lease on a shed and yard where vehicles and tools and supplies could be stored. He'd brought that into the new company, as well as his landscaping experience and his horticultural knowledge, and his brother Ben had brought cash, had bought in as a partner.

There are companies that will do your shredding for you. He has seen the trucks. And companies that will come and take away your trash, recycle what's useable, deliver the rest to the dump. He could just do that. He'd really like to do that right now, just call a truck and have it come and take everything. Every single thing that's in the garage, whoosh, into the back of some big dump truck, maybe one with a crusher. Yeah. Just *whoosh*, and the garage clean and empty. He'd like that so much.

They were supposed to be partners, he and Ben. But Ben had done less and less of the work – even the managing work. He'd taken company funds, been careless with them. He'd lost them the company.

Even after several years, the thought of what Ben had done sends a tightness up Cliff's torso and shoulders and squeezes his neck, so that his vision blurs for a few seconds.

He had trusted Ben, and Ben had screwed him so badly he will never recover.

Worse to think of it because Ben was his little brother, his lost little brother. He'd been adopted out of their family as a toddler. Cliff couldn't remember him very well – he'd been six at the time. But his sisters, Cleo and Mandalay, had never stopped talking about their lost baby brother. And then Ben had showed up, the golden boy, raised by wealthy parents, and had worked his way back into all of their lives.

That's what made it worse. That he had been so happy to find Ben, his long-lost brother.

Then Ben had fucked the company, spending all of his time snowboarding and surfing instead of working, and helping himself to funds, and they'd almost gone bankrupt. Ben's adopted dad and a partner of his had taken it over. They'd agreed to let Cliff stay on as manager, but then he'd had his accident, and they'd turned around and sold the company to a couple of Punjabi brothers.

South Asians, Cliff's sister Cleo would say, but his wife, Veronika, and the guys Cliff knows from the coffee shop all say Punjabi.

Yeah, he should just call one of those trucks that will come and take everything away.

They could take the other stuff, too – the house stuff, Veronika's stuff, as he thinks of it, though he knows there are plenty of things of his mixed in. He'll have to talk to her about it first, though, and he guesses it's a pretty sure thing she won't want to let go of it.

But he has to ask Veronika. Some of it's her stuff. He has to ask her. And she'll linger over her sorting; she'll keep most of it. Even though they need to clean out the garage to park her car in it.

The accident: his own fault, he guesses. Though it wouldn't have happened if the company hadn't been falling apart, then. His employees laid off over the Christmas holidays, to save money. Cliff had gone to a job site on his own, a problem site in West Van, where some deforestation had made a steep grade unstable. Cliff had been working there alone, and there had been a landslip, tons of mud and stones and broken roots and nursery plants not yet established had slid down the side of the mountain.

He can still see the buckling of the earth, grey and shining with clay, swimming toward him. He had run across the slope, run for his life, but he hadn't been able to get completely clear, and the avalanche of mud had pulled his feet out from under him, and had tumbled him arse-over-teakettle for about twenty metres. Luckily, he'd been able to pull his arms up around his head and face. He'd hit some stone and chunks of tree on the way, and had broken several ribs and cracked his pelvis, but had survived.

They said he was lucky.

It was his spine that was unlucky. Soft tissue damage, they said. Nothing broken. But he'd come out of his cast to excruciating pain; ongoing, excruciating pain across his back, when he tried to walk or bend or move. There's been a little reprieve, but no real improvement. He's been now to a few doctors. They try different things: they've done some surgery, which made things worse; they've sent him to physio; they've given him painkillers, which, if he takes enough to cut the pain, make him dopey; they've even sent him for acupuncture.

Nothing works. The pain has settled into his body like a conjoined twin. He carries it everywhere; it's the last thing he knows at night; the first thing he's aware of in the morning. It decides everything about his day.

An evil conjoined twin.

And he has not been able to work since. His company sold, anyway. His one good shot in his lifetime, probably, sold to the Punjabi brothers.

He doesn't like it, not working. He's not like the guys at the café, who seem to have learned to make a career of it. He needs to be doing something, making something. He wants his company back. He'd even go back to working for someone else. That's what he has, the memory in his hands, his fingers, of the texture of soil and the health of a plant; his eye for a pleasing sweep of botanical colour and texture. It's all that he has ever had.

Something else that is in those grey steel file cabinets: all of his notebooks and drawings, for all of the gardens he has made. The woodland pool; the hidden garden of moss and fern and white fritillaries; the box garden, the flame garden that bloomed in surges of scarlet and orange and crimson for six continuous months, before the colours were taken up by foliage. The owner had made a time-lapse video of it.

He shouldn't throw away his notebooks, maybe. Though he doesn't imagine he will design a garden ever again.

Well, he should clear out the garage. It's something he can do, anyway. Something that needs to be done. Though the contents clutch at him, entangling him, holding him in place, like some old unpruned untamed overgrown bramble thicket. He'll never get out. He can remember freedom, lightness, a meadow aglow with darts of purple, but he'll never get there. He can't think how to find his way back.

4

THE VISIT GOES BY QUICKLY, but smoothly, for the most part. Olivia sleeps late, goes out, late, with friends. Cleo has to work, anyway, so she can't spend the days with Olivia, but she wonders if she will see Olivia at all over her week's visit. Cleo plans family dinners, coordinating with Trent over picking up ingredients, scraping the barbecue grill. Olivia says: You guys don't need to go to so much trouble! I'm used to eating much later! She eats very little, or not at all, and then heads out with friends, stays out late.

She's pleasant enough, puts together a salad one night with Cleo; makes conversation with Trent about sub-prime mortgages and with Sam about new bands and YouTube things they follow.

Trent comments to Cleo that Olivia has matured — that it's a pleasant change. But to Cleo it feels like a niece is visiting — a niece with whom she had a close relationship years ago, when the niece was a small child, but whom she doesn't really know very well anymore.

Cleo's friend Lacey had said, last week at yoga: I miss Claire viscerally when she's away. But I still miss her when she's back visiting. Do you know what I mean?

She asks Olivia to stay in, to have one family dinner, and Olivia says she will.

She sets the table herself for dinner, using the aqua-blue Denby, which she still loves; the aqua and cream and sand-colour checked napkins, bought in a shop in Sechelt years ago, on their way to Butterfly Lake; the heavy plain Swedish cutlery; the wooden trivets made by Olivia in ninth-grade shop class. She hears Olivia and Sam laugh at something Sam is streaming – Olivia's throaty chuckle, Sam's giggle – and the sound makes her so happy (as she stands at the cook top stirring puttanesca sauce) that she is able to restrain herself from calling out to them, from suggesting that they should cast the program, show, whatever, onto the big-screen TV.

Over dinner, they talk about family trips. They laugh; they share family jokes. Cleo feels content. This is good.

After dinner Olivia volunteers to help Cleo clear up, and over the dishes she asks if Cleo has time for lunch the next day, just the two of them.

That is a lovely idea. Cleo feels alight, inside. Everything is going to be alright, after all.

SHE HAD THOUGHT that Olivia might stay in this one evening, but she leaves, again, late, picked up by someone Cleo doesn't see. A car in the driveway, Olivia's phone pinging and then Olivia out the door. Who are you going out with? Cleo had asked, the first evening, but Olivia had stared her down, raised her eyebrows, to let Cleo know it was a faux pas, and Cleo, suddenly tired, had not pushed it beyond saying that she meant it only as polite conversation.

Cleo has cleared her evenings for the week, so this evening, as the others, she feels adrift.

She checks in on Sam, who is in his room, which is almost a suite, really, at the computer, his head encased by large headphones with an attached mic. Typing rapidly, multiple windows open on his screen. He's giving commentary to some unheard, unseen listeners. As if he were piloting a craft through space, maybe. Or an employee in some call centre? And he'll spend six or seven hours like that, stopping only for food. There's a pyramid of empty soda cans on his desk, she can see in the twilight their metallic sides reflecting the coloured LED lights of Sam's keyboard.

He has called for her to come in, at her knock, and removes his headphones, but looks at her as if he's waiting courteously for her to state her needs so he can get back to his work.

Want to go for a run? she asks.

Oh, no, sorry, he says. In the middle of something. Why don't you ask a friend?

She does that. She calls Jennifer, a friend from the old neighbourhood who has also moved to this more upscale suburb. Jennifer says she can't: she has to finish something for work and she's already been to the gym. She says: I thought Olivia was visiting this week.

She is, Cleo says, but she's gone out every night.

I wouldn't stand for that, Jennifer says, and Cleo knows she is right.

Jennifer's daughter Maddy who has also returned from school back east – McGill – is somehow more compliant. She will live at home, working, over the summer. She has not, Jennifer says, got high enough grades to get into grad school, but Mitchell, Jennifer's husband, has got Maddy a job at his friend's company, a PR job.

Jennifer has said, lightly, making joke of it, that Maddy partied her way through university, was probably drunk every weekend. Jennifer had not seemed worried at all by this. But Jennifer and Mitchell are so well off that it doesn't matter if Maddy parties all through her twenties.

No running with Jennifer, tonight.

Cleo finds Trent in his den, watching golf on TV, and asks if he wants to go for a walk. *Now?* he asks, as if it were two in the morning, instead of eight in the evening, and still light out.

Never mind, she says. She retrieves from her bedroom her new hooded jacket – she has learned, the hard way, to keep anything new and fashionable in her room when Olivia is around – and her running shoes, and heads out into the street, which is lined with wide boulevards and blossoming trees that, against the deep blue of the evening sky, look like an image from a tacky aspirational poster.

Self-pity begins to tighten her throat as she runs. She works so hard for her family. What has she got to show for it?

It's a common complaint, she knows, among her friends, the other working mothers she knows. They are treated like staff, or unpopular schoolmates, or doddering distant relatives, by their young-adult daughters.

Some kind of karma, for the way we treated our mothers? someone had joked.

Cleo does not think that she sneered at and criticized either her mother or foster mother, when she was younger. She wouldn't have dared. It wouldn't have occurred to her to do that.

Of course, she has had little contact with her birth mother since she was twelve. But she sees Crystal once or twice a year, and is, she thinks, unfailingly polite and kind. And Cleo had made many visits to her foster mother — out of duty; there wasn't anything in it for her — after she left her foster home at eighteen, and could have chosen not to.

Perhaps it is payback for Cleo's absenting herself from her mothers, her would-be mothers, that Olivia must be so difficult to live with.

But Cleo survived by making herself invisible, throwing up a cloud of ink and disappearing. Cleo had had to work to survive; she had had to plot and strategize to get into university, to get through her undergraduate and graduate degrees. She'd had to teach herself how to interact with people with enough sophistication to get jobs, to move up the career ladder. Even to have friends. To create the middle-class suburban home in which she has raised her children.

Olivia has never had to do that. She doesn't have to be silent, unobtrusive, self-abnegating. She has never had to work harder than everyone else in the room just to be acceptable.

And that is a good thing. That is what Cleo has wanted. Olivia has a sense of entitlement, maybe. But she is strong, self-confident.

She is her own person. What Cleo missed out herself, she has ensured for her daughter.

So Cleo reminds herself, as she runs through the quiet streets, meeting few neighbours, passing, on this evening, nobody that she recognizes, so that she could be running in a city anywhere, so that she feels strangely detached, not a citizen, not belonging, somehow, at all. Responsible to nobody, for nobody.

CLEO HAD HOPED THAT Olivia would meet her in the office; she had fantasized mildly about having her beautiful slim poised daughter admired by her colleagues, who have known her since she was in her mid-teens, but Olivia isn't up for that, and Cleo has to admit it's not Olivia's job to be shown off like a new bicycle or puppy. They'll meet, instead, at the restaurant. And Cleo reminds herself (freshening her lipstick, tidying her hair in the bathroom before she leaves her office) to just enjoy the afternoon, be in the moment. In the cab to the restaurant, she checks the restaurant's lunch menu so she won't be annoyingly indecisive, then puts her phone on vibrate and zips it away in an inner compartment of her handbag.

Olivia arrives on time, just after Cleo has been seated, and they hug, lightly, briefly, an unfamiliar, new ritual. Olivia admires the décor of the restaurant, and Cleo feels a sense of achievement. She had put a lot of effort into it, guessing that Olivia would have moved on from the industrial-chic aesthetic she enthused about the year before, asking around to find out what was the new "it" place for people in their mid-twenties. This restaurant has velvety flocked and gilt wallpaper and an assortment of antiqued and gilded antique furniture, faux-French Provincial, chandeliers decorated with painted metal foliage and fringed shades, and a trompe l'oeil mural. It seems a bit tacky, a bit seventies-motel décor, to Cleo, but Olivia looks around her approvingly. She likes it. It is new, to Olivia's generation. Or perhaps interestingly retro.

The menu offers fish and seafood, Provençal style, and Cleo steers Olivia toward the bouillabaisse, having looked up reviews in the taxi. Olivia says she's heard of bouillabaisse, but never had it. She seems pleased. She's in a mood to be pleased, a mood in which Cleo likes her best: open, innocently happy, eager to be delighted. Her true, sweet girl.

She remembers to ask Olivia questions that will lead to conversation, to Olivia being comfortable, being able to shine. She turns down a glass of wine, partly because she is working and wine leads to sleepiness; partly because she can be more pleasant with Olivia if she doesn't lose her inhibitions. It takes a lot of attention to keep from saying the wrong thing, she has learned.

And she is successful. Or semi-successful. Olivia doesn't really talk about herself; she never has. But she talks about her projects; she tells funny rueful stories about getting ideas in the middle of the night and deciding, last-minute, to change her whole focus; about almost losing a file; about leaving her poster project on the bus. She's being funny, self-deprecating, charming. Cleo does not once comment that Olivia should pay better attention, manage her time better. She does not even let herself think those things. Olivia is doing fine.

Cleo feels aglow: this is what she has wanted, this connection. The feeling that there are no barriers between them. That she and Olivia are still connected in that fundamental, perfect way. And reassurance that Olivia is okay, of course. That she is happy and confident and resilient. Which she seems to be.

It's not a given, Cleo knows. Even with a stable family, sane parents, all of the advantages, it's not a given that a child will grow up okay. She thinks of her friend Stephanie's adopted daughter, Ocean, whom Stephanie supports, who has a toddler whom Stephanie cares for while Ocean does Office Management courses at the community college. Ocean is Olivia's age. And Stephanie is a smart and good woman, who had homeschooled Ocean until she was eleven; had arranged therapy for Ocean's compound learning difficulties; had raised her without anger or belittling or indulgence, in a sane, caring way.

She thinks of Olivia's elementary-school friend Laura, sweet gangly Laura with her grey eyes and open grin, who had been loved, for sure, who had been in dance classes with Olivia. Laura, whose mother had got a portfolio of professional photos done, and had shopped them around agents, confident that Laura would get work in movies. (The other dance moms had smiled – anyone could see that Laura was the least coordinated of all the little girls in their jazz slippers – but nobody had openly laughed, because Laura was a sweet child.) Poor sweet, knock-kneed Laura, who had been arrested one night, when she was eighteen, with her boyfriend, as they committed an armed robbery at the Circle K all-night convenience store.

Olivia is doing well. She is on track. She's doing well in economics, after her false start in engineering. She'll likely go into law – economics is often a precursor for law – and have a solid career and find a well-matched partner. (And then what?) But focus on now, on this moment. On not wrong-footing this perfect moment.

They finish their perfect salads and bouillabaisse and chewy artisanal sourdough bread and sorbets.

Cleo tells Olivia about her current project. Olivia is impressed; she says so. She says that she wishes she could have seen the site. Then she reminds Cleo that her dream is to live in a tiny house on a piece of land. Cleo knows this, and forebears to say that it's everyone's dream, at twenty-two, to claim a bit of wilderness for one's self; look out on a sweep of meadow or lake or trees and not see other humans; to live without garages and closets and, presumably, cleaning supplies. I'm glad you're designing this consciously, Mom, she says. I'm glad you're trying to help fix things.

The things Cleo's generation messed up, she means. She lumps Cleo in with the baby boomers, though Cleo was born a few years too late to fit into that group. According to Olivia, the baby boomers have caused all of the world's current ills. In vain Cleo points out the sexual revolution, second-wave feminism, and the environmental movements of the late 1960s and 1970s, all wrought, surely, by the boomer generation. But Cleo won't argue about this today.

Then the cab back to Cleo's office and the nearest SkyTrain station, and that's where Olivia finally says what she has come to say.

Of course there was going to be something, Cleo thinks. An ask. A substantial ask. And Cleo has known her daughter for twenty-two years: has been nanny, cook, maid, teacher, bodyguard, personal assistant, therapist, chauffeur. And also: advocate, prosecutor, judge, and parole officer.

I have been thinking, Olivia says, that I want to take a sabbatical this coming year.

Cleo does not react. She has worked very hard to be able not to react. Oh, yeah? she says, neutrally.

Yeah, I think I want to rethink my direction before I've invested too much more time in it.

Hmmm, Cleo says. What would that look like?

I've been thinking, Olivia says, that, you know how everyone says students don't live in the real world? I want to go travelling. I want to take a year, maybe two. I want to see the real world. I want to go to, like, developing countries and see how people really live, in favelas and so on. And there are these matriarchal societies, you know? In Asia. Where people are doing something different. Their lives aren't just about making money and having stuff. They're about community and intangibles and connection. I want to go see that. I want to be part of a different way of seeing the world. I don't want to get caught up in the machine, like everyone else.

Cleo feels her chest constrict. She glances out the window. Only a few blocks to her building, thank goodness. A few blocks.

She says: We should discuss it with your dad. Her voice sounds flat, false, to her own ears. It's the best she can do.

Oh, but Mom, Olivia says. I know what Dad will say. I talked to you first because – I knew you'd get what I'm saying. I knew you wouldn't just be all prejudiced and reject it. It's really important, Mom. I want this more than anything else in the world.

Olivia is tearing up: real tears, Cleo thinks, though not with complete conviction. She's touched, anyway. There's something in Olivia's plea that's reaching her. She does want to talk about it more, not just so that she can disabuse Olivia of some of her naïve ideas, but also so that she can connect with her on this new level. It's something that's been missing in their lives, she sees suddenly: discussions about purpose, about the world beyond what is practical and obvious and maybe deeply flawed. Call it philosophy, maybe. Because that is what it's all about, isn't it? The beauty and meaning of humanity. It's like a window has been opened between them and she has seen that Olivia is entirely different inside than she thought.

No, that's a bad metaphor.

Of course, it's not going to fly, as a plan. Trent will hit the roof, for one thing.

Would you go alone? It's a silly question, she realizes, as soon as she's asked it.

Some friends are planning on going. They've invited me.

I see, Cleo says.

You think it's a really bad idea, don't you? Olivia says.

Only one block to go. Cleo says: It's a surprise. I need to process.

IT'S A REALLY BAD IDEA. Olivia needs to go right into law school or a Master's degree. You can't get into a profession without one, these days. She has to stay on track, now, as they're supporting her financially, she and Trent. They've budgeted enough for her degree and law school and she has already cost them an extra year, switching majors.

Trent isn't as outraged or dismissive as she'd anticipated he'd be. Well, he says. She's free, white, and twenty-one. We can't really stop her.

Can we really use that phrase anymore? Cleo thinks. But of course, that's true: Olivia can make her own choices. And then she realizes, that the obvious hasn't occurred to Trent.

She's going to want funding. You can't travel on nothing, these days.

Oh, of course, Trent says. Well, she'll have to fund herself.

Olivia has the summer job, but most of what she makes goes for her rent and food. She really doesn't save much. Cleo feels simultaneously a wash of relief: *Yes, that's the answer. That will decide it,* and a jagged streak of disappointment: for what, she doesn't know.

And then, a kind of disdain: Trent always sees things in black and white. Things are always simple to him. A simple matter of economics.

How much would it cost? Olivia will have it all worked out; she knows how to make a spreadsheet. Probably not more than her tuition and living expenses come to, now. Cleo could give her a year. Cleo herself could fund a year. She is making good money.

But she is trying to pay off the mortgage and the line of credit for the improvements on the house. She had taken that on: she'd made that deal with Trent, when they bought the house. She would cover the extra, because Trent didn't want a fancier house. Trent didn't want to take on a big mortgage. She had done that, and she is paying for it. And they have a very tight plan for Olivia's and Sam's education, and for retirement.

It's a foolish idea. Olivia can wait a year – take a year off after her graduation, work. Or do law school in Van, live at home, work part-time. There are options. It's best if everything isn't just handed to her, anyway. They can't encourage the expectation in her that they can just pay for everything, all of her life.

Cleo herself had to work very hard all during her teens and her university years. There was no money for trips or gap years. She had to work her butt off to keep her scholarships and to afford her rent – and always in shared accommodation – and food. She didn't have a car or eat in restaurants or buy nice clothes.

Not that her child should have to undergo the same hardship, of course.

But it doesn't even sound *safe* – her mention of Tibet, Brazilian favelas. Not even feasible, in fact.

And then there's that vague word *friends*. Cleo has been young. She knows the usefulness of that phrase, *with friends*. She sees suddenly and clearly that Olivia is planning to head off with some boy, probably a selfish, New-Age liberal arts student (she can picture him, his pretty face, his long hair, his faux-shabby clothing) with a moderate drug habit and a trust fund behind him. It's about the boy, not the trip, Cleo guesses: hence the vagueness, the flakey global-studies speak.

Is it prudent to let Olivia waste a year or more of her educational time, and her money, to accompany a spoiled dilettante on a tour of global drug culture? No, it is not.

She says she'll tell Olivia. Better that than risk a huge argument between Olivia and Trent. The two of them seem to be getting along better now, but it's only been a couple of years since their screaming matches ripped the house apart. Better to take it on herself. She can talk to Olivia, maybe suggest some smart compromise.

SHE DOESN'T FIND A GOOD TIME, unfortunately, to talk things through with Olivia before she leaves, and so has to do it over a video call. Cleo stays home, on a Saturday, setting her laptop up in the kitchen, waiting for Olivia to get up, even though it's three hours later in Ontario. It would be better if they could do this in person. If they could at least go for a walk. But Olivia is a few thousand miles away. It's just the way it is.

She hopes that Olivia will manage to get up in time. Cleo has also to conference with a client, today. She has to get this contract underway, ready for the lawyers. It's already delayed; it's costing them thousands a day.

On the screen, her daughter looks younger. She's still tousled from sleep, not wearing makeup. She looks like her ten-year-old self, in a way that clutches at something in Cleo's chest.

Cleo takes a deep breath. She says: We aren't rich. We don't have the kind of money that your friends' parents do. She says: You need to make good decisions. This is the crucial point of your life. Everything you choose now is a path. Can you see that? It might feel like you have endless options, but very soon most of those options are going to close down.

I don't feel like I have endless options, Olivia says. I feel like I have a couple of options right now, and only one that really interests me. Her voice is wobbly. Maybe it's just the speaker in Cleo's computer? Cleo makes an effort to focus.

But is it a good one to pursue? Cleo asks. Can you see that it leads to a good outcome?

I can't see where anything leads, Olivia says. I think it is a reasonable option.

You really can't afford to make a bad decision, Cleo says. She glances at her laptop; the email she has been waiting for has come in. She should follow up on it.

I don't know how to tell, Olivia says. I don't know how to tell if it's a bad decision. She's crying, now.

It's just probability, Cleo says. She can see that Olivia wants to get into an hours-long conversation, but she doesn't have time for it. She needs to get to work. It's all she can do not to open another screen on her laptop while they're talking.

Olivia doesn't know what she wants, as Trent says. She's been indecisive, uncommitted, before. At this point she just needs a little parental guidance, a little encouragement to stay the course.

Cleo agrees. Olivia is almost finished her degree. To a twenty-two-year-old, time seems infinite. The possibilities seem endless; sticking to one thing seems a drag. But Cleo knows: a couple of years is nothing, in the bigger scheme. Olivia will be done her education in a couple of years. She can wait it out. She'll survive.

We can't support you, she says.

Well, then, I can't go, Olivia says. Her voice is flat, but she's not crying anymore, or having a meltdown, thank goodness.

She'll see that it's the sensible decision, Cleo knows.

It's important to stay the course, do the sensible thing. Not to go chasing after every interesting new idea.

But a greyness falls over her, as if a door has been shut, suddenly, against the sunlight.

5

BELINDA HAS SUGGESTED THEY MEET UP in the morning for tea and a walk. She's better in the mornings, Belinda says. On this day Belinda is feeling well-*ish*, as she says. She's in a cheerful space. Not pretending her illness is not there; that never happens; just focussing on the rest of Belinda's life, which is going on around her illness, the healthy life around the damaged centre, Mandalay thinks. Belinda is good at this. She is good at being brave, or something.

Happy birthday, darling Mandalay, Belinda says.

She has a gift for Mandalay, or rather, two gifts: a book Mandalay has been longing for, but not able to afford, on West African batik patterns, and a bottle of Spanish champagne.

Belinda is wearing a new knitted hat, which she is joking about, but which is rather fine. Even in her illness, Belinda would not be likely to wear something that wasn't aesthetically pleasing. The hat is knit in a pleasing pattern of cables and raised stitches, out of very soft-looking yarn, in a a warm wine colour that suits Belinda's brown, freckly skin.

The knitted hat was a gift from another of Belinda's friends, and Mandalay is fleetingly jealous that someone else has found such a great gift. She and Belinda discuss what the shade of wine might be – Merlot? Cab Sauv? – and whether or not it could be called a tuque.

They have had so many thousands of these light discussions, over the years, riffing off each other, stimulating each other to greater and greater wit and recall of associations, chasing topics down rabbit holes and returning to the main trail, usually, eventually.

I think I'm going to get eyelashes tattooed on, Belinda says.

That's a thing?

Yes, indeed. I looked into extensions, but you have to have eyelashes already to glue the new eyelashes to.

The way you have to have money already to get a loan, Mandalay says.

Exactly, Belinda says. *What good does that do me?* I said to the eyelash technician. And she suggested the tattoos.

It sounds a bit sadistic. How do they manage to do it?

I don't know, Belinda says, suddenly sounding bored, which means, Mandalay knows, that she has run out of energy, not interest.

They walk along the sea wall, this quiet afternoon in early spring. Flowers are abloom in the parks: camellias, crocus, some sort of fritillary. It is almost warm.

Belinda is Mandalay's oldest and best friend. She and Belinda had met while both were pregnant: Belinda with her daughter Harriet; Mandalay with her twins. Belinda is an artist, and an art teacher; it is she who has mentored and encouraged Mandalay all of these years, has prodded Mandalay to finish her degree, has used her connections to get Mandalay part-time teaching work, and shows.

And now Belinda is sick, and Mandalay feels inside herself a deep dread every time she thinks of her or sees her, and the temptation is to push the existence of Belinda outside the little globe of her everyday thoughts, to find excuses to avoid seeing Belinda, to build stories about their interactions (which are not always happy, these days) that would allow her to detach from Belinda, to safeguard her own feelings, but she must not. Belinda is her oldest, her dearest friend. She will not abandon her. She will not cut Belinda adrift with the pretext of setting her free.

Doing anything this weekend? Mandalay asks.

Aside from puking and lying very still?

I thought your chemo was next week.

No, this week, Belinda says. Tomorrow.

Mandalay feels useless, and blindsided, in a way that is dispro-
portionately intense. She has Belinda's chemo dates circled on the
calendar in her kitchen. She knows which days will be the worst,
afterwards – the third and fourth days – and which days Belinda
will feel up to walks or going for lunch or to a gallery. She *knows* this.
She makes a point of knowing this – of bringing a meal over to the
house on the worst day, not that Belinda can eat it, but it takes care
of her partner, Joe, and her daughter Harriet. But somehow she has
lost track of her weeks.

Aarrghh, she says. I'm so scatterbrained. I have it on my calendar.

I know you do, Belinda says, affectionately.

Mandalay feels relief at the softening of Belinda's tone. But it is
not Belinda's job to make her feel better, she reminds herself.

Are *you* doing anything this weekend? Belinda asks.

Lunch with Duane, Mandalay says.

Oooh, Belinda says, sarcastically. What's he got up his sleeve?

Mandalay doesn't know. Something about the boys, of course.
The only interaction she has with her sons' father is when he wants to
add a new set of complications or controls to their lives. She smiles,
though. She loves how Belinda always takes her side, always has her
back, when it comes to Duane.

Where are you going for lunch? Belinda asks.

Mandalay sees a bench in a parklet ahead, and steers for it. Belinda
doesn't always remember to rest. The Alchemist, she says, as they sit.

Belinda leans back, closes her eyes, lets the sun fall on her lash-
less, browless face. The fibres of her scarf and her wool coat and
her tuque blaze in the sunlight, and her facial skin glows, hairless,
anointed with many creams, Mandalay knows, against the assault on
her cells of the chemotherapy drugs.

The Alchemist, Belinda says. That's fancy. Make sure you have
the risotto with the bone marrow.

Is it the most expensive thing on the menu? Mandalay asks. It's an old joke between her and Belinda.

No, Belinda says. That's probably the caviar. But you can order that too. As an appetizer.

They both laugh.

Oh, lord, Belinda says. This sun sure feels good on my bones. I guess this is a foretaste of old age, eh?

Mandalay feels awkward, suddenly, as if her body has been stiffened by a chill. It's very, very unlikely that Belinda will see her sixties, even. "Old age ain't no place for sissies," Mandalay says, quoting Bette Davis, maybe not very appropriately.

Yeah, Belinda says. But what's the alternative?

Impossible to keep going on like this, with dark knowledge dogging every move. But what's the alternative, again? If there's a way to keep the knowledge out of her conversations, her interactions with Belinda, she is not capable of discovering it.

How's Harry? she asks, meaning Harriet, Belinda's daughter. Precocious, androgynous, amazing Harriet, who used to be Mandalay's twins' favourite buddy and playmate.

Last year, when Belinda got sick, when she had been starting her first round of chemotherapy, she and Joe had given in to Harriet's long-standing, Hogwarts-inspired fantasy of attending boarding school, and had sent her to Scotland, of all places, where she, by all reports, is thriving.

Mandalay still feels a little squeamish about the decision. Won't Harriet, somewhere down the road, suffer from it? Is illness something you should hide from your child? And if Belinda dies when she is away, isn't Harriet going to feel robbed of the years she would have had with Belinda? And isn't she going to feel that she was rejected, or abandoned, at some level?

Harriet has never even seen Belinda sick – she's been away during all of the chemo rounds.

It's not Mandalay's issue to worry about, of course. As Belinda's friend, her job is to support Belinda, to have Belinda's back. Not to judge her decisions. She is very fond of Harriet. The three children, Harriet and Mandalay's sons, had grown up together, close as a litter of puppies, Joe, Belinda's partner, always said. In their mid-years they'd stayed close, had lived in a world of their own. For a few months, actually, they'd all had Elvish names, devised or dug up by Harriet, a voracious reader and creative myth-builder.

At some point in the last couple of years, they had begun to abandon their imaginary play, or at least Aidan and Owen had, and they stopped wanting to spend time together. Perhaps they just outgrew each other. That's all it was.

But then Mandalay misses the space that they had. She misses the childhood of her children, which seems to her now like a walled, enchanted garden.

All is loss, Mandalay thinks, for a moment. A shadow moves over her, again: a chill.

Harriet is thriving, Belinda says, as she always does. Harriet has the lead in the fifth-form play. Whatever that is.

She looks at Belinda. Her friend's eyes are closed. She looks aged, her skin dry, thin. Mandalay takes her hand and squeezes it lightly, and Belinda returns the pressure.

You will get better, Mandalay thinks fiercely at Belinda, holding onto her for dear life.

Belinda opens her eyes. Mandalay, she says. Have you heard back from the gallery, about a show next year? Maybe you should call them again.

I'll call them, Mandalay says.

It's going to be so great, Belinda says. She leans her head back, closes her eyes. What a perfect day, she says.

6

ON THE FLIGHT TO TORONTO, Cleo and her husband Trent enjoy, side-by-side in business class, complimentary meals of sole amandine and Salisbury steak, served with orange rubbery cubes and green rubbery globes that are meant, Cleo guesses, to approximate vegetables. With the sole, there is a little half-glob of yellow rice sprinkled with coloured flecks, a roll, a piece of chocolate cake, a glass of wine. Trent's meal of Salisbury steak is accompanied by a mound of mashed potatoes.

Cleo says: This is the worst food I have ever eaten.

Trent frowns. Oh, I don't know. It's edible.

But Trent doesn't really notice what he eats, as long as the food has no strong, unfamiliar flavours. He doesn't eat fish. He doesn't like wine, either, but accepts the complimentary mini-carafe, gives it to Cleo.

I can't drink all of that wine, she says. I need to get some work done. She has her laptop in a bag at her feet, handy.

Oh, relax, Trent says. Just relax, for once.

They are flying to Ontario for Trent's mother's funeral. Cleo considers: drinks the extra glass of wine, buys Trent a beer from the bar service.

Trent gets up to rummage through his carry-on, in the overhead compartment, and retrieves a pad of ledger paper and a pen. He says: Can you help me with my speech?

You haven't written it yet?

No. I thought I would do it on the flight, when there's nothing else to do.

Cleo puts her laptop away. She's not going to be able to work. Even with the extra width and legroom of business seats, Trent is bumping her with his elbows, flinging his jacket across her, getting up again to rummage in his bag again, rustling, scratching, making sounds with his mouth.

His mother's funeral, she reminds herself. She must cut him some slack.

Should she open her laptop, do some work, while Trent is making his notes? He doesn't seem to want her help, after all. Or maybe get out her paperback. But she's saving that for bedtime, for the hotel. And if he does want her help, he'll be irritated. When she's reading, she doesn't always hear his voice.

Are you going to tell some funny stories? she asks. Maybe the one about your mom leaving you on the train when you were little?

I'll think of some, he says shortly.

He's irritated, she knows, because his older brothers and his sister are all going to speak, and they will tell all of the stories. Trent, a late last child, an afterthought, born when his mother was in her forties, will have none left to claim. All of the good material will have been appropriated. They will have shared it among themselves – a tightly-knit group of siblings in their sixties. They had formed a club, figured out their roles, long before Trent was born, and they're still close, living near each other, seeing each other often. They're all talkers, too – voluble, social, used to giving speeches.

Maybe you could just let Bob and Tom and Caroline do the speeches, she says now. You could play something on the piano. Some of your mom's favourite music.

I haven't practiced anything, he says.

They have a piano, now, a baby grand, bought second-hand from one of Cleo's clients. Trent plays, sometimes.

Beside her, Trent wriggles and flexes and breathes through his mouth. In the pocket in front of her is a newspaper left behind by a previous passenger and not cleared out between flights. Cleo picks it up, opens it to the crossword puzzle. Someone has begun it and abandoned it. She reads a clue: *He went skyward at 50 metres in the middle.*

One of those. She detests cryptic crosswords, with their dissolution of meaning into individual syllables, their reliance on puns and aural tricks.

The Sudoku, then. Good, it's untouched. And rated Diabolical.

Her brain begins noting patterns and possibilities. She's a problem solver, an engineer. It's what she does.

Trent says: How's this?

She puts down the newspaper, reads from Trent's screen.

THERE ARE WAYS of doing things, like funerals, that the old moneyed families of Ontario know (Cleo thinks), which have their advantages. There are no awkward gaps. Everything has its place. Cleo appreciates that.

Here Trent's family all are, now, filing into the grand Romanesque-Revival church. United, of course. In spite of its great age and architectural grandeur, it has an air of having been purposed for the occasion, with many flowers. Here are Trent's brothers, dark-suited, on the verge of being elderly, now, themselves. His sister Caroline, silver-haired, in a dark tailored dress. Their spouses; their children, all grown now, mature adults, with children of their own. They all move with ease, greeting each other with decorous affection, appropriate solemnity.

Cleo is glad she has worn her new suit, which had seemed like overkill, for a funeral, but fit her nicely and was the best thing she owned. She'd worn it out of respect for Gwendolyn, whom she *had* respected, perhaps more than liked, but she sees now that anything lesser would not have done for the venue.

A woman who Cleo thinks is her own age approaches and embraces her and addresses her as Auntie Cleo. Belatedly, she recognizes a niece-by-marriage. Goodness, that feels shocking. A sister-in-law asks about Sam and Olivia. They had elected not to attend. Trent had wanted them to, but both had said that it was a bad time; they were in the middle of term end. Can't you get extensions from your professors? Trent had insisted, but Olivia had laughed, derisively: saying your grandmother has died is such a cliché. If you even think about using it as an excuse, you'll never get any of your profs to write you references.

Cleo says: Both of them have term end. They couldn't afford the time.

Ours are all here, the sister-in-law says.

Of course they are, but for them, it's a two-hour chunk out of their Wednesday – they all live in this city. For Cleo, Trent, and Sam, it's a multi-day trip, containing four-and-a-half hour flights, as well as the concomitant waits at airports and getting to and from. Not to mention the expense. Even for Olivia, missed classes and travel.

She remembers now why she had stopped going along on the annual visits to see Trent's family at the cottage. There was a pack mentality, and she and Trent outliers, hangers-on. Once she had stopped going, Olivia and Sam and Trent had lost interest, quite quickly. It was a long trip. The children's cousins were so much older. The brothers and brother-in-law played golf together regularly, both in Toronto and at the lake. They had a fourth, an old friend of all of them. After golf they sat in the clubhouse or on each other's decks and drank whiskey and talked business. No room for Trent, really.

And the trips with the children were hard for Trent, without her along to organize things, to keep track of belongings and suitcases, to administer regular meals and sunscreen and bug repellant and baths. The kids got sick; had tantrums; left favourite possessions on planes.

She knows that it's her fault that they didn't go. But maybe not her responsibility.

The funeral progresses.

There is organ music, played by a family friend – classical selections that Cleo isn't sure Gwendolyn would have recognized. (Why not play the top hits of the 40s and 50s, which Cleo had heard Gwendolyn sing to her children, sometimes, when she didn't know Cleo was listening? But those might not have sounded fitting in this cathedral-like edifice.)

Trent's eldest brother Bob gives the eulogy. The older siblings have decided, it seems, that they'll do this, instead of individual speeches. Somehow Trent didn't get the memo. (After all of that time I spent on my speech, he had fumed.) The speech is very impersonal. There are no funny stories at all.

Bob speaks: Their mother's energy, her breadth of interests, her membership in many clubs and charitable organizations. Her long marriage; her devotion to her children and grandchildren.

She'd never had a career, of course.

At the end, there is a procession, in which the casket is carried out to the hearse by Gwendolyn's sons and grandsons, though the hearse will take it to the crematorium, not the cemetery. The ashes will have a green burial, Cleo has been told. Very popular now.

There's supposed to be an order to the procession: Trent's father will lead it, supported by Trent's sister Caroline; then all of the grand-children will file behind, in order of age, and then the spouses. But then, at the signal – the minister in her robes lifting her hands, *up*, there is a commotion. Bob, Trent's father (there are two Bobs, of course, Senior and Junior) doesn't want to walk down the aisle of the church with Caroline. Too much fuss, he says, loudly. Too much fuss.

Trent's father is ninety-five. He seems to have all of his marbles (Trent's words), but Cleo has noticed that when he isn't actively engaged in conversation, a bewildered look comes over him.

At the gathering at Trent's sister's house, the evening before, Bob's children had said that it was a pity he had outlived their mother.

He had been completely dependent on her, they said, in a tone of pride mixed with something Cleo couldn't identify. And then one of the daughters-in-law, after maybe one too many glasses of wine, had said that it was a pity he couldn't have died years earlier, so that their mother could have enjoyed a few years of freedom. Everyone had ignored that statement.

Now, as they form up for the procession, Bob Senior balks.

What, then, Dad? Caroline asks him, in a tone stripped of impatience, but perhaps also tenderness. Caroline, who runs a large investment company.

Bob Senior looks around wildly. He doesn't know where he is, someone murmurs. But no, Cleo thinks, he does. He knows very well. He just wants things to go differently. He wants to create a wave.

Here, you, he says, pointing at Cleo. You can walk with me. Be my partner.

Caroline raises an eyebrow, from behind her father's back. She doesn't like this, but there must be a minimum of disruption.

Cleo reluctantly makes her way over, takes Bob's arm. He has shrunk, in the past few years. His suit is too big. His head is smaller. Age spots show through the thin hair on his crown.

Bob Junior's wife does not like this substitution. She offers a granddaughter, two granddaughters, in place of Cleo.

No, Bob Senior says. This lovely young woman is who I want.

There can't be a visible flaw in today's performance.

Cleo walks beside her father-in-law, feeling radically angry. Such a ruckus he has caused, her father-in-law, who all of his adult life has insisted things be decorous and appropriate. Maybe it wasn't about decorum, after all. Maybe it was just about being in control. Making the world around himself predictable and safe.

Trent's mother had done that for him: it had been her job.

Gwendolyn had been a resourceful, competent woman, with a life of caring for children and then grandchildren, friends and social activities and charity work, and taking care of Bob had been just one of the jobs she had carried out with grace and aplomb.

She is not going to be forgiven, Cleo sees, for their dependence on her.

On the flight home, Trent says: How did you end up at the front of the procession? It didn't look good.

It was the most elegant solution, she thinks. Doesn't say.

7

MANDALAY IS NOT SURE that her lunch with Duane, her sons' father, is a birthday lunch. He doesn't mention birthdays. He says he needs her to find some documents, some tax receipts. Something about claiming the boys' education expenses. (She registers a slight tightening of her shoulders at the prospect of looking for these things, but makes a reminder note in her phone, allows the tension to dissipate.)

Duane says: What are you not eating, these days? Are you going to be happy with the menu, or do you need something special prepared for you?

His tone is very light, very smooth, but Mandalay has known him for a very long time.

You're confusing me with one of your — *girlfriends*, she says, letting whatever word he wants to imagine drop into that little pause. She's a little disappointed, though. That's an old gibe; he could do better. He's letting himself get out of date.

You sure? he asks, holding up the menu like a piece of evidence.

Absolutely, she says. This is a very nice restaurant. The food is lovely, here.

She can see that he's disappointed, too, in her blasé reaction. So, your department covers your lunches at the Alchemist, he says. Good use of taxpayers' money.

In fact, it *was* a department lunch, but the one for a high-profile visiting artist, and she suspects the chair paid for some of it out of his own pocket. She's nettled, but lets the annoyance float by her. She smiles at him lazily. She doesn't care.

Seventeen years ago, she'd worked at a café as a baker, and Duane had pursued her splashily, taken her out for many expensive meals, not to mention concerts and charity galas. He'd enjoyed that. She had too, of course, but she thinks now, has thought for a long time, that he enjoyed it more. It was Duane's way of controlling a situation, paying the bill.

Paying the bill, but making sure you knew the amount.

The restaurant has lovely food: things like lobster and sablefish and wagyu beef, all of which cost about what she spends in a week on groceries, but as Duane is paying, she won't worry about that. She orders a salad and scallops with tarragon sauce and a mushroom risotto.

It sort of works, their long-standing truce. They've both accepted that they can't change each other. Though each will, occasionally, still erupt with incredulity and derision at the other's extravagances, it's more a ritual, now. And she'll admit that Duane has been right about some things, even things she thought were really, really crazy.

Right to move the boys to the private school, where they have smaller classes and specialist teachers, where there is money to support teachers. She still doesn't agree with private schools in principle. They breed entitlement; they perpetuate the gap between classes. But she can also admit it has been a richer experience for the boys.

She concedes that Duane might have been right, also, to put Owen, at eleven, into Pee Wee hockey. It *had* helped with his coordination, though it wasn't true, as Duane insists, that Owen couldn't walk across a room without falling down, before hockey. And he might have been right, too, about coercing a very shy thirteen-year-old Aidan to sign up for debate club. Aidan has done well. He has developed a lot of social confidence. But she misses the sweet intuitive Aidan who spent his time curled up on the sofa, reading books way above his level, by the bagful. Doesn't she? Everything has become a debate, in his mid-teens. It's exhausting.

It's Aidan that Duane wants to talk to her about, today, or rather, Aidan's tuition and education credits, which Duane wants to claim. It's astonishing, what Aidan's tuition, at his private school, costs.

Duane is an attorney, and as far as she knows, makes an obscene amount of money. She, on the other hand, is a new academic, without tenure.

He must have set up some way of making his income look less, some kind of tax shelter. It's disturbing, talking to Duane, to find out how much effort people like him spend in avoiding paying taxes. She disapproves on so many levels of how much Duane makes, as a lawyer, and how good he is at avoiding contributing to his society.

She disapproves, and yet she is really enjoying this twenty-five-dollar salad.

Alright, she says. Just let Trent know.

Trent, her sister's husband, is an accountant. He does her taxes. Or rather, a twenty-two-year-old articling with his company does them, Cleo had said. But they are done for her. It was either that or use Duane's accountant, and that seemed all wrong.

Now Duane wants to discuss the boy's university applications, though they are at least a year and a half away from that.

Dalhousie for Aidan, Duane says. My alma mater. They have an excellent law school. Aidan can file clerk for one of my colleagues over the summers.

She has imagined art school for Aidan. He has always loved to draw and has good spatial sense. And a local institution. She feels a painful pull, like a muscle strain, in her viscera if she thinks of Aidan being in another city. And Dalhousie is on the other coast, thousands of kilometres away.

We'll see, she says. It annoys her that Duane has a say in the boy's lives. It has annoyed her for many, many years. She had not intended that, but he had used his money – he still uses his money – to control things – to offer the boys the things she can't.

She wonders if he's going to make any comments about the house finances over lunch. It's another bone of contention between them. Not really a bone, because here again, he has the power. Duane had bought a house, when the twins were born, and had given her half of it, as a settlement. It had seemed a big gift at the time, and she had taken it, because she really didn't have many options. House prices have risen so much in the past sixteen years that he must have doubled his investment. But Duane expects to get income from the house, as well. He has insisted that the basement suite be rented, and has kept reminding Mandalay that she is supposed to be paying half the taxes and upkeep. She doesn't have the means to do that, and he clearly does, so she hasn't worried too much about it. It is just there, the issue of the house, and what she owes him, and he likes to raise it once in a while, to wield power. Because she owes him, has never been able to pay her share, she hasn't been able to prevent him from making decisions about their sons.

They share their sons biologically, but they are *her* children: they had grown in her body for all of those months, when Duane hadn't been interested at all. She had been the one to feed them and hold them and dress them, to change their diapers, bathe them, be there for them day and night. She is still the one who looks after them, feeds them, is emotionally present for them, cleans up after them. Duane had come waltzing – well, strutting might be a better word – back into their lives when the boys were four and a half, and had been trying to take them over ever since.

It's hard to connect the endless struggle with the short-lived affair that had produced the twins – had ended, actually, before she realized she was pregnant with them. There seems to be no connection between the two things.

It had been the kind of affair in which a wealthy older man showers a young woman with the kinds of things she can only dream of, in return for sex, she guesses, though it hadn't seemed like that to her at the time. It hadn't been material goods that she'd accepted from Duane, but rather experiences – concerts, plays, amazing meals, a kayaking trip in Haida Gwaii – that she had thought of as mutually enjoyable – things that Duane wanted to do, and enjoyed significantly more because Mandalay could share them with him, and was knowledgeable and aware enough to appreciate them. She'd thought he liked her for her cultural capital, her ability to discuss a show intelligently, as well as for her body, her looks. And she'd thought – she'd been convinced – that his attention to her pleasure, in bed, meant that he cared about her. That he loved her, even. She hadn't realized that it was only part of his own satisfaction.

They'd had an affair that had lasted a matter of months, and she had thought it meant something more than it did. Even though he had hinted, and even said overtly, that he wasn't interested in a committed relationship, she had imagined from his generosity, his ardour, that he cared about her. And then he had let her know – he had in fact told her – that he was done. Just like that. Finished with the relationship and with her.

And of course, when she told him about her pregnancy – she hadn't wanted to, but had realized that she had to; she was too impoverished to have a child on her own, and she wanted to have the baby – he'd shut down like a vault. Of course he had suggested the obvious solution – had even pressured her a bit.

If they'd still been a couple, maybe she would have gone along with his wishes, to please him. Would she have? The idea chills her now. But he had rejected her so completely and coldly, and she had gone through the pregnancy and the years of the boys' infancy without him.

Though not without his money, as he so constantly reminds her.

And now he wants to direct where the boys will go to university, and as he can afford to help them financially and she can't, he automatically can suggest to them more attractive options.

She had thought it too early to start these conversations, but now that she knows Duane has an agenda, she will have to start bringing it up with Aidan, start talking about art school. Not to unduly influence him, of course – just to counteract the messages he's going to be getting from Duane.

It's Aidan's decision. Her role as a parent is to support who her sons want to become, not to steer them into her own preconceived ideas of what is appropriate for them.

And then there's Owen, who plays for a Midget hockey team. It wasn't supposed to come to this. He'd been drafted by a high-ranking team, the year before, and suddenly what was supposed to be a hobby, an amateur sport interest to help with Owen's coordination and fitness, had become – well, a job. He is working. School now comes second, though Owen pushes himself to do his online work. She doesn't have to remind him. But the courses are bare-bones – none of the enriched science or English classes he'd had, at least, in the private school. No gene-splicing labs or authors in residence. Owen is a worker, at not-quite-sixteen – or, as he isn't paid a wage, maybe an apprentice? A slave? He's making money for someone, she is sure. Tickets to the games are sold. Someone is making money from his physical labour.

She has argued this with Duane, already. His answer is that Owen's league doesn't make anything significant in ticket sales or advertising. The player's costs are covered. Their travel expenses and uniforms covered.

What is it all for? But he can't answer that, satisfactorily. He is wrapped up in some mystique of the game. A game that is nothing more than organized aggression, a manifestation of a militarized society, of toxic masculinity.

She can only hope Owen will tire of it soon and quit, before he absorbs that culture completely.

She doesn't bring up Owen with Duane, though maybe she should. Find out what he is thinking. Forewarned is forearmed.

How she dislikes the terminology of sports — drafted, defence, battle, defeat. It's partly why she has resisted learning very much about the game. She doesn't actually go to Owen's games — she'd make it clear from the start that she wouldn't do that. It was Duane's domain. She knows that Owen was disappointed, at first. He has accepted it, though, she thinks.

She has temporarily tuned Duane out, and only really starts listening again because she hears him say something close to what's been running through her head.

He's actually asking her to go to a game. An important game, he says. She should really come and see Owen play. His team has made it to the finals this year.

You should really see your son play, Duane says. It's quite beautiful, really. It's an art form.

She snorts.

You should come for his sake, Duane says. He'll always remember, you know, that you didn't support his interest.

Your interest, she corrects.

Mandalay. He wouldn't have done so well if he weren't completely committed. You should see it. He has passion. It's something to watch.

It wasn't the deal, she says, but even now she is thinking that she has demanded flexibility on some of their deals; that this is perhaps not a fight she wants.

And there's the issue of how much time she spends with each of the boys, how invested she is in their separate interests. It's so much easier to spend time with Aidan. She and Aidan share so many interests; they get each other. She's conscious that Owen is short-changed. It's harder for her to get enthusiastic about his hockey, and she knows she doesn't give him as much time as she does Aidan.

But *hockey*. I will think about it, she says.

I have tickets, Duane says. I'll pick you up.

8

CLEO HAS WORKED FOR NINE YEARS now with Aeolus, an architectural firm. She's an engineer, part of a team of engineers and technicians. She has no input into the original designs, but it's her job to figure out how to execute the architects' visions. Alex Olson and Larry Schiff are the architects. AOLS. Aeolus.

Right now, she's working – the firm is working – on a really big, multi-year project – a block of condominium apartments being constructed where once twenty or so wartime bungalows had quietly decayed, cellars and joists and beams aging out even under the facelifts supplied by various short-term owners over the decades. A block of single-family houses has been razed, and the apartment block will take its place, providing housing for many times the people, as well as commercial space at the street level. And parking!

She needs to make a site visit on this morning, and cabs over from the Aeolus offices. She has a favourite approach; she tells the cab to stop a block away, so that she can see how the profiles of the buildings frame the view, the skyline with the trees of Queen Elizabeth Park rising behind the site. Against a sky of stacked clouds – it will rain, soon – two twenty-storey towers have risen, canted away from each other slightly, formally acknowledging each other's existence, but agreeing to maintain a respectful distance, to accommodate each other's orientation, each other's need for psychic space.

She walks to the site, toward the towers with their raw concrete shells and still-decaled windows, under the scaffolding of the westernmost tower, where workers in orange vests squat, applying ceramic tile cladding. The glaze on the tiles had been developed especially for the project — a cream-and-sepia swirl with a passing skim of iridescent slate-blue. Some of the team had thought the samples looked like parking-lot puddles — muddied water with oil slicks, and the iridescence had required an expensive metal component in the glaze, driving up the cost of the custom ceramic facing significantly. Now that the tile is being installed, though, Cleo can see how well it works — how the earth colours ground the building, and the iridescence looks like reflected sky and water. It's successful.

Sepia. From the ink sac of a particular cuttlefish species, she remembers, from a nature show watched, years ago, with her son Sam.

Along the sidewalk, behind plywood hoardings, is the ground floor, where shops will create a pedestrian neighbourhood. The site manager meets her at the construction entrance, a double-locked steel gate. Inside, then: hard hat donned, riding the freight elevator up to the top floor to see the view; then back down, all the way, to check the underground parking with its car elevators and EV stations and brightly-lit, finished walkways. Next, to the space between the towers, where a starfish-shaped structure, with beautiful angles of steel and glass, will house an indoor market, a food store, a clinic, a library, a gym with pools, a daycare centre. The floating sweep of roof, with its planned gardens. And finally, the show suite, with its elegantly high ceilings, its energy-saving fixtures, its renewable-resource finishing.

This is where she must focus her attention, today. Something has not been functioning, with the HVAC. The builder thinks that the problem is structural: the building is designed in such a way that airflow will be supported by natural force directions: gravity; the moving angle of the sun during the day; the direction of land and sea breezes. The natural airflow is supposed to cut down on the energy required to move air with the mechanical systems. The show suite, whose finishing is being expedited so that pre-sales can begin, is also a test unit for the HVAC and other systems.

Cleo had designed the passive airflow system herself, spending hundreds of hours drafting, researching, testing. It had better work. The firm is applying for a platinum LEED rating, a signifier of leadership in green design, and most of their dossier weight is in the passive air movement systems.

It will work. She has no doubt. If there's a problem, it's likely in the mechanical, which has just been installed.

She talks to the builder, the HVAC installer. She rides back down to the mechanical room; she logs into the computer that will run the systems.

What is happening is that the mechanical isn't working properly, although it tests out normally. It's simply not delivering nearly the volume it should be at the level of the show unit. It's a serious issue; the system won't work at all, if it's not working now.

She checks the controls, the vents. Short of crawling into the ducts herself, she can't think what is happening.

She looks at the plans again, on her own laptop. Rides down to the mechanical room, again.

Can I borrow a measuring tape? she asks.

The site manager doesn't have one. A call goes out; a construction worker comes by, all stubble and too-new leather pouches, and produces a shining yellow-and-chrome version.

We do have laser measures, the site manager says. More accurate.

Cleo shakes her head. She doesn't need accuracy for this one.

She checks, double-checks. There it is. The mistake.

She shows the project manager. The project manager shakes his head, mutters some curses. He's not too upset, as he's able to move the blame downward, onto someone he can unload upon. But he's a little embarrassed. At some level, he's unhappy that Cleo has discovered the error.

She has to deal with this all of the time: project managers who take her for a secretary, a sales rep, an insurance adjuster, a caterer, or a nosy journalist. She is almost never recognized for what she is, the senior engineer of the architectural firm. And when she needs to correct some installation or construction issue, which is frequently, because nobody seems to be able to read a blueprint carefully, she feels an extra layer of resistance, of resentment, possibly, from the contractors. There's a look they get: a blankness of expression. They won't meet her gaze. Sometimes, they don't respond to what she says.

There are initiatives to encourage more young women to go into the trades. Cleo wonders how that is going.

She's showing the project manager, now, on the blueprint, where the error is. She points out the dimensions that were stipulated. She uses a nice voice. She is careful to avoid any hardness, but also any up-talking, any doubtful raising of her voice at the end of sentences.

His face is so expressionless, so absent of engagement, that she wants to pinch him.

He's not happy about the situation, in any way.

He'll just have to deal with it.

Waiting for the cab, Cleo blows on the tips of a pair of imaginary pistols before sliding them into their imaginary hip-slung holsters. Only in the cab does she let herself remember that she has just spent two hours identifying and fixing someone else's mistake, and she can't even bill for this kind of thing.

9

VERONIKA HAS TO DRIVE to the arena, as the action of pressing down the pedals causes Cliff intense pain in his back. Also, he's afraid that his leg will seize up and he'll cause an accident. It has almost happened twice. He doesn't say this to Veronika, though, because she'll try to stop him from driving altogether. And then where will he be?

Veronika's a too-careful driver, having come to driving too late in life, he thinks. She's not confident enough. He has to coax her to pick up speed, to change lanes. She's not happy driving on the freeway or in downtown Vancouver. She's not happy even making this drive to the next city. He can see the tightness of her shoulders, her grim concentration. But it was her idea to go to the game. She insisted. So she can't complain.

Take the Pitt Meadows exit, he says. You want to get onto number seven. You'll want to get into the right lane. Speed up. Okay, yes, there's a truck on your tail. You can see him in your mirror now. Put on your signal. Keep your speed up. Okay, you need to change lanes now. Now! Keep your foot on the gas. You can't change lanes and then slow down. Yeah, well you kind of cut him off there. That's why he honked.

It's hopeless. She's too timid, and that makes her erratic, slow to react. She needs to make her moves and follow through more decisively.

You make me nervous, she says.

You make *me* nervous, he says.

It's very inexpensive to go to minor hockey league games, especially the Midget and Bantam ones. And the hockey, in the triple-A leagues, is pretty good. It's pretty good to watch. He enjoys it. Veronika likes to do it; she likes to go support their nephew, she says. He looks around and they spot Owen's father, Duane, coming into the stands. Veronika complains that Mandalay, Cliff's sister, doesn't ever attend her son's games, and neither does his other sister, Cleo, nor any of Owen's cousins. Nor his twin brother. Nobody has any family feeling, Veronika says.

He sees his nephew Owen skate onto the ice, slow down, look right at him, raise his gloved hand. Veronika waves back, overdoing it, maybe.

Yours? The woman next to him asks.

My nephew, Cliff says. It's a great feeling, to say that.

He's always thought that if he had a son, he'd want him to be like Owen.

They're not going to have kids, he and Veronika, he guesses. He's never known exactly how old Veronika is — she has let slip that the date on her Estonian birth certificate isn't accurate — but Cliff is forty-two and he thinks Veronika has a few years on him.

That one's talented, the woman next to him says, meaning Owen. He'll be in the NHL one day, for sure.

That would be great, Cliff says.

He hasn't been to an NHL game in years, not since, maybe, that time with Ben. Yeah, that would have been it. His younger brother Ben, who had been adopted by another family when he was a baby, a family who possessed things like a corporate box at the NHL games. Ben's adopted dad had brought Cliff and Ben to a Canucks game, must have been around 2003–2004. The West Coast Express, Bertuzzi and Näslund. The ten-game streak. And the team in the run for the division title, until Bertuzzi lost it and attacked that other player. What was his name? One of the Flames? No, he was on a US team.

Landed on him, flattened him. Broke his back. *Avalanche*, that was it. An accident that had turned out so bad the guy had been paralyzed. Just bad luck, the way he fell. But Bertuzzi had punched the guy from behind.

Anyway. Years ago, now.

That was the year that Cliff had inherited the company, the landscaping company he worked for.

Ben had gone back to school, to law school, after they had gone bankrupt. Cliff hears news of him, occasionally, from his sisters. He doesn't go anywhere that Ben might turn up.

His company; he has worked for it, in one form or another, for over twenty years now. For Mrs. Cookshaw, for himself, for Ben's dad, for the Singhs.

Over twenty years.

The whistle blows; the game starts. Owen's team is at the opposite end of the ice in the opening period, far down the arena.

Veronika says: Why doesn't Owen get to score some goals?

Oh for god's sake. He's a defenceman. You can see that. It's his job to protect his own goal.

That doesn't sound as good.

It's just as good, he says. But he knows what she means. It's the offence, the players who get the goals and assists who get the most attention, who are the media stars. They're the ones whose names everyone knows.

But it's just as important to defend your own end, isn't it? To defend what you have. Because anything that's yours can be lost.

10

THE SOUND OF THE ECHO inside the building, the smells, decant into Mandalay's mind a memory: herself and Duane, seventeen years ago, in a different arena. A Stanley Cup game, was it? Mandalay had not wanted to go, but it had been a big deal for Duane, having tickets, and she had been his girlfriend, so she had ended up in some special box near the ice belonging to a millionaire client of Duane's. She'd smiled and stayed quiet to cover her ignorance, and had drunk the alcohol that was offered her, and wished she was anywhere else.

And now here they are, she and Duane, about to watch a game in which their son is playing. How had that happened? They'd been romantic partners for such a short time – eight or nine months – and in the weird adversarial position of joint custodial parents for almost two decades since. And Owen a hockey player! That's not something she had intended for him.

She sees in another section of the stands (are they called stands? Or bleachers?) her brother Cliff and his wife Veronika. They're waving to her. She waves back.

Duane says: They come to every game.

That's just weird, she says. She knows Duane means it as a dig, a comment on her not attending. She watches them now, Cliff sunk, brooding, in his wheelchair; Veronika knitting. Watching Owen play with some sort of strange sense of ownership. She resents it.

She doesn't know where she has got the image that Veronika is knitting. She's not a knitter. Once, Mandalay had asked Veronika if she could knit – there was something about Veronika's broad neck and upper arms, her stolid filling of chairs, that suggested the idea to Mandalay. But Cliff's wife had sneered. Knitting, handicrafts, she had said. For children in nursery school, or great-grandmothers too old to work.

It's her cell phone that keeps Veronika's hands busy, her eyes and fingers moving, Mandalay sees, now.

She watches the two teams file onto the ice, shake hands. Owen's team is the one in red with white and black trim and a logo of a Native American with feathers in his hair. She's not sure how they are still using that logo. How Owen, with his private school courses in social justice and cultural awareness can think it's okay. She can't tell the boys apart and has to find Owen by his number, which is 17. There he is. She feels she ought to be able to identify him by the shape of his body, or the way he moves, but she can't. There's too much padding, too much altering of the natural shape and posture.

She ought to just *know* intuitively, because he's her son, half her heart, but she doesn't. She can't pick him out of the line, without the number on his jersey.

Maybe she could if she were more interested. If she didn't have so much aversion.

The boys are breaking the line now and skating around the oval; they are being introduced by the announcer. Owen begins his loop. When he passes in front of her and Duane, he slows, she thinks. Under his raised visor, she can see his eyes crinkle at her. He's surprised, amused. He ducks his head. He skates on.

The teams take their formation; the extras skate off the ice. The whistle blows and the puck drops. The game is underway.

She doesn't find beauty in the game. She sees short, violent slaps of the sticks, ungainly dashes, random movement. It's all about violence and brute force, to her – she can't see any finesse or strategy. And even if there were, there's no point to it. Nothing is created. Controlled, commercialized militarization; that's what it's all in aid of.

She had helped Owen wash and repair his clothing and equipment, had got up early to make him breakfast on practice mornings. She had bit her tongue. But she had not liked it.

She'd hoped that he would give it up, after the first year or so, but he'd kept going up through the age levels, Pee Wee, Bantam, Midget. In his second year he'd moved from a house league to a competitive league, which had Owen and Duane happy, and her really unhappy. She'd been able to accept his hockey, just, as a non-competitive sport in which he'd make friends and get some coordination. She'd agreed to it on those conditions.

Then she'd felt trapped: she really, really didn't want Owen to play competitive hockey. And he really wanted to. Oh, she'd been angry at Duane, in those days.

She is still angry with him, she guesses. She is just too tired to be as angry. It takes too much energy.

It's something she needs to let go of, this anger.

She watches Owen — she's not always sure it's Owen — skate back and forth, chasing the puck. As there is only one puck, and several players of each team on the ice, most of the boys' time is spent watching the movement, chasing, waiting for the puck to near them.

Watching a black rubber disk flung around the ice, and occasionally attempting to hit at it with a flattened stick. How was that in any way a meaningful activity?

She watches the player she thinks is Owen skate back and forth, back and forth.

She directs attention to her breath. She directs awareness at her blaze of anger. She imagines it burning under a jar, a little flame that will burn itself out.

Beside her, Duane is completely focussed, his posture and gaze and even the movements of his body tied completely to the game. The whole crowd is like this. The spectators turn their heads, lean, gasp, cheer, fist-pump, get to their feet, almost as one.

It's terrifying, isn't it, to see a whole arena full of people reacting as a single mindless organism?

She has been to music concerts where this happens, but it's not the same.

At the end of the first period, Duane gets up and stretches. Want a coffee? he asks.

She does not want a coffee.

An acquaintance of Duane's leans over, congratulates him on Owen's playing. Duane goes off with this man, comes back with beer breath, and a bottle of water for her.

She's glad of the water.

The teams change ends. She looks at the scoreboard, to see who is winning. It's a tie. Owen isn't on the ice, at first. She thinks another player, roughly his size, with the same shade of dirty-blond hair emerging from the back of his helmet is Owen, but then she sees he is not, and she intuits from Duane's body language that Owen isn't actually playing.

When Owen skates back on, she both hears and sees it. He's down at the other end of the ice from her seat. She keeps her eyes on him.

He's playing a position that doesn't get to score goals, she sees. He's mostly on his own team's end, and goes into action when the other team starts rushing toward the goal. She thinks, *get out of the way!* when the other team rushes, but in fact Owen goes intentionally toward them, uses his body to be in their way, slaps and hooks his stick at the puck. There are a lot of collisions. He gets shoved, a lot.

Owen gets the puck and there is nobody near him for a second or part of second, and he's moving down the ice toward the other goal, now – is he allowed to do that? – and then the buzzer goes. The play stops, right where it's at.

Two-thirds over.

When the third period starts, Owen is back at her end again. She can see him more clearly – see the movements of his hips, his knees, his arms, as he watches the puck. He's responding to its position, its movement, she sees, as if connected to it by an invisible thread. At the same time, he's registering, in the same instinctive way, the movements of all of the other people on the ice.

She watches, from a little behind and to the right of him. She can hear, now, the slap of Owen's stick on the ice. She sees the spray of ice shaved up in a sparkling parabolic fountain, from the side of his skate. She hears the sound his skate blade makes shaving the ice as he brakes and turns, a satisfying hiss. She begins to feel it, then. She feels the movements of the players, of the small hard black disk, of Owen's body. It's as if she has one of her hands on his back and is picking up all of his sensory information, the way she used to when he was very small, when he was beginning to walk.

When the player from the opposing team comes at Owen from the side at great force and speed, she notices only at the instant Owen does, and flinches sideways as Owen is bodychecked into the boards almost at her feet. She can't breathe, and Duane leaps to his feet. The sound of Owen hitting the boards repeats in her ears.

He's on the ice, on his side. A whistle blows.

He has bounced back to his feet. He's upright. He shakes himself, shakes his joints loose again. (She knows that gesture; her body shakes off the impact, too, sympathetically). Someone in black and white stripes skates over to him, asks him something. He shakes his head. He adjusts his helmet. The whistle blows again. He skates off.

Duane is sitting down again. He has beads of sweat at his temple. She's clutching his hand, or he's clutching hers.

She frees her hand immediately. Breathes.

She has to disentangle herself from Duane.

And the hockey has to go.

2017

11

THE 737 BEGINS ITS DESCENT hundreds of miles to the west and north of its destination: it is flying so high, twelve kilometers high, that it will take an hour to drop safely to earth. On the screen in front of her seat, Cleo can see the plane icon: they are somewhere above the Atlantic. They have flown directly from Vancouver, curving up over the Arctic, which shortens the distance, belying the scenario of the flat map, and are now somewhere west of Britain, the map on the screen tells her, although through the window, she can see only cloud.

She imagines a conversation with her son, Sam, about the flattened poles of the planet. It's difficult to remember, having seen only flat, distorting maps and rotating globes, that the earth really resembles a mandarin orange. Sam would know the data about the earth's shape: the reasons for it, the measurements. He would be quick to counter her statements – to contradict or refine on them, in his didactic way. He would lecture her for some time on the earth's curvature, if she were to ask him.

She thinks of Sam, home in Vancouver, so many hours away from her. She will turn on her phone once she lands in Copenhagen, and can connect to Wi-Fi. She'll check her messages, to see how Sam is faring.

She has made the trip to Copenhagen twice before: she flies there for work, to meet with a furniture design company that she does business with. She's too busy to travel much, outside of business trips. Cleo's friends, her colleagues, her brother Ben, even her daughter, Olivia, seem to globe-trot on a whim: *I decided to hop to Paris*, they'll say.

I changed my mind at the last minute and took the train to Barcelona.
We had a day to spare so rented some bikes and cycled through Wales.

She can really only justify the time when she's travelling for work. And neither her husband, Trent, nor Sam likes flying, so they don't go abroad for holidays.

The plane doesn't descend smoothly, it seems, but rather in stages: they will drop a bit, then level off. It's probably something to do with other planes. She can see them, sometimes. There are thousands of flights crisscrossing Europe on any given day. The drops are not enjoyable. Her body doesn't like the drops.

But she'll be on the ground soon, soon.

The woman in the seat next to her wakes up finally and heads for the washroom. Cleo stands up too. She has wanted to go for a while, but hasn't wanted to climb over her sleeping neighbour. The woman's seat area is a swamp of crumbs and wrappers and airline blankets and earphone wires, of magazines and bags spilling their contents. Cleo's things are packed away. She sees the woman's glasses, or the case for them, under the aisle seat of the row ahead. Should she mention them? She's not sure her seat neighbour speaks English. Cleo's reading glasses are put away properly in her carry-on, along with everything else she has brought with her.

The fasten-seatbelt sign comes on, just as she is returning to her seat. Her seat neighbour rises to let her slide in. The woman begins to collect her things, twisting and bending in the small space. Cleo shrinks away from her jutting elbows. She says, Your glasses are on the floor in front. She points. The woman can't see, or perhaps doesn't understand. Cleo says it again, in French. Cleo leans over, half across the woman's knees, and retrieves the glasses case. The woman looks annoyed; she doesn't do the abashed smile and I'm-so-careless pantomime that most people would. She just looks annoyed.

Cleo has avoided looking at, or speaking to, her neighbours, for the duration of the flight. She has spent the last nine hours within a couple of feet from them, but couldn't describe them, or pick them out of a crowd. It feels unnatural, a kind of torture, to be crammed so close to strangers for so many hours. Even in business class, there are too many strangers, too close.

There is still some time before they land. A flight attendant comes by, gathering plastic juice glasses and food trays and paper coffee cups and crumpled paper napkins. What a lot of garbage this trip has generated. She wonders if the paper and plastic is recycled. She thinks probably not. She thinks of the jet fuel, the carbon footprint. Is this trip necessary? Possibly not. Probably not.

For a few moments a kind of panic fills her. She can feel it seep in, like a gas, like pressurized air, she thinks. It takes the form of a growing dismay, a growing sense that she is in the wrong place. The fasten seat belt lights come on and she buckles her belt, presses herself against the seat back, grips the chair arms. Cold sweat breaks out on her forehead and chest, and she feels that all of the blood has drained from her head.

A flight attendant, checking seat belts, asks if she's okay. You're a little pale, he says. He indicates the bag tucked into the pouch of the seat in front of her.

She's okay. It's not queasiness that is assailing her, not air sickness, but a strange desire to throw herself from the plane, or to at least run down the aisle toward the back, clawing her way, screaming to be let off.

She would never do anything like that, of course.

She always forgets this part of the trip, and it's getting worse. She should ask her doctor for a prescription for Ativan, maybe. Only, how to explain it? She doesn't have a phobia of flying – not at all. It's rather something existential. She is too far from home. Too far from *home*, and a kind of visceral animal panic just can't deal with it. It's too silly, really to tell anyone about.

Now she can see through the little window they have dived below the clouds, and the aircraft is tilting over the deep clean tourmaline water of the Øresund, then the harbour of Copenhagen, with its modernist abstract forest of pure white wind turbine towers emerging from the surface. The bump and thump of the plane on the runway. Still, the sensation of being disastrously dislocated doesn't fade.

It has passed, eventually, on previous trips. She knows it will pass. She must just breathe through it, go through the necessary familiar motions of disembarking from the plane, passing through customs (a mere nod, in Copenhagen, unlike in Frankfurt or London – why is that?), finding her way to the train. Eventually, it will pass. She won't really recognize when it leaves her, when it disappears, but all at once, she will feel attached to her surroundings again. Grounded. That's not quite it, though. She just feels the absence of the dysphoria. That is it. She feels fine, again, as if she has rebooted.

THIRD TIME LUCKY, Cleo says to herself as she waits in line to buy her train ticket from the airport, which is in a satellite town called Kastrup, to downtown Copenhagen. The first time, she had stared at the bank of ticket machines in complete incomprehension. They looked nothing like the rapid transit dispensers in Vancouver. She could not make out any of the Danish. A tall woman behind her in the line had stepped forward and with a mixture of embarrassment, impatience, and politeness had helped her. Cleo had not been embarrassed at all. Why should she be? She did not expect to be proficient. But the Danish woman had been embarrassed for her.

She had noted that. A useful bit of knowledge.

The second time, Cleo had known from her previous trip how to work the machines, and had bought her own ticket, without making anyone in the line behind her antsy. (She had done the logical thing, on her first trip; she had gone back to the train station on her own, had found a time when there was no lineup, had figured out the machines, had taken photos of them with her phone to remind herself.) She had purchased the ticket easily, and then had gone to the platform to wait, but the train had not arrived. There had been an announcement, in Danish. The people on the platform had left. She had gone back to the main concourse, too, and looked around for a train office, some sort of representative, but there were none. Eventually, she'd asked a woman her own age, in English: What happened to the trains?

The woman had looked at her wide-eyed, and again, she'd sensed the woman's embarrassment. The trains have just gone on strike, the woman had said.

A wildcat strike. Why had the woman been embarrassed? How could Cleo know? And she has been assured that everyone her age or younger has learned English in school. As a country with a population under six million, Danish people need to know another language, she had been told. They even use English to communicate with the Swedes and Norwegians. Presumably it would be expected that a visitor might not speak Danish, might ask for a translation?

Again, it had been mystifying, but useful information.

This third time, Cleo knows a little Danish. Only a little, but she has bought an online course, practiced reading and hearing and speaking basic sentences and phrases useful for travelling. She had learned French and German easily in high school, finding the courses slow, undemanding, and again, she finds she can pick up the nuances of sound and inflection, can understand the logic of the grammar rules, very easily. What's different is that she doesn't have the retention for new information that she had in her teens. But she has more discipline. She has more focus.

She buys her train ticket. The unintelligible choices now make sense to her, and she chooses, easily, one adult ticket, no return, to *Køben-havns Hovedbanegård*, Copenhagen Central Train Station. She feels a little glow at her own competence. She is happy not to disconcert the tall elegant competent Danes. She appreciates their rigorous personal boundaries.

CLEO HAS NO MEETINGS this first day; she has booked herself time to ground herself, to recover from her jet lag, so once she has checked into her hotel near the station – Wake Up, the hotel is called – she sets off to make the most of the day, to learn something more about the city. She has a guidebook; she has a day pass for transit. She has walking shoes. She'll avoid the tourist places, the Top Ten Sights, as she's been to most of those before, on previous trips.

She had not travelled in her teens or twenties, as so many people she knows had done. She should have, then, when she was younger, more impressionable. Less anxious.

Yes, she is anxious, though she throws herself into things. Brave, but anxious. She is afraid of upsetting the Danes with her mistakes.

It is a grey day, with lowering clouds, but a good day for walking, for photographing, if she wants to do that. She downloads maps and walks to the city centre, the older parts of the city. She walks along canals and stone sidewalks. The public buildings are all fortresses: even the storybook castle ones are heavy, solid-looking, built of dark, earth or ash-coloured stone and brick, with heavy, metal-banded doors and small windows trimmed in dark colours. It's all a bit grim. It looks like it was built by people who feared their neighbours, feared the gods, never laughed (or only laughed at others' misfortunes). The private houses are a bit less formidable. Occasionally is there an elegant Palladian-style terrace house with tall windows, a pretty gabled and tiled roof, plastered in yellow or salmon or slate blue.

But then, surprisingly, a building so ultra-modern as to appear futuristic: a high-rise near one of the canals is shaped like a tall wedge of cake or cheese, and sheathed entirely in glass panes. And then buildings so old that she can't imagine they still stand: some timbered medieval houses, a Romanesque church. Cobblestones prevail on even the main streets and squares.

And everywhere, of course, bicycles.

She walks along a canal and sees on the other side the row of tall painted 18th-century houses that look to her like doll's houses. Four storeys high, with attics. They must have been cold in winter, the attics, where servants or impoverished artists would have lived. In one of the houses lived Hans Christian Anderson, who wrote about lonely children and poverty, and a kind of pre-Christian magic connected to the earth and the elements and the human heart. Cleo had read those stories, as a child, and had read them to her children. She remembers their eeriness and otherworldliness. The row of red and yellow and blue houses brightens up Anderson's dark images.

She has lunch in an outdoor café, where she's offered a soft woolen blanket against the cold.

IN THE AFTERNOON IT RAINS, and she goes to the National Museum and looks at the aurochs and the bog mummies, the bronze-age shields and lamps, the lumps and ornaments of amber (amber that is blood-coloured, not golden) and the Viking maps and ships and buckets of buried gold. Sam would like this, she thinks. She should have taken him on this trip. He's old enough that he could have amused himself in Copenhagen while she was in her meetings. But it hadn't coincided with his school break, and he was reluctant to miss classes. He's big on rules, Sam is.

She and Trent have never travelled. They had agreed when they got married that this was something they would do. But first, they couldn't afford it, and then, it was too much trouble to arrange, with children, Trent thought. Now he says he doesn't like flying. She thinks that he never really meant to go. He didn't want to go. It's a long-standing, low-intensity point of contention between them.

She reads the text in the guidebooks and on the plaques on the walls, in the museums. It seems that most of the skeletons or bog mummies have grievous head injuries, but it is unclear whether or not they died of their injuries. Sometimes the skulls show signs of bone healing. Did the Neolithic and the Bronze Age people that lived here routinely bash each other over the head? Were their short lives in a state of constant conflict ending in a painful death?

There's a female mummy found buried in an oak log, partly preserved by the tannins. A small skeleton, the size of a ten-year-old, although that of an adult woman, reposing in a glass case. Sleeping Beauty. Cleo reads that she was found with a little cap, a cap made of kingfisher feathers, which would have flashed an iridescent blue. She can see the cap, dull now, in the case, next to the woman's skeleton. The cap would have hidden a big dent in her head, from a blow with a weapon. She had survived the blow for many years, but she might well have been visually or cognitively impaired, Cleo reads. The damage to her skull was that severe; the blow was that severe. But somebody took care of her, the placard says. She was loved; fed; clothed. Someone sewed her a little cap of iridescent blue kingfisher feathers to wear on her dented head.

Cleo, standing by the glass coffin, feels tears spring to her eyes. She feels her chest ache, as if something inside her is trying to batter its way out. She does not know why these fragments of story, from several thousand years in the past should affect her.

She is tired, that is all.

But the sense of dislocation that had possessed her on the plane has passed. And in its place another sense: that her life back home, her life in Vancouver, has ceased to be real. She experiences this sensation, now, too.

THE FIRST DAY OF MEETINGS starts with a brief coffee session and introductions and greetings by the company directors and designers, which Cleo is glad about. She has sort of forgotten who they are, since her last visit – has forgotten exactly what they look like, what their roles were. But in the conference room, she remembers them: Anders, Karsten, Pernille, Jonas, and Louise, whom she met two years ago. And Camilla and Mads, who are new. Anders and Pernille are around Cleo's age; Karsten maybe a few years younger, in his early forties. The others are younger, in their early to mid-thirties, perhaps. They are all architects and designers. Cleo is technically a client of theirs. Or the company she works for is a client of their company, and she is the representative.

They are all strangers to her at first – she has almost forgotten them – but then they transform, they assume, or resume, familiar shapes and faces and voices, to the degree that she is able to recognize that Louise has a new hairstyle and Jonas has new glasses.

They transform themselves back into acquaintances.

Cleo has been involved with this company, Mogun, for nearly fifteen years now, since her early days at *re/vision,* her previous employer. She'd been the only person to *get* her boss, Kate's, concept for creating a partnership with the little Danish start-up. Everyone else at *re/vision* had opposed it, on mostly reasonable grounds. It wasn't Canadian; it used a lot of particle board (sawdust and glue, they had said), so was disposable, and not environmentally friendly; the company was too new, too small.

Kate had patiently gone through all of the objections with the designers at *re/vision.* They used waste wood product and non-toxic plant-based glue; their woods were sustainably sourced, fair-trade. They had a platinum safety and emissions record, and paid their employees European-scale compensation and benefits. Their products – the office fittings and furniture – were modular, and could be re-configured, re-used. And as for disposable, Kate had said: they all knew, being in the commercial space renovation business, that expensive, several-lifetimes-durable oak and maple and mahogany panelling, desks, credenzas were continually being ripped out of office space, and usually not recycled. Steel chairs, leather sofas, whose expense someone had justified because they would never need to be replaced became unfashionable and ended up at the scrap dealers.

Why not use products that were cheaper and would not outlive their usefulness?

Cleo had got it right away. The decision had been a good example of the things she had admired about Kate – her ability to see what was coming, what was just on the horizon, and to take the opposite stance to the prevailing ethos or beliefs. Kate has long since moved on, reinventing herself, serially, as a partner in an upscale architectural firm, the presenter of a house-and-garden channel renovation show, a producer of other lifestyles television shows, and a brand of trendy housewares. Cleo, whom Kate had brought along to Aeolus, the architectural firm, and then left in her wake, has remained the contact person for the Danish company, Mogun, encouraging her firm's designers to choose it for their clients.

She had inherited the contact with Danish company, though not Kate's vision and *chutzpa*, which might have been useful.

But a few years ago, Mogun had suggested that Cleo fly out to meet with them (as Kate used to do). Cleo had done that, and all at once the names the designers and the sales people and managers with whom she'd been communicating for years, whom she'd known only as names, had become real people.

This visit starts, as the previous two have, with meetings, charts, PowerPoints. There are discussions of issues of the past couple of years: a shipment gone astray, a design flaw, some problematic connectors and a dye lot change in one of the laminate colour options, which isn't supposed to happen. If a client bought cubical dividers in *Katost* pink fifteen years ago, they should still be able to get matching *Katost* credenzas. It's one of the company's selling points.

Of course, the other colours from the *Earth and Farm* series still tone up with the originals, one of the designers says. *Selleri*, or *Cassis*, or *Moss*, for example.

They take the change very seriously. They are apologetic; they discuss options in minute detail.

There will be a nudge toward increasing the orders: some offers, some incentives, but that won't happen until the last day.

They are methodical and intense, these lean polite Danes with their Viking jaws and cheekbones.

After the review of issues or problems, the changes in production and shipping processes, and then the projections. And then the introduction to new products, and finally the sales pitch. It's very in-depth. It takes three days.

Cleo likes that she knows what to expect. She settles herself more comfortably in her vegan-leather chair, which is very comfortable and has patented microscopic pores so that it breathes. The chairs are engineered ash and grey-teal upholstery, and the boardroom table around which they're sitting is ash with lighter teal panels. They are part of the *Nordsøen* collection, and the anchor colours are this dark grey-green, *Nordsøen*, North Sea, mist-greys and blue-greens, and that really nice *Søgraes* orange: kelp orange. She has this combination in her own office. It's her favourite.

IN THE EVENING, they all go out to dinner. Pernille picks her up at the hotel, in her Volvo.

At the restaurant, which is Danish, minimalist, expensive, they have foods that Cleo has never eaten before, or at least, never eaten in this form. First, marinated cod, which is cod fillets sliced very thinly and dressed with onion and orange and fennel and juniper berries. She's nervous; is it really okay to eat raw cod? She remembers live worms in cod fillets she has bought at the supermarket, at home.

Pernille says: Yes, but you must buy it very fresh. It must smell of the sea, not the harbour. And Karsten, who is next to her, says in a low voice: It is a different kind of cod, I think. Mads, two seats away, breaks off the conversation he's having to say: I believe there are many types of fish that we call cod. And it's back to Pernille, who adds: And one fish that is a cod, that we call pollock, in Danish. I don't remember the English word...

It's also pollock in English, Mads says.

Cleo feels herself sinking into a deep pool, a deep spongy mossy pool of comfort. These are her people. She could listen to them discuss cod all night. How civilized, how elegant, to know about the different species of cod, the different words for them in various languages, their history and the preferred way to cook the fish in various seasons.

After the appetizers there is asparagus with a hollandaise flavoured with an unfamiliar herb – chervil, Pernille says – and a dish of smoked eel. Do you know, Mads says, people used to think that eels at their different life stages were different species, they transform themselves so much?

Potatoes and peas that taste of early summer and garden; a cake of rhubarb and cream and puff pastry, all layered; an elderflower sorbet. Simple garden or countryside food, made magical.

Cleo likes table d'hôte, likes to have courses and wine chosen for her. She likes the conversation, which trickles here and there, impersonal, apolitical. She likes the Mogun people, who are so amiable to her, though she knows that they are courting her business, her patronage.

She likes that, within a safely inscribed set of boundaries, she doesn't know what is going to happen next. That new things will happen.

Her third evening in the city, after the second day of meetings, Cleo will be given dinner again, but this time by just one of the senior members of the company and his or her family, not the whole group. On her first visit, four years ago, Anders and his wife and their two grown sons had taken her to a loud bar with a lot of hard liquor brewed in local distilleries, and food that she had thought of as Danish tapas. There had been a DJ, and Anders, his wife, and the sons had all danced with Cleo, in turn, solemnly, punctiliously, flawlessly, as if she were being included in a rather esoteric church service, some rites important to the family, hidden from daily life, but close to its heart. Afterwards, she had hyperventilated in the taxi all the way back to her hotel, overstimulated.

She'd kind of dreaded the evening out with a colleague, which was evidently a ritual, the next visit, but it had been different. On her trip two years ago, Pernille had invited her for dinner at her house, *en famille*. Pernille was a single parent with two teenaged children, similar in ages to Cleo's own two. Pernille had ordered pizza. After dinner the children had disappeared and Pernille had opened a third and then a fourth bottle of wine, kicked off her high-heeled boots, tucked her feet under her on the sofa, and told Cleo about her divorce, which had been precipitated by her husband's infidelity, and about which process Pernille seemed to have no ambivalence, no self-doubt, no second thoughts. The story was a lesson in determination, in sensible pragmatism, Cleo thought. She wished some of her friends, who had been caught for years in indecision over their unhappy marriages, could have heard it.

This year it must be the turn of Karsten, the third senior partner, unless they are going to skip him and turn her over to one of the younger colleagues.

Karsten, she gathers, is a bachelor, and possibly gay, though she's not good at reading metrosexual Europeans. Karsten is the most reserved of the designers, the one who says least, but whose opinions seem to cut through to the heart of things. She feels that he does not waste time on what doesn't interest him, or what someone else could do as well.

She doesn't know why she has assumed he is gay, either. He is very good-looking and well-dressed, though all of the designers are dressed in hip, interesting, well-fitted clothing. He seems very intense and private though, and maybe it's those qualities that make it hard to imagine him wanting to entertain her, one-on-one, for an evening.

She remembers now with some embarrassment that she had remarked to Pernille, on her last visit, when they'd been on their second bottle of wine in Pernille's living room, that she thought Karsten was exceptionally attractive. Pernille had raised her eyebrows. I do not think so, she had said.

Had there been an implicit message for Cleo in her response? It seemed obvious that Karsten was attractive. But maybe Danes had different standards of physical beauty.

No, that's a silly thought. But there is something – something she can't put her finger on. And she can't imagine that Karsten will either go to a gin-and-jazz bar or curl up on a sofa with personal disclosures. So maybe it won't be Karsten.

But she doesn't mind. Everything so far, everything her hosts have planned for her, on all of her visits, has been useful and interesting. She has enjoyed herself.

Pernille had also said: Karsten always says *we should* when others say *we shouldn't*.

Had she meant he was an iconoclast (a good thing in a designer, surely) or that he was just wired a bit differently? But Pernille hadn't elaborated.

Karsten is a bit of a mystery. Cleo isn't sure how a private dinner with him will turn out. But it is all an adventure, a break from her real life. Nothing that happens will have great consequences.

When she reconnects to her hotel Wi-Fi that evening, Cleo has messages on her phone from Sam, Olivia, and Trent, besides her work messages, which she can mostly defer answering. What time is it in Vancouver? Mid-afternoon: while she was in meetings, earlier today, they were all still asleep. While she was at dinner with the Mogen gang and during her trip there, they have all awakened, begun their days, decided to message her. She feels, again, the gap, the slippage in what is real.

Olivia's message is chipper: *Hope you're having a fantastic time! Buy yourself SHOES!* Olivia's in Toronto, and only six hours behind, instead of nine in Vancouver. Sam wants to know if she can WhatsApp with him, this evening, her time. If she isn't busy, he says, politely.

Trent's is just — Trent: *Hey, Crystal called at about five a.m. She seemed to have no idea how early it was, or that you were away! Off her meds?* Trent trades in the shared jokes of ten or fifteen years earlier, as if he's unable to sense that things change, people move on. He never gets when things are no longer a joke.

She sends back to Olivia a smiley emoticon, a heart, and the message *In your size, I suppose?* Trent's message, she'll ignore. She's tired, but she'll talk to Sam. She has always answered a call or message from one of her children. It doesn't even feel like a decision, to be available to her children. It's just an integral part of her, like breathing.

Her friend Mira had once said to her: You're only as happy as your least happy child. It was an observation, not a boast or piece of advice. It's true, she thinks. If something is bothering Sam, she will listen. She will take it on, to a certain extent.

She is a good mom. Better than a good-enough mom, she hopes.

She is not such a good sister or daughter or wife. And why should she be? There are limits on what one grown adult can expect from another, aren't there? She wouldn't expect anyone else to drop what they were doing and look after her needs.

Knock on wood.

One's children, though — that's different. There's some obligation to see them through to independence. One could even say it's a pragmatic choice.

Sam will graduate from high school this year. He'll go to university in Vancouver, and he'll get a job when he graduates — he's in computer science, he's good at it. He'll get a job, and he'll grow up, and move out. Not necessarily in that order. But he'll become a functioning, independent adult, as Olivia has.

It's only a short time now.

And then with her youngest child out on his own, she'll be free. Only a short time.

12

MANDALAY SAYS: I thought your dad was picking you up for your driving test.

No, Owen says. Max is. But we're going to swing by Dad's and pick up his vehicle, as it's the one we practiced in.

Well, that's nice of Max, Mandalay says.

It's useful that the boys organize their own lives, more or less, these days. The years of complicated arrangements via telephone calls, of the careful creation of a network of drivers and at-home parents and favours and obligations, which had been necessary to manage the boys' lives and which had fallen to her to manage, have suddenly (it feels like) evaporated. Now, if she's lucky, she is informed whether or not either of the boys will be home for dinner.

Not like Duane to miss out on this kind of milestone, though. What's up with your dad today? she asks. It's not her habit to ask about Duane, and she sees Aidan, hovering over the toaster, glance at her quickly, as if startled.

Or as if wary, maybe. She and Aidan, so closely connected, intuitively: it's like there's still an umbilical cord between them. A ghost umbilical cord.

Owen, energetically spreading peanut butter on a stack of toast already on his plate – he's eating it faster than Aidan can produce it – says, cheerfully: Dad was going to take us, of course. But his surgery got scheduled for today.

Oh, his surgery, Mandalay murmurs. (Has she heard about this?

Is she supposed to know? Sometimes, lately, she tunes out things the twins tell her. Just sometimes. But they don't tell her everything.)

Yeah, surgery, Aidan says. He looks unhappy, his lips pressed together, his eyes round behind the round lenses of his glasses. He won't say anything more, Mandalay can tell, but she thinks also that she reads embarrassment, rather than dread, in his expression. So maybe not serious surgery, but something personal? Colonoscopy? But Duane would have rescheduled. Something to do with the prostate? She had recently heard one of her students refer to someone having "ass cancer." Much better to have some delicacy, though she doesn't want Aidan to feel that any part of the body is shameful to discuss.

Yeah, Owen says, talking with a mouthful of toast and peanut butter. Dad's got ear cancer.

Ear cancer? Is there even such a thing?

Moron, Aidan says. It's skin cancer on his ear. The top of his ear.

Well, that's not surprising. Duane has been bald for decades, and he's always out in the sun, sailing, kayaking, windsurfing, whatever.

It's funnier to say ear cancer, Owen says.

It's not funny, Aidan says. You can die from skin cancer. Melanoma.

So Aidan is upset, not embarrassed? Had she read him incorrectly?

Yea, Owen says. But he's just going to get a piece of his ear cut off. He laughs.

That's kind of lacking in empathy, Owen, Mandalay says. To find it funny.

Owen shrugs. That's how it struck me.

She dislikes her son, at this moment. And yet, of the two, he is the closest to his father, and more vulnerable to any kind of bad news. She has tried to discourage it, in her sons, this jokey, callous response to emotional events. It's a form of toxic masculinity, to minimize the feelings, to distract oneself with jokes, to pretend insensitivity. She has tried to show them a better way, but it's all around them.

She can't control everything they come into contact with. She has tried, but she can't control every influence.

That's scary, Owen, she says. Do you know if he will be in the hospital long? Will he want visitors?

Mom. It's okay, Aidan says. Just lean out a bit, okay, Mom?

It's none of her business, but she needs to know, somehow. She'll call Taylor Gibbons, maybe. The other twins' mother. It would be Taylor who has arranged for Max Gibbons to take the four of them – her sons and the Gibbons pair – for their driver's tests, as a group, when Duane couldn't do it. Taylor who arranged the tests all together in the first place. Max is a businessman who could talk any deal into being, but it is Taylor who manages the household, in that traditional arrangement, and the family money, in a not-so-traditional arrangement. Taylor had dusted off her CPA licence, back in the crash of 2008, when Max had gone bankrupt, and supported them all for a couple of years, until Max was back in action. Now his bankruptcy looked more like a small blip in his rising fortune, but back then it had been pretty devastating.

Taylor had also kept up the friendship between her twins, Galton and Mahalia, and Mandalay's sons, via much ferrying of the four of them in her car, signing them up for fencing and pottery and drama and sea kayaking classes. Duane paid, of course – Mandalay had even paid, for a couple of things – but it was Taylor who searched out the opportunities and booked them and got the kids there.

Mandalay does not like to admit what she owes Taylor. Of course Taylor is extremely wealthy – domestic-staff-level of wealthy – but Mandalay would not have done all of that arranging even if she hadn't been in school or working, probably. Taylor runs rings around Mandalay, as Duane has pointed out.

Taylor will know what's up with Duane. Mandalay will call her, when she finds a moment.

In fact, it's Taylor who calls Mandalay. About Tuesday, she says.

She's always to the point. As Max is taking the kids to their test, could Mandalay pick Duane up from hospital? Taylor would herself, but she's committed to a board meeting.

Of course she is. Taylor is on the boards of a number of charities. Doesn't Duane have other friends? But Mandalay has to say she will, in the face of so much benevolence. I don't drive, though, she says.

Yes, I know that, Taylor says. You'll have to take a taxi. The hospital won't release him unless there's a responsible adult who can stay with him.

Mandalay isn't teaching that day. She can hardly say no.

Of course, Duane won't ask for help, Taylor says.

But doesn't he have a girlfriend or something? Mandalay wonders, but doesn't say.

You know how he is, Taylor says.

Yes, Mandalay knows how Duane is. He would lie down and bleed to death, probably, before he would ask for help. He can't bear to be in anyone's debt. He can't bear to be vulnerable in any way. He would not want a girlfriend, if he has one, to see him in a hospital bed or unable to drive – he wouldn't accept that abnegation of power.

It's really the last thing she wants to do – take on the job of seeing a belligerent Duane home from day surgery at the hospital. But she really doesn't see how she can refuse.

I'll text you the details, Taylor says.

Mandalay would rather not take on a new intimate role with Duane. But she remembers always the two sets of twins growing up together. Taylor and Max Gibbons, Duane's friends, embraced a sort of rich, privileged liberalism (she is momentarily ashamed of thinking so judgmentally, but that's what it was) and eschewed, as Mandalay did, conventional gender roles and colours and toys for their twins. The four children had grown up all together, all encouraged to play with building toys and dolls, all sporting the same haircuts and jeans and T-shirts. They'd all bathed together until they were ten or so, and still have sleepovers. (She suspects that they also still skinny-dip together in the Gibbons' pool, but can't really ask, can she?)

Mahalia is definitely embracing a more feminine look, though, now. Are either of her sons attracted to her? Or would there be, given their history, a sort of kinship taboo?

(Back off, Mom, she hears her sons say. Lean out.)

What will become of them all, these seventeen-year-olds, born at the turn of the millennium? They are very polished and confident, Galton and Mahalia. They have a certain gloss about them, a perfection of dress and grooming and manners and speech. They have been able to hold their own even in a group of adults since they were pre-teens. It is not difficult to be ultra-confident, socially, Mandalay thinks, when the world seems to belong to you.

She wants, and doesn't want that for her sons.

MANDALAY DOESN'T LIKE HOSPITALS. Possibly most people don't like hospitals? But for her it's something visceral – her knees shake; she can't breathe; her vision blurs.

The nurse at the station says: He's a bit groggy, still. But you can see him.

A row of curtained cubicles, like change rooms in a department store. Some are open to the corridor, and in them she sees tubular steel beds on wheels, carts with apparatus, handles and spigots and signage on walls. The nurse twitches open a blue curtain hanging from an aluminum track. Duane? Are you decent?

In the bed, between the raised rails, an elderly man with one side of his head bandaged, asleep.

No, it's Duane. Oh, lord.

His skin, under the pitiless hospital fluorescents, is greyish, and sags with gravity toward the side closer to the bed, as if it's slipping from his face. The stubble of his beard is white, and a few white hairs curl out of the neck of his hospital gown.

Oh lord.

She can hardly bear to look. Has to sit down. No seat, only a commode chair. Is she allowed to sit on the bed? The bandaging over his ear makes a large lump, as if there's a protective cage inside it.

Pull yourself together, she thinks. She recognizes her own panic but can't move away from it. Can't get even the space of a breath between her and the shock or fear or whatever has leapt at her and is squeezing her chest.

The nurse is a calm man, well-groomed, alert-eyed. He could be one of Duane's colleagues, if he were in a suit instead of scrubs. Time to wake up, Duane, he says.

No, not a lawyer. He has somehow scrubbed authority from his voice.

Duane's eyes open, close, open again.

Hi, Mandalay says. Her voice is squeaky. She clears her throat, begins again. How are you doing?

Duane moves his head, focuses his eyes. And act of will, she can see. His lips part.

He can have some of that water, the nurse says. There, with the straw.

It feels an act of violence, of unspeakable boundary crossing, somehow, but Mandalay lifts the cup and brings the straw to Duane's lips.

The nurse lifts a blood pressure machine from the wall and wraps the cuff around Duane's arm. Mandalay can't watch even this procedure. She feels light-headed. Sits on the bed.

It's too warm. She's sweating in her vegan-leather jacket. But Duane's hand, when he reaches to take the cup from her, brushes hers, is cold.

You need to start waking him up, the nurse says. He has to be walking before he can go home.

He looks like he should be in a hospital bed for several more days, Mandalay says.

Oh, yeah, the nurse says. Patients always look like that. It's surprising how quickly he'll look better once he's sitting up. Anyway, we need to move him out. Day surgery.

Factory, Duane whispers.

You got that right, the nurse says. Assembly line. But hey, you get to go home.

There are forms with starred sentences that Mandalay has to initial and sign. It's really difficult to focus on words. She balances the clipboard on her lap and tries to make sense of what she's reading.

Don't sign anything, Duane rasps. She looks at him. Crooked smile. Okay, then. She sits, quietly, focussing on her breath. The panic begins to ebb.

Move your fanny, he says, presently. I want to sit up.

He's wearing track pants and a T-shirt, under the gown. And socks. She passes him what must be the rest of his clothing, in a clear plastic bag on the end of the bed. He undoes the fasteners of the hospital gown, slips it off, pulls on a shirt. Sits a moment. She doesn't offer to help him. She can see that he is exerting all of his will, his considerable will, to pull himself out of the thickness of what is left of the anesthesia.

He pulls on his leather loafers.

She hands him his watch and his phone and wallet and keys, which she has retrieved from the little locker in the cubicle. He says, I want to use the john.

To the left, she says. Around the corner.

He lurches a bit, grabs a rail. Mandalay hesitates, then follows him, waits outside the lavatory door. He looks more like himself already, standing up. He's going to be alright. Well, she doesn't know that. He's going to be alright today. Now.

When he comes out of the washroom he says, I can call myself a taxi. We can drop you at your place, if you want.

Nice try, Duane, she says. I'm going home with you. You're not supposed to be alone for twenty-four hours.

It's not that she cares, but she has promised Taylor, whom she owes so much.

He shrugs, but doesn't protest.

She doesn't stay overnight, of course.

She rides with him in the taxi, and pays the driver with his credit card. At his condo, she helps Duane take off his shoes, because he's not supposed to bend over. He asks her to put his shoes in the closet and she does. She puts the prescription painkillers and package of gauze on Duane's granite counter. He says he wants to sleep; insists he'll be fine. He'll talk to her later. He clearly needs to sleep, and seems fine, and she says she'll call in a couple of hours, and he'd better answer or she'll send an ambulance, and he grins absently and tells her to go.

And she does. She's glad to go. She is suffering severe generalized anxiety. She can still hardly breathe or think.

She takes a cab home from Duane's, lets herself into her quiet house. It's only late afternoon, but she wants a drink, to take a pill and be unconscious. She can't settle to anything, so has trouble distracting herself. Settles on the yoga mat, and finds some relief, moving through positions, focussing on her breathing, her alignment, her body sense.

Had she left, really, because she felt something of their old attraction surface, between herself and Duane? She doesn't want to encourage that. It is just attraction, a random kind of chemistry. She doesn't want to get close to Duane again.

Some quiet, before the twins return from their driving tests, triumphant.

13

DURING THE LONG SLOW DAY, in the spare bedroom that he uses, or used to use for an office, Cliff sits and clicks through links on his laptop, moving from one article to another. He has bookmarked many of these sites already: he's finding that as he clicks on links that take him to different sites, he ends up, more and more, where he began. Is this a good or a bad thing? On the one hand, it's reassuring to find the familiar. He thinks: Yes, I know this. He's familiar with some voices, some terminology. On the other hand, he's starting to get this nagging feeling that the whole thing is just one big circle or cycle. That the same few people are just referring to each other for evidence or author-ity, cycling him around the web.

It's a little bit similar to the process of trying to get to talk to a live person at a government service: the endless menus on the phone or website, the clicking through choices only to cycle back to the original menu. *Please enter your PIN now. If you are calling regarding a PIN, please press 5 now. To receive a PIN, please enter your temporary authorization code. To receive...* He has spent many hours, over the past few years, trying to talk to government ser-vices. Workman's Comp, which changed its name to Worksafe. Ha. Disability services. Medical services. The tax people. So many people, so many forms and documents and numbers. A cycle that exists just to keep itself going.

Or it's like the life cycle of this African parasite he watched a documentary about. Snails, waterfowl, humans. Snails, waterfowl, humans. What's the point? It exists only to make new parasites, in complicated ways.

The websites and the items on them proliferate, but he is learning the paths, now. He follows them. It gives him something to do.

Well, it's more than that. He's learning something. He was never one for politics. He had his job; he liked his nature shows. But now he's learning things. He always felt a bit stupid when people talked about politics. He found it very confusing. It was mostly over his head. But now he's beginning to get it. He can understand it; he can understand what's going on. He'd rather not know, in some ways. But it's clear, and it's something you can't *not* see, once someone points it out to you.

Some of the types who post online go a little too far. He'll admit that. But in general, he thinks that what he's reading makes sense. It's not what you'll see in the mainstream papers, of course. But they're all controlled. On the internet, people can talk about what's really going on. People can say what they want. Most of what they want to say is that other people are controlling what you can say, but it makes sense, doesn't it? Too much bureaucracy. The government is trying to stop you from making or keeping your money. But some postings say that handouts are bad, are making the country weak. He doesn't know if that's true, being one of the people on disability. Likely, though, lots of others are collecting money fraudulently? Welfare mothers sitting on their asses, one of the postings he's read says. He doesn't agree with that opinion. Of course, many of the people who post things are in the United States, and he understands things are different there.

It's clear that someone is controlling things, anyway, and that people like himself have no say anymore.

On regular days he doesn't have as much time on the computer, but he has time on his hands, now. He's going to have another back surgery, and in the meantime he's already off work, already trying to fill in the minutes and hours. He's had three back surgeries, already, not counting the first one that he guesses saved his life, and also involved some surgery on his pelvis and shoulder. It's like they can't get it right. They go in, they chop away at his bones, they fuse this and stabilize that. And he feels better for a while, but it doesn't last. Or, usually, he doesn't feel better. He feels better, but only until the physio and the painkillers wear off. Then he feels worse. But he goes back to work anyway, and keeps at it until he can't anymore.

He feels the hot sting at the back of his nose, and gives himself a little slap on the face. Stupid useless clod. Stupid crybaby.

It hurts, his back, and pain runs down his arms and legs. He works through it until he's too tired. That's the thing about pain; it makes you tired. You can push through it but it grinds you down. This time he wasn't even in worse pain than usual. He'd got off the mower, went into the truck to get his lunch, and he just couldn't go back. Usually if he felt like that he'd just go somewhere, lie down for half an hour, even on the ground, put his legs up on a box or something to take the strain off the sciatic, wait it out. But then one day he can't. He can't make it back onto the tractor. It's not his body, but something in his mind that says no more.

It's the pain, but it's the tiredness, really.

He reads some new posts in a thread he follows about the press only supporting the left, criticizing the right. The press and the universities, the postings say, with links to online articles, are all in cahoots; they all hoodwink the public about the way things work. They attack the common working man, the family, religion. They have a stranglehold.

Cliff isn't sure if that's true. He's not much for religion, having had some bad experiences with it as an adolescent. But it seems clear that freedoms are being controlled, that only certain viewpoints are being allowed, anyway. That isn't right. It's not democratic. And it's clear that ordinary people like him are struggling. Things are going downhill for people like him. Honest working guys. This is the fault of rich liberal intellectuals, who want to turn the country (not his country, but the States) into a communist regime by breaking down the businesses and the working man. He's not sure he can see how this happens – the whole life-cycle – but there are sure a lot of articles about people doing really bad things, crazy, perverted things, all the while being supported by taxpayers' money.

He thinks of his brother Ben, with his expensive stuff and education, and how he fucked up Cliff's company, the only chance Cliff has ever had to make something of his life.

He finishes the article about the stranglehold of the press and shuts his laptop, just before Veronika puts her key in the lock. He can time his life by her.

How was your day? she asks, poking her head around the door of his office.

He doesn't know how to answer that. How does she think? Anyway, she definitely doesn't care. Doesn't want to hear his complaining after a day at work. She works as a care aide, driving from home to home looking after sick old people. He guesses that she listens to complaining all day long. Doesn't need it from him.

She's taking off her coat and her shoes in the entry. She makes the same pattern of sounds every day: the rub and rubbery thump of her white runners coming off, the yawn and buckle of the closet door, the jingling of the clothes hanger. The rustle of her lilac polyester uniform, the padding of her slippers, the firm click of the bedroom door as she goes to change. All a pattern he knows like the rhythm of his own body.

Did you enjoy your lunch? she asks, coming to the doorway again. She means the sandwich she left him, plated, in the fridge this morning.

Yes, he calls back, thank you. He's sick of sandwiches, he thinks. The endless chewing, the stickiness of the cheese on the palate, the slime of the ham.

The bread was dry, he says to her.

She doesn't answer. He hears her go back into the kitchen, begin opening cupboards. She shouldn't have to cook, after an eight-hour shift.

You don't have to cook, he says.

Who else is going to do it? she asks. I don't see a maid.

That's a low blow. He gets to his feet. He doesn't like this shouting at each other from different rooms. Things get lost in translation. He stumps his way to the kitchen. It hurts, to get up, especially for the first few minutes. His legs move like some stupid robot legs. He sat too long, but whatever the hell is he supposed to do all day? If he lies down, things go sideways. He falls asleep and then can't sleep at night, when it's worse to be awake, when his moving around or even having his laptop on disturbs Veronika.

Clomp, clomp, his feet go. He feels his pants slipping. He had undone the button of his pants while he was sitting at the laptop; the waistband dug into him. He is doing up the button when Veronika finally turns around to him.

I should get you some elastic-waist pants, she says. More comfortable.

She means he's getting fat. Yep, that's what happens when you can't work or get any exercise.

Did you walk a bit? she asks.

No, he didn't. But he should. He knows he should.

Take some laps up and down the hall while I put supper in the oven, she says. Or at least get out from underfoot.

He taught her that phrase, get out from underfoot. He learned it from his foster mom, likely. It makes Veronika sound like a native English speaker when she says it, though maybe one from an older generation.

He turns to leave the kitchen as she comes toward him with a casserole dish. He turns too quickly. There's a sensation like a sword slash from his waist up to his shoulder, and for a moment, he's paralyzed.

He hears himself shriek. It's like being reamed in two. It's pain like a streak of white-hot light cutting him in two.

Veronika puts the pan down and says, Come, take my arm. We will walk it out.

But he can't move. He sees that he is clinging to the refrigerator door, and he can't move. He's locked in place.

Veronika moves around in front of him, plants her legs apart, locks her arms around his chest and back, under his armpits. Forward! she says.

They have done this before. He shuffles one foot an inch or two along the floor, then the other. It takes him a million years to get anywhere, but if he moves his feet by more, his body seizes up entirely, and he loses balance.

Shuffle, shuffle, they move through the kitchen doorway. Like robots, like huge ungainly animals. Walruses locked in combat; that's the image his mind is going for. Two walruses, massively heavy, awkward on land, thrusting against each other in mortal combat.

Except Veronika is moving backward, sliding her feet backward, supporting him. Bed or sofa? she asks.

Sofa, he thinks. Sofa. He can at least see the television, if he's stuck there for many hours.

When was your last pill? she asks, meaning the anti-inflammatories with the analgesic. He can't remember. Morning? Afternoon? He can take them every six hours but he doesn't remember the last time. He's had some today, though, he thinks.

Veronika lowers him to the sofa, her face reddening with the effort. She gives him a pill. He should give you something stronger, she says. A proper painkiller. Oxy or something.

No thanks, Cliff says. He's read about that, people getting addicted. That's all he needs.

The pain or the anti-inflammatories wipe out his appetite, but he eats the food Veronika brings him, anyway: the steaming cabbage rolls, the pleasant grainy texture inside the slightly bitter leaf, the spicy tomato sauce. It's a warm comfort, going down. And it passes the time until the news.

What did you do today? Veronika asks, as they eat their dinner.

He can't answer that. Her question is an assault. He says: Oh, sat around twiddling my thumbs, as usual. He means it as a joke but it comes out a little harsher than he intended.

Veronika is silent. Then she says: My day was okay. Mrs. Clark offered me a cup of tea. When I made her tea she insisted I sit down for ten minutes and have tea, as well. Take a load off, she said. I never heard that saying before. Take a load off. Then Mr. Dalgleish, in the afternoon, he asked if he could have a hug. I almost cried. Think of that; he is so alone that he has to ask a stranger, someone paid to clean his house, to give him a hug.

Cliff doesn't want to think of that, of Veronika as paid help for some old man. It wasn't supposed to be like that.

Did you give him a hug? he asks.

Of course. But I thought about it. Such a tragedy, to be that lonely.

Ha, Cliff grunts.

It's a basic need, Veronika says, not looking at him. Watching the TV, chewing. Human touch.

If you say so, Cliff says.

14

AT LUNCH, CLEO WONDERS whether Karsten will invite her to dinner, or something else will happen.

Lunch happens democratically in the company cafeteria, with its clean playful décor, in which all of the employees eat — the machine operators, the secretaries, everyone. There are even small children — employees collect their offspring from the on-site nursery and lunch with them at brightly-coloured, child-height tulip-shaped tables. They are like bright summer flowers, the tulip tables with the parents and children around them, eating, conversing.

It occurs to Cleo that her colleagues take their leisure time, their private time, more seriously than their work time. The work sessions are very light, very casual, but there is a focus to the interactions with the children at the lunch break, though the parents are all gentle and playful. She feels a kind of pang, an envy, that she had not experienced this culture of relaxed parenting with her children, who are now grown. It is not something she has seen in North America. Is it new? Or very old? Or maybe cultural?

Karsten appears at her table with his coffee and open-faced sandwich. May I sit here? he asks.

Please, sit, she says. She has been expecting him to approach her, and here he is. She likes that she was able to predict the social schedule.

So, about dinner tomorrow night, he says, not looking at her.

She feels a slight sinking in her chest cavity. He's so diffident. He's trying to get out of taking her to dinner, as she suspected he might.

But almost immediately, the sensation leaves. It doesn't matter. Nothing matters, except that she doesn't behave too unprofessionally and damage her relationship with Mogun, because nothing is real, here. Very little is in her control, and very little will matter, in a few days, when she returns home. It's a dream, a temporary vacation from her real life.

If Karsten does not want to take her to dinner, that is fine. She does not mind being in a restaurant on her own. Usually, she gets put at a nice corner table and is served more quickly, perhaps out of pity, but nevertheless conveniently.

She smiles at Karsten with good humour. But they are interrupted by Jonas, whom she has not met before this trip, and who reminds her of her son Sam, with his enthusiasm, his lack of self-consciousness. Jonas pulls up a chair, sits. And then others join them.

So, Jonas says. We have the same surname; did you know that? And are you Danish too?

Swedish, I think, she says. My father came to Canada from the town with the same name, in the 1950s.

Oh, super cool, Mads says. Is the house where he lived still standing? What neighbourhood?

To Jonas and Mads, she thinks, the 1950s are the far past, like the 1920s would have been to her.

Cleo admits that she doesn't know; she has never been to Sweden, or to Lund.

Karsten says: You've never been there? But it's less than an hour's drive from here.

It's in Sweden, though, Cleo says. In another country.

Karsten laughs. Sure. But it's also just across the bridge. Really, you can be there in less than an hour by train.

I should go, then, she says.

Karsten brightens. Or, you know, we will drive there. We will go there for supper.

She'd had no idea it was that close. She'd like to go, of course. She says that, impulsively. She laughs. She has no idea if his suggestion is serious or not. It's a thing that would normally make her anxious, the absence of a plan, but really, she doesn't care.

Okay, Karsten says. I guess we can go, then.

He's intense, but also diffident. His intensity isn't personal. She can't tell if he really wants to do it, or if he felt he must make the offer. But she doesn't get tied up in finding out; there's no point in her dancing around, or overthinking this. She really doesn't mind, either way. She has nothing riding on this. She has no anxiety about pleasing Karsten. It's like she's dealing with one of her friends' husbands, or one of her son Sam's friends – someone with whom she has a very casual but friendly relationship, right?

You really didn't have a plan for dinner, did you, she teases him, smiling.

Karsten laughs. He puts down his sandwich and turns his hands over, palms up, in that ageless *no weapons* gesture. You have found me out.

The others think that Karsten and Cleo going to Lund for supper is a good idea.

Is it really feasible? Cleo asks.

Oh, yes, Mads says. They go to his girlfriend's mother's house in Falsterbo for Sunday lunch, often, he says. It's no further. The others chime in. Everyone agrees that they must have a Swedish meal. Anders recommends a place called *Mat och Destillat*. Food and distilled liquor, Cleo understands, from the few words she knows, and suppresses a shudder, remembering her hangover from her first visit. Pernille says, but don't go to the place by the cathedral: the portions are very tiny and the waiters very snobbish.

But what is in Lund? Cleo asks. What do we go see?

There is a Romanesque cathedral, Karsten says.

There is always a Romanesque cathedral, Jonas says.

But it is eleventh century, Mads says.

Everyone is delighted to suggest things to do. It occurs to Cleo that it must be a responsibility for this small firm to entertain her for days, to make it worth her trip. They take it seriously, as they do their process of consensus. They are all happy to participate in planning this outing.

And there is an open-air museum, Jonas says. Almost as good as the one in Stockholm. With houses from medieval to 1930s.

But is it feasible? Is there really time to see these things?

We will compress the afternoon meeting, Pernille says. We will cut it short. Anything we don't cover can be postponed until the next day.

Everyone agrees: they will cut tomorrow's agenda a little short, so that Karsten and Cleo may have an early start.

I believe there is a television series, Karsten says, featuring this bridge. A detective series.

Oh, yes; Cleo has not seen it, but she remembers her book club talking about it.

You talk about television shows, in your book club?

Well, yes. In fact, it should probably be called a television club. Only Cleo would be excluded, as she doesn't really watch any television.

I do not either, Karsten says. Except for football, soccer I mean, and the news. And golf, recently. And handball. And international hockey, of course. He gives her a shamefaced grin.

Cleo laughs. She would find this claim, so clearly compromised, annoying, at home, but here it is just absurd. Delightfully absurd.

Because nothing is at stake.

They have left Copenhagen in late afternoon, and traffic is heavy, and when they make Lund, there is only enough time to visit one attraction before closing time. *Kulturen* or cathedral? Karsten asks.

Cathedral, Cleo says. It's raining.

Cathedral it is, Karsten says. He is driving a black Volvo which seems to be the default car, in Denmark or Sweden. How do people find their own, in supermarket parking lots? Karsten had offered (weirdly, but maybe sweetly?) to let her drive, and held out his key fob, but she had declined. Driving in a foreign country, where the street signs are in an unfamiliar language, does not appeal to her.

I can't read the traffic signs, she had said.

Sure you can, Karsten had said. They are all cognates, no, those traffic words?

There are all of those o's with slashes through them, Cleo said. They give me dyslexia.

The *eueh*, Karsten said. They are nothing. Just an extra vowel. He had laughed.

It occurs to Cleo now that Karsten imagines she travels in Europe frequently, rents cars and zooms from place to place, sluicing through those strange roundabouts and knotted double overpasses as if navigating her own suburban cul-de-sacs. It's charming, that he would make that assumption. She doesn't mind. It's enchanting, to feel that she is that person, even in someone's imagination.

Lund is a university town, full of students, international as well as local, and therefore the kinds of shops and cafés that appeal to students, which gives it a kind of holiday vibe, Cleo thinks. Much of the old town has been preserved: there are winding cobbled streets, half-timbered houses painted Falun red, the deep Swedish house red, and golden yellow.

Karsten drives smoothly, efficiently through the town. They park in the cathedral parking lot and get out. He is wearing, Cleo notices, dark jeans that may have been pressed, a subtly striped grey cotton shirt, a tan jacket. She hopes she has dressed appropriately. Linen trousers; dark beige; an off-white cardigan; a t-shirt the colour of spruce trees. Simple, rather expensive, but well-made things she had bought in Denmark on her last trip.

She pays attention to how she dresses, and notices others' clothes. Clothing is not just a consumerist means of self-expression, but for her, another skin. Also, she had been poor, as a child, and not allowed to choose her own clothing, as a teenager. She likes, now, to wear things that are beautifully made, simple, sustainable. She has had these items for four years, and they show no sign of wear or becoming dated.

The cathedral is very old: nearly a thousand years old. It's difficult to get her mind around that. She tells herself: the people who built this were alive a thousand years ago. She knows that she is not really processing that idea, though. What she feels, really, is a sense of randomness, her own randomness. So much time, so many lives. And hers is just one, a chance occurrence.

Karsten says: Some of your ancestors might have stood here, in this building.

That is an intriguing thought. She knows so little about her father's family that the idea of ancestors is vague. What would it mean, to have that sense of — what? Belonging?

What is striking me, Karsten says, is that it is very modern. Clearly an Italian influence. The apse, those Corinthian columns. That would have come up the Rhine. But it has also picked up something from English churches — you see that in the towers, I think. And the groin vaults evolve a bit, as we walk from one end to the other. Whoever built this thought in a modern way — they adapted to change, to improvements that came along.

Cleo has not travelled. She realizes, now, that the groin vaults, the arches that hold the building together, are an engineer's language — they are transparently mathematical, the way music is sometimes. She imagines workers without laser measurers or power tools or cranes building airy, load-bearing stone structures hundreds of feet high.

She reads that the walls are composite, hollow sandstone filled with much more available fieldstone and mortar.

Also a concept that we think of as modern, Karsten says.

Inside, there are too many stone sculptures, too many carved wooden seats and choirs and pulpits to take in.

There's the famous statue, Karsten says. Danish legend is that it is a troll who fought with the clergy who wanted to found the church.

I think it's meant to be Samson, from the Bible, Cleo says, peering at the oversized, long haired figure clinging to a pillar. No, chained to it, with carved stone chains.

Of course, but it is both, Karsten says. It is the wild giant who must be subdued, for what is civilized and orderly to be created. But it also must tear things down, so that creation can happen, so that there can be change.

Karsten looks a little embarrassed, after that, as if he has made a social *faux pas*.

And a *Danish* legend, had he said? Cleo asks, extending to him a subtle exit. Not Swedish?

Yes, Karsten says. Lund used to be part of Denmark.

Denmark? Goodness; she has always thought that she was half-Swedish. But Danish? Though that would make sense.

Until 1668, Karsten says. But it was all one country until the fifteen-hundreds.

Oh, well, then. That's another thing. Countries in Europe have changed borders frequently, and from her perspective, it seems, arbitrarily.

Do you notice? Karsten says, when they are back outside, heading for the car: the parts of the building seem separate entities from one another.

As if you could take it apart and reassemble it, Cleo says. Modular.

Exactly, he says.

Suddenly she feels the connection, viscerally, with the anonymous medieval architects who designed the church, the eighteenth-century builder who had renovated it. She can imagine them creating the plans, working out the design problems, detail by minute detail, in the fierce joy of focus, of things coming together. The passion to marry beauty and function.

She says this to Karsten, feeling some trepidation as she does so. Speaking of the emotions, an imagined connection with people long dead seems a leap outside the parameters of their conversation so far, a breach of the unspoken agreement to speak only of impersonal subjects, material things, facts.

Karsten doesn't recoil or freeze up or look at her with that Viking embarrassment, though. Instead, he puts an arm around her shoulder, as if she had confessed to him a great trauma, or a great passion or affection for him. Which might, in his mind, amount to the same thing. She leans into him a little, experimentally. This does not feel odd or strange. She thinks: It's pathetic, how nice it feels to be touched. Trent is not physically demonstrative, and even Cleo's kids, once they were teens, had chosen to avoid being embraced. She herself is not an enthusiastic hugger.

Karsten points out some more architectural features, medieval engineering feats. They discuss esoteric aspects of arches. Dusk begins to fall. They return to the car, still talking. This is quite pleasant.

The restaurant they go to next is housed in a converted warehouse or factory, a brick building with high, black-mullioned windows. Inside, the walls are white plaster, except for one in various colours of limestone, grey through cream through honey. The floors are also limestone tiles, highly polished, and the tables are plain rectangles of blond wood, surrounded by high-backed chairs that are slipcovered in black or white canvas, with exposed, industrial zippers up their backs. The lighting pendants hanging from the very high ceiling are a sculptural mystery, which Cleo must look at for a long time before she realizes that they are cylinders of something transparent – probably a kind of plastic – roughly wrapped and tied in burlap, which breaks the light into layers and gives it a golden cast.

I get it, she says. It's about the cathedral.

Yes, Karsten says. A kind of deconstruction of the medieval cathedral.

Re-envisioned in modern forms, Cleo says.

Yes. And so, a comment also on historical form and material. But not so serious.

Are we here to steal ideas for Mogun? Cleo asks. A new line, maybe?

Karsten laughs. We could be, he says. He looks like he wants to say something else, but thinks better of it.

In fact, he says, I know the person who designed this place. So you are right about the inspiration.

A competitor?

A competitor, yes, now. And actually, my ex-girlfriend and former partner. But we are on good terms. We have even collaborated on designs.

So not gay, then? Cleo feels her perception making a small, and perhaps illogical adjustment. She wants to ask if he's involved with anyone else, and how long it has been since his former relationship, and much more. Is it permitted? She remembers Pernille's frankness, that evening a couple of years ago.

It was our everyday living that was the problem, Karsten says, as if she has asked. She likes more social interaction than I do. Going out with friends, parties, always the summer house filled with visitors. We could not compromise, so we decided to separate. Distance not disrespect.

Something in Cleo's mind clicks into place: a missing puzzle piece, a thumbprint on a sensor, a key in a lock.

BUT ON THE SUBJECT OF new lines, Karsten says.

They are driving back, now, to Denmark, over the high bridge with its wash of lights reflected in the waters below.

The company is going to offer you something, Karsten says. On Thursday.

Thursday: day four of the visit. Of course.

A new line?

Bigger than that, Karsten says. His eyes are glinting sideways at her, and he is grinning, with teeth. The overhead lighting of the bridge glistens on the whites of his eyes and his teeth, and throws hard shadows from his prominent brow and cheekbones and jaw. She feels her heart pound for a few seconds, as if she's on the edge of a precipice. Viking smile.

I'm not supposed to talk about it yet, Karsten says. But it is one-third my company, after all.

At her hotel, Karsten pulls up in front of the entrance, reaches across and takes her hand. I hope you will like our proposal, he says, gazing at her intently.

Viking, she reminds herself. Marauder. Though in the museum she had read that Vikings also traded and cultivated farms, in the lands that they had moved into.

I hope you will take it, he says. He's still holding onto her hand.

She realizes that if she were to invite him up to her room, he would accept the invitation. The knowledge, the sudden revelation of his interest in her, ignites something. She can feel it. Is that all attraction is, then? The mirroring, or even the misreading, of another's interest?

She could do it. There would be no repercussions; she can see that. It would be, at the very least, interesting.

She looks at Karsten's face, now. Meets his gaze. He is holding an expression that reads to her as open, but not needy. Not too expectant. There's something on offer, an overture, but he will not be offended if it is rejected.

She imagines going up in the elevator, to her little perfect minimalist room, to the no-frills built-in bed with its small flat pillows and meagre duvet. Imagines their bodies, not so limber, not so lean, manoeuvring around on that high box of a bed, the indelicate adjustments, the inevitable bumping and mistiming, the very small space in which clothing would have to be retrieved and reinstalled after.

If she'd had one more drink, she might have managed it. But as it is, it seems — not repulsive, not wrong, none of those things — but just insufficient. Not offering an experience rich enough for the occasion.

She withdraws her hand.

I know that you are married, Karsten says. I felt that it was finished for you. I had that impression. Forgive me if I misunderstood.

He has, she sees, opened himself to that most dreaded of things — an awkward social interaction.

She doesn't know what to say. She can't, actually speak: can say neither Yes you are right that it's finished, or Yes, I am married and therefore not available. She feels herself flush, now. She has clearly been giving unclear signals, which is tacky and unfair.

Karsten gets out of the car all at once and comes around to open her door. He holds her gaze, when she is standing next to him. He says: I will be in such trouble with the company if I have done something to offend you now. Please forget it. I'm clumsy. I'm out of practice with my manners.

But he is neither clumsy nor unmannerly. Tears sting Cleo's eyes; she looks away. She says: You haven't offended me.

What is wrong with her? Jet lag, still, she imagines. And too much wine, even if not quite enough. But his courtly response touches her. He could have been chilly, and he isn't.

She says: You haven't offended me. I'm just not in a position to...

Not in a position to what? She doesn't know where she was headed with that statement. And now she's torn between wanting to say something encouraging, and thinking that she really must not confuse this nice intelligent respectful man any more than she has.

She wants to say that she owes him an explanation. She wants to apologize, to have some reassurance that she has not offended him. She wants to say no while inducing him to reassure her that he still desires her.

All of those impulses are wrong. Something about her is wrong.

She says goodnight, in Danish, abruptly, and moves toward the doors of the Wake Up Copenhagen hotel.

THE MOGUN TEAM don't have a new design to launch, this year. They have some add-ons to existing lines: a new colour, Sand Dollar, which is a greyish cream, for the *Nordsøen* line; a standing desk attachment that can be added to any of their conventional modular desks. They are going to phase out the *Earth and Farm* line, despite their company promise never to make any product obsolete, but they will do it very gradually, keeping some stock for the next seven years.

They run through these changes, and then they look expectant, as if there's going to be a surprise birthday cake.

It's the proposal. She tries to keep a neutral expression, so as not to give Karsten away.

Karsten, it appears, is too nervous to speak. He opens his mouth, closes it, gestures toward Anders.

Anders clears his throat. We think, Anders says, that you have given us some very good ideas in your feedback over the years we have been working with you. We think you could help us adapt our product more to the American market. We'd like to talk to you about working for us as a consultant.

You wouldn't have to live here full time, Pernille says. You could fly back and forth.

We'd be looking for inspiration from you about the American West Coast, specifically, Anders says.

Also perhaps the Prairies and the Rocky Mountains, Mads says, almost bouncing in his seat with excitement. And the deserts. All of those places.

You can tell us how people live and work, there, and what colours they respond to, Camilla, the younger woman, who has, like Cleo, an engineering background, says precisely. What sizes of spaces, what configurations are popular for the North American office space.

Cleo feels herself flush as if she's just been plopped in a steam room. She has not expected this proposal, and so it seems unreal, but no more unreal than anything else that happens in the jet-lagged, dream-filtered visits. It seems perfectly plausible that this offer should be made, and also perfectly impossible to process it in relation to her real life.

Her heart is beating so quickly that she thinks it's skipping beats. She has forgotten how to breathe. She has just enough presence of mind to say nothing. She eases her face into a smile, a non-committal, but yet encouraging smile, she hopes. Why is so much at stake? It's just an offer. And obviously impossible to even consider.

15

TODAY BELINDA IS WRAPPED UP in a mustard-yellow blanket on her sofa, her bald head cozied in a yellow toque. She is tired, occasionally groping for words, but that's the chemo. She's nearing the end of her second run, and it's always hardest near the end. There's a flood of afternoon sunlight slanting in through a window, falling across Belinda's lap, and in this patch of sunlight, Harriet's cat, Clytemnestra, lies watchful, her yellow eyes glowing against her black fur.

You're an amazing composition, Mandalay says.

I know, Belinda says. I call us Study in Black and Gold.

Very Klimt, Mandalay says.

A little too Klimt, Belinda says.

Mandalay has brought her popsicles, which Joe says are the only thing she can really enjoy. Belinda opens her blanket cocoon and extends her arms for a hug, and seems delighted about the popsicles. She chooses one and Mandalay puts the rest into the freezer.

I think I could eat a little something, Belinda says, after they talk awhile.

Mandalay mixes a smoothie for Belinda with banana and avocado and probiotic yogurt. She rubs Organic Hemp Cream onto her feet and hands, which look like they've been blanched in boiling water and then peeled. Belinda says: I think my digestive tract, from my teeth down to my anus, is in the same shape as my hands and feet. She says: Did you know – my oncology nurse told me this – that the gut and the skin are one continuous organ? That the same cells form both, in utero, and then the gut tube forms like someone poking an indent in a lump of clay on the wheel.

Belinda is her normal alert and enthusiastic self today. It's a good sign. Mandalay feels brighter.

It's something to do with neuropathy too, Belinda says. Then she closes her eyes for a moment. The sunlight slants across the angles of her collarbones. Mandalay sits, watching her.

Belinda opens her eyes as if a silent alarm has awakened her.

My chemo-brain, she says. Let's talk about your show, though!

Are you going to be there? Mandalay asks, letting herself sound plaintive. She has never before done a show of her work without Belinda organizing it, curating. Now she has an opening at a public art gallery coming up, and it's kind of terrifying.

Wild horses won't keep me away, honey, Belinda says. Nor Avastin nor Carboplatin.

Belinda has so much spirit.

How is Harry? Mandalay asks.

Doing a tour of Greek archeological sites, Belinda says. That's not surprising, is it?

Mandalay wonders if Harriet will come back soon, and is just thinking about how to phrase the question when Belinda answers it for her. At the end of summer, I think, Belinda says. Before her university term starts. I should be feeling better then.

What kind of cure is worse than the disease? Mandalay thinks. Perhaps she is exaggerating? But it seems that Belinda's treatment is exacting cruel and unusual punishment on her body. Why are there no better treatments for cancer?

She is not sure that she believes, anymore, that Belinda is going to get better. She isn't sure at all. But what then will have been the point of this terrible struggle?

MANDALAY IS NEARLY finished writing a batch of crits for the summer course she's teaching, has maybe an hour of work left, when her phone plays the rackety little tune that lets her know she has an appointment. Damn it; she could have finished today, been able to get back to her own work first thing tomorrow. She has promised the boys a meal together tonight; Owen is home for a few days, between the end of season and training camp.

It's a meeting with her department chair – the usual year-end review she has to do as an instructor on a short-term contract. They'll go over her teaching evaluations, her peer evaluations for the two courses that she has taught this term. The chair – Felix, a photographer eager to get back to his digital editing, his own work – will suggest some phrasing for his write-up for the dean, and she'll nod, and that will be about it. Pro forma, and largely a waste of time. But she has to go through with it, to be offered more courses in the fall term. It's a hoop. She resents the time it takes, and the discomfort of scrutiny and judgement, but she understands it's necessary.

Felix makes her wait ten minutes while he finishes a conversation with a couple of his own students, then lets her in with a mild air of surprise, of having forgotten the appointment.

Felix has to dig through oscillating towers of paper on his desk to find the envelope with her materials in it. Mandalay knows that there is no department office anymore, or a secretary. Belinda had told her about those gradual erosions – the lunch lounge, the reserved parking, the secretarial support, the storage space.

I should tidy all of this up, Felix says, looking around helplessly.

She likes Felix, with his wild greying ginger hair and beard and his eccentric clothing.

Here we are, Felix says, pulling an envelope out of a pile.

He undoes the waxed green thread that's wound around a cardboard button. I always like these envelopes, Felix says. A genius kind of design. Functional and beautiful.

It's clear that he has not looked at Mandalay's evaluations yet.

He pulls out the sheets of paper, scans them. Hmm-hmm, he says. Hmm-hmm. The usual.

Just as Mandalay has expected.

Felix pulls out a sheet of paper that is coloured, unlike the other. A notice or letter. He reads it, passes it to her. I didn't realize, he says. Good thing somebody in the dean's office keeps track.

Mandalay reads the notice. Reads it again. It's in officialese, and cites the collective agreement rather often ("article 6.3.5.1") but seems to be saying that, having taught a number of courses for a number of years, she is entitled to apply for continuing status in the department.

What does that mean?

Oh, Felix says. They convert you. Your salary goes up, you get benefits. You'll know in May instead of August what you'll be teaching the next year. You'll have to start being on committees. That's about it.

Huh. Mandalay has always imagined that she would have to compete with a hundred and fifty new-minted MFAs for a real job.

Of course there's a first-year probation and a review, Felix says.

It's a little much to take in. And anti-climactic.

The forms are on online, Felix says. Probably self-explanatory.

Huh.

There must be some catch.

16

TRENT'S FATHER DIES just under a year after Trent's mom, after a fall, or because of a stroke that caused him to fall – it's not clear. Trent flies back to Ontario alone. Cleo really can't take more time off. The funeral, as well, won't be as grand. A small family event at a funeral home.

Trent says he's surprised: his dad was an important man in Toronto, he says. Lots of things are named after him. Lots of businessmen owe their careers to him.

Cleo suggests that the family might be exhausted still from arranging Trent's mother's funeral, which had been elaborate and well-attended. They probably don't have the energy to do it again. And Bob had retired twenty years earlier, and none of his cronies are alive.

Well, I'll be the same, Trent says. I definitely won't live as long, but there won't be anyone at my funeral, either.

He says this while he's packing. Cleo has heard it before, in various forms. She is waiting to drive Trent to the SkyTrain station, from which he will take the train to the airport. She doesn't contradict or question him.

He outlived his usefulness, that's for sure, Trent says.

Don't forget your blood pressure pills, Cleo says, calmly. She's not going to engage with Trent's self-pity or whatever it is. She'll look after him in the ways that make sense, but she's not going to indulge his anxiety or depression, or get sucked into it.

When she's tidying the bedroom that evening, picking up the items that Trent decided against taking and left strewn on the bed and floor, she sees that he has left (and therefore taken with him) one black dress shoe and one tan. One of each.

She sits on the bed and laughs out loud. Poor Trent. She can feel sympathy for Trent, for his being distracted. For his shock and grief. He has just lost both parents in a matter of months.

In the past, she wouldn't have been able to summon up that emotion; she could only feel impatience with him. *Typical*, she would think. *Trent never focuses on what is happening around him. He refuses to make the effort to pay attention to what is going on, to process emotions. He's just never there. He has basically skimmed through the entire twenty-five years of their marriage, not really there.* And then she would feel that familiar cascade of resentment and despair. It had been a bad idea, she knew, to go with these thoughts; they had led to contempt, a dead-end street. And yet she hadn't been able to act on her own contempt; she had believed at some level that it was not justified, perhaps, and so she wasn't able to use it as a basis for action. She had been stuck. She had been stuck for so long.

But she is doing better. She is learning to manage better. To let things go; to be kinder; to see the humour in things.

Trent texts her a photo of his mismatched shoes and a crying-with-laughter emoticon, plus the line *At least I have a left and a right*, and Cleo catches herself smiling and feeling benevolent. She likes Trent's humour. She has always liked his humour. And they communicate better when they use text, as when one of them is away. (Could they have a relationship confined to communication by text message? What would that look like?)

Distance rather than disrespect. (But she won't let herself think about Karsten, in Copenhagen. That's a door she chooses not to open.)

She feels hopeful about their marriage. If they could just give each other distance, communicate in carefully-edited telegraphic witticisms, they would do alright.

How would that look, in realistic terms?

17

OWEN IS STRETCHED OUT on the sofa, taking up the full length of it. He's wearing black jogging pants, a black sweater without a logo. He looks completely at ease. Even his phone is resting face down in its metallic black case, on his chest. From the papasan chair, in which it seems only yesterday she used to curl up with both boys, Mandalay smiles at him. She wants to hug him. She wants to tell him to get up off the couch; she wants to towel and comb his hair, but she refrains. She wants him to be small enough again to sit on her lap, to throw his arms around her neck, to fall asleep on her shoulder.

What do they call that colour? she asks. Your phone case.

Oh, the skin? he says. I forget. A mineral name, I think.

Skin. That's an interesting use of the word. Skin, she says.

Owen takes up space the way Duane does. As if he owns it. It's a big part of Duane's personality. Comfortable in his skin, she'd have said, but it is more than that. It's a way of holding the spine and pelvis. Could she get it down on paper, the line? Her fingers itch, momentarily, for a pencil.

Don't you have something to do? Owen asks. Could you make me some lunch?

She gives him a look. They have an agreement: she doesn't prepare lunch or breakfast. Also, it's late afternoon.

It's actually annoying, that need to dominate a space.

I'm sore, he says. I took a hit last night.

Are you bruised?

No, he says. Not much. Padding. But then pulls up his sweater and shows her: a bruise on his hip, a purple stain on his pale skin. In spite of the padding.

I knew you had a bruise, she says.

You think you can read me, Owen says, lazily. Women always think they can read minds.

He's having sex, she realizes suddenly. Well, he is seventeen. He is a hockey player.

You're completely an open book to me, she says. And you always will be. When you're sixty and I'm ninety-four, I'll still know everything you get up to. I'll know what you're thinking before you think it.

Even when I'm sixty? He laughs.

Even when you're sixty, she says.

Nah, Owen says. You know nothing about me.

Yes, he's having sex. She doesn't see girls in the house, but she's not home during the daytime. And Owen is on the road often. Hopefully (her chest contracts a little) hopefully, besides taking the obvious precautions, he is also being careful of others' feelings, and of his own emotions?

But it's taking on too much, to follow one's nearly grown sons into their private lives. Time to detach.

Honestly? she says to Owen. I think I'd rather not know.

Good call, he says.

You're going to get covered in cat hairs, lying on that sofa, she says.

Ma, he says. The cat's been gone, what, two years, now? You need to get a new couch.

She probably does, but it's not something she thinks about. The old sofa is comfortable. Maybe she can find a new blanket to throw over it.

Are you going to get another cat? Owen asks. You should, now that you're alone a lot of the time. A kitten.

She has not been thinking about getting another cat. Sophie had been her familiar, a nice talkative tabby, growing more human over the years. She'd inherited Sophie from Cliff, when he and Veronika had moved in together. Veronika did not like cats. Sophie had lived to be twenty, a great age for a cat. But Mandalay is hardly home, now, and the boys are both gone much of the time, too. A cat would be lonely.

And she doesn't really want to have someone to look after, right now. Aidan and Owen are finally grown enough that she's able to come and go as she likes. She doesn't have to think about anyone else's needs.

She says: Maybe I don't want to take care of anyone or anything, now.

Oh, you know you want to take care of us forever, Owen says, grinning.

Anyway, he says. You don't have to cook for me tonight. Aidan and I are cooking. Dad's coming over. He wants to have a family powwow.

That's probably not a phrase we should appropriate, Owen, she says.

She doesn't like Duane coming over, especially without notice. He sneers at things, criticizes things. She doesn't like Duane in her house, stirring things up, starting arguments, getting the boys agitated.

So you are going to cook for us all? she asks. What are you planning to make?

Owen grins. Linguini and clams. I've got it under control.

Okay then, she says.

Don't feel embarrassed to offer to help, he says. You can make a salad.

I can do that, she says. And adds, craftily: you'll need to clean the kitchen before you start.

Oh, Aidan's going to do that, he says.

(Where is Aidan? He's usually back from school by now.)

But then, right away, Aidan's coming through the back door into the kitchen, in his school uniform with its tie, his oversized backpack, his glasses. He drops a grocery bag onto the counter. Your clams, he says to Owen.

Mandalay catches Owen's eye. He lifts his eyebrows at her, grins. She wants to hit him with something. She wants to wipe that grin off his face.

Aidan looks tired. He has a huge cargo of homework every evening, it seems, though his school term is nearly over. She has never had to remind him to do homework; he's self-motivated to the point where sometimes she wakes at two in the morning to find him finessing an essay, even if it's not due for a couple more days.

Come sit for a minute, Aidan, she says.

He shakes his head, hoists his backpack again, heads down the hall toward his room. But then stops and looks at her, smiles. I will later, Mom, he says. I want to change, and I've got to send my lab write-up in by five.

She hopes Duane won't bully Aidan over dinner. He needles Aidan; he likes to get Aidan upset, riled. He talks over him, uses fancier language, is faster and more experienced with his reasoning.

That whole business with the American election the previous fall had been demoralizing for Aidan. Duane had played devil's advocate so heavily, forcing Aidan to defend himself. More than that, push him to argue, to do verbal combat, the way he argued, or pretended to argue, in favour of the ridiculously impossible candidate for the US election. Pretending to be pro-Trump, just to make Aidan argue.

And Aidan had got so... invested in the whole thing. When the election results had come in, Aidan had been sick. Pale, shaking, vomiting. Aidan, she had said. You're sixteen. This election is happening in another country, and you can't even vote yet. She's not sure he's over it yet. He seems to have lost some hopefulness about the world, the future.

She hates to see it. She doesn't want it happening in her house.

Her house, which is half Duane's, still.

Maybe now, though, if she is being converted to full time at the art college, and has a gallery to represent her and sell some prints, she will make enough to buy Duane out. Get him out of her life. Ha! That would make it worthwhile.

She launches herself off the papasan chair and heads upstairs. She also wants to change her clothes. She hopes she has something decent and clean left in her closet.

She'd be happy if the boys didn't feel they should invite Duane to the house. If he didn't need to be in her house ever again.

It is her home. She has made this house a home.

DUANE SHOWS NO EVIDENCE of his recent surgery, and doesn't mention it. He has a neat piece of gauze taped over the top of his ear. It's hardly noticeable. He doesn't reveal whether he's going to be doing any further treatment. He wants to talk about the boys' futures, it seems. During the preparation of the linguini and clams, which Duane takes over – she knew he would – she can sense that he is building up a speech in his head, marshalling the arguments he intends to use, reviewing and dealing with possible rebuttals. He's always chatty, glittery, all surface when he's doing that. And just as she expects, they're no sooner seated at the table when he launches in.

What are Owen's plans for next year? Duane asks, blandly. Does he want to stay in Vancouver, do engineering at UBC? Or maybe U of Alberta? If he wants to do some house league hockey, Edmonton might be a better choice. Is he getting bored of hockey, now? He would have had a choice of universities if he were going to graduate from his private school, the best ranked in the province, but his grades seem adequate. Should he pick up a couple of science courses? Has he thought about what he'll need to take in his final year?

Mandalay thinks: This is going to go fine. She had thought that Duane would be on Aidan's case about his wanting to do a Liberal Arts degree. If they can just keep on the subject of Owen's plans, things will be fine.

Engineering is one of the fields Duane considers a viable option:

that, medicine, or law. Owen has already said that he thinks he'll do engineering. So for once this discussion should go down civilly. They should all be on the same page. And maybe Duane will be so happy that he'll approve Aidan's plans too.

Owen says, cheerfully, I'm probably going to get drafted by the juniors next year. And then, I hope, maybe the NHL.

Duane grins, his eyebrows raised to the ceiling. That's your plan?

That's what I'm hoping for. The draft happens in spring.

Duane says: I get it, but what's your backup plan?

I'll think about that if this doesn't work out, Owen says, cheerfully.

So you don't have a backup plan. What is the likelihood of this *turning out*, as you call it?

Mandalay winces. She can't stand it when Duane takes this tone with the boys, but it just makes it worse if she attempts to intercede. Duane just gets more aggressive, and often the boys turn on her, too.

I don't know, Owen says. Pretty good, I think.

Pretty good. That's hardly an analysis I'd like to base a life decision on, Duane says. You can look up your stats. *I* can look up your stats. Look at your ranking. Do you know what that number means? It means that's how many players, your peers, are considered better hockey players than you. Now find out how many players in your division are drafted each year, on average. Is that number higher or lower? It's not brain surgery.

There are other factors, Owen says. It's not just stats. He has reddened and is sounding surly.

Are there? And how do you measure those? How do you think managers make decisions about investing millions of dollars in draft picks?

Mandalay sighs. Okay, Duane, she says. You've made your point. Now you're just bullying.

It's a life decision, Duane says. He needs to put more thought into it.

So you don't want me to play hockey, Owen says.

I didn't say that. I want you to have a backup plan.

Duane, stop, she says.

Duane simply raises his voice over hers.

Duane! she says.

I don't need your permission, Owen shouts.

Aidan is looking nauseous, has stopped eating.

She says: Owen, you do have plans. Maybe we could talk about them, instead of going through this stalemate. You do have a sensible backup plan. You're just using the draft as a smokescreen.

She realizes, even as the words are coming out of her mouth, that she has not chosen her words well. That she sounds as if she's on Duane's side.

Owen looks at her now with a mixture of irritation and surprise, and maybe something else. What do you mean? he asks.

I phrased that wrong, she says. I'm sorry. I just think you could enter this discussion with good faith.

You don't have to always make it so obvious that you don't approve of me playing hockey, he says.

Okay, she says. I don't. But this isn't about that. It's about what you're going to do with your life. Where you're going to go to university.

I'll deal with that if I need to, Owen says.

She wants to say: But you'll have lost other options. You'll have closed doors.

She does not speak.

She needs to remove herself from the situation, she realizes. There's some power struggle going on here, and somehow it's including her, against her will. She gets up, finds her coat and umbrella, heads out the door.

It's too windy for an umbrella, and the rain blows down her neck and puddles splash up her legs as the cars go by. Though it's dark, she turns down a quieter street.

She doesn't get angry at her sons. She always finds her centre, finds a way to listen and understand. She doesn't know where this is coming from.

She has been walking for nearly an hour, has turned to head home, when her phone rings. She digs it out of her shoulder bag. Aidan.

Hey, Mom?

Hey, Aidan, she says, reaching out toward him with more warmth (more neediness?) than usual. (Aidan, her wise, sensitive son.)

Aidan says: I think you should come back. Owen has taken off. He says he's going to stay with a friend.

Everyone's just upset, Aidan, she says.

But she calls Owen. Don't leave, Owen, she says, sounding pathetic even to her own ears. Don't leave like this.

Owen says: I guess you'll have Aidan for another year, anyway.

Owen. We need to talk. This isn't the way to handle things.

He doesn't reply. She walks on: her anger cools, as she had known it would, but is replaced by a kind of cold plug in the bottom of her stomach.

Owen turns up to retrieve some of his belongings a couple of days later. He seems neither angry nor distressed, but there's some difference about him. Some minor shift. Something withheld. Is it her imagination. No, she knows Owen, knows when he's holding back.

It will pass. Intuition tells her to let it go, let it pass. But she can't let him leave like this, with space between them. Are you angry with me? she asks.

No, Mom.

But there's some new wall up. Owen is generally open about his feelings. He'll tell her when he's angry — at her or at Duane. He always has.

Okay? she asks Owen, meaning, Are we okay?

Owen's hug is brief, and he's out the door sooner than she expects.

Guarding against her. Guarding himself against her.

18

TRENT SAYS, IN AN ACCUSING VOICE: I have not felt any real warmth or affection from you in years.

Okay, Cleo says. She remembers not to react, to let a little space follow his words, to let a little space open between the jolt of them and her own response, as the therapist has been suggesting. She stays still. She envisions the space. They are sitting at the dining table, just the two of them, the smeared and daubed dishes and the scraps from the meal still on the table. She has a glass of wine, her second; Trent, the remains of his carbonated drink.

They have begun to have these conversations, lately. Well, since Trent's parents died in close succession, and he began to have sleeping issues, and starting seeing a therapist, and then had asked if they could see a therapist together. Which they have done exactly twice. The whole session had been spent on communication techniques, which Cleo had initially thought was reasonable, but then had wondered about, because the therapist had focussed more on her than on Trent. He hadn't understood, which should have been obvious, that it was Trent who had the communication problems, who needed to learn how to listen and also to edit himself.

But she had participated; she has been practicing the key takeaway concepts. And the one about leaving space between her experiences and reactions is a useful one. She's read it elsewhere, too.

How long, she had asked the therapist, should this space be?

The therapist had looked confused.

If you can't measure it, Cleo had explained, it's hard to believe in.

Five minutes, the therapist had said. Try five minutes.

So she listens to Trent. Okay, she says again, and nods. It occurs to her now that this isn't a fair statement: that she does nothing *but* express care for Trent. She takes care of the house and meals. She took time off work to fly to Ontario with him for his mother's funeral. She works full-time, brings in as much as Trent does, pays half of everything.

But she does not say this. She doesn't dwell on it, either, but puts it in a kind of mental box – a clear plastic one, so that she won't lose track of it, won't forget about it – and focuses on keeping the empty space. It's a funny sensation, unnerving, to do that. But she can do it.

Trent says: I realize I've wasted my life. I'm fifty years old. I don't care about my job. I have no friends. I don't have a marriage. When my dad died, I realized: I'm next in line at the checkout.

Now into the space, a trickle of sympathy. Yes, she can understand what Trent is saying. She does feel for him. She sees him now for an instant as a vulnerable human being, and her heart contracts for him.

But the five minutes are not up. She has to hold the empty space, can't let even this positive response seep in. She gives it a box, its own box.

The thing is, Trent says, I can't keep waiting for you to be there for me. I can only control my own response.

He sounds like he's repeating something he has been told, but only half-remembered, she thinks. Typical. And, typically, so wrong. And then: *keep the space empty*. Another box. She remembers to put a label on this one: a label for her own emotion, which is probably *contempt*.

Five minutes is an awfully long time.

I'm sorry, she wants to say. She just wants to make it all stop, now. I'm sorry; I'll try harder. But she holds her tongue. There is something that she may say at this point, but she can't remember what it is. Oh, yes.

I'm listening, she says.

The thing is, Trent says, the thing is, this isn't working for me anymore. I've decided I want to move out.

Okay, she says.

One more minute. But a grey mist is rising now, filling the space. How will she live? Can she afford the mortgage on this very expensive house, on her own? Likely not. And there is the kids' education, which they are not nearly through yet.

She's going to have to lose her house, her beautiful house.

The minute is not up. *Breathe*, she reminds herself. *Breathe.*

What she experiences now is something like a near-death experience; it *is* a near-death experience, perhaps. The whole history of her marriage to Trent, their twenty-five years together, flashes before her mind.

She sees their wedding, impromptu on Kits beach, a couple of colleagues as witnesses, a wedding that had been so offbeat, so out-of-the box, that she had thought (and Trent must have, too) that it presaged a different life together than what they had actually had.

She sees Trent's face, open, ecstatic, alive, at the births of Olivia and Sam. She sees him lying on the floor, both children astride him, flapping his arms. (Had that happened only once, or had it been a favourite game?) She sees him look up, or fail to look up, a thousand times from his screen. She sees his lips curled in disgust (fear?) at her suggestions for trips, decorating plans, art movies, jazz clubs, overtures to new acquaintances, moves to the city, moves to rural areas, unfamiliar foods, social or philosophical or psychological theories or revisions, alterations in sexual positions, and proposals for exercise.

She sees his shoulders slide inward and earthward slightly, each morning, as he picks up his laptop case and lunch bag for two hundred and fifty working mornings a year, for twenty-five years.

Six thousand mornings. (Six thousand mornings of processed cheese on white bread.) She sees herself turn away from his awkward, unskilled, but ineluctably hopeful questions, complaints, jokes, embraces, a thousand thousand times.

It is her Damascus moment. She sees this.

But the five minutes are not up. And into the last few seconds of their space, what flows into her mind and body is not love and light and optimism, but only a slight shift, as of a lens being twisted into focus. A new image, herself for twenty-five years trying to read Trent, to shape herself into the space she has imagined around them both.

Trent stops speaking. She says nothing. She looks into his eyes and nods.

Trent's face twists with some emotional force she can't identify. Fear, or resolution, or both. Fine, he says, as if she has made a statement. I'll pack and be out in a couple of days.

And now the space opens wide, and she could not cross it with a simple reaction if she wished to. She does not know what this means, or what she feels, only that it is a change, an opening of something, and that it is happening. That is all.

Okay, she says. Okay.

19

THE SPECIALIST SAYS: I don't think that there's anything more we can do.

Cliff has been expecting, and not expecting, to hear this. It seems that he has always known — from the time that wall of mud began crimping itself in folds, sliding toward him. Known even before that. Known since he saw that building site in West Van with its steep drop of raw earth, the gaping sockets of the arbutus and maple and cedar and salal that the oversized excavator had ripped from the soil and heaped for burning.

Known years before that, when he was falling backward down the stairs at Loretta's place, falling forever toward the floor below, the place that was determined to connect with the back of his head. Known when Loretta's hands shot out, as he stood at the top of the landing telling her he was going to leave. He's always known that at some point he will hit the ground and not get up again.

But at the same time, he's always believed that this surgeon, who has touched the secret places of his spine, who has traced the branching roots of his nerves, like the root ball of a sapling, who has peered at the open front of Cliff's brain, would always be able to repair him.

Nothing more, Cliff repeats.

What does that mean, nothing more?

It means there are no more surgeries I can do that will change anything, the doctor says.

He has a heavy seeding of white hairs, and Cliff thinks: The first time I met him, he was younger than I am now.

There are x-rays and MRI scans both in Cliff's patient folder and on the computer. See, here, here, the doctor says. Cliff doesn't know what he is looking at, but nods minutely. The doctor isn't trying to make him feel stupid, but he knows he is stupid.

Veronika has come along, to drive him into the city, to ask the questions he will forget to ask, but she is feeling stupid too, he can tell. They had been expecting that there would be another surgery. They had tried to prepare for this pre-op consultation by remembering all of the things that happened the last time, and the time before that, but now that there will be no surgery, they can't think what to ask.

The doctor says, I'll refer you to the pain clinic. I'll give you another prescription.

Well, you see, it's not so much the pain, Cliff says. He sees the doctor's face tighten a bit, there. They've had this conversation before.

It's the pain that inhibits your range of motion, the doctor says, as if he has memorized that line. It's what he always says.

I'll refer you for more physio, he says.

Cliff has tried the physio. It cost two hundred and fifty dollars for one visit, and wasn't covered by his insurance, and it didn't do anything.

In the car, Veronika says: You could ask for a second opinion. Veronika is addicted to hospital dramas on television. She thinks she knows something about medicine.

I already see the best neurosurgeon in the city, he says.

That may or may not be, she says.

He'll let that go. It was ignorant, but he'll let it go.

Veronika says: In this country we have permanent disability payments from the government. You will get that. It's lucky.

If you say so, Cliff says.

You can tell those Punjabi brothers that you quit, Veronika says. No more getting the crap under-the-table jobs. You can just say I quit.

He has not, in fact, worked for the Singh brothers for years, though he does own still a small interest in the company, and on paper, at least, he is an employee. He does not want to think about that, his non-job in the company that used to be his. Keep your attention on the road, he says.

How are you feeling? Veronika asks.

How do you think I'm feeling? he says. He is not going to be robbed of his right to feel the way he does right now. Though what he feels, exactly, he can't really say.

Veronika thrusts out her lower jaw and sucks her lips in. It's a particularly unattractive look. She's sulking, that's all.

IN THE NIGHT Cliff wakes with a surge of intention. He needs to get the paperwork done for the permanent disability claim. It will be less money but he will have freedom to do what he likes. He can take courses, maybe learn to make something. He can refinance the house; the mortgage is almost due, and if he takes a longer term, the payments will go down, even though he'll end up paying more to the bank in the long run. He can change the insurance on his truck to pleasure only. He needs to get the damned garage cleared out. Maybe he'll just hire a hauling company to take it all away. He'll give Veronika notice. Or maybe she can just stack her boxes along the wall.

He should get his house in order.

He should get another dog. A pup. Their little dog Buster had died a few years back and Veronika hadn't wanted to get another one: she was worried about who would take care of it when they were both at work. But he could have one, now.

He could look into getting one of those scooters.

Things will get better with Veronika. He knows he needs to be nicer to her.

HE FALLS ASLEEP AGAIN around six a.m., and doesn't hear Veronika leave for work. When he wakes again, it's mid-afternoon. He's really thirsty, and has a caffeine-withdrawal headache, but other than that he feels pretty good. He has a plan; he's going to get a grip on his life, now. Wrestle it into shape. Things are going to be better.

Veronika will be gone awhile yet. Maybe he'll make dinner.

He showers and dresses and goes to the kitchen, which is very neat, as always, dishes washed and put away, countertops wiped, chairs pushed neatly under the table. He'll make coffee; he'll make himself some breakfast. Then he'll see what he can find to cook for dinner.

On the table is an envelope with his name on it in Veronika's printing. He opens it. A note, not a card. He reads it twice, but it doesn't really make sense, except, finally, as a dull clanging in his diaphragm.

She can't really do that, can she?

But a part of him feels that he has known all along that she would leave.

20

BELINDA IS LYING DOWN. She looks shrunken, yellowed. She can't talk long, Joe says. Her mouth sores. Joe helps her sit up, props her up with pillows.

Mandalay needs to talk about her work. Nobody but Belinda understands what she's trying to do. She will distract Belinda, anyway, by talking about art making.

I don't know what I want to do, Mandalay says. I need a new topic. I've done the shelter thing to death, I think.

Belinda looks bemused, as if Mandalay is telling her something fabulously irrelevant.

I mean, Mandalay says, I have so many ideas running through my head all of the time, or I did when I was younger, but now I really have to come up with something, my mind is blank.

Belinda says: Process.

What do you mean? Mandalay asks.

But now Belinda just looks bored or irritated. She says: Call Joe. I need to. Lie down. My meds.

Mandalay says, Belinda, what can I do to help? Tell me what I can do.

Belinda shuts her eyes.

Joe comes in. A difficult day, he says. She is not feeling so well today. Tomorrow will be better.

What Mandalay is feeling is something like panic. Belinda, her mentor, her friend, her guide. She needs Belinda to get better.

At least to come to her show, which is only a week away. Her first show. She has been counting on Belinda to be there.

She feels those things, she knows, because other things are crowding at her consciousness. Easier to fill the space with the current feelings, refuse to let the more painful feelings in.

She remembers Belinda blurting out — it would have been four years ago — uncharacteristically rattled, her eyes wide with her news *something odd on my mammogram*. They had been walking along False Creek, East through Charleston Park, as they often did, Mandalay finding Belinda in her office, after her class, the two of them setting out in the sunshine or drizzle, whatever was on offer. Herself saying, I've heard that happens often, really high rate of false alarms, it'll turn out to be nothing. At the same time, the cold finger of fear in her innards.

Then the succession of bad news: disturbing ultrasound, disturbing biopsy, disturbing margins, disturbing number of affected lymph glands. Surgery, radiation, chemo. Mandalay holding Belinda's hand while a technician threaded a tube through a small incision in her arm, up a vein into her neck and back down to a larger vein in her chest. Had brought her smoothies and taken Belinda and Joe's daughter Harriet, the same age as her twins, overnight and organized a casserole drop-off and found a bong.

And Belinda had got better: she had grown eyebrows and sported a chic buzz cut; she had cut out alcohol and gone on an Ayurveda retreat and a trip to Columbia, and she had returned to work. A good two years. And then the cancer had come back, in Belinda's spine and pelvis and liver and brain, finally, as if enacting a scorched-earth retribution, and in spite of the chemo it had persisted.

Now Belinda has collapsed in on herself, has from one week to the next given up walking, stopped eating, lost the ability to form complete sentences. How can that happen?

MANDALAY CAN'T FIND THE TIME to go to visit Belinda for a few more days, and when she does, there are many people in Belinda and Joe's house. She finds her in a rented hospital bed in the living room of her house, which never was really a conventional living room anyway, and now has become a sick room. There's a bag of dark orange fluid hanging under the bed, and she thinks it's blood, but then realizes that it is very, very dark pee. There's a morphine pump connected to a tube that disappears somewhere into Belinda, into a PICC line, Mandalay knows.

Belinda is propped up on pillows, and her skin is deep yellow, as if she's been gilded.

She can't really speak. She can't form words. Harriet, her daughter, is home, now, stunned, bruised-looking. The shock, Mandalay thinks. She should have been brought back months ago, so she could spend time with Belinda before she became too ill to interact. She should have been allowed the time to get used to Belinda's dying.

Mandalay must not stay long: she must leave time for Harriet, now. She'll come back, she promises Belinda. Belinda nods, grimaces. Harriet's cat Clytemnestra is lying on her chest, purring, kneading a little. Belinda strokes the cat's fur, occasionally. Her hand is a yellowed claw.

Two of Belinda's sisters, women who are brown-skinned, freckled, with Belinda's kinky hair, and the same wide, graceful swing of her shoulders and pelvis, have come to help. They are both nurses, Mandalay knows. They are there so that Belinda can stay at home. They can administer the morphine pump. They can make sure Belinda is peaceful. They moisten Belinda's lips with ice chips; they sponge her face.

One of them, Andrea, gives the pump mechanism a little pat, and in a few seconds Belinda's eyes close.

It's very difficult to witness, Mandalay thinks. That this is what we come to, pain and oblivion. She hates the deep yellow tinge to

Belinda's skin: it's as if she has been painted that colour by someone who doesn't know her. A brilliant and hard-working and generous woman, who lived richly and loved fully, ends up dying this way, body wasted, mind shutting down.

There's the sound of someone arriving, being admitted through the front door. Joe looks in the doorway of the living room (the dying room) and says: The priest is here.

Priest! Mandalay thinks. If Belinda was against anything in her whole generous life, it was organized religion, priests. But the men who enter are shaven, barefoot, in yellow-brown robes. Buddhist monks. They aren't Asian, Mandalay sees, but Caucasian; they have Canadian accents. Vancouver accents. Of course. She has forgotten that Belinda and Joe are Buddhists.

One of them says: The cat needs to be put out of the room.

Belinda's sister says that the cat is comforting for Belinda.

The monk says: Her soul might be attracted to it and enter it, when it leaves her body.

Mandalay rolls her eyes at Andrea and Lorna, but Joe says: Take it out.

She had always imagined that Joe and Belinda's Buddhism was of the secular type. Balance and boundaries, meditation and prayer-flag bunting on the deck, and vegetarian curry suppers. It seems not.

Mandalay reaches for the cat before Andrea or Lorna can move. She picks it up, cradles her, walks from the room. She passes Harriet in the hallway. Harriet, who has been called home almost too late. She hasn't seen Harriet for a couple of years, and the girl has grown up. She's taller, more muscular, her facial structure stronger, more defined. She has cut her long hair, and wears it in a straight, chin-length bob tucked behind her ears. Her clothes are androgynous, almost severe. She's very pale, but composed. Too composed. She looks somehow unreal, bloodless, a ghost.

What has happened to Harriet?

Harriet says: That's my cat.

Mandalay hands Harriet the cat, as if she's handing over a baby. She finds her boots in the jumble by the front door, opens the door, walks down the steps. She is not grieving, now, only furious, burning, flaming with fury. She does not know why. She thinks that she will ignite anyone who comes near her.

MANDALAY'S JOINT SHOW is called "The Places We Live." Mandalay likes the title: it's unpretentious, but resonant enough that it catches the imagination. The places we live: yes. More to it than you might immediately think. The places we live are not necessarily physical structures, though they may be those too. The show is about (so the catalogue copy says) the places, physical and conceptual, that twenty-first century West Coast culture has constructed as home. *Home* could have been the title of the show as well, but the curator and the artists all agreed that it was too loaded a word: too highly emotional, too freighted with cultural meaning. The chosen title, deliberately a little clumsy, a little vague, opens the idea up, a little. That home is not necessarily *home*, after all, is one of the things that the new title acknowledges.

It's her first show at the big public gallery, and so, even though she's sharing it with two other artists, it's a milestone, a tangible recognition. She has dreamed of this all of her life. The opening of the show, this evening, has been anticipated for a year, and here it is happening now. Her show. The curator in her electric-blue cheongsam and lug boots bustles around, the technician sets up the microphone and the interns double-check all of the text placards, the catalogues. It feels that the event will never begin; time stretches impossibly.

The two other artists who are part of the show are fussing over last-minute details. They are also Vancouverites, and she knows each slightly. Madeleine Chen, Davigny Purcell. (We could have all been chosen for our fancy names, Mandalay thinks.)

Madeleine is a painter, and her canvases are big, showy. She has embraced glossiness. Her trademark black backgrounds are mirror-like, almost glazed, and against them, jots and splashes and streaks of rich colours — cobalt, alizarin red, chrome yellow, metallic gold — make you think of calligraphy or embroidery, the decoration of two-dimensional objects.

It's almost too pleasing to look at, for Mandalay. It will be the most popular work in the show, of course, but it's almost decorative, almost too easy to picture hanging above an Italian leather sofa in a twentieth-story Coal Harbour condo. She knows that Madeleine has done commissioned work for commercial spaces — banks, brokerages — that are even larger than the pieces in the show. Her work sells for a lot.

Davigny's work is three-dimensional, positioned in vitrines on black columns around the room. Davigny tends to work very small — she's a miniaturist — but they've used her larger pieces for the show, which is just as well, as they might otherwise have been dwarfed by the other work. In the vitrines are fantastical sculptures — each one a little fantasy or sci-fi movie, almost — of hallucinogenic versions of sea creatures. The sculptures are made from porcelain, finely detailed in the extreme, translucent in places, bristling with impossibly delicate protuberances. Mandalay wonders how they can even be safely transported.

They are convincing, biologically, in a strange way: they remind a viewer of the bizarre, phantasmagorical creatures that have been photographed in the deepest marine trenches. But they are not scientific replicas; they are inventions. And they too are about containment: all of the imaginary porcelain creatures are based on organisms that build shells or tests. Snails, urchins, barnacles.

The works of the two co-exhibitors are good juxtapositions for her own work, Mandalay sees. Madeleine's glossiness and Davigny's encrustation are both foils and reference points for Mandalay's print-collages. They make her work seem more organic, more intel-lectual. Don't they? She thinks they do. Anyway, the built-up textures and hard architectural lines of her pieces are very much emphasized by their context, and by the lighting, which has been well-designed.

Here is the past eight years or so of her work. About half of it has sold and is on loan from owners; it's great to see some of the older pieces, again. To see an evolution. She had begun as an art student in her early forties to create this work. All of her pieces are prints, hard-edged prints in the industrial colours of a city – black, grey, park-bench green, hi-vis orange – made from her photographs of buildings and architectural drawings. She has made these in the traditional ways, with resist gels and etched plates. But overlaid are other prints – bits of texture, of found objects whose shapes she had chosen for their forms, but that work also as cultural references.

She had begun, eight years ago, with the decaying, ineptly-repaired craftsman-style houses on her own city block, and had used objects from her own life for added dimension. A bit of lace from an old bra; a scab from her son Owen's knee. She'd made block prints from things like these, added them in. Pulling enough useable prints, assembling them, had taken her hundreds of hours. In her more recent work, she has used digital media – photos of objects that she has manipulated. She has also moved out of her own neigh-bourhood and used other buildings – monstrous new houses in West Vancouver, warehouses on the docks, tarpaulin shelters in Downtown Eastside alleys with dumpsters. She'd spent some time with the inhabitants of the Downtown Eastside, before she took the photos and collected the objects she needed. The work was seen as a commentary on homelessness, of course, but her prints show some-thing else: resourcefulness, adaptability, the choices necessitated to survive without a house or apartment in the city. She had focused in on the intrepidness needed to secure a tarp against the rain and wind, on structural shapes and knots. The street-dwellers had told her about their possessions. Even the winged-out ones, the scruffy men and women whose cognitive skills had been scoured out by psychoses. Everything meant something. She'd recorded them, taken photos, careful notes. She'd had a grant, and had spent almost all of it on food and coffee for her subjects. She had also given them cash, though she had been advised not to; she had withdrawn stacks of twenties from bank machines, and every day, had slipped them to the different people she spoke to, whose shelters and possessions she had photographed.

She likes those pieces. They are honest work, but they don't sell very well. Her sister Cleo says that they're a niche market – the people who would buy them are architects with strongly developed libertarian biases and equally strong stomachs.

The show opens. The crowd of invited gallery members trickles in, with their Burberry raincoats and cashmere scarves, to look at the works, to stand holding stemless wineglasses while she and her co-artists give their carefully-pitched and timed talks, to mill around before dissolving into social conversations.

Mandalay gives her talk. She circulates. Her son Aidan has come; Owen has a game. Her sister Cleo; some people she knows from the college; Max and Taylor Gibbons. Duane has not come, though he raised an eyebrow when she mentioned the show, a few months ago. She is pretty sure that he'll take time to see it on another day, and then drop a mention of it – not necessarily positive – into their next conversation.

Cleo drifts up to her, dressed in an off-white wool sweater and trousers, gold earrings, new tan leather ankle boots. Cleo's hair is even blonder than before; Mandalay feels momentarily frumpy, in her forgiving black Gap stretch jeans and flowing bronze-coloured silk shirt and long greying ponytail, but lets the thought evaporate.

So, Cleo says, are you happy with the gallery work? Is there good press coverage? Will you get some sales?

She doesn't know. Cleo makes her aware of aspects of the show over which she has no control. She doesn't want to think about those things.

A short stout woman with very heavy black-rimmed glasses, à la Iris Apfel, and cerise lipstick to match her cerise dress strides over. Mandalay knows who she is. Her heart begins to beat a little too quickly.

Denise Paumgartner, the woman says, putting out a hand. Mandalay extends hers, and her fingers are briefly squeezed and released. This is a person who shakes a lot of hands, who has pared down her handshake to conserve energy.

Who represents you? the woman asks.

Mandalay knows that Denise Paumgartner would have already ascertained this information. She smiles in a way she hopes is ironic, but not too cynical. She says: I'm not represented.

Denise Paumgartner makes a gilt-edged business card materialize from thin air and passes it to her. You should come and see me, she says.

I'd like that very much, Mandalay says. She hopes that she is not grinning too crazily. She reminds herself to stay cool but not zone out; to maintain eye contact but soften her lids; to breathe.

Denise Paumgartner owns what is likely the most prestigious gallery in the city.

She says, now, showing teeth somehow miraculously not coloured by their proximity to the cerise lipstick: I'm very interested to hear about what you're working on now. A slight flick of her chin indicates the work hanging on the wall. Mandalay reads the gesture: This body of work is admirable, but you're finished with this subject now.

Mandalay swallows and hopes that it isn't too obvious. Of course, she says.

Great, Denise Paumgartner says. Ring my assistant to make an appointment sometime in the next week or so. And disappears, despite the cerise dress, back into the crowd.

And that's it.

She might collapse.

Cleo comes back, says: Is that who I think it was?

Mandalay says: She wants new work. I don't have new work.

Don't be ridiculous, Cleo says. You'd better have new work. Chances like this don't come around very often. Am I right?

Mandalay suddenly sharply misses Belinda,. Who would have said: Of course you have new work. It's just in your unconscious still.

Why doesn't she have new work? Because it's only two years since she made the Shelter prints, and the time has slipped by so quickly that she hasn't even noticed. Because she doesn't have studio space now that she's no longer a student. Because she has two teenaged sons, and is menopausal, and has been working as an art instructor, and her best friend is dying. And because as hard as she tries to live in the present, the years slip by, just like that.

She doesn't look at her phone until the end, when most of the attendees have gone, and the curator is pressing her interns to take home the leftover hors d'oeuvres. Then it's with a casual, automatic gesture. She has had no premonition.

Belinda is gone. What now?

2018

21

BEN, IN THE CHEAP SEATS, thinks he sees Alison across the arena: Alison, with a strange man. But it's probably just a tall slim woman with long blond hair. He hasn't seen Alison in, what, ten years. Since they'd come back from Nicaragua and she'd broken up with him.

The woman is laughing, bending toward her companion. Moving the way Alison moved.

Will she see him, sitting here with the boy. He wishes he hadn't come. It had been a mistake, he thinks. A stupid idea. The kid is too young and not the right kind of kid to bring to a hockey game. He is sitting back in his seat, not even on the edge, his legs sticking out, huddled in his puffy coat. His hands are folded together. He has not touched the drink or the bag of mini donuts. His mouth is held in a straight line, like he's waiting for the dentist.

Crap, he'd better make sure the boy enjoys himself, or it will be even harder to talk Tiffany into letting Ben have him for a couple of hours next time. And if he doesn't keep it up… Panic roils around his chest. He's in such a bind.

Well, he can't get out, so might as well face it, get through it. Anyway, it might only be for a couple more years. A few, at worst. They can't live much longer, the old man and the old lady. He just needs to hang on, get through it.

Hey, he says. Don't you want to watch your cousin play? It's not every boy who can say he has a cousin who's a hockey star. Come on. If you try it, you'll like it.

The kid sighs, slides forward in his seat, pushes his glasses up higher on his nose.

The glasses are so dorky. There must be less dorky styles for little kids, but he can't say anything. The kid's eyes magnified behind them. Too much oxygen, at his birth. Damaged from the start.

He can't think of that. Aren't you happy you can see your cousin play? he asks.

Which one is he? the boy says.

Crap, the kid is small. He can barely see over the heads of the people seated on the tier below them.

I told you, number seventeen, Ben says. In the blue, see? There he is, see? It says Lund on the back of his jersey. See, there, skating toward the goal. Why can't the kid see?

The kid chews his upper lip with his lower teeth. His teeth are tiny, like a cat's teeth or something.

I can't read it, the kid says.

What? You're not looking. There. He's got his back to you.

I can't read, the kid says.

Oh, for fuck's sake.

Number seventeen. You can read the number seventeen, can't you?

The kid shakes his head, minutely.

For fuck's sake. Is he handicapped? How old are you? he asks.

Without turning around, the boy holds up one hand, four fingers and a thumb splayed out.

Can't kids read by five?

The kid looks like he's going to cry.

Hey, Ben says. Get up on my lap. You'll be taller.

The boy does so, slowly. His little weight on Ben's thighs.

Okay, he says. He takes out a program, points. Look at this line. See it? And the bent line next to it? Straight line, bent line. That's seventeen. Now look over on the ice. Do you see that same number on the player's jersey? His, uh, his shirt?

The kid looks in the direction he's pointing, finally nods.

You see him? Okay, that's your cousin.

A thought strikes him. Do you know what a cousin is?

The kid shakes his head.

Okay, it's a relative. It's like, well, I'm your dad. And then I have a sister. Do you know what a sister is? Okay, good. My sister's boy — her son — that's him. Number seventeen. That's your cousin. Got it?

The kid nods.

It's too complicated. What if the kid wants to meet his relations? Well, you *have* met them. That's what he'll say. You just don't remember.

Kids can't remember being babies, can they? He can't remember anything before he was in school.

The boy sits back against him, then. Should he put his arm around him? He's kind of leaning into him. The lightness of him against Ben's chest.

He'd better not fall asleep and piss his pants, not on Ben's lap. Kids do that, don't they? But it's good he's making himself comfortable. There will be a good report.

He remembers now the twin, the hockey player, climbing up on him like this. Or the other twin, maybe. He could never tell them apart. Before his sisters cut him off. Well, basically cut him off. Took Cliff's side. Blamed everything on him.

Fuck, the time has sure gone by. His life, flowing down some crummy gutter.

On the way out of the arena, the kid says he needs to pee, so they take a side route. It takes so long. Ben needs to get home now; he's getting jumpy, and being reminded of Alison hasn't helped.

Ben pushes through some glass double doors, quickly, and then hears behind him a thump, and sees a shocked look on the face of a woman coming toward him. The kid on the floor, flat out, on the other side of the doors.

His hands are shaking. He kneels by the boy, sits him up. A bruise is coming up on his forehead, already. Shit. The kid looks dazed.

The woman hands him the kid's glasses, which must have gone flying. I can't believe you did that, she says. You let the door swing back on him.

Typical man, another woman, says.

The rage is like a soft-nosed bullet expanding in him. But his other need is more urgent, distracting him. He picks the kid up. Sorry, bud, I thought you had it, he says.

The woman who picked up the glasses plants herself in front of him. Her mouth is ugly. What's his name?

What?

What's the boy's name?

Fuck, she thinks he's abducting the kid. As if.

Oscar, he says. It's Oscar.

Is that your name? the woman asks the kid. Do you know this man?

The boy looks terrified. Thanks a lot, crazy bitch, Ben thinks.

But the boy nods. He gets a grip around Ben's neck, and he nods.

22

MY GENERATION, OLIVIA SAYS, is the first one in ninety years that will be less well off than our parents.

I think that's an oversimplification, Cleo says.

My generation won't be able to afford to own a house, Olivia says. We won't have pensions. *Your* generation, Olivia says, has destroyed the environment and blown up the economy. Now we have to deal with it.

Cleo feels her muscles sag, her bones turn to lead. She wants to sit down, to lie down, but they have only started their climb. She can't stop yet.

It's not that she hasn't thought much of this herself. She's quite aware that expansion can't be maintained indefinitely. It's that she can't bear the blaming. It's not fair. She thinks of her birth family, living off-grid, eating what they grew, wearing hand-me-downs. And her foster family, frugal and practical farmers. Cleo had not owned a new article of clothing until she was twelve; she had worn Zellers jeans and sweatshirts until she went to university. She had been given a radio-CD player for her sixteenth birthday and had bought a used electric typewriter in grade eleven, to type up her assignments.

I had much less than you, growing up, she says. My generation had very little compared to yours.

It's not about what you gave us materially, Olivia says. That only raised our expectations for a standard of living that is unrealistic for us.

I don't think it's that simple, Cleo says. You can't lay everything on one generation.

It's your generation that has enjoyed the best of everything, and caused huge economic and environmental problems.

Hardly, Cleo says. I was born in 1968. You have an overly simplified grasp of history.

You are so naïve, Olivia says. I find it difficult to talk to you.

Cleo doesn't have the words to describe the sensations running through her at this moment. Alarm? Anger? Panic? Nothing is adequate. Also, there would be an appropriate way to respond to her daughter's rudeness, but she can't think right now what it would be.

Right now she has to concentrate on getting up the Grouse Grind.

Olivia is home for a brief visit. She's assiduously dividing her time between Cleo and Trent, although staying at Cleo's house, her own home. Cleo has booked the week off work, this visit, to give herself more time with her daughter. To be available when Olivia wants her to be.

It's early May, and a day borrowed from summer. Warm already, and cloudless. A week day, but the trail is busy with climbers. Cleo hasn't climbed Grouse Mountain for years, probably not since she was in her thirties. It's fierce. The trail is steep and twisty and knotty with roots of arbutus and pine. Olivia's idea, and Cleo was glad to take her up on it. Olivia likes to do things outdoors; she's in a better mood when she's doing something physical, even strenuous. But it's requiring a lot of exertion. Cleo runs a couple of times a week, but not up steep hills.

She says nothing, for a few minutes, just climbs, tries to keep up with Olivia, who is climbing effortlessly ahead of her in her Lululemon shorts and tank top and her deep-treaded running shoes.

Olivia calls over her shoulder, Am I going too fast for you? She doesn't slow.

Nope, Cleo says. I'm fine.

What does Olivia want from her?

Olivia has just finished the first year of her master's program in economics. She has chosen to go further in that field, rather than apply for law school. She has a research job that pays her tuition and part of her living, and another job that covers the rest. She knows more than Cleo does, now, about her field – she quotes experts and has theory at her fingertips. Cleo is not uninformed; she reads. But Olivia dismisses her contributions to the conversations.

More unbearable than Olivia's rudeness is the idea that her daughter feels so hopeless about the state of the world, the future. Her own future.

An hour into the climb, Cleo feels she has finally got her second wind. Endurance has always been her specialty. Now she's right behind Olivia, keeping a good pace.

Cleo says to Olivia's back: I think things are actually getting better. People are trying to do financially and environmentally responsible things. We've learned from the last couple of recessions. And cars are going electric, and there's so much research and new technology in building, these days.

You don't know anything about it.

But I'm agreeing with you, Cleo says.

No. You clearly don't understand anything about it. You shouldn't pretend you do.

Why are you so gratuitously rude? Cleo asks. She has asked this more than once. She makes an effort to keep her voice light, to express curiosity rather than accusation.

I'm sorry if I seemed rude! I'm just being blunt.

It's rude and hurtful, Cleo says, mildly.

Olivia has stopped and is standing, legs apart, a little above Cleo. She has taken out her water bottle; she unscrews the lid, though it's one of the straw types, throws back her head, and drinks deeply.

Cleo stops climbing, though it's difficult to do that on such a steep stretch.

Olivia's poise is victorious. But what has she won? Why beat down Cleo?

Cleo climbs up the few meters that separate them and sits on a gnarly root. She takes out her own water bottle.

Is this climb too much for you? Olivia demands.

Maybe Cleo's daughter is just a bully.

Trent is often bullying, and Olivia used to pick on Sam mercilessly.

But she was a paragon of sweet reasonableness and gentleness, according to her friends' parents and her teachers.

It's only with Cleo now that she shows her teeth.

What does she want?

They're two-thirds of the way up. Cleo doesn't remember the mountain being this steep or high. She pauses to catch her breath; other hikers and even runners surge up past her.

Olivia looks back at her. Are you going to make it?

Is she going to make it?

She remembers Trent saying to her: Why do you even get into those discussions with her?

Think of something else.

It's difficult; Olivia sidesteps questions about her courses, her social life, even her pastimes.

Cleo says: Oh! I heard from Lacey that Claire and her fellow are planning to get engaged! Is that even a thing? Doesn't getting engaged just mean planning to get married? How can you be planning to get engaged?

I wouldn't know, Olivia says.

Claire had been Olivia's best friend, up until high school at least.

I just thought it was a bit absurd, Cleo says.

Olivia stops, turns. I don't find gossip very interesting, okay?

Cleo says: I don't understand why you are so rude. You speak to me so disrespectfully.

You're just so frustrating, Olivia says.

I can guarantee you, Cleo says, that if you speak to a partner the way you speak to me, he will leave you. Guaranteed.

A spasm passes over Olivia's face. I don't speak to anyone but you this way, she says, furiously.

Right, then, Cleo says.

She can feel the sting of tears, and hot hard lumps have risen in her throat. Her legs are like heavy pegs. She stumps past Olivia on the pathway, forges upward doggedly.

IN THE EVENING Cleo cooks dinner while Olivia and Sam play a complicated board game involving tokens, dice, game cards, and several different kinds of possible moves. It's like a mashup of several different board games and Cleo, playing with Sam, has never quite managed to get her head around it, but her two offspring play it very fast, with much laughter.

Cleo hears Olivia's infectious, throaty chuckle. Olivia has always laughed a lot. Cleo has never known a child who laughed so much.

Why does she seem so unhappy with Cleo now? And what is Cleo to give this adult child of hers to satisfy her?

It's not as simple as boundaries, she thinks, though the time of unconditional love is drawing to an end. It's every parent's job, of course, to show their children that balance between overweening confidence in their own opinions and respect for the opinions and experiences of their parents and other adults. But with Olivia, she is stymied. She has no clue.

It's probably too late to repair the mistakes she has made. Perhaps all that she can do is carefully, carefully avoid blowing up any bridges.

At the top of the mountain, Olivia had flung herself down onto a patch of grass, and Cleo had sat down beside her, cautiously, silently.

Are we going to take the cable car down? Olivia had asked, presently.

It's either that or roll myself over the edge, Cleo had said.

And Olivia's laugh, so spontaneous, so joyful, so delighted, that the other hikers passing them had smiled.

SHE ASKS OLIVIA: Do you need any money? Can I pay for your trip? Do you need anything for your apartment?

They are doing up the dishes: Cleo washing, Olivia drying. The dishwasher has broken down again. Cleo will have to get a new one, though the expenditure will be inconvenient. Olivia says, stiffly, No, thank you.

Aha, Cleo thinks. She says: I'd be happy to help out.

I don't need it now, Olivia says. It would have made a big difference a couple of years ago, when I wanted to travel with friends for a year, but now I am paying my own way, and I'm doing fine.

You don't have to do it alone, Cleo says. I want to help you out.

It's important to me, Olivia says. It's a point of pride.

The footing is very slippery here. Cleo must guard herself so carefully. But she's moving over completely unfamiliar terrain, and in the darkness.

It occurs to her that her concept of family, of friendship groups, even the workspace, has been one in which normally, any member can make certain reasonable assumptions. There is a shared language. If one or more members disturb the assumptions, the unit's shared, unspoken constitution is spotlighted, shaken out and dusted, and whether or not members want to, it's up for review. It can feel as though this member has made an attack on the institution itself.

And for the member who challenges the group assumptions, the institution, it can feel like personal existence itself is at stake.

So we come to war with one another.

It's a long way from this thought, though, to the conversation that is happening at her kitchen sink. And she needs to meet Olivia where she is, for once. To engage with her as a fellow human being: to see past the various bombasts and bombardments.

I'm truly sorry, she begins, and then stops herself. Amends a word she had almost spoken. Not *if.* Not *if.*

She looks directly at her daughter. I'm sorry, she says, that I have not given you the support that you needed.

Olivia's face changes: her forehead scrunches up; the corners of her lips pull down deeply, and her chin forms itself into a little puckered ball. Cleo looks back at the sink. A silence hangs between them, transparent, fragile, trembling, begging to be breached.

Cleo normally fills that space with a reasonable explanation.

Her lips are actually parted, and she's about to continue: But I did the best I could at the time. Which is true.

Or maybe not completely true. Or maybe, just irrelevant, at this moment.

She closes her mouth.

She hears Olivia, to her right, draw air in through her nose, expel it through her nose. Again.

Olivia says: You're just so critical. You're so judgemental of everything and everyone. Nothing is ever good enough. I'm afraid to tell you anything about my life. You make me feel bad about everything I want to feel happy about. You're so hard on Sam that he's afraid to get off his computer or come out of his room. You try to be a good mom but you just drive us away.

It must be like this to be shot, Cleo thinks.

I've given twenty years of my life to taking care of you two, she says, calmly, though Olivia is sobbing, and she can hardly speak. I stayed home with you when you were little and after I went back to work, I spent all of my weekends and evenings doing things with you, taking you places, making sure you had everything you needed. You were the focus of my life.

I know that, Olivia sobs. But you're so mean. You're so mean.

I just want you to succeed, Cleo says. To have good options. It's a tough world, and if you don't succeed, you're vulnerable to terrible things.

But even as she says that, she recoils. She knows this, of course. All of her life she has seen this: anyone who falters, even a little, will likely crash and fail. She has seen it in her parents' lives and in the lives of the troubled boys at her foster home, in the mishaps of her neighbours' and colleagues' kids and in the news.

But what a thing to believe, and what a terrible view of the world to impart to her children. Because that is what she has done, she sees. She has tried to manage and insulate and contain; she has tried to intuit potential dangers, predict faults, engineer against all possible failure. And she has not been wrong to do this, but she has not done it skilfully enough: she has let her anxiety be her blueprint; she has overdone.

She has assigned herself responsibility for fixing the world, and has convinced her children that it is her job.

There is nothing she can say that will change this. And so many things she might say that would achieve complete demolition.

Sam comes in from putting out the trash cans, making so much noise washing his hands in the powder room that he must have heard them, wanted to give them warning.

Cleo thinks: I must find a way to defuse. But it is Olivia (wiping her eyes on the dish towel, leaving mascara streaks) who says: Why don't I put the kettle on? Does everyone want tea?

And so they manage to go on.

23

MANDALAY IS PUZZLING OVER a first-year portfolio. Something is off –
there is something she doesn't quite understand, doesn't quite know
how to articulate – but that is common, in first-year portfolios. What
she must do is see it clearly, as a whole, as its individual components,
as an item in an almost infinite collection of like items, the early
attempt of a visual arts student, and then, having seen it, articulate
its strengths and weaknesses to the student in a way that will both
make sense of the grade she's going to attach to it, and illuminate the
work to the student, hopefully with the result that the student will
discover other possibilities and want to learn more.

The grade, she has already decided, is B. It's a useful grade, a
grade for a student who has done careful, competent work, who has
met the criteria for the assignment, and shown that she has considered
the discussions, the lectures, the slide shows of the term in her own
output, but who has not, actually, made something unique to herself.

She hates this part of her job, having to assign a grade to a student's work, having to judge it and measure it.

I'd like to see more flow, more expression, in your line, Mandalay
types, in her comments. Try to translate the feeling of the weight, the
mass of the hand, into varying pressures on your pencil. Try to feel
the line as language to communicate mass. Will this communicate
to the student? She has grave doubts.

She flips through to a block print in the student's portfolio. The
print is technically fine: no bleeding or blank spots; well-matched

layers showing a precise use of register marks; an appropriate design, one which allows the student to create texture out of their lino block. But again, there is something expressionless, mute, inert about this image of a skull. It adds nothing; it's a pastiche of the skull logo popular with brands of surfing (or is it skateboarding?) merchandise.

At least the student had not added a heart and rose to her design, as some others had done.

Now she is feeling disrespect for the student, and that is not a good place from which to teach. She flips to another assignment. She must get faster. She has a stack to finish, and then a department meeting, and she's helping to set up the graduating year-end show. And she needs to return to her own work, to the next of the series of prints she's making.

She is fifty-two years old, and still an apprentice at her job. Still new enough that every task requires a million separate considerations. She'll get better. But she is starting out in a teaching career at *fifty-two*. It's the hardest thing she has ever done in her life.

She has had many jobs; she has raised two children. She has been practicing her own art for decades. She is employed at a provincial college that pays well, has a good union. The students are mostly talented; some are gifted. But teaching art is very hard.

She is lucky to have a teaching job at all, of course. But what is expected of her, the managing of several first and second-year studio classes, the administrative work, the grading – especially the grading – has been an assault on her equilibrium. She feels at the end of each term that she has pulled a handcart carrying all of her students – a few dozen – up a steep hill.

And this last year, not only struggling, but alone. She pauses from her engagement with the B portfolio to let the wave of sadness settle over her, as she knows it will, as it still does, every now and then.

There isn't adequate terminology, let alone a cultural space, for the grieving that happens after the loss of a close friend.

For a spouse or child or parent, even a sibling, yes. But no place or name for the bereavement of a friend, even if that friend was the person with whom you spent most of your free time, shared your innermost thoughts, relied on most in the world for understanding and encouragement and the occasional motivational kick in the butt.

She's trying to avoid the emotion, sidestepping it with interior peroration, but better, she knows, to just let it wash in.

Belinda, her friend, mentor, colleague, her office just down the hallway, empty now. Belinda's stacks of books, her walls papered with overlapping thumbtacked images and quotations, all cleared out; Belinda herself, in her thrifted T-shirts and unfashionable jeans, her corkscrew hair, her freckled, café-au-lait skin, her irreverent, salacious observations, her laugh like a stack of Jenga blocks falling off a table, her all-seeing, all-accepting dark eyes, the humour, the generosity, the *light* of her, gone, extinguished forever.

The dark wave pulls at Mandalay, empties her out, drags at her heart, recedes.

She gets up, goes to the washroom and mops at her face with damp paper towels. Descends the lesser-used stairs at the far end of the building to the coffee machine, punches the buttons for hot water in a cup, creeps back up to her office to add a bag of tea, not black, which she's had enough of already today, but her weird catnip-smelling Indian herbal tea, which may or may not work but at any rate will distract her until she can return to the portfolio.

She is so lonely, without Belinda.

Mandalay sits back on her chair, puts her feet in their scuffed and dusty Blunds up on the stack of folders on a chair and sips her tea. Her office is extremely untidy: she pretty well lets it go until end of term, then spends a day hauling out old projects, filing paperwork, re-shelving books, picking up the various bits of detritus that had found their way onto desk and floor.

But she hadn't bothered, at the end of the last term: Belinda had been dying, had died. Mandalay hadn't got a thing done. Now two terms' worth of clutter choke the small space. She'll clean it, after she gets through the final grading. She has a high tolerance for clutter, which is lucky for her. Not so lucky for people who have to share a space with her, perhaps.

She sips the slightly fetid tea, nudges the cup with its tea bag to a corner of her desk, where it will evaporate slowly in the humid coastal air, the teabag growing a coat of grey fur, so that it looks exactly like a dead mouse. Allows the images to fade naturally, her mind not able to sustain them indefinitely.

She picks up the B portfolio again. Engage with the content, she hears Belinda's voice say. Ask questions.

Mandalay writes: *I wondered what you felt about this hand, and what you want me to know about it.* The words emerge painfully at first, but then more easily. She praises the effort she sees, even while she points out the limitations.

She knows, now, what to say. But it is so tiring, to engage in this deep necessary mode with student after student. How can she be completely present with, and see, so many human beings, in such a short space of time?

MANDALAY EMAILS HER SON AIDAN. She does this once a week, whether or not he has replied to her last email. He does not often reply. She is conscious that she might be giving him too much freedom, too long a leash, as her sister Cleo would say. He has just turned eighteen. He is far away from her for the first extended time of his life.

But what has she left to give him but his freedom?

She had been hurt when he left: she had not been prepared, had thought she had one more year with him at home, just the two of them. It had been difficult to accept that Owen was moving out and would be living in another city, with another family, as a billeted hockey player in the Juniors, but she'd had the consolation of her other son, she had thought.

Aidan had announced, in late January, days before starting his final term of high school, that he already had enough credits to graduate, even to get into a good university, and he was going to quit his last term. He would go travelling.

Mandalay hadn't reacted very well. He had made his decision when she was vulnerable, still numb and grieving for Belinda. He hadn't thought of it that way, she knew, and she hadn't mentioned it. Children should be the sun in their own universe; they shouldn't revolve around their parents' lives and needs. She *wanted* him to focus on his own wants and needs, to be essentially oblivious to hers, outside of the requirements of basic human respect. But it had hurt her that he wanted to leave so quickly, and she had been angry with Aidan, and told him she was angry. She'd criticized him; she'd said that he was privileged, and didn't deserve his privilege; that he was wasting opportunities other people would never get; that he was rejecting everything she had done for him.

She shouldn't have said those things. She had been grieving for Belinda, and angry about Owen's decision to continue to play hockey, and also, she sees now, angry about her brother Ben, who had also had all of the privileges, and seemed to be spiralling downward, causing increasing damage to himself and others. She can see that now: she had been angry and grieving, and had not given the attention and objectivity that she should have to Aidan, and had done damage herself, which has not been reparable.

And Duane, of course, had been coldly bullying: Aidan would have to fund himself. But not out of his university savings account. And Aidan would also have to fund himself for whatever bullshit university he could get into, later.

Whereupon Aidan had said that he would just go, backpack and work his way around the world. They wouldn't hear from him.

He emails her, occasionally, from various places. He has lost his phone, or turned it off, perhaps. He seems to be using internet cafés.

He is gone too, she thinks.

But she continues to write him, to make herself vulnerable, to express herself in a way that asks him to engage. He does not engage. If he would only argue with her, castigate her, she would feel that they were connecting. But he does not. He doesn't write at all, except to say that he has moved on to a new place, and that he is fine.

She has lost him, perhaps, but she will not let go of him. He is her son, the son with whom she has the best rapport. He is closer to her, emotionally – or she feels closer to him, which, she admits, is not the same thing – than is anyone else.

She asks Aidan questions that she hopes will elicit responses from him: questions that she thinks he will be so compelled to answer that he will answer her email. Questions about his take on books they have both read, on how to make his famous green sauce, on whether she should renovate the kitchen. She writes of her work, the ideas, the conversations and images she comes across. She is careful to avoid anything that could be read as critical or overbearing or prescriptive.

What has happened to Aidan?

She had thought that because she had such healthy boundaries with her sons – she never lost her temper, never allowed barriers against them, never criticized them or pushed them to be what they were not – that they would skip the need to separate emotionally from her. But this does not seem to be true.

Her son will not communicate with her, and will not tell her why.

She writes Aidan that Harry's cat, Clytemnestra, has settled into the house. Harriet had moved in, briefly, with Mandalay and Aidan, after her mother's death. She had brought her cat, and then left it with them.

Mandalay has wondered if Harriet's stay, back in the winter, had dislocated Aidan somehow. They had always been good friends, as small children, but they had seemed different, in the weeks after Belinda's death. Of course, Harriet had been grieving and in shock.

She writes: Tell me what you are doing. What you are thinking. Tell me you are safe.

But he does not respond. He can't be enticed out of hiding, even though she enacts, over and over, the bond between them.

Duane says that Aidan is fine; that he is accessing his bank account, but not spending much. Duane isn't angry at Aidan any longer; in fact, Aidan's stock has risen, in Duane's estimation.

Terrible language to use, about the dynamic between father and son. *Stock. Estimation.*

She has an empty house, now. She spends a lot of time at work, on campus. She is able to do her own print work in the campus studio, which is not always convenient. She can't keep things there: her prints or her supplies. Too many people, students and faculty, use the studio.

She could fill her sons' empty rooms with her prints and her supplies. She could, as Duane suggests, rent them to students. But she leaves them empty.

She finishes her email to Aidan, which he may not read, which he will not respond to. She presses send. She sits by her computer, in her office. She waits for something to happen that does not. She returns to her work.

24

CLIFF HAS AGREED TO MEET BEN at the McDonald's at Kingsway and Victoria Drive, a location that's on his way, heading home from the clinic where Cliff has had a physio appointment and accessible, he guesses, by bus, and suitable for the boy, whom Ben has said he'll have with him. Cliff expects Ben to be late or not show at all, but when he walks into the low, functional-looking building with its red trim, he sees Ben already there, in a dirty suede jacket, towing a small boy, who is Oscar. The boy has an envelope of fries in front of him, which he is eating delicately, dipping each a precise depth into the pleated paper cup of ketchup. He's in a grey sweatshirt that's not really warm enough for the day, and looks dirty.

Cliff pulls up a chair at the next table, not getting too close to the child, who doesn't know him.

Hey, bro, Ben says. Thanks for coming.

Ben looks terrible. His hair is unwashed; he's got stubble, deep shadows under his eyes.

Cliff reminds himself to be guarded. *There is nothing Ben won't do*, he recites silently, *to take advantage of you.*

Ben asks if Cliff wants some food; Cliff doesn't. But he thinks that Ben does. He's willing to spring for a McDonald's meal. He orders four big burgers and a large fries and coffee and a small milkshake, brings them to the table.

Ben gives him a grateful, abashed look, and dives in. The boy looks inside the milkshake container dubiously. He peels back the bun of the burger Ben has passed to him and examines the innards. He's a very small boy, kind of quiet. Ben makes a deal of introducing him to Cliff, telling him that Cliff used to look after him when he was little. Cliff doesn't contradict him, though maybe he should. The boy doesn't seem to be paying a lot of attention. He doesn't touch the hamburger, but continues to eat the fries methodically.

Ben says, wow, you're a lifesaver, Cliff. I don't know what to do. I'm just down on my luck.

Down on your luck, Cliff repeats.

Well, yeah, Ben says. He looks at Cliff soberly. It's more than that, you're right. I've fucked up again. You're right. He drops his gaze to the table.

You should watch your language around the kid, Cliff says.

Ben winces. Did I? Oh, f... Oh, man, I'm sorry.

Cliff waits. The appeal or whatever is on the table will come, soon enough. And then he'll say no, and give Ben the two hundred that Cliff has taken out of the bank machine and has in his wallet right now, and he'll walk away. He has already made this decision. He can't really spare the two hundred, but Cleo has said she'll pay him back. He won't take the money from her, of course, but he has to give it; he has no excuse.

Ben has two ploys, Cliff sees. One is to be abjectly honest, or maybe more accurately, honest-seeming. He says: I f... I messed up. I let everyone down. I let you down. I let myself down. The other is to try to get Cliff and Oscar interested in each other. Ben is working both angles.

Cleo has given Cliff a sketch of the arrangement Ben has with his parents: he's on an allowance (which they can easily afford, Cleo had said, so don't feel bad for them), and the conditions of the allowance are that he maintain joint custody of Oscar, and bring him to visit them. In order to do that he has to be sober for a week out of every month and keep his apartment in decent shape for a child.

That should be easy enough, but he's clearly on the edge of not being able to manage it.

Cliff doesn't let Ben know that he's aware of the situation. He doesn't respond to Ben's admissions of failure, nor his apologies, when they start. My heart is stone, he thinks. It's harder to resist interacting with Oscar, though the boy seems to want to keep his distance.

What is it going to be this time? Cliff wonders. What is Ben going to try to steal from him this time?

Ben says: I've got a big problem. I've been locked out of my apartment. A misunderstanding with the owner. No, I'm lying. It's my own mess. I didn't pay the rent. But it was kind of a miscommunication. The bitch is really riding me. Sorry. And I could sleep anywhere, you know; I don't matter. But I've got the kid this week. I can't subject him to, you know, anything like that. I've got to protect him.

What about your parents? Cliff asks, though from what Cleo has told him, Ben won't want them to know that he has been evicted.

Ben says, Oh, you know, I don't like to ask. Makes me look bad. I've f... I've screwed up so much here that I don't have any more chances, you know?

What do you need? Cliff asks.

A place to stay for, like three days, Ben says. I wouldn't ask you, of all people, but I know you have a nice place; maybe your wife won't mind. Oscar is very quiet. She likes children, doesn't she, your wife?

Doesn't he know? Cliff is sure he must. But he says, coolly: Veronika and I have split. I have a one-bedroom apartment in Burnaby. It's not great.

Three days, max, Ben says. I just need a sofa. For Oscar. I'll sleep on the floor. And a shower. I can get my shit together in three days.

Ben and Oscar stay for a week. Cliff thinks, frying up eggs and bacon, wiping the toilet and the floor around the toilet, buying more shampoo and bread and milk, that it is what he owes the universe, for the times he himself has been cared for. He keeps his wallet and bank information and all of his other personal papers locked up in an old briefcase under his bed, and takes the briefcase with him when he goes out. He doesn't give Ben a key.

Cliff sees Ben look around at the apartment – the holes in the walls, the chipped countertops, the stained and torn carpeting. He does not ask Cliff for money.

At the end of the week Ben and Oscar look a little healthier. Cleaner, anyway. Cliff has washed their clothes – what they have on their backs and in Ben's backpack. Not much. Ben uses Cliff's razors and hair products, and leaves whiskers in the sink but he looks, when he leaves, a lot shinier. He looks like Ben, again.

He knows that Ben will go visit his adoptive parents now, bringing Oscar, to keep getting money from them. He has helped Ben clean up enough that he can visit his parents; they won't guess that he's been locked out of his place. They'll give Ben a check, or pay his rent directly, or whatever, and Ben will be back in play.

Cliff buys them tickets and puts them on a bus for downtown. Oscar still hasn't really spoken to him, but Cliff feels he has known the boy forever: the weight of Oscar's eyes, watching him, summing him up.

He watches the bus leave and gets back in his truck and drives home. He had expected to feel relieved, but actually he feels something unpleasant, as if he has lost something. When he gets home, he checks his entire apartment. Nothing is missing. But he feels he has not seen the last of Ben. He feels Ben is going to surprise him again, not in a good way. And he feels, sickeningly, that he has not done nearly enough about Oscar.

25

CLEO, IN HER OFFICE, hears her phone buzz and sees on the screen that it's a call from Crystal, her mother. She normally lets Crystal's calls go to voicemail, and calls her back when it's convenient. But the call comes between two meetings, and Cleo answers it, thinking that she might as well deal with whatever it is right away.

Crystal's voice is shrill, thin. Darrell is dead, she says.

Darrell, Crystal's partner of many years now. Cleo half doubts her, half knows that it's true. But is cautious. Is he missing? she asks. It's possible that he's away, on a run – he drives a logging truck – and Crystal is confused and panicking.

But Crystal is lucid. The police came, she says. I didn't believe them. He was fine when he left in the morning.

I don't know what to do, Crystal says. Cleo understands this to be true.

I'll come up, Cleo says. She begins, automatically, to scroll through the calendar on her phone. What will she have to cancel or postpone?

Her birthday, her fiftieth birthday. No, she can be back for that. Can't she? It's possible that a party is being planned for her, by her friend Stephanie, or by Lacey and Mira.

It will just have to be forgotten.

SORRY, MAN, SORRY, Ben says, three or four times. I slept through my alarm. I do that sometimes. Sorry.

It's the first time Ben has ever apologized to him, Cliff realizes.

It makes him want to overlook the fact that he has been waiting for Ben for half an hour, pressing the buzzer for his apartment and phoning him. And that they will have missed the ferry he was planning on, so they'll be waiting for the next one, and nothing will connect well for the whole trip.

He says: You still want to go, though?

Yeah, yeah! Ben says. Just need to shower and grab some things.

Yeah, good, Cliff says. He would not wait, but he wants Ben to be at Darrell's funeral. It's going to mean a lot to Crystal, their mother. Also to Cliff's sisters. It's the least Cliff can do – round up Ben and get him to Butterfly Lake. It's the least he can do.

Though he still feels the wash of the dismay that filled him at Cleo's call. Darrell, their mother's second husband, had died, suddenly – a heart attack while on the road. He drove logging trucks. He'd pulled over at a rest stop, not feeling well, likely, climbed down from the cab, taken two steps from the truck and keeled over, dead. Even if a medevac helicopter had been right on the site, even if the best heart surgeons in the country had been right there, they likely couldn't have saved him. Blew out his aorta.

A good way to go, Cliff thought, but hard on whomever you leave behind. In this case, Crystal, who, Cleo said, had come apart. Wasn't coping at all. They all needed to come up there, organize a funeral, and see what they could do to help Crystal out.

It's a frightening thought, though, something like that happening. That some part of you could just blow, like a gasket, and you drop dead.

Crystal in shock, no wonder. Darrell wasn't old – only in his mid-sixties, and seemed fit and strong as anyone, though he had a good beer gut, a neck as thick as a thigh. How will Crystal run the place without Darrell? he wonders. She's seventy, getting skinnier and loopier every time he sees her.

His sisters will work it out. They're always able to manage that kind of thing better than he is. Cleo had insisted he come up, and she's probably right he should be there. It's going to be difficult, driving all of that way. His leg still wants to go numb, at times. But can he trust Ben to share the driving?

He tries to concentrate on that while Ben gets ready – very slowly, it feels like. He concentrates on his job, which is to get Ben to Butterfly Lake, which means not letting him off the hook, not letting him find a reason to change his mind, to pick an argument, to say he won't go. Even though Ben seems to be very distracted, stopping to scroll and text, wandering around the rooms picking things up and putting them down, pausing half-shaved to watch something idiotic-sounding on his phone, Cliff does not say a thing. Does not let himself betray by a gesture, even by his breathing, that he is worried that they will miss the upcoming ferry, as well.

Ben's apartment is not large. It is new, though, a lot newer than Cliff's. It has high ceilings and modern fixtures, cultured granite countertops, stainless appliances. It's also quite dirty, surfaces marked with grease and fingerprints, corners black with grime. There are two bedrooms, one of them very small, barely wide enough for the single bed and dresser and desk that it holds. All new-looking, flat pack furniture, as if the person living here had previously lost everything they owned in a fire. The boy's room. There are toys, a small pair of running shoes. A large TV, gaming equipment, cords everywhere. Cliff is suddenly grateful for the bland tidiness of his one-bedroom, which has at least pictures on the walls, a couple of plants, some rugs, a few pieces of furniture from his townhouse.

He looks around, tries not to seem impatient.

When they're finally on the road, Ben seems edgy, as if he's worried he's left something behind. He checks his pockets, his bag.

If you've forgotten something, Cliff says, we can stop for it in Powell River.

He can't remember driving with Ben as passenger at any time in the past. They squeak onto the Horseshoe Bay ferry, only two hours later than Cliff had hoped. He loses Ben on the ferry, but then through a window sees him sitting on the outside deck, on a bulkhead. It's raining, lightly, but the part of the deck near the windows is under cover, and a few passengers have congregated there. He sees Ben, cross-legged, in a fleece jacket with the hood up, speak to a dreadlocked, backpack-laden young couple, bearded and dreadlocked. Tree planters, maybe. Ben looks up at them, says something Cliff can't hear, of course. Something muttered, supplicant, though, by the angle of Ben's head, the movement of his lips. The male partner shakes his head; the female's face goes stiff; she turns it away. All of this in a couple of seconds; then Cliff pushes himself to move on, not to be caught by Ben in the act of watching.

The rain follows them as far as Sechelt, then disappears, though Cliff can see it still hunkering darkly in the sky, in the rear-view mirror. It's not sunny out, but rather the clouds have grown thin, inconclusive. Ben asks if they can stop in Sechelt. He says he's hungry. Needs a coffee fix. Cliff looks at his watch. They are in time for the Earls Cove ferry; if they miss it, it'll be two hours till the next one.

We can stop in Powell River, he says.

How long is that?

Ben is like a kid, Cliff thinks, not making an effort to work out the trip in his head, just along for the ride. He relents, pulls over at a gas station near Madeira Park where they can grab a cup of coffee from a machine, and a donut or something, in a couple minute's stop. Even then he sees Ben wander off, get into conversation with a hitchhiker, and has to chivvy him back into the truck.

The long coastal drive northward, though trees. Ben is edgy, again. Cliff asks him about the boy, tries to distract him. Ben answers in spurts: monosyllabically, then in rushes, contradicting himself, leaving sentences unfinished. Oscar. Well, he's a kid. He's in school, yeah. Ben thinks so. Yeah. He is supposed to have him alternate weekends, now because he's in school. School comes first. Weekends are not so good because hey, that's when a guy needs time. But it's a kick having him. Yeah. It's really...

Cliff imagines that when you have kids you wear them 24/7, like organs that have grown outside your body, organs that have no protective shell, are squishy and vital, like your liver. You have to walk around with them protruding from your body and you can't ever forget that you need to keep them hydrated and nourished and protected from getting banged or crushed. Even if you want to forget, you can't.

Cliff has lived with small children. After his first accident, a fall down a flight of stairs, he had lived for a few months with his sister Cleo. Her children, Sam and Olivia, and been little tykes, then. He'd been very aware of them — how Cleo was always there listening for them, watching them, feeding them, cleaning them up, talking to them, all of the time, when they weren't in daycare or kindergarten. Even at night. Sometimes, wakeful in his basement bedroom, he'd hear Olivia's or Sam's feet padding overhead, Cleo's or Trent's voices, the creak of a bed, water running. Singing. As if this other life was going on in the night. And then Cleo and Trent would be up early in the morning, dressed, perky, heading out with briefcases and the children in coats, as if that life of the night was a dream of Cliff's.

It seems impossible to do. It seems too difficult to do without making mistakes all of the time. Think about it: you'd have to have a 99% average, or better. You couldn't let yourself get distracted or lose your temper. You couldn't forget to show up or wake up, or to lock the door or keep sharp tools put away. You couldn't procrastinate getting food or doing the laundry. You had to be watchful 100% of the time of stairs, traffic, pools, doors, things that could be put in the mouth, climbed up on, pulled down.

And you had to keep your crap together, even if you were sleep-deprived or over- or under-stimulated. Not overly critical or competitive. Not saying *no* too often but not saying *yes* too often either. Never having a meltdown or retreating into a sulk.

It's completely too much. Even keeping a child alive for the first few years is too much. It shouldn't be expected of anyone.

Cliff had wanted to have a child, but it had not been possible. Veronika had been past it, she said. He didn't inquire into the details. It used to make him crazy, that some people had children and didn't care for them properly. But now he thinks: it is too hard. And nobody should be punished for messing it up sometimes.

When they get to the town, he stops, and Ben disappears for a bit, gets something to eat, maybe, and is more cheerful when he comes back. More talkative. Cliff grabs some groceries so that they don't make too big a dent in what Cleo and Mandalay have brought. Milk, bread, fruit, cereal.

Cleo says: That's just what we needed, thanks, Cliff!

As if she's in charge.

But then, she always is.

CLEO MAKES A LIST: *copies of death certificate, bank, title, will, vehicle registration, pension.* Crystal is distracted, not much help. Mandalay wrapped in the duvet – the house is cold in the morning – drinking coffee, which at least she has made for everyone, as she is not really contributing, otherwise.

Ben still asleep.

Cliff, looking over her shoulder, says: How do you know how to do all of this?

It's just a matter of systems, Cleo says, looking up opening times for businesses on her phone. Every system is different, but once you understand a few of them, the rest is easier. You recognize patterns. You know what to look for.

She feels tired, though. She has done Cliff's paperwork for him for years. Decades. And often helped Mandalay.

Mandalay says, now, from her duvet cocoon: I have form dyslexia.

That's not a thing.

Yes it is.

Cleo hates the way Mandalay reverts to adolescence when they are at Butterfly Lake, leaving cups of tea and half-eaten peanut butter toast and clothing everywhere for others to pick up, and monopolizing the bathroom. Cleo has sensibly taken a motel room for herself. It's clean: the best that can be said for it. It's new, not more than seven or eight years old, but it seems to have been built from something porous, like metal grating. Cold damp drafts and highway noise seep in. She had been awakened at five by a car alarm in the parking lot. It's still better, though, to have a good bed, a tidy space to retreat to, than to stay at the house with Mandalay and Cliff and Ben.

Crystal alternates between bright-eyed, perky uselessness – bringing Cleo scraps of things, old phone bills and property tax statements, prescription receipts – and tearful paralysis. I don't know; I don't know, she wails, when Cleo asks her, for the fourth time, where certain documents are kept.

Let's be compassionate, Mandalay says. Cleo thinks she has been very patient.

Crystal doesn't want Cleo to look through cupboards, but Cleo can see there are stacks of paper everywhere, bills and documents, letters, clippings, flyer coupons. Everywhere. In boxes, in drawers piled on desks. She'll need to get Crystal out of the way so that she can figure out their system. She'll need to find Darrell's passwords for the computer and for the utility accounts.

Mandalay and Cliff both look at her doubtfully when she proposes that they take Crystal out for a few hours. You can get some groceries, Cleo says. Given the right ingredients, Mandalay is likely to cook exquisite meals.

I need to go through Crystal and Darrell's papers, Cleo says.

Why does it have to be now? Mandalay asks.

Cleo explains: Because Crystal will need to be able to access money, pay bills, deal with Darrell's new pickup truck, which likely has large payments owing, and will need to be sold.

She'll send them on errands, she thinks, now. Besides groceries, they can pick up the copies of the death certificate, forms from the bank.

When she has got them all out the door, including Ben, who woke up and wanted to go along, who first needed to have coffee and food and a shower, she scours the house for documents.

It's a disaster. Well, it's not that dirty. And underneath is some sort of system of organization: she finds the documents she needs. But on the surface, everything is cluttered, mixed together without any rationale she can see. Legal documents and flyers are jumbled with tools and cutlery and string and batteries in the kitchen drawers; the closets are stuffed with recycling and clothing that needed to be given away decades ago. It's a nightmare.

She makes stacks of documents that Crystal will need to settle things, clips them together. Finds Darrell's passwords in a little moleskin book in his desk, where she'd predicted they would be. Checks the accounts. Internet and phone provider are in Darrell's name; everything else, Crystal's. Automatic payments from bank accounts. All good, those things.

She'd love to clean out all of the drawers, but there isn't time.

She finds a square tin box about the size of a large shoebox, recognizes it. She'd been fascinated by the clasp and lock, as a kid. On the lid is a label, printing almost faded away: *Privat. Lars Lund.* She finds the key, a funny little antique one she remembers, in a ring of keys in a drawer, opens the box.

Inside, the title to the property – the house and a few hectares of bush – and her father's old passport and birth certificate, among other things.

Among other things. Something slips sideways in her sense of boundaries. She pockets everything that belonged to her father. She'll say nothing to the others, just yet, she thinks.

Only when she is finished, when she has found the documents that are needed, does she have thoughts about privacy. She imagines what Trent would say, or Olivia. She has, she supposes, been trespassing. She decides she won't say anything to the others.

Mandalay says: Aren't we going to organize a funeral?

So there is that too. Cleo feels herself actually sagging, as if she has picked up half a house in her arms.

She stiffens her spine. She can do this.

If not her, who?

CLIFF JOINS HIS SISTERS at the table, where they're looking at old photo albums, trying to find some nice shots of Darrell to scan and put on a PowerPoint presentation for the funeral. Cliff is looking over Mandalay's shoulder as she turns the stiff pages with their crinkled yellow plastic protectors.

Mandalay stops at a page of photos of a young man, perhaps in his late twenties, with curling, untrimmed blond hair, a tanned, bare torso, frayed denim cut-offs, crouched on the roof of the garage, wielding a power nailer.

Cleo says: There are some photos of Ben in here. Ben working on the garage. See? When did this happen? It looks fairly recent, of Ben.

Mandalay says: That's not Ben. That's Darrell. He's building the garage. It's a photo from the 80s.

No, Cleo says. It can't be. How would you know?

Partly, Mandalay says, because of the type of photoprint used and the way the inks have deteriorated. But mostly because I was there when Crystal took those photos.

It can't be Darrell, Cleo says.

But Cliff knows, already, that it is. Take away the balding pate, the big beard, the extra forty or fifty pounds, and it's Darrell. The squint of his eyes, the slightly overlapping, though very white, front teeth, the polyhedron tattoo on his bicep.

But it's also Ben.

Mandalay is looking at the photos now, one by one. In this one especially, she says. Cleo nods.

Something is falling away from Cliff, dizzyingly, as if he's on a fairground ride.

I never noticed, Mandalay says.

I think that it wasn't apparent, when Ben was younger, Cleo says.

And there's a resemblance to all of us. So he just looked familiar in that way.

Cleo turns now to where Cliff is leaning over her shoulder. Do you think this looks like Ben, Cliff?

Of course: that's the real question, isn't it. Not whether the young man in the photos is Darrell, but whether there's an obvious resemblance between him and Ben. Which there is. Which means, what?

Maybe, Cliff says. He looks at the photos, again. It seems clear. He doesn't say anything. He'll let his sisters decide what it means. He'll let them tell him.

Ben – Bodhi – was over a year old when Dad died, Cleo says. And Darrell and Mom got together, what a couple of years after that?

Mandalay says: Darrell was around, though, before that. Don't you remember him?

No, Cleo says. I don't remember seeing him until the first time I came back to Butterfly Lake, when I was eighteen. He was there, then. That would have been '86?

He was around before that, Mandalay says. In the late 70s. He worked with Dad at the mill, maybe? He came to the house once or twice, I think. He had an old Camaro.

Cleo says she doesn't remember. He was staying at Myrna Pollard's. He came to Butterfly Lake when the mill reopened. He helped build the new playground at the school.

Mandalay says: Yes, Darrell was around when I was still in elementary school. I remember him working on the playground, when the community built it. I had a crush on him.

You were thirteen, Cleo says.

Yeah, but.

You and Crystal both, I guess, Cleo says, tossing the photos back onto the table. I remember trekking Cliff and Bodhi home from Myra's after school. I don't think Darrell was around then.

Was Darrell around, when Dad died? Cliff asks. Was he in Butterfly Lake?

I don't know, Mandalay says. Wait. I think not. I think that when I came back, after I was released from foster care, he was just back from somewhere. Why does it matter?

It matters, Cleo says, because if he had been here, maybe Bodhi wouldn't have been given up for adoption.

Well, obviously he wasn't, then, Mandalay says.

We could ask Myrna Pollard, Cliff says. If she knew.

We could, Cleo says, but is she even still alive? She seemed old, back when I lived here. And that's nearly forty years ago.

We could ask Crystal, Cliff says.

His sisters both look at him with alarm.

Oh, we could, Cleo says. But.

CRYSTAL SAYS: I don't know. Then: I think he was already living here when I came to Butterfly Lake. This was his house. I moved in and sewed new curtains.

I think that was Dad, Cleo says. Dad lived here, in this house, and you moved in with him. It was after Dad died that Darrell moved in with you.

Oh, you're mixing me up with someone else, Crystal says, laughing.

Our dad, Cleo says. Lars Lund. Your first husband.

Oh, that man, Crystal says. Whatever.

Focus, Mother, Cleo says.

I don't think this is a very nice game, Crystal says.

Maybe try later, Cliff says. She's had a big shock.

MANDALAY SAYS: Why is it so important to you, Cleo? You can't go back and change the past.

I'm trying to piece this together, she says to Mandalay. So Darrell was in Butterfly Lake around 1977. Say, spring and summer? Maybe for a few months? Somehow he had an affair with Mom, and she got pregnant with Bodhi. Then he left? Maybe he didn't know she was pregnant? Anyway, she was married. She pretended the baby was our dad's –

Or didn't know, Mandalay says.

Or didn't know. Then she had that breakdown in 1979, when Bodhi was about a year old, and we were all scattered.

Or, she did know, and told Darrell, but he didn't come back for her, Mandalay says.

Maybe Darrell knew but couldn't come back for some reason, Cliff says.

You lived with them for a couple of years, Mandalay, Cleo says. Was there any talk about Bodhi?

There was talk, alright, Mandalay says. All Crystal talked about, to anyone, was getting her baby back. About how she had been tricked or coerced – her story changed – into signing away her rights. And having her tubes tied.

She was involuntarily sterilized? Cleo asks, shocked. I don't think that was still happening in the 80s.

Cliff feels muddled. It's all such a muddle. And he's not sure that it matters, somehow.

All of Crystal's stories are suspect, I think, Mandalay says. And there's a big grey area in her mind about what was done under her own volition. We know that. There has always been a sense that she has never chosen freely.

Cliff feels a vague pervasive discomfort, as if he's been sitting too long in the same position. A cramping, a need to stretch in new directions.

Maybe she never has, Cliff says. Never has chosen freely.

Well, Cleo says. That's a deeper discussion than I'm up for today. She looks at her phone. Two more days? Do you think we can get things wrapped up in two more days?

But they have just opened a can of worms, Cliff thinks. Can they now just wrap things up? As always, when he talks with his sisters about the past, there is a gutted feeling in him, a feeling of loss all over again, he thinks. He recognizes it, now. And thinks: it isn't fair.

The question that his emptiness always funnels down to comes again: Why couldn't he and Cleo – or even just he – have gone back to Butterfly Lake, once Crystal was back, living with Darrell? Mandalay had been allowed to leave foster care and had gone back; his older brother Che, long dead now, had gone back. Why hadn't Crystal asked for him back?

Because all of her attention and energy was being spent on trying to get back Bodhi – Ben – her youngest child. (And, it looks like, Darrell's son.)

She had wanted Bodhi, and Cliff had been forgotten.

It doesn't occur to him for several hours that the photos have another meaning. That Ben is not Cliff's real brother. Not his full brother.

He's not sure what to do with that information.

CLEO SAYS: Can you at least take Crystal off somewhere so I can search for the documents we need?

Mandalay can do that. She says to Crystal: Let's go for a drive. Let's go shopping and for lunch. It's like someone else is talking, maybe some pale copy of Cleo, efficient, cheerful, practical. But she can do it.

Crystal brings along a pair of boots with a broken zipper. She says she wants to take them to the shoe repair shop; she will wear them at the funeral. The boots were nice leather boots at one time; Mandalay thinks she might recognize them from the mid-nineties. But the leather is cracked, now – the bonding split, scuff marks wearing through the toe and heel, creases permanently ridged into the shank. A mouse or something has nibbled at the top edge of one boot. They need more than a new zipper, she says.

I don't like to waste things, Crystal says. I haven't got a rich boyfriend, like you.

Ha, Mandalay says.

She drives around and around Powell River – which doesn't take that long – but there is no shoe repair shop. She thinks finally to look it up on her phone, and gets no results. Of course there would not be a shoe repair place left in a small town. It would be generally cheaper to replace shoes than to repair them, these days. She imagines the labour required to replace a zipper in a pair of tall leather boots.

She says: Let's go buy you a pair of boots at the mall.

Oh, I have lots of other pairs of boots, Crystal says, laughing. I just like this pair, you know?

Mandalay laughs. It's not funny; Crystal's plight isn't funny. But it's weird and cracked and crazy, and it's the first thing she has been able to feel a response to in days.

She takes Crystal for lunch and orders the platter – prawns and popcorn shrimp and scallops, clams and calamari. Crystal says: Aren't you living high on the hog.

After, they walk along the shore, as far as they can go, then sit on a log. It's not the most prepossessing view. The sea is grey and flat on this day. Seagulls and crows peck at the clots of seaweed that have washed up. In the distance, there's a smudge of grey-green that is Texada Island and beyond that, further west, a smear of blue-grey that is Vancouver Island.

Crystal fishes in her coat pockets. She says: I want a cigarette.

Mandalay laughs. You don't smoke. I've never seen you smoke.

Oh that's an old story, Crystal says. A story written on water. Do you know what I mean?

Yes, Mandalay says. I think I do.

Anyway, Crystal says. You seem nicer today. I think you have changed something. Is it your hair?

Maybe.

We have the same hair, Crystal says, and Mandalay sees that it is true: she and Crystal both wearing their long dark iron-streaked hair in braids today. She had braided Crystal's hair this morning, then her own. We could be sisters, Mandalay says. (Why has she said that? All of her life, it feels like, she has been resisting, resenting her mother's inappropriate tendency to see her as a sibling, a rival sibling.)

We *are* sisters! Crystal says. Then she looks doubtful. Under the skin, I mean.

Oh, definitely, Mandalay says.

She feels her mind-fog shifting now, dislodged by something warm and splintered and painful, but painful in a bearable way, perhaps. Or bearable at least in this moment.

She says, Crystal, you're a lot of fun.

I try to be, Crystal says, pleased.

CLIFF SAYS, FIRMLY: there's something wrong with Crystal. She's losing her marbles.

Crystal has always been kind of flaky, though, Mandalay says.

That's an understatement, Cleo says.

It's different now, though, Cliff says. She's forgetting things she wouldn't have in the past.

She's just had a big shock, Mandalay says.

No, it's more than that, he knows. There's something missing. She's forgetting the rhythm of the days, yeah. Darrell must have held that together for her. But she's also completely forgetting conversations of a week earlier. And she's losing the ability to tell fact from fiction.

I don't think that Crystal was ever that good at telling fact from fiction, Cleo says.

This is different. She had told Cliff, in a normal conversational tone, that a man had shown up from the lottery place to tell her that she had won a trip to Manitoba. The same man, it seemed, was going to drive her there. She had to pack. She was worried about who will feed the dog. She was worried about the lot of them being in the house, while she was gone.

Is she being scammed? Cleo wonders.

I don't think so, Cliff says. I don't think there was any man. Cliff had said: Did you dream that? But Crystal had been definite. Also, very excited. Joyous. And then, a couple of hours later, she'd forgotten it.

She had told him, in an injured, grieving tone, that some children, a little girl and a little boy, had walked into her house and took her favourite ornaments out of the china cabinet. She told them not to, but the little girl stuck out her tongue and said she could do what she liked. A woman had come in to clean — one of those foreign women, Crystal had said. She didn't know where from. Brown-skinned. She had been very bossy. She had hidden some things, or taken them.

What things?

Crystal had started to cry. The toilet brush. Some photographs. Her favourite shoes.

The thing is, Cliff says. She speaks with such conviction. I believe her. And then I realize that something is off. I don't know how to separate what's true from what isn't. He hears anger in his own voice, as if Crystal is doing this on purpose.

He's not angry at Crystal. He's angry because Cleo and Mandalay aren't listening to him.

He says: I think there's something wrong. I think she has dementia.

There's a long silence; then Mandalay says: Actually, I think you're right. I was trying to tell myself that it's just Crystal being Crystal.

Cliff wants to cry with relief, and something else.

Cleo is silent for a moment longer, then says, slowly for her: I think what we have to do is get her assessed. Then find an assisted living home for her, maybe? Or someone to come in? Someone should stay and take care of things.

Mandalay says: I can't stay up here. I've got classes.

Cleo says she can't either, she says; she's very busy, at work.

I'll do it, Cliff says. I can stay on a few days. One of you needs to take Ben back, though.

Oh, Cleo says. Cliff. Well, maybe.

CRYSTAL SAYS: Those people who were here, they left my kitchen in an awful mess.

Who, Mom? Cliff asks.

She says, in an injured tone: If the person who is taking my things would just *ask*.

She says, in businesslike voice, at breakfast: I guess I should call that fellow to come and remove his truck. I don't want that pile of junk rusting away in my driveway forever.

She means Darrell's truck.

She says: I would have thought my sisters would have bothered to come.

Which sisters, Mom?

You know. Those girls. They live down by... the river. The place that sticks out into the water.

In between these statements, she converses normally about lunch and whether or not it's going to rain and if Cliff should mow the grass.

Something else Cliff notices: she doesn't finish her sentences, and if you don't do it for her, or guess from the situation where she was going with them, there are big gaps. Words she can't find. Can you put this on the...? Someone needs to go to the... That was when your dad was working at...

She says, again in that aggrieved tone: Someone came into the house and gave me a big whack on the head with a stick. I have such a headache.

Has she fallen in the night and banged her head? He looks over her scalp, tenderly.

She says: I'd like to see Bodhi. My son.

He was just here, Cliff says, unthinking.

He was not! Crystal blazing at him, now.

He's in Vancouver. I'll see if he'll come up, Cliff says.

Crystal laughs, mocking. They won't let a little boy travel on the Greyhound by himself!

She needs to see a doctor. Can she find her doctor's phone number? Can he get her there? Cliff's chest clamps up. What will he say? What will happen? He begins to search for something – a list, a little book – in which he'll find a doctor's number. He finds drawers full of screwdrivers and old bills and bank statements, flyers. Bits of paper or used envelopes with messages written on them in Crystal's looping hand. Her name. Statements like "born 1947." Words like *pension, bank account*, circled over and over.

Finally, a small address book. Out of date: it has his last, not current address in it. There's a doctor's number. He calls it; finds it out of service. Looks the doctor up online. Retired; his practice closed. He notices a new drop-in clinic in Powell River. They won't know Crystal there. Will they think he's trying to pull some scam, a middle-aged man saying his mom has dementia? He has an image of not only Crystal but himself seized, incarcerated, not allowed phone calls. His old fears of authority figures, of being unfairly accused, of being unwittingly guilty.

A South African man, Cliff's age, maybe, with greying hair and very blue eyes takes them into the office, asks questions matter-of-factly, walks Crystal through a test. Cliff has done this test himself, after a couple of his accidents. He sees now what it looks like from the outside. Questions so simple that they seem insulting. What's the date? Where are you? What's your address? Draw a clock face showing this time. Remember this list of three words I'll ask you for at the end.

On the way home, Crystal says: I failed that test, didn't I?

You did fine, Mom, Cliff says. He isn't sure what he should say. He says: You have some memory loss, Mom.

She makes a dismissive sound with her mouth, like a bird spitting out a seed. That's just the stuff they did... when I was ill. After you were born.

She needs twenty-four-hour supervision, the doctor had said. She can't live alone. He'd given Cliff phone numbers, geriatric mental health specialists, the regional health people.

When they get back to the house, Crystal is exhausted, sunk into herself. She says to Cliff: I'll have a nap now. In front of him, she takes off her clothes.

In the yard outside, he clutches his head, walks in circles on the patchy, unkempt lawn. Around him, Crystal's flower beds choked with weeds, the cultivated flowers wilting from lack of care. He's hyperventilating. Because there's nobody around, he lets out a moan. He moans again.

He is losing Crystal again. When your mother forgets you, do you exist, anymore?

But there is only him, Cliff, to look after things now.

26

CLEO ARRIVES AT KASTRUP, at the airport, a few days before her meetings with Mogun, this visit, and boards a train heading directly for Sweden, for Malmö. In Malmö she rents a car, and drives to a little town called Östra Sandby, where, she has discovered, at long last, not without some difficulty, her father was born, in 1925.

There's no hotel in Östra Sandby, but only a bank, a church, the usual ICA general store, a sports club, a garage, a school. There are nineteen-century brick houses, a little repressed-looking, but mostly respectably prosperous. Everywhere, trees, shrubs, hedges. Yards well kept: the almost oppressive neatness and lack of eccentricity that she has noticed in Denmark and Sweden. A shopping plaza, also of brick, with no little exterior advertising and no windows: it's very unappealing.

There would be little temptation to shop for shopping's sake, in Östra Sandby.

It's the parish church she's after. She finds it on Kyrktorget, Church Street, a decorous white clapboard building with arched windows, a porch, a belfry tower topped with a steeple. It's immaculate, plainly elegant, grey-roofed, perfectly proportioned, as Swedish buildings, even sheds and barns, tend to be. She has been able to find online the hours it's open, though not the name of the pastor. She parks her rental car – a black Saab; she'll never be able to find it in a busy parking lot, though this one contains only one other car – and walks in through the main door, where a sign says *Välkommen,* a pretty easy cognate.

The pastor is a woman perhaps a few years younger than Cleo, in her mid-forties, with neat brown hair, dressed in a Fair Isle sweater, a corduroy skirt, opaque tights, tan ankle boots. She speaks English fluently, is politely happy to help Cleo with her quest.

The parish record books are kept in a vault, she says, in the church basement. Well, not so much a vault. A dry room, with metal shelves. She will bring up what Cleo wants. The books are indexed by years covered. If Cleo could tell her a year...

She says: 1925. She might want other books, but that's the only date she has, to start. Her father's birth year.

They put on cotton gloves, and there's a magnifying glass. The pastor says it's an odd thing, but village pastors, besides being ministers and social workers, are now expected to be archivists, as well. Do you know the month, she asks, and Cleo does. Or thinks she does. She has always remembered her father's birthdate: April 4. But is that it, really?

The pastor turns the pages gingerly, using a tool that she says is a piece of antique ivory. It does not tear the pages, nor deposit acid on them. She finds the pages for 1925, and then the page for April. Lots of deaths, always, in April, in the past, she says. One would have thought that in spring, people would be healthy, full of optimism and vigor. But no. They are worn down from winter, and then the warmer weather brings the spread of viruses, cold and flu, and they succumb.

What is the name? she asks, but there is only one birth registered for the village, for April 1925.

The pastor says: Can this be? Truly? Your father is Lars Lund?

Why? Cleo asks. Was he the village criminal or something?

The pastor is silent for a moment. Cleo looks at her, thinks: She is praying. Or she is allowing that space to exist between herself and her emotions, her realization and her response.

After a moment the pastor looks at her. She's a bit pale, Cleo thinks.

Lars Lund was my grandfather, she says. *Morfar:* her mother's father.

Cleo says, What?

IN THE PASTOR'S OFFICE, they have coffee and some sort of pastry, and Cleo listens. Her hands shake, on the mug. She has to put it down. The pastor had introduced herself, initially, as Margaret Dahlström, but she had paid only minimal attention. Now she repeats the name to herself: *Margaret.*

It's not a good story, Margaret says. It will likely distress you.

Tell me, Cleo says. I've heard worse, I'm sure.

This is what my mother and aunt have told me, Margaret says. Their parents, Lars and Gunnel, were married in 1943. I can probably find the record. I have a copy of the certificate. I don't know if the early marriage was because of the war, or not. There was a child born in fewer than nine months, though – my aunt Katrine. After that, four more, in fairly quick succession: my mother; my uncles Johan and Jakob; my aunt Louise. Lars worked on a farm. They did not own the farm, but he had a steady position as a farm worker. His wife, Gunnel, was a cook at a hospital, until she had the children. They were, I think, quite poor. I have seen the little house in which they lived, but it is no longer standing today.

In 1957, Margaret says, sometime in the fall of the year, I gather, Lars did not come home from the farm one evening. This had never happened before. The boys were sent to the farm to see what was holding him up, and were told that he had left the barn where he had been fixing the turnip-harvester at noon, on foot. He had not said where he was going, but the others on the farm assumed he was going to the blacksmith's to get a part. The family checked in the village, and he had been at the blacksmith's, but had left. Someone remembered that there had been a transport truck passing through the village – a rare thing. It had stopped for something at the blacksmith's – perhaps some repair, as the blacksmiths were becoming garages, then. It was thought that Lars had taken a ride – hitchhiked – with the transport truck to Malmö to search in the city for the part for the turnip-harvester, though this seemed an unlikely trouble to which one would go.

The driver of the transport truck was traced, and confirmed that he had given Lars a ride to Malmö, but nobody had seen him after that. The police and hospitals in Malmö were contacted. Nobody meeting Lars' description had been seen.

Eventually, Margaret says, it became clear that he was not going to return.

And your mother's family never found out what happened to him?

No. And as you can imagine, in a small, insular Swedish town, in the mid-twentieth century – they suffered. There was judgment, censure. None of the four older children finished school – they all went to work in their mid-teens. My aunt Louise, the youngest, was adopted, though, by childless relatives, and had a more privileged life. When she was in her thirties, she hired a detective who was able to find out somehow that Lars, or a man called Lars Lund, the same age, had signed on as a seaman on a ship that was sailing from Copenhagen to Canada. And that was as far as she got. It is possible now, I think, to trace people who have immigrated to a country, so we could make sure that he landed and where he went. And then perhaps to find his steps, in Canada. But the family lost interest, then. It was enough to know that he had gone so far away, I think. That he had abandoned them so thoroughly.

Cleo thinks: It's too much information. I can't process it all.

But at the same time, her mind is taking it all in, quite clearly.

Is your mother still alive? she asks. Are your aunts and uncles…

Oh, yes, Margaret says. All alive, except my uncle Johan, who had a motorcycle accident. All still living in Östra Sandby still, or nearby. I came back to work in this parish – I oversee a few village churches – so that I could be near my mother and aunt Katrine, you see. They are getting older. They live together and manage quite well, but they are now in their mid-seventies, you know, and I like to be near them.

And your mother and aunt are my... Cleo's mind won't quite close the loop.

Your sisters. Your half-sisters, to be precise. And you are my aunt.

That's the only part that's very difficult to take in. It's impossible. Even after Margaret has shown her the other entries in the register – her father's marriage to his first wife – his only wife, if one wanted to be technical – and the births of his other children. Those other Lunds, the oldest of them senior to Cleo's mother Crystal.

You will notice that I can tell the story in great detail, Margaret says. That is because I listened to it over and over, as a child. It is largely what shaped me. What was he thinking, Lars Lund, my grandfather? I wondered, over and over. It was inevitable that I would become either a psychologist or a priest.

What had he been thinking, Cleo's father, Lars Lund? He had simply walked away from his life, at the age of thirty-two. Walked away from his wife and five children, without a word.

The terrifying thing is that she understands it only too well, that urge to simply vanish, to deal with problems by walking to a place in which they did not exist.

IT IS INEVITABLE that she must meet Margaret's mother and aunt, then – Cleo's half-sisters. Margaret makes the arrangements; Cleo will get a hotel in Malmö and drive out the next day to see them.

Cleo messages Mandalay, who doesn't seem surprised at all about the revelation. I absolutely knew it, she says. I knew Dad must have left some secret life behind. I always suspected we had half-siblings somewhere.

In her hotel room in Malmö Cleo scours her laptop and her Facebook account and Mandalay's as well for family photos, downloads them to her phone. She doesn't sleep much.

Margaret says that her mother and aunt don't speak English, having left school early, and worked in rural jobs. They are shy, she says. They are feeling intimidated, perhaps.

Are they angry? Cleo wonders. She remembers, now, her decades of resentment at the couple who had adopted her younger brother Bodhi and renamed him Ben. And she and her siblings had taken more than that from her father's first family in Sweden. How they must have suffered. What opportunities they must have missed.

Margaret says: You can do them a huge kindness by speaking openly of your father's life in Canada. Tell them everything, the good and the bad. They are starved for news of him. They have been, for sixty years.

IN THE LATE 80S, when she was in university, studying engineering, Cleo had told stories of her childhood in Butterfly Lake to the friends and acquaintances she socialized with, editing, shaping the stories to shock or awe or elicit laughter as she wanted. She had got better at it, over the years, as she moved from her undergraduate to graduate programs. She got better at choosing words and details, at leaving things out and exaggerating others, at finessing her timing. A roommate who was a graduate student studying English literature told her she had invented a new genre, West Coast Gothic. She had told the stories in different ways to Trent, when she began dating him; then to new friends, the friends of her life as a young mother in the suburbs; then again to therapists she had talked to. And differently again to her friend Stephanie, who is a sociologist. Stephanie was interested in how the population of rural communities like Butterfly Lake became marginalized, and the statistics of abuse in communities with resource-based industries. Stephanie had been interested in learning about the Aboriginal adoption scoop of the 60s and 70s, about counterculture, personal freedoms, social dislocation.

And to her children, who loved going to Butterfly Lake, Cleo had downplayed the hardship, and recounted instead magical stories of living in nature, of her encounters, as a young girl, with various wild creatures.

And now Cleo will tell the story again, as a story of – what? Of wilderness, of dysfunction, of poverty? Of karmic comeuppance? Will she stress the strange, the exotic, or the similar and familiar? And how much will she talk about Crystal, her mother, who is younger than some of Cleo's newfound half-siblings, and crazy, and increasingly vulnerable?

SHE IS WELCOMED INTO a neat little brick house with a green-painted door, pristine white window trim, a hipped gable over the front door. In the parlour, which is not quite the same as a living room, there is department-store Danish Modern furniture, plain and modest rather than sleek and dashing, furniture that might have been bought in the 1980s, but has been kept in new condition. On the walls, some prints of landscape paintings, and some old photographs that have been enlarged and framed. It's all very clean and respectable, Cleo thinks. The whole point is to be irreproachable.

And then Katrine and Ilsa, Cleo's half-sisters.

Katrine is small, frail looking – she has the body of someone who has done physical work and not had enough to eat during her adolescent growth spurt. Ilsa is a little taller, a little more relaxed or confident. They both look familiar: they look like Cleo's dad, and also like Cliff and Mandalay, and, she supposes, like herself.

Her sisters, but she can't quite get her head around that: doesn't feel that fits. Aunts, maybe. It's their age, the generation that separates them.

They must all speak through Margaret, as Cleo speaks no Swedish, and Katrine and Ilsa no English.

There is coffee, and cheese and a hard dark bread, prepared ceremoniously, carefully, by Katrine – there is some matter of status, of territory, here, that Cleo doesn't completely understand – and then they look at the photos of Lars Lund's first family. These are black-and-white, deckle-edged, sparse. There are photographs from the early 1940s, in which Lars, a very young man, looks broodingly at the camera. It's a shock to see these. Cleo has never seen a photograph of her father as a young man. Photos of him and his wife, Gunnel, who is as tall as, and broader than Lars. And older, possibly. Their children, who look in some photos like Cleo and her siblings as children, and in others, not very much.

Did Lars belong to this life, or the one he had in Butterfly Lake, with Crystal and their children?

And what does it say about a man who walks away from a life of poverty and hard labour and five children and travels over seven thousand kilometres, presumably in some desperate bid for freedom, that he ends up again in the same situation?

Cleo wants to ask Katrine and Ilsa about their mother, Gunnel. She looks formidable, in the photo: grim, humourless, unyielding, though photographs don't always show character. She wants to ask what Gunnel was like, if she drove Lars away. She realizes that she can't really ask this. She says, instead, to Margaret: I suppose the family suffered greatly from material want, after Lars left?

Margaret translates, and Katrine begins to answer, but then Ilsa interrupts, vociferously. The sisters begin to argue. Ilsa laughs: a mean laugh, Cleo thinks.

Margaret interprets. Katrine has said that they all pulled together. They were poor, but had what they needed. And Ilsa disputes that: she says that they were pulled out of school by fourteen, sent out to work. They had no opportunities, any of them, except Louise. Their lives were blighted.

Katrine's lips thin, and she adds something. This time, Cleo understands what she has said. Maybe it's the context, or maybe she has just learned enough Danish, which shares roots with her half-sisters' language. There was no room for sentiment, Katrine has said. We had to support our mother.

They have had a life of privation, and their privation was the cost of Cleo and her siblings' existence. It is a hard thought to consider.

Cleo wants to say: *Our father loved you. He thought about you. He missed you.* But she can't say it with conviction, and they will not believe it. She has already told Margaret that her father kept his early life a complete secret.

Had there been any vestige of his first family? Any sign that he had thought of them and missed them?

She remembers: My sister Mandalay's middle name is Louise, she says. She must have been named after your younger sister.

This is pleasing to the women. But a crumb.

CLEO SAYS: Lars ended up on the West Coast of Canada in the early 1960s. He got a job in a sawmill in a remote community and bought ten acres of land. No, not a farm. It is forest. Coastal forest by the mountains. It's rainforest.

Oh, yes, rainforest, the sisters murmur, and Margaret says: They watch a lot of nature shows on TV. They have seen your western Canadian rainforest on the screen.

There was a small community of loggers and draft dodgers and artisans and hippies, Cleo says, in Butterfly Lake. Lars built a house there, a wooden house, with a steep roof. Chalet-style. My mother came to the community in the mid-1960s. She was very young, hitch-hiking. She fell in love with Lars, I guess, and moved in with him. My sister Mandalay was born in 1966, and I in 1968. And then there were three boys: Che, Cliff, and Bodhi.

Here Margaret gives a nod, and translates what she has just said. There are responses from Katrine and Ilsa, and Cleo tries to interpret them. Shock, then laughter. No doubt, she thinks, they would be both surprised and amused by this story. And then both are speaking, asking questions.

Margaret translates, and then indicates for Cleo to continue.

Cleo has thought for hours about what she would say about her family.

Tell the good and the bad, Margaret had said. She will do that. Something has flowed into her, this day: the story she has told so often, to herself, to others, has shifted, as if it has been only a light refracted through a prism, the kind of crystal drop that people had hung in their windows, when she was young.

She holds it in her mind, this image, a moment or two, while Margaret is translating. For the first time, she sees it as a story, a story that happened to someone who she no longer is, a young, frightened, naïve, resourceful little girl. That is not her, she feels, now, inside herself, for the first time in the four decades since. It is not herself, adult Cleo, to whom it is happening.

Something falls away from her: something constricting (but also reassuring, maybe).

She says: When Lars – our father – died, our mother was quite ill. We children were all taken into care.

She remembers her childhood in extremely vivid visual detail. The house they lived in, unfinished, a small cabin that had been added onto, inexpertly, haphazardly. It was impossible to keep clean, with its hodgepodge of linoleum and carpet remnants, its expanses of gapped plywood, the rough timber bunkbeds the children slept in and the bench that they sat on to eat. There were no cupboards or closets, just shelves made of strips of plywood, shelves that bowed in the middle, lengths of pipe suspended from wire to hang clothes on. The windows had been obtained at flea markets and renovation sites, and took a variety of shapes and sizes, were mostly not curtained, but stapled over with thick polyurethane sheets to keep out the cold. Doors were not plentiful; curtains were strung across doorways. Everything unfinished, second-hand, ramshackle.

Her father, who worked sometimes in the lumber mill and sometimes driving a logging truck: remote to her and her siblings, impatient, frustrated with the endless chaos and incompetence of the house. Her mother, who was in and out of psychiatric care, suffering from depression or bipolar disorder or maybe just exhaustion. Cleo and her sister Mandalay, from a young age, had to try to keep the house together, to look after her younger siblings. Disaster ensued, of course.

When Cleo was twelve and her older sister Mandalay thirteen, their youngest brother still a baby, their mother Crystal had to be hospitalized for a few months. And then their father Lars died, suddenly, of a heart attack. Cleo can call that day up in too-vivid detail, still: Mandalay had been at high school in town, then, an hour's bus ride away, and Cleo trying to deal with the younger children, her little brothers, the freshly-butchered chickens, the stinking bucket of cloth diapers, when the RCMP and social workers had arrived.

They had all been taken into care, the five of them. Mandalay and their brother Che (who was younger than Cleo, and who died, at nineteen, in an accident) had been allowed to go back to Butterfly Lake, a year later, to live with Crystal and her new partner, Darrell. Cleo and Cliff had stayed with their foster family in the Fraser Valley, not visiting, not having contact with their mom and siblings. And the baby, Bodhi, had been adopted by a wealthy childless Vancouver couple, and had become Ben.

She says: The youngest, my brother Ben, was adopted, but we found him again. Or he found us.

Margaret translates. Ilsa and Katrine hold an animated discussion.

The sisters are remarking on parallels with their siblings' lives, Margaret says. Cleo is also aware of these: the order of girls and boys; the loss of the eldest brother; the adoption of the youngest child.

The sisters want to know about her and Mandalay's and Cliff's and Ben's marriages, their children, Margaret says.

Cleo is filled for a moment with guilt and shame – something she has not felt before. It is the age, the sense of respectability, of propriety, that attends Katrine and Ilsa and even Margaret, she thinks. She says: None of us are any longer with our partners.

There's a moment of tension, of discussion, while Margaret translates, she thinks. The two older women look, she thinks, disapproving, or shocked, or something. But maybe it is only concern, sympathy.

Cleo remembers the multitude of pictures that she has put onto her phone. She has put them into a folder, all she can find of her siblings and their children, the house and forest at Butterfly Lake. She passes her phone to Margaret, and Margaret passes it along, to the narrow hard-looking sofa where her mother and aunt are sitting, and so they pass the phone, and the photos, among them, asking questions, commenting on resemblances.

Cleo is so tired. But they must continue, it seems. And she has only these couple of days before she must be in Copenhagen, a couple of days, which she imagined would be easily sufficient to track down the parish records of her father's birth and origins.

Katrine has a final question for her, as she is leaving: Were you happy?

Cleo understands that she means, was it worth it? Was there anything good that came out of our father's crazy impulse, his devastating abdication?

She says: I loved my dad more than anyone else in the world, when I was a child.

She says: He was a complicated person. He gave us all what he had to give.

She says: Lars rejected mainstream culture. Our mother was a flower child, an artist. We grew up in the rainforest. Our childhood was completely free. My siblings and I could do almost anything we liked. We played in the forest. We built things using our father's tools and scraps of lumber we found and dragged home. We wandered freely in the woods. The trees are very tall, cedars, and they shade the ground. There's moss, ferns... the forest is very dense. We picked blackberries and mushrooms. We saw wildlife every day – jays, owls, deer. Sometimes black bears, who also liked the blackberries. Once, a cougar.

She says: We were, I think, very poor, but we didn't know it. We knew everyone in the community. We wore everyone else's clothing. It was given to us or gleaned at the church rummage sales. We had no television set – TV being an instrument, Lars thought, that the government was using to stupefy the population. Our parents both liked to read, though, and lugged home used books from everywhere. There were no rules about what we were allowed to read. We read the children's books first, but moved onto the others when those were done.

She says: One of my most enduring memories is of my family, in the evening, curled up in quilts on the sofas – one, with holes in the upholstery, so that you could see the interesting substructure, wood frame, springs, foam and cotton padding, if you removed the faded, fringed, jacquard bedspread that covered it; the other an IKEA-style platform with a mattress. All of us, big and little, curled up on those makeshift couches, with quilts against the cold, a little fire in the woodstove.

She says: I think I have never since felt such intense happiness and well-being as in those moments.

Margaret translates, and Cleo sees Katrine and Ilsa nod, solemnly, but oddly with something like relief smoothing their aged faces for an instant. It is so little, and the barriers to communication so high, and she feels the generational and cultural gap so much more strongly than she feels any kinship. She has, perhaps, given them what they needed.

ON THE TRAIN BACK to Copenhagen, to her meeting with Mogun, Cleo thinks: I am fortunate.

Perhaps it is not a thought but a feeling, a kind of welling up of understanding that is deeper and more intense than thought, that contains the rational but also more.

She doesn't know that she has ever felt this before. She *is* fortunate. She has had many opportunities, much freedom, in her life. She feels she is held on the shoulders of her parents and grandparents, her ancestors who lived and worked within much more limited horizons, under much duller skies. She has this life, which is a result of the lives of many others.

It's a new feeling, a kind of expansion inside her. She will see where it goes.

CLEO HAD IMAGINED, had resigned herself to the inevitability, even, that once she and Karsten could actually spend time together, after the months of messaging, the occasional unsatisfactory screen time, they would have nothing to say; the little flame they had been nourishing would have burnt itself out, or would be too feeble for the force of physical presence. They meet up at a café, once she has arrived back in Copenhagen. It's awkward, for sure. He's there when she arrives, has got a table. She spots him instantly, the shape of his head, the angle of his shoulders and back instantly familiar, though she had wondered if she would even recognize him. He's wearing a grey jacket over a green flannel shirt, jeans. He sees her as she begins to walk toward him, and rises from his seat, not taking his eyes from her face.

She wonders if there will be some awkwardness about hugging or not hugging, but Karsten takes both of her hands, kisses both of her cheeks. Pulls out a chair for her. Stay, stay, he says. I'll get the coffee.

Breathe, she reminds herself. *Breathe.*

It's impossible, of course. At her age. And given the geographical distance. She must be unconsciously driven to choose a relationship with insurmountable constraints. What does that mean? That she doesn't want a relationship, doesn't want to be partnered?

She wants, and doesn't want.

Karsten returns with the coffees. He is slightly flushed, she thinks. He is possibly experiencing the same emotions. It would be easier if they could each admit that, talk about it. But as she feared, the banter that they had achieved over messaging is not available to them now. He is looking at her anxiously, too seriously, and she is aware that her own expression has formed itself into a kind of panicked blankness, and if she tries to force a smile, it will manifest only as a horrible grimace. It's all very well for simpletons to say things like *a smile is the best cosmetic, and free.* When one can't smile easily, there is no remedy.

She thinks about the messages they have sent. The deep intelligence and sweetness in Karsten's. She remembers him writing about fishing with his father, as a boy. What he had said: that he felt the knowledge of the world was being transmitted to him through his father's fingers touching his as he learned to tie on a fly.

She reaches across the table, her palms turned upward, open. Karsten takes her hands, and in his grasp there is an instant, deep sensation of familiarity. Of comfort. Of *rightness.* Then they can't stop smiling, either of them: smiling at each other, flushed, holding each other through their gaze.

Oh dear, Cleo thinks. I have it bad.

It can't last.

She has a week: it's all the time she was able to book off. A couple of days for finding her father's birthplace, and then the week in Copenhagen.

There are the meetings with Mogun, again, and the renewed offer of a role in the company, which she says, this time, that she will give serious thought to. There is the electricity of her and Karsten's physical awareness of each other, in any room, which she feels must be visible to the others as a kind of phosphorescence. There is the time after the meetings, when sometimes the group all goes out together for a drink, and sometimes Karsten walks with her to her hotel room, or drives to his apartment, which is on the outskirts of the city.

From the very first they go to bed with such ease that they might have been lovers for years. Their very skins seem to have been engineered to fit together. They find each other's rhythms easily, as if they have always been known, and the impetus is not so much to extract or induce pleasure but to voyage toward something inward, intense, transcendent. Cleo marvels: This is what it is meant to be, this fit, this drive toward connection.

But it can't last. It can't work, this long-distance folly.

At the end of the week she gets on her plane in a fog of sexual and conversational satiation and sleep deprivation. They will find a way to be together for longer, for more often than every other year, they have promised. She doesn't really believe that they will.

27

IN THE EVENINGS, NOW, Mandalay works in the campus printmaking studio. Her prints are coming together, slowly. Each one takes weeks to build up, of course, but she's also feeling her way into something new. She had been doing her shelter and cityscapes pieces for several years, and had explored so many aspects, but always thematically-connected. Now she has found her way, through a few false starts, into a new emotional universe, she thinks.

Like the early explorers of a coastline, venturing without map or satellite photo, she does not always know if some promising idea is a little bay or inlet, charming but soon completely charted, or the mouth of a major river that will sustain exploration for years, will lead her deeper and deeper into the heart of the territory.

What she wants to explore is the idea of skin, or rather, through the metaphor of skin, ideas about autonomy and connectivity, self-expression and conformity, interpenetration. She has found her exploration constrained, interestingly, by the difficulties of representing skin, a surface, through the medium of print. The texture of skin has been an obvious element, but, in fact, skin does not have a great variety of textures. Even fingerprints, notoriously individual, are, in terms of visual affect, exhaustively similar.

She had brought in tattoos, a study of tattoos, in itself problematic, as tattoo art is already processed, already representational. She had learned a lot about tattoos, but had not found very satisfying ways to talk about them in her printmaking. She had explored the forms and textures of leather goods – starting with those cracked and worn-out boots of Crystal's – but had been conscious that her images could be read as polemics on the use of animal skins, which she had not intended.

She had thought about Duane's melanomas. He's had a few surgeries, now. There is a danger of metastasizing, she knows. It hangs over him; he has to have frequent tests. She thinks about the mechanics of skin cancer, the proliferation of cells into something malign. Skin cells replace themselves often; it is their job. But in their frequent work of replication, there is increased chance of errors being made, and the skin also takes the brunt of agents that can damage cells, disrupt their intricate coding.

She had thought about the covers of cell phones and the friction strips used by skiers, both of which, she has learned from her sons, are called *skins*; of the uses of phones and skis to interface with others, with the space of internet and the space of nature; of the possession of these items by her sons as symbols of their interface with privilege. She has thought about the outside surface materials of buildings, which Cleo tells her are also referred to as skins. She has considered onionskin, which she uses in creating transfers; of tree bark and the tensile surfaces of fluids; of surfactants; of mosquitoes; of ice; of the cosmetic and dermatological interventions accessed by her acquaintance Taylor and other well-off women; of a phase Aidan had gone through, a year or so ago, of waxing his entire body, to the detriment of her bathroom (gobs of hairy wax everywhere, like melted spiders); of exoskeletons and the current fetish for Japanese wrapping paper and the swollen, hairless body of a dead dog she had seen cast up on a beach.

She is caught up in the study, if that is the right word, of the meaning of skin, and also its whatness. She sees texture, permeability, pigment. She thinks about appearance, image, boundaries, porousness, illness, identity. It's a very large topic, one that she could explore for the rest of her life, she thinks. It's important to have time, to let all of the options, the little stubs, develop.

She is hungry now for time as she has never been before in her life.

MANDALAY GETS AN EMAIL from the dean's secretary, requesting her to have coffee with the dean. This is kind of a command, she realizes, not an invitation, though it is phrased as one. She hasn't met the dean, but has seen her in meetings. Claudia Trimmer is tall, substantial woman, always in a suit, perhaps ten years younger than Mandalay. In meetings, she seems to be very focussed, organized, well-informed, adept at running things. She doesn't appear to have a sense of humour. She is rumoured to be fond of committees – of having people serve on them.

Mandalay is invited – instructed – to meet the dean at a café that's in a strip mall near the campus. It's awful, really, plate glass on three sides, so bright that on sunny days dark glasses are necessary. Students don't frequent it, even though it would be a nice clean well-lighted place to study, because it's just a little bit far for a walk between classes, because it has no dark nooks, because the proprietors discourage lingering. There's even a sign advising patrons that a certain amount must be spent per hour. *No Computer!* another handwritten sign says discouraging would-be scholars.

The dean gets tea and chooses the table furthest from the espresso machine. Mandalay orders a latte – the café does them nicely, uses decent coffee – and a carrot-coconut muffin. She carries her items over to the very clean glass-topped table, sits on a tubular metal and plastic chair, offers the dean a piece of her muffin, which is large and glistens with calories ready to leap onto Mandalay's upper arms.

Maybe, the dean says, briskly. It looks delicious.

Call me Claudia, the dean says.

Claudia says that she wants Mandalay to join several committees. Bodies are needed, she says. Women are needed. She lists the committees, outlining the amount of work, the frequency of meetings, before the committee function. It will help your regularization application, she says.

Mandalay thinks: Do I want to be regular? She says: When do I have time to do my own work? I come home from a day of teaching and meetings, and the original, creative part of me curls up somewhere and regrets that it's unable to come to the table.

I hear you, Claudia says.

Does Claudia have kids? Mandalay wonders. She knows she's not supposed to ask that. It's not supposed to be relevant for women, anymore. Women are not supposed to be asked this. They are not supposed to ask each other this.

I also see you haven't signed up yet for the Identity Sensitivity Workshop, the dean says. All faculty are required to take that. It's a full week just before the start of classes.

Mandalay groans. She had been counting on another week in the studio, before classes started up again. A chunk of her summer has been used up going to Butterfly Lake and organizing the funeral. And Aidan is going to be home for a brief two weeks. He has emailed her; he will come home. They will talk. She is longing for time with him, time to mend whatever has broken between them, before Aidan goes away to start university.

It's important, the dean says, to become aware of others' viewpoints. That in any dealings with students or each other, faculty must approach the issue with the awareness of every marginalizing experience the student may have had. With the understanding that the institution, and oneself, represent entitlement and power that in themselves disempower the other.

I am not entitled, Mandalay thinks. I have lived below the poverty line all my life. I have been dependent on those in power. I have always lived by an ethics shaped by an awareness of gender and racial equality. I do not think I am uninformed, nor that I have displayed a lack of sensitivity towards any of my students or other faculty at any time.

It's important for everyone to participate, the dean says. We work alone most of the time, in our offices and studios. It's important to come together and create community.

Can they really do that, ask her to give up the last week of the summer break? She doesn't think it's in the contract.

AIDAN SAYS THAT she should go to her workshop. He has stuff to do, anyway.

He had scoffed at her meeting him at the airport and had just taken the bus and Skytrain home. She meets him at the door, though, and wraps her arms around him unabashedly. He has grown, in his six months of travelling and working on farms. He's muscular, sun-tanned, has some beard and hair long enough to tie back with an elastic. And he's taller. She hadn't thought he was still growing, but he's actually, noticeably, taller.

Two inches, he says. He's proud of it.

They stand in the hallway, grinning at each other.

Thanks for all of your letters, he says.

She can't ask him now why he left. It's not that it doesn't matter anymore – it does, this breach between them. But she thinks she will wait to for him to bring it up. She must leave it up to him.

It's so lovely to have Aidan in the house again. They have long talks; they go to a new gallery; they shop in dark obscure ethnic grocery stores and Aidan cooks new things he's discovered; they go shopping for clothes, because nothing in Aidan's closet fits him anymore, and the clothes he worked in are worn threadbare and stained with ground-in earth. He doesn't need much, he says: he'll buy clothes in Halifax, when he gets there. He has enrolled, after all, in his father's choice of university.

The workshop she has to attend, Mandalay finds, runs only a few hours a day; by the time she gets back, Aidan is just up and having breakfast. He spends an evening with friends and another one with Owen, and has lunch with his father, but most of the time he is hers.

They have long talks, but they do not talk about his defection.

On his last day, she trims his hair, as she always did when he was young.

Leave it long, he says.

I'll just tidy it up. Clean up the split ends.

He sits in the kitchen, a towel around his bare shoulders. She sections his hair off, pins, lightly snips. His hair, streaked by the intense sun, lightens as it dries. She cuts it as he has asked, in a bob that brushes his jawbone and tucks behind his ears.

There, she says. You look like an Italian playboy prince.

But really, she is reminded of Harriet.

He lowers his eyelids, pouts his lips, holds his hand out for hers. Ah, bella Signora, he says.

So suave, she says. Let me get a Q-tip for your ears. Bits of hair have got inside.

So lovely to have him home.

And then she almost ruins it, by asking if he has heard from Harry, if he knows how Harry is doing. His expression closes off, and he says shortly that he does not, and she can see that he has put up a wall between them, and she must accept it is there, unpleasant as it is for her. She says, only: I was wondering if she wanted news of the cat. Of Clytemnestra.

That sounds lame even to her, and she sees Aidan glance at the cat, who is stretched out along the back of the sofa like a fur stole, but he says nothing.

28

MARLENE, WHO IS BEN'S ADOPTIVE MOTHER, calls Cleo one evening. She says: Such a silly thing. I got a new phone and I forgot to transfer Ben's new number to it. And for the life of me, I can't remember it. You know what it's like; everyone's on speed dial these days, and we don't memorize the phone numbers of the people closest to us.

Cleo says, I don't think I have Ben's new number. (Does Ben have a new number?)

I'll call you back, Marlene, she says.

The thought of Ben, a sore tooth the tongue won't stop probing.

She'd felt torn, keeping up the relationship with Ben, after the loss of Cliff's business, after Cliff's terrible accident. Cliff had said Ben had screwed him over, misused business funds, not taken on his share of the work. Sucked the business dry. And Cliff had been stranded – financially, emotionally, physically – while Ben, apparently, had walked away from it. Had enrolled in law school, in fact, his adoptive parents' money a good safety net.

She'd spoken to Cliff of Ben, a few months after Cliff's accident. She had said she was worried about Ben; he seemed to be in a downward spiral. She had not said to Cliff: maybe because you've cut him off, or maybe because he feels so guilty about everything. She wouldn't have said that, wouldn't have laid that guilt on Cliff, even if she had believed it was true. She had just thought that maybe if Cliff reached out to their brother, Ben could find himself. He could get better. She'd just said to Cliff: Ben has dropped out of school. He seems lost.

And Cliff had screwed up his face and then said: Good.

It's not good, Cliff. He's our brother.

Not really, Cliff had said.

Ben had called her, she remembers. After months of not calling, not returning her calls; had invited her for coffee. He'd looked clean, well groomed, if thinner. But somehow dried up, rigid. Bent on some goal that required her, but didn't include her. His eyes and jaw moving in new ways. The small muscle movements off.

Are you working too hard? she had asked.

Something like that, he'd said. He always had this manner, she had realized, a thinly-veiled attitude that she needed him more than he needed her; that he was doing her a favour by giving her his time and attention. She had always thought it was the effect of his having been a longed-for, late, only child, for his wealthy adoptive parents. Clearly, they had spoiled him; indulged him, made him feel too much that he was the centre of the universe. She had thought that. She had not seen that his manner said something else: it said, I know I don't really mean anything to you, so I won't pretend you are important to me.

It's the attitude of someone with an attachment disorder, Mandalay, who had taken courses in psychology and sociology, had said. It's damage from Ben's being taken from his family as a toddler.

He'd asked her for money. She'd been surprised; he'd always seemed better off than she was. He said that he'd had some bad luck, that he was embarrassed to go to his parents. That he was articling soon; that he had a great job lined up, that he'd pay her back. He'd said he was embarrassed to go to her, but he didn't have any other options, and he knew she'd be there for him. She always was.

She had given him some money. A few thousand, which was as much, she calculated, as she could afford to lose, and enough for Ben to live on for a few months. It was a pinch, even then, but it wouldn't damage her in the long run. Trent had okayed it. They each had their own bank accounts, but an agreement to confer over large amounts, since at some level, it was family money. After that, she hadn't heard from Ben again for months; hadn't been able to contact him.

She'd felt sick about the money. It wasn't that she couldn't spare it, though she and Trent were frugal, would have put it towards something important to the family. It was the realization that Ben had seen her as a dupe, an object to exploit, all during their conversation, when she had seen herself as unselfish, generous, a good sister. That was hard to get past.

She has helped Cliff to get back on his feet more than once. After an accident in the late nineties, when he'd fallen down a staircase and fractured his skull. Then after the landslide at his job site, where he'd been tumbled down a steep slope along with many tonnes of clay soil, tree limbs, and boulders. She'd let him stay in her basement for a few months, recovering from his first accident. She'd helped him with all the application forms for disability support, for grants for house accessibility renovations and a wheelchair. The forms had been complex, beyond Cliff's or Veronika's ability to finish them. She'd also loaned Cliff money, and he had paid her back.

Cliff was always grateful, always tried hard to help himself. It was a natural, simple thing, to help Cliff.

Then, shortly after Cleo had given Ben the money, Mandalay had said: I heard that Ben has bottomed out. He's in rehab. Mandalay had heard it from Duane, who had it from the grapevine at work. Both Duane and Ben's father were lawyers.

Cleo had said, Oh, that can't be true! She had tried calling Ben, again, fruitlessly, and then had called Marlene.

Cleo had said, Hello, this is Cleo Lund, I'm calling about Ben, and Marlene, not hearing her properly, or maybe not registering what she had said, had responded, in a tight, high voice, an unnaturally hard voice, that Ben didn't live with her, that she wasn't responsible for his financial obligations, that she would not be a reference for him.

She had been taught to say that, Cleo had realized, later —
taught by a tough-love counselor, or by experience. At the time, she
had been shocked, appalled. She had said, Marlene, it's me. Cleo.
Ben's sister.

Marlene had sighed. She had said, You have no idea, Cleo. She'd
asked Cleo to talk to her husband, to Ben's adoptive father, and Cleo
hadn't wanted to, had avoided it, and then he had called her, instead.
Don't give Ben money, he had said. I hope you haven't been giving
him money?

Cleo had not confessed to the money she had given Ben. It
seemed paltry, now. Mandalay had told her that Duane had estimated
the price of the private rehabilitation clinic to be something like fifty
thousand dollars.

She had asked, and Ben's adoptive dad had told her, what drugs
Ben was using. A partial list, probably, he had said. She had not heard
of some of them. There was a hardness in his voice that she had heard,
at the time, as lack of caring, and later, as the effect of endless worry,
endless disappointment. A necessary armouring of the heart.

The rehabilitation program had seemed to work, though. Ben
had called to thank her, to apologize, to promise to pay her back.
To tell her about his new job, his new girlfriend. She had not been
impressed with Tiffany, and was sorry that things had gone wrong
with Ben's previous girlfriend, Alison, who had been wonderful.
She'd gone to his wedding to Tiffany and to the baby shower for his
son. She had made a point of inviting him over, getting Mandalay
to invite them to her parties, as Mandalay lived in the city, more
conveniently. She had invited Ben's wife for coffee, once in a while,
tried to be supportive.

She had some reservations about Tiffany. She'd said to Mandalay:
Something's off about that girl. She's a bit dim, isn't she?

Mandalay had said, Cleo, you're so sheltered. You really don't
know anything, do you?

But there was the baby, Oscar. Cleo loved the baby. Trent and her own, grown children had teased her: she wanted another baby; she was hungry for grandchildren.

She thought that if she were there, a benevolent aunt, no harm could come to him.

It was when Ben dropped away the second time, a couple of years ago, that Cleo had begun to understand his adoptive parents' responses. She's heard an expression, before, in a novel or a movie: *a blow upon a bruise*. Now she understands it: there's a particular pain that comes when you have put everything you have into forgiveness, into trusting someone again, and they disappoint you again. It shouldn't be worse the second or third or fourth time, but it is.

Now Marlene calling. Cleo pictures her. She'd be standing in the living room of that very expensive Point Grey house. Cleo has been there. It's a West Coast style house, and the living room has twenty-foot ceilings, a view of Burrard Inlet and the wooded rise of Stanley Park. Large windows; modern furniture. A Poul Henningson Artichoke chandelier.

It occurs now to Cleo that it was seeing Ben's adoptive parents' house that had made her fall in love with her own mid-century modern, architecturally-designed house. Hers was a more modest version of Marlene's.

Marlene is tall and angular and dresses in bespoke wool suits and handmade silk shirts. Ben had said that she wore dresses, not slacks, even to cook and garden. That he had never, not even as a small child, seen her without her hair and makeup done.

She wonders what Marlene thinks of Tiffany. Of course she had spoken to Marlene at the wedding reception, at the baby shower for Oscar, but Ben's adoptive mother curates her emotional expressions as she does her appearance.

Cleo has spent much of her life imagining Marlene – her lifestyle, her emotions. And her house. Both disdaining and desiring, she has to admit. Marlene, who, not satisfied with a successful career, a life of privilege, had appropriated the treasure of Cleo's birth family, her little brother Bodhi.

Well. That is not completely true, Cleo knows. Marlene and her husband, in their early forties, unable to have, but desirous of having a child, had been offered a little boy, a toddler, who, they had been told, had been found in a state of neglect, whose birth family could not care for him properly, who came with risks, but needed a good home. They had adopted Bodhi, had changed his name to Ben, had given what they had to give. They had done their best, according to their beliefs and abilities. It had not been enough.

But Cleo now knows: what we give our children is seldom, if ever, the correct thing.

She calls Marlene back. She says, I don't have a new number for Ben. I haven't seen him for a few months.

The last time she had seen him had been in Butterfly Lake, hadn't it?

She says, maybe we need to join forces to find him, to see if he's okay?

Marlene's voice quavers. She says: My husband, Ben's father, isn't doing well. He wants to see Ben.

Cleo can hear how Marlene hates not being able to suppress the quaver. They must be in their eighties, now, Ben's other parents.

Marlene had said to Cleo, once: It was my husband who wanted a child. I was happy. Ben cried constantly for weeks, and I didn't know what to do with him.

Cleo says, Do you have Tiffany's number? Her mother's? I'm going to try to track Ben down.

CLEO REMEMBERS MEETING Tiffany's mother, the woman who comes to the door, once she sees her. She is dressed too youthfully, Cleo thinks: in very tight black stretch jeans, high heels, a ruffled and appliqued and rhinestone-embellished blouse. A lot of very straight, pale-blonde hair, false eyelashes.

Tammy: that's her name.

Tammy has a collection of birthday cards on a credenza in her living room. Nifty Fifty! Most of them have bawdy messages, comic photos of elderly women in underwear, or references to wine.

Happy birthday, Cleo says.

Oh, Tammy says. It was last month. I just haven't got around to cleaning all of this up. My friends took me out; it was such a... Her voice trails off into laughter.

I also turned fifty this year, Cleo says. Shocking, isn't it!

Tammy looks at her, squints her eyes. She's trying to tell if Cleo has had work done, Cleo thinks. She thinks that Tammy has. There's a certain shininess, a certain pneumatic quality. But also, a hint of ravage.

Tammy says in response to Cleo's inquiry about Ben: That bastard. That asshole. I should have known. I've got the gift for falling for real losers, you know? Con men. Druggies. Alkies. Looks like my daughter has it too. It's like we're magnets for every guy with a problem. Every guy on his way down.

She says that she hasn't seen Ben for nearly a year, now. She doesn't know where Ben is. She doesn't care. All she knows is he hasn't sent the money in a few months.

She says that Tiffany is in the hospital.

Which hospital? Cleo says, feeling alarm. Which is worse, she thinks. Which do I least want to hear — that she is ill or had an accident, or that she is in rehab? Which is the worst news?

Tammy tells her the whole story. Ben's drug use; Tammy persuading Tiffany to leave him; Tiffany with her own substance abuse problems.

But is she okay? Is she going to be okay?

Oh, sure, Tammy says. She just needs to get out there again, meet someone else. But she's being stubborn right now. She won't eat, she tried to do things to herself. She has to stay in the hospital until she gets her act together.

And where is Oscar? Cleo asks, finally, after holding off as long as she can.

He's playing in his room. He's a good, quiet kid. Doesn't ask for anything. She yells, Oscar!

And here he is, a little taller, less chubby, than when Cleo saw him last. He is what, seven, now. He's wearing camouflage-patterned pants and a sweatshirt with an image from a video game on it, and someone has shaved a zigzag pattern on the sides of his head and left the hair at the top long, like a bird's soft crest, but he looks like Cleo's children, like Sam and Olivia. And like Aidan and Owen. She can see all of them in his face, his gestures.

He shakes his head when she asks if he remembers her. She wants to touch him, to hug him, but he keeps a wary distance.

Tammy says: Who's paying me to look after Oscar? I should be getting paid. I have to live my life. Who's looking after me? I deserve to live my best life, you know.

Cleo could take him. She can see that. She could transfer Tammy a few thousand dollars right now, and Tammy would scoop up all of Oscar's belongings into a couple of bags and let Cleo take the boy away with her. He would be safe, at Cleo's. He could stay with Cleo for a long time. Sam is there to help look after him; Sam is great with little kids.

No doubt she could get Tiffany, and Ben too, to give her custodial rights. Oscar would be safe, cared for. He'd have a better school, a greatly enriched home life.

She must be looking at the boy too speculatively, for Tammy says: I don't know when Tiffany will be out of the hospital. I'm sure she wouldn't mind if Oscar had a little visit with his auntie.

Do you remember, Cleo asks Oscar, do you remember when your mom and you and I went to the Aquarium? Do you remember that you liked the otters? And you got an otter stuffy?

His eyes are wide, now. And she is stooping low, reminding him of the toy she bought him.

Oh, your otter! Tammy says. That's your favourite, isn't it! Why don't you go get it and show your auntie?

He shakes his head. He doesn't know me at all, Cleo thinks. A year is a big chunk of his life. I'm a stranger to him.

She could take Oscar with her right now. She knows how to raise a child. She'll cut back her hours at work; she'll be there for him. And she'll find Ben; she'll get him into a good rehab. She'll give him — and Tiffany — every support.

But Oscar doesn't know her at all. And he doesn't look underfed or uncared for. His body language toward Tammy is perfectly relaxed.

Cleo pulls out her business card, the cash she has in her wallet. Not much; a couple of hundred. She says to Tammy: Call me if you hear from Ben. Let me know how Tiffany is. Call me if you need help applying for assistance. If you need anything. If you want a break.

From her car, she calls Marlene, tells her that she's on the track. That Tiffany is in the hospital — she doesn't say why. And that Oscar is at Tammy's, that he seems okay.

She is so tired. She can feel waves of tiredness tumbling her, like the surf on a beach. And then a kind of anger. Dammit, she has worked hard all of her life — well, all of her adolescence, all of her adult life, to be a functional person, to look after herself and everyone she is responsible for. She should not have to clean up other people's messes. She should not be driving through a tatty part of Vancouver to check up on her brother's family after working for ten hours.

She can't do this much longer. She's fifty years old and she's been taking care of other people's shit for the last forty. When is she going to be able to take a break? When is she going to be able to focus on herself?

I deserve to live my best life, you know? she says aloud, in her car. She feels her face split into a grin, then — a huge, humourless grin that hurts the corners of her mouth. If anyone could see her, they'd think she was off her rocker, grinning away in her car like that, in the evening traffic heading east out of Vancouver.

CLEO HAS WON AN AWARD for her company, Aeolus.

It's a design award, an international award for green design. Cleo has created a new system for heating and cooling multi-story buildings; one that uses air flow, the natural inclination of drafts, to move cool and warm air throughout the building.

She has used ideas from around the world, but synthesizing them into something new, something unique. Aeolus had patented the design. It will probably make them some money. Cleo had written up the application for the patent, and for the prize. Alex and Larry have invited Cleo to sit at their table at the ceremony, which will be held in Los Angeles. She doesn't care so much about the ceremony or going to Los Angeles, but she thinks that this might be a good time to approach them about shifting her role in the company.

She'd joined the company passively, about a decade ago, as a part of a merger, as a drafting technician. Because of her structural engineering degree, she could be also thrown other jobs: she could do some design, particularly things like foundations and HVAC work, that Larry and Alex, the two architects who own the company don't do. The boring bits. But she has loved being part of an architectural company, which has in recent years become a design and build.

But she'd like to do more design, to be more involved in the building concepts. She has done her apprenticeship. She has, on her own initiative, taken courses in design, and has become fluent in the aesthetics of the company; as well, she has some ideas of her own, for new directions. And now she is going to ask to be recognized, rewarded for her contributions to the company. She's going to ask to be made partner. She would rather they had approached her, but she knows that doors only open for those who knock.

She has prepared a presentation, of course, with both slides and hard copies, because Alex loves digital and Larry does not. She has booked a time with them; she has prepared well; she has had sleepless nights, but she thinks she will convince them. How could they not be convinced?

And here she is now, at the table, the highly-polished rosewood table in the partners' boardroom, moving through her presentation, remembering to pause, to engage, to sell herself in the most effective way possible. (She has taken courses in that, too.) She knows how to do this. She pulls everything she has ever learned together, and she surpasses herself. She summarizes all of her contributions, her innovations, her billed hours. She shows some of the new ideas she has. Her graphics and slides are impeccable; her pace and tone, practiced for days, are convincing.

And at the end, she can see by their faces that it's going to be a no. They have already decided, without speaking to each other, somehow, her bosses, whom she has served diligently for ten years.

She can read their faces so well, that she knows their answer, even while she is gathering up her materials, putting them into her beautifully-tooled Danish laptop case, along with her laptop, suppressing a chill, because this room is always cold, and she has dressed lightly, in a silk-and-wool blend shift and blazer. She doesn't need the interview that happens later the next week, Alex calling her into his office as she passes, as if for a casual exchange. She doesn't even feel any anxiety, during the interim, because she knows that they have already decided *no*.

No, because what she's describing would involve a partnership, and they aren't willing to take on another partner. No, because they need her to keep doing the structural engineering work. No, because she is so good at managing the technicians and the junior engineers. No, because she really doesn't have the design cred that their clients are looking for. Of course she can do good design, but it's all about brand, these days. Aeolus is a brand. That's what they are selling.

They offer her a raise — not as generous as she would have expected, for their *no*.

HER SON SAM SAYS: Maybe you should quit your job.

She can't do that, can she? Anyway, she likes her job. She has worked at Aeolus for ten years now. She's making good money, as an engineer, there — an income she needs to pay the mortgage. Of course, there are things she doesn't love about it. The scrimmages with the project managers, who can't seem to read her blueprints properly, who assume that they know what's on them. Who put heat pumps into the wrong shaft, or build electrical rooms six inches too small, so that nothing works, or the whole building plan shifts. They are always respectful and polite, the contractors she works with. They just don't listen to her, or pay close attention to the designs she gives them.

She is contributing something important to the world, through her engineering ideas, she knows. She's creating new ways to move air through buildings, to heat and cool them. That's important and useful; environmentally sound.

What would happen if she quit her job? She'd get another, but maybe not for a more interesting architectural company, not in Vancouver, at least. It's hard to move between architectural firms at a senior level: they are entities with their own distinctive flavour. Their own brand. She'd end up taking some city planning job, probably. Nine to five, at a desk, at a lower salary.

She makes an Excel spreadsheet to calculate how much she needs to make to keep paying her share of the mortgage on the house. Her beautiful mid-century house. She will not be able to do this if she doesn't have a high enough income.

She cannot quit her job, though something defiant and wilful in her wants to walk away from Aeolus, right then.

It's what she has: the ability to work hard, to take care of the needs or demands of others. Those are her gifts: what she knows she must exercise in her life.

THE FINAL PAPERS for her divorce arrive in the mail. Cleo has read all of the documents already, of course, but she opens the envelope and scans the copy anyway. It has all been very straightforward, very civil. They have split things equitably, dealt with each other without rancour.

They've got along better, in the joint project of dismantling their partnership, than they had for years before. It's this she thinks of now: the amicable meetings over lunches; the shared jokes about their lawyer's orthodontic appliances and her grammar errors; the unspoken agreement not to trash each other to their children.

They could have tried harder, maybe. Where was this goodwill when they lived together?

She doesn't regret the split. Things had not been working between them, and she has a peace now, a feeling of relief in her own home. She has been glad of that, this past year; she has grown into this new space, felt her own sense of self-acceptance, of spaciousness, grow.

But twenty-five years of her life, the prime of her life, wasted.

CLEO IS ON THE FREEWAY when she feels it. At first, she thinks *stroke*. She's fit and only fifty, but anyone can have a stroke.

She's in three lanes of traffic on the Trans Canada east of Vancouver, a stretch of highway she has driven hundreds of times, in the far-left lane, the passing lane. On her way to work. An ordinary day. October. The leaves of the poplars and the alder fiery against the deep blue morning sky. Mist rising from the fields as the air warms. The traffic is heavy, as always, this time of day, but it's an ordinary day. She is not especially worried about anything, either at work or at home.

It takes over her as she's passing a row of semis. The trucks loom over her. They are all going as fast as she is, about 120 kilometres an hour, but she doesn't like being behind them, not being able to see what's ahead. She always passes. She zooms past a long line of them, easily, all of her attention engaged on the manoeuvre. But they are passing each other, too, pulling in and out of lanes. For a moment she's hemmed in, the body of her new-model import suv dwarfed and blocked by the high walls of the surrounding trucks.

She thinks later that it isn't this situation that causes it, but it's the moment it happens, whatever it is entering her heart and lungs and bloodstream. Her heartbeat first quickening, as if she's had a near miss with another vehicle, which she hasn't. And then not subsiding, but picking up, thudding in her chest as if she's been on the StairMaster for too long.

She tries to slow her breathing, to calm her mind, but she isn't really feeling agitated.

Then the dizziness hits. She can't see. Everything around her jiggles and swirls. She's beginning to black out.

She has to pull over. She can't see and she's passing out, but she has to get over to the slow lane, find a widening of the shoulder where she can pull over.

She fixes her gaze on the painted lane lines, though they buckle and waver. The world inside or outside her head is surging, disintegrating. She is going to black out. But she is driving 120 kilometers an hour in heavy traffic.

She signals, shoulder-checks, slows, waits for a gap. The truck behind her looms suddenly in her rear-view mirror, honks, a loud deep complaint. She slides her vehicle to the right. Another blast. She's not going fast enough. Cars passing her now, almost veering around her. She slides right once more. The sight of the grassy verge, even with the deep ditch beyond, is a slight respite. She can focus on the edge.

But the dizziness persists. Her face and hands are numb.

She sees a pullout, but she's not quick enough, is still going too fast, doesn't make the turn, and the chance goes by.

Her eyelids are starting to close against the blurred and leaping road. She must pull over. She puts on her signal. Slows, slows. More horn blares. Then a widening of the shoulder, just a small bulge of the pavement into the grass and brambles. She slips in, comes to a stop, pulls the emergency brake. Breathes.

Trucks roars by, only a few inches away. She should put on her hazards, but she can't remember where the switch is. She puts her head forward.

The dizziness abates, after a few minutes. She doesn't feel normal, but she can see. She can feel her hands. She doesn't feel that she is losing consciousness.

She should get back on the highway, make her way to a safer pullout, at least. And maybe it's over, whatever it was. Maybe she can make it to work now.

She signals, releases the emergency, watches, over her left shoulder, now, for a long enough gap in the stream of vehicles. Slips back into the stream, accelerates hard.

And within a hundred metres is blacking out again.

She tells herself that she didn't pass out earlier; she won't now. It feels like she will, but she won't. She won't pass out. She won't. She's shouting, *Won't, won't won't*, and that somehow helps, keeps things intact. And then she she's able to pull over again, this time in a slightly wider place. She turns off the engine. Puts on her hazards. Closes her eyes.

She doesn't know how long she waits there, in her car — fifteen minutes, only, perhaps — before the cruiser pulls up behind her, lights flashing. A pleasant, matter-of-fact woman around her own age appears at her window. Cleo opens it, looks up at her.

Do you need some help? the woman asks, conversationally.

Cleo says: Yes. Yes, actually. I can't seem to drive my vehicle, this morning. I get dizzy as soon as I get back into the traffic.

Will she get a ticket for pulling off onto the shoulder of the freeway?

The police officer says: Do you need an ambulance? Are you having symptoms of stroke or heart attack?

Cleo doesn't know. No, she says. I'm fine, sitting here. I just can't drive.

The police officer seems to find extricating drivers stuck on the shoulders of the freeway in morning rush hour an everyday chore. She blocks off the shoulder with some orange cones, calls for a backup to drive Cleo's vehicle, gives Cleo a ride home.

Cleo calls in sick, feeling fraudulent. She is fine. She feels perfectly fine. The next day, Saturday, she is able to get into her vehicle and drive herself to the plaza to get groceries. On Sunday she puts her bike and Sam's on the back of her SUV and drives to the park on the inlet where they can ride. She has no difficulties driving.

On Monday, she gets in the SUV again without even thinking about her Friday trip, makes it as far as the same place on the freeway, and has to pull over again. She is dizzy, she can't breathe, she is falling forever into darkness.

SHE CANNOT DO THIS ANYMORE, she realizes. She must take a break. She must rethink how she lives her life.

What does she need, after all?

She can sell her house. She can buy instead a small apartment. Sam is twenty; he can live by himself, now, or with friends. Olivia is nearly finished her master's, and will be self-supporting soon.

She'll give up her house. She won't think about it too much, because she is very, very attached to it. But she can live in a condo: maybe one of the ones she has helped design. She can exchange her house for freedom.

She writes up her resignation from Aeolus in about two minutes, presses *Send*.

29

CLIFF HEARS IT BEFORE HE SEES IT: the roar of the chainsaw, the crash of the tree. Then he smells it, raw cedar raking the sinuses.

Someone is felling trees on his family's lot.

He throws the emergency brake, leaps out of his truck. For a moment he is undecided: should he check at the house first, or make for the woods, see what the hell is going on?

The door of the house opens, then, and Crystal steps out, Maria right behind her. Crystal beams at him. She's dressed neatly in clean slacks, a T-shirt, a cardigan, her hair in a braid. She has put on a bit of weight; the hollows in her face have filled in.

Crystal runs down the steps and across the yard. She hugs him — girlishly, he wants to say — then looks up at him, alight.

There's something different. It's in her gaze, he thinks. He can't describe it, exactly, but as close as he can get it's that she is not looking at him as if he is Cliff. It's something you don't notice until it's gone, but everyone looks at you in a very specific way, which indicates how they see you. How they feel about you. There has always been an expression in Crystal's eyes that is like a private message for him, maybe. That identifies him: *Cliff. My son.* Or maybe just: *You.* He's never thought about it before — except that maybe Veronika used to look at him like that, and then had gazed at him without any warmth, any recognition — those last few days before she had left. He had never noticed it consciously, though, how Crystal had a certain look for him, but he can see that it is gone. He is gone from her eyes, and that feels more than odd. He feels that he isn't Cliff anymore, that he has been erased, lost.

It's Maria, still standing at the top of the steps, who says, Ho, Crystal, your son Cliff. Isn't it great! And then Crystal looking at Cliff the familiar way, and laughing, and hugging him again. Well, she says. You have been gone a long time, haven't you?

Neither Maria nor Crystal can tell him anything about the logging. Cliff sets off down the deer path he and his siblings used to take, the shortcut through the woods, and comes upon them quite quickly, the two men with the chainsaw and the Cat. They've smashed a track in from the road, and have already managed to take out three or four of the giant cedars. The woods are gashed open, where they have been working – not only the big trees down, but the smaller ones, the maple and young Douglas fir, the under-growth of salal and waxberry, all ripped and crushed where the trees have toppled down through the delicate interlocking layers of the forest. The earth ripped up, the air sharp with the stink of diesel and smoke. At the edge, a stack of trimmed cedar logs, each thirty metres long and at least two metres in diameter. Giants, hundreds of years old.

The man not using the chainsaw sees Cliff approach, holds up a hand, points: get out.

Cliff shakes his head, keeps walking. He'd normally not walk into a situation like this, wildcatters, two of them against one of him. He keeps walking. These woods are not for cutting. They are his.

The man with the chainsaw now looks up and stops the machine. The mangled space echoes still with the sound of it. Cliff says: You're cutting trees illegally on my land.

The first man waves a hand. Nope, he says. I bought the wood rights. All legal.

The man with the chainsaw just stares at Cliff, like a bully dog.

Cliff says: Can't be right. My family owns these woods. We haven't sold any wood rights. You must be on the wrong property.

The first man windshield-wipers his hands, shakes his head. Nope, he says. I fixed it up with the son of the old lady who lives here. I got paperwork.

Cliff says, she can't sign things. My sister and I have power of attorney. It's our family land. We own it. I've never seen you before in my life.

I got the rights, the man says. And paid a lot of dough for it.

I think you should stop, Cliff says.

The men look at him appraisingly, derisively. He should not have come down the path alone, Cliff thinks. One of the men takes off his hard hat, puts it back on. They both stare at him, something bovine in their faces.

My family owns this place, Cliff says. You can't cut here. He turns, clambers over the fallen brush, makes for the path. Doesn't let himself turn around.

Cleo says, on the phone: call the police and lawyer who did the conveyancing, and then she looks up the numbers for him. Cliff's call-in is answered quite quickly. It must be a slow day in Powell River. A patrol car pulls into the yard, in front of the house, with two uniformed officers, in under an hour.

But in that time Cliff has heard another tree fall. And thought: Ben.

The Mounties are a man Cliff's age and a younger woman, in uniform. Heavy lumpy flak vests, like carapaces, and stiff leather holsters at their thighs. These are reassuring. They scarcely look at the document on his phone – the title deed, he thinks. Like in the Westerns he and his brother Che used to watch at Myrna Pollard's when he was little. The deed. The power of attorney document. They look at the documents and at his ID.

He leads them into the forest, past the ranks of salal and sword fern, the maples and Douglas fir and the giant, ancient cedars. His woods. They can hear the chainsaw, the snap and rustle of branches being trimmed away from the fallen tree.

Into the clearing. This time the guy with the chainsaw sees them first, and turns off the machine. The other guy looks up. Then it's all *Shit, a misunderstanding, we were scammed* from the two loggers. The female police officer takes photos. The older male one calls in the licence plates for the loggers' truck and the serial number for the bulldozer. He asks for documents, confiscates the chainsaws and saw and the keys to the bulldozer. Cliff stands back, out of the way, as he has been told to by the younger officer. Something like boiling pitch is running in his veins.

30

DUANE KNOWS TO RUN BACK UP the stairs between the bleachers and down the passage to the dressing rooms and the ice, but Mandalay doesn't know that route. She runs down the steps to the glass barrier around the rink, presses herself against it as if she can force her way through. She is screaming, but she doesn't know this until later, when she watches the video and sees herself, the camera zooming in on her. Someone puts an arm around her shoulder and says something she can't understand. Come this way, he says, but she can't pull herself away from the Plexiglas, from what is happening on the other side of it. He's trying to steer her with his arm, but she can't leave, can't take her eyes off Owen, who is lying on the ice, immobile, partly blocked from her view by the ref and attendants and the managers, who have clustered around him, and by the purposeless, confused milling of Owen's teammates, their helmets and padding making no visual sense.

She sees Duane walk out onto the ice and realizes that she has gone the wrong way; there is another way to take, which would lead to Owen, to her son, there on the ice.

The man behind her takes her shoulders, gives her a little shake. Come on, Mandalay, he says.

It's Max Gibbons.

Come with me. We'll get you to him. Come with me. And then he pushes her, holding her by the shoulders, up the stairs, to the doorway and passage she didn't know about, and as they pass through the crowd there is a kind of shock wave of silence that follows them, and she knows that they are all aware of her in a way that she has not experienced before.

From the opening to the ice she can see that Owen is lying on a red arc. It's like blood. It isn't blood. It's like a red strap holding Owen down. It's a circle painted on the rink, under the ice. Underglaze. Owen's helmet is off, his eyes are open, but not focussed. Duane is on his knees, is saying something; the manager is saying something. She thinks: He isn't breathing. She can't get to him, though, because Max Gibbons has a grip on her upper arm. She sees Duane lean forward over Owen's face, and then there's a pulse of movement behind her, and a quartet of paramedics races past pushing a gurney on which various implements swing and bounce, and Owen disappears under the scrum of uniforms and arms.

THE HOSPITAL CORRIDOR is too bright. Everything is too shiny, too smooth, too hard-edged. There is nowhere to find comfort, to ground one's self.

Duane is pacing. He can't stop moving; he is angry, she thinks, as well as afraid. Or maybe just afraid. Anger is fear, she reminds herself. They have had a string of bad news: from the emergency room physician, the report that Owen had stopped breathing again in the ambulance, that he was unresponsive, that they had intubated him, that he would have an x-ray and a CAT scan. From the radiologist, who had come into the waiting room to find them, in her white coat, to show them the pictures, which she didn't have to do, Mandalay realized, and so maybe portended some worse news for which she wanted them to be able to prepare themselves. The x-rays showed such a tiny anomaly: a winglet of a vertebra folded down at a different angle to the rest in the row. But the CAT showed some swelling around the spinal cord; that was bad. Duane kept asking, which vertebra, is it C5? But the radiologist said that the orthopedic surgeon would explain things more. Then the medical team was waiting for Owen to stabilize, so that they could operate safely. And after that, he was going into surgery because he was not stabilizing.

Each piece of new information an assault.

And in-between the runners with their news, Duane had watched the replay of the accident – they have to call it an accident – over and over on his phone. The sports news and the local channel both replayed it, with adjusted commentary and increased speculation. Mandalay had looked over at the screen only once; had seen the slowed-down video footage of the other team's player skating into Owen like a runaway train; Owen flying up and backward into the boards, bouncing off the boards, his head in its helmet snapping backward; Owen flung out in a sort of twisting arc and dropping onto the ice. (It was then she had seen the other camera view cut in: the spectators moving forward as if propelled by some sort of shock wave, then herself pressed up against the glass, her mouth open.)

When he was not watching the updated video replay, Duane had paced. Mandalay had moved a few seats away from him, pulled her tuque over her ears, to muffle the sound. She already had the few seconds of the impact scratched deeply into her mind. She does not need to watch it again and again.

Owen's team had been in the playoffs in their division, an away game for him, in Vancouver, and Duane had got tickets and said she should come and watch. Max and Galton Gibbons were going, too. It was a big moment in Owen's life: she should be there.

Okay, she had said. She always has this sense of guilt around Owen: he's harder to know, harder to understand. She doesn't have the kind of easy rapport with him that she can have with Aiden – about books, art, music, their ideas melding, flicking off each other, the two of them paired in their similar ways of seeing the world. With Owen, it's been harder. There's always been a little gap, a disjunction. She has always been conscious of this, aware that Owen feels that she is closer to Aidan, that he feels second to her. She knows that she needs to make that up to him.

So she had gone, had been sitting on a hard seat under hard light, between Max and Duane, watching this game that doesn't always make sense to her, watching her son on the ice in his ridiculous padded uniform, his helmet, his futuristic skates. And then the bodycheck, the opposing player careening into Owen, sending him into the boards.

Her son has been irrevocably, terribly injured. He might die, or he might be left in such a state that dying will seem the better option. In a few seconds, his life, her life, her other child's life, have been changed permanently.

No, she will never get that image out of her mind. She'll never stop experiencing this night as if it's happening still, the brutal realization slamming her, over and over.

And now they have been in this space for a whole night, and Duane is still pacing. She knows it has been a whole night because her phone is buzzing and vibrating. This is limbo, and there is no time, only eternity, but her phone is buzzing, so she knows it is morning. Or morning in another time zone, where Aidan has woken up and heard the news.

Aidan, she says. Yes, I'm here. Yes, hospital. No, still in surgery.

She had not thought, and Aidan's fear and grief now is a new onslaught of the unbearable. She thinks: *I will die.*

31

CLIFF TRACKS HIS BROTHER BEN down by means one of his social media accounts, on which, recently, a young woman Cliff doesn't know, with improbable breasts and eyelashes and lips, has posted. They are off on a snowboarding holiday, Cliff gathers, to one of those expensive places in the Rockies, where guests are helicoptered in so that they can ski or snowboard on pristine snow. So they can be in nature without people around, the young woman says, on her own account, which has no privacy markers, and a great number of selfies. YOLO, Ben has posted, himself.

Cliff can wait. He can bide his time.

It's almost too easy to track Ben's girlfriend, Ashlee, online. She posts something almost every hour. She skies. She doesn't ski. She drinks in hot tubs. She has a massage, a pedicure. She's always looking at the camera, her face, which is as smooth and pore-less as a plastic doll's, her puffy, shiny lips, her stiff black lashes obviously manufactured. She has one expression: widened eyes, mouth in an O – which looks ludicrous and lewd at the same time. Her comments are all misspelled and followed by winking emoticons. Who is this girl? What is Ben doing with her? Ben, who is paying for this trip, winky-wink. Though Ashlee is making it worthwhile, winky-wink.

What is Ben up to this time?

The hotel, Cliff discovers, runs several hundred a night. Just the hotel. Then there are the meals, which Ashlee photographs and posts, as well. She boasts about the amount of liquor consumed, and the diamond earrings for her birthday. (How much did Ben get for the trees?) What is he doing? He can't possibly think he can maintain this lifestyle beyond a week.

He catches a post that says *Last nite in this paradice* and guesses they will be flying back the next day. He looks up flights. Cranbrook to Vancouver, he guesses. Not first thing in the morning. Midday, maybe. He finds a flight arriving at 12:15. That will be it.

He drives to the airport, walks in, his pulse racing but his mind curiously flat, finds the Arrivals waiting area. He's sweating. He feels he needs to calm himself; that something of his emotional state is visible to people around him, airport security.

The monitor shows that the plane has landed. Cliff drifts back into the crowd, slightly. Positions himself behind an elderly couple and a woman with two small children.

What does he plan to do?

He has thought out a few scenarios. None are dignified or dramatic enough to stir his imagination. He trusts he'll know what to do when he sees Ben and Ashlee. Perfidious, betraying Ben. His brother Ben, who is responsible for pretty well all of the losses Cliff has sustained in the past ten years.

It seems impossible that he'll be able to get to Ben in this crowd, inside the airport, but he could tail him to his car and approach him there, where there's space, and Ben will be off guard.

He wants to knock him down, he thinks. Kick the shit out of him. Kick him in the face; wreck his lying perfect face. But he also wants to yell at Ben, to give him a piece of his mind, to tell him finally and forever that he is a shit, that he deserves to die in a gutter, that the world would be a much better place without Ben in it. He wants, also, to spoil Ben's little ride with Ashlee, to let her know that Ben's a thief, that he has no money to spend on her, that he will end up taking everything she has. He's not sure this will help Ashlee, but he'd like to see Ben discredited in front of her. He'd like to see Ben punished by Ashlee's disgust.

The frosted doors from the Arrivals corridor now show dark moving shapes, like fish in murky water.

Likely the girl already knows what Ben is. Knows, and can't be surprised. Is just taking what she can get, as Ben is.

The doors open. The passengers from Cranbrook (he guesses; there are so many flights, so close together) begin to file out of the long passage.

He spots Ben almost instantly, the girl just behind him with a small wheeled suitcase. She's shorter, plumper, than she appears in her selfies. He sees now that she has used some app to elongate or narrow her face, to enlarge her eyes, in the photographs. She's absorbed in her phone, even as she walks along. He sees her almost trip. Ben, ahead of her, seems in no way conscious of her.

Cliff stays behind his human screen. He can envision himself, a slightly overweight middle-aged man, with an ordinary face, in a cheap navy windbreaker. He's invisible.

He can't see any satisfactory outcome.

He can follow them out. At the least he can confront Ben, make his day unpleasant. Why should he be allowed to enjoy this day, or his ill-gotten trip?

He watches his brother move through the concourse toward the exit: his tall, lean, well-dressed body, his shining thick sun-tipped hair.

Cliff knows that there's nothing he can do that will make himself feel any better. Nothing that will bring back his company, or a pain-free body, or a stand of old-growth cedars. Nothing he can do that will bring back his townhouse, his fleet of trucks, his wife Veronika.

And there's nothing that he can do to Ben that has not already been done. He has known for some time now, he realizes, that this gap in Ben, his inability to see anyone's interests but his own, is only a small shadow of what it is like to be Ben, to have his insatiable and remorseless need. Ben will take and take, but never will be filled up. Will always have a huge hole inside of him, like a child's hunger.

He will not harm Ben. He cannot do it. And from this moment, he will not bother to be angry, even at Ben. This is for his own sake, not his brother's. He will let go, in himself, of all of the hurt that Ben has done him.

He will not trust him again, no. That would simply be stupid. But he will not wish Ben harm. He imagines the would-be loggers will sue Ben. Or maybe worse. He could warn him. He could do that. He might do that. But no, he will not. It is Ben's world; it is something Ben has set in motion, in his own world.

He sees Ben's fair head disappear out the exit doors, in the crowd. He will not follow him. He feels something move in his chest. An impediment, like a stone in a creek bed dislodged. There's a kind of vacuum, in its wake, a kind of pain. But he feels also life begin to move, to resume, to tick forward with its own natural momentum. His own life.

32

MANDALAY SITS BESIDE Owen's hospital bed, which has side rails, so he can't fall out. He is surrounded by machines: machines that apply traction to his fractured spine, fluids and nutrients to his cells, suction to his airways; machines that track his blood pressure and pulse rate; machines that take away his urine. She keeps vigil for hours each day. If she is not in her classroom, she is here. She has come to know this room, which is so awesome in its functionality that it is painful, as well as any room she has known. She can identify within the first few seconds of arriving any changes to it: a new device, a different blanket on the bed, another card added to the collage that decorates the wall.

She has come every day now for — how many days? More than ten, she thinks, but fewer than thirty. It is as if she has travelled to a foreign country and has had to learn new customs, a new language, a new job. Every day, she sits beside this bed and talks to Owen, strokes his hands, his feet, his back, his shoulders. She has to move around the nursing staff, who connect him to the machines, clean and turn him. It is their job to maintain Owen's body, to make sure it keeps functioning while he is not able to look after it himself.

And it is her job to bring him back, to cajole and entice him to return to them.

There is a good probability that he will wake up, return to them, they say. There have been seizures; there is damage that she doesn't understand. Even the specialists with all of their experience and knowledge don't know yet how the healing will progress. But they think it may progress. She can hear that tone in their voices; she thinks it is authentic.

She sits by his bed for hours each day and talks to him, sings to him. She has done this before, when her twin sons were infants, toddlers, growing children, she had interacted verbally with them as much as possible. She had talked them into consciousness. And now she can do it again.

She knows that she must go back with Owen to his childhood, to a time when he was dependent on her, not wholly in control of his body, his limbs and tongue. She must return, descend to that place and bring him back again. She doesn't want to do this: every part of her resists, but she must descend, strap him to her back, her six-foot-one infant, and lug him back up to the light.

She is afraid. She is afraid because Owen might never completely recover, might never be fully Owen again. She is afraid that she will be lost, if she returns to that buried place of her sons' dependency on her. But she must try; she must not give in to despair, must not give up. She must not cease to look forward in hope. She must descend to the dark chaos, but not give into it.

Duane comes too, she knows. Her son Aidan comes; he had flown home, as soon as he had heard. Her sister Cleo has taken a couple of shifts: get some rest, Mandalay, she had said. And Mandalay had trusted Cleo enough to do this, to lie down for an hour, two.

But mostly it's Duane. She doesn't know if he talks to Owen, if he stays long, if he sits by the bed in a heap of remorse and despair. She doesn't care. She hopes he feels remorse, that he realizes that if he had not put Owen into hockey class – against her wishes – this would not have happened. But she hopes it coolly, in a detached way. She doesn't care much about Duane right now. They have arranged their visiting times so that they do not overlap. They don't meet each other. Her classes are in the afternoon, so she takes mornings. Duane is often in court; he comes when he is freer, in late afternoons and evenings. They do not meet.

The night of Owen's accident, as they had sat and waited to hear if he would live, she had not thought about Duane's guilt. They had been allies, sharing the one thing most important to either of them, in a moment of crisis. After, when Owen had stabilized, the hospital social worker had sent them home. You will need your health, he had said. It will be a long journey. Others had come to relieve them, to stay at the hospital: friends, family.

Duane had driven Mandalay home — it had been morning, mid-morning on a week day, not a time when Duane was ever at her house. The neighbourhood had been quiet, deserted. She had been dazed with trauma and lack of sleep, and Duane had opened the car door for her and walked her inside, and then they had turned to each other, without a word, and embraced, not comfortingly (she thinks now with a little shame) but with fierce arousal, and had gone to bed, had long satisfying sex, for the first time in nearly nineteen years.

It was after that, after Duane had woken and dressed and left, that she realized that he was to blame for the accident. She is not angry; it is simply a factual realization. It is his fault.

The thing is, she has no space for extra anger toward him. She had already, for the last eighteen years, blamed him for everything. There was simply no space.

She sits beside Owen's hospital bed and holds his hand. He is asleep, breathing on his own, the cervical collar removed, but his head bandaged. It had not been what they feared most that had threatened him, after all. The high cervical spine had not been broken; the spinal cord had been bruised, but intact. He had not been anoxic long enough to suffer brain damage: the quick attention on the ice, the quick arrival of paramedics, had kept him breathing. The damage had already happened even with a helmet: his brain, that three-pound double-handful of matter, as the neurologist had described it, had rotated and moved inside his skull, banging into the inside of his skull. The axons and blood vessels had been stretched and torn. Later, in hospital, in spite of steroids, his bruised brain had swelled, cutting off oxygen to some areas, temporarily.

Traumatic brain injury. Closed-head injury. Diffuse axonal injury. New language with which to describe the end of the world.

There had been surgeries, hopeful reports and then less hopeful and then hopeful again. A roller coaster of emotion, as they say. She has learned to attach to nothing.

She sits by her son's bed, holds his hand. Sometimes he squeezes back, infinitesimally.

She has learned not to attach too much to that.

2019

33

MANDALAY HAS an early-afternoon studio class, but stops at the hospital before to hang out with Owen for a couple of hours before heading to campus. She can see from the outset that it's not going to be a good visit. Owen is reluctant to wake up. This happens. Mandalay would have let him sleep, but the hospital staff are pretty strict about schedules – they work around the surgeons, the physiotherapists, the neurological therapists, the nurses tell her. On this morning Owen is resisting the nurses' coaxing, and turns away from Mandalay when she sits down on his bed.

Sometimes when she visits, she finds him curled in fetal position. Sometimes he whimpers, won't look at her, won't let her see his face. It hasn't happened recently, she reminds herself. And when it happens, at least he is no longer in a cervical collar or a special helmet. No longer in an artificial coma, on a ventilator. At least he *can* curl his body up and whimper.

On this morning, she says to the nurses: I'll just talk to Owen for a moment, and they nod and move off to the next bed, a thin young man in pink scrubs, a woman with a luxuriant russet braid of hair and upticked eyebrows. Someone has cut Owen's hair very short since her last visit, and the shaven part is growing out, so the surgical site on his scalp is no longer as visible. There's still a scar, a red ridge of flesh running from just in front of one ear across his crown and down to the other ear. It will be hidden, soon, she reminds herself. It will shrink; it will become a thin white scar, hidden until he begins to go bald, if he does, in middle-age.

She strokes his back. He doesn't push her hand away. She says: You've had a haircut. She wants to put her hand on his head, but he doesn't like to be touched there.

She remembers how his entire head fit into her hand, when he was a newborn. She remembers in her palms and fingertips the weight of his head, the texture of the fuzz that clung to it.

But here is her adult son, trapped, enclosed, locked down by the damage of his accident. Her adult son, who must be coaxed out of the case of fragments that holds and limits him.

She rubs his back between his shoulder blades, as he has always liked her to do. He groans and rolls toward her then, clumsily. His hand reaches out, bumps against hers, as if it is a blind creature navigating through some thick substance. That gesture has started a couple of days ago. It's less purposeful, today. She takes his hand, wrapping her fingers around his.

The nurse in pink is back, suddenly. We want Owen to do the grasp himself, he says. We're working on him completing the action.

She decides to ignore the nurse. She is tired of listening to the nurses. Have you had breakfast? she asks Owen. The staff doesn't always get him fed this early, understandably. It's a time-consuming process; they are short-staffed, they say. Sometimes, she'll help him, but lately he hasn't wanted her to. It's a messy business. They give him soft food, mushy food, because there's still a choking hazard. He doesn't have perfect control of his swallowing. And they want him to feed himself. A lot of food ends up on his face and the bib. He's not fond of the bib.

Hungry? she asks. He shakes his head. No, he says. He doesn't want to eat in front of her, these days.

That is a good sign, she reminds herself. Self-awareness; a sign that Owen has a sense of himself, has some pride. The head-shake, the controlled movement of his head from side to side: that's good too. A few weeks ago, he had been able only to thrash around, spasmodically, to grunt, to screw up his face and cry.

What do you feel like doing today? she asks. She has a hard time doing that, but the therapists have suggested it. Push him a little, all of the time. Bring him back.

Do you want to play a game? Do you want to draw?

He shakes his head, grunts. She can tell that he is frustrated. What does he want?

His face turned toward her with an expression that she remembers from his early childhood.

You want a cuddle?

She sits on the bed, gingerly, then snakes herself under the tube and wire that still connect him to machines. She wraps herself around him. He turns; he tries to manoeuvre his body so that she can spoon him. She has to lift him a little, but she does it; she nestles up to his back, puts one arm under his neck and the other tightly around his chest, tucks her legs into the backs of his, pushes her face into his spine. Ahh, she says.

She feels him relax into her. She feels her body relax, sympathetically, as if it's been clenched for months. It's like some warm fluid beginning to flow after long cessation through her own spine and limbs. Ahh. Ahh.

There's a beeping, and the nurse in pink comes in.

Pulled your wire loose? he asks, neutrally. He reattaches something behind Mandalay. The beeping stops.

Owen's wearing pajama pants, only. She can feel Owen's body heat, his familiar texture in his bare back and chest. She can smell his familiar smell. She feels their deep connection, mother to child. He came from her body; they shared blood, nutrients, a system for carrying away waste. He had been the more physical of the twins, always lying on her, plastering himself to her, when he was little. Even now – even recently – an enthusiastic hugger.

Her son. Her flesh and blood. They lie, skin to skin.

MANDALAY SITS BY OWEN'S BED. She rummages in her shoulder bag. Look what I've brought. He's not interested. A couple of weeks ago she could catch his interest: she brought in the treasures of his childhood, his stuffed bear, his recorder, his Tamagotchi, small toys to encourage him to focus his eyes and attention and memory. He'd always brightened, when she said *look what I've brought,* and that had been a hopeful sign. And now he's jaded, he's been through them all, the forgotten pleasures. He has exhausted them.

He has outgrown his toys, a second time.

She has brought something today, anyway, though when she rummages in her bag, she can't locate the object by feel, and stabs a finger on some unidentified sharpness. She begins to extract items one by one, to lay them on the blue woven blanket that covers Owen's legs and lower torso. Wallet, keys, glasses in their battered case, ancient granola bar in a creased wrapper.

Owen eyes the granola bar.

I don't think I'm supposed to give that to you, she says. Choking hazard.

Pens, notebook, change, loose paperclips, bus tickets.

Here it is. It's Owen's old phone, cracked screen, worn-off number keys and all. He'd left it in a drawer when he got a new one. It doesn't work as a phone anymore, has neither phone minutes nor data, but all of his favourite music from when he was sixteen is still on it. She has brought earbuds, as well. She plugs them in, turns on the phone, puts the wired buds in Owen's ears.

He listens, grins.

She holds out the device, tells him to take it, which he does, swatting at and catching it as if he is wearing catcher's mitts. He listens for a few minutes, and she watches him listen, imagines the music, with its freight of associated memories, seeping into his brain, waking up synapses.

Then he swipes the earbuds from his head with a rough, impatient motion, slaps the phone across the bed.

No? she says. Not that music?

Owen shakes his head, with more vehemence, less control than before.

Okay, she says. She feels tears sting the inside passage of her sinus. She can't give in. Can't indulge her own disappointment. She puts away the phone. Owen turns his body back to the wall.

She says: I saw the oddest thing on the way here.

Owen moves his face almost imperceptibly toward her.

It was near the corner of King Edward and Knight, she says. Do you remember? There's a kind of makeshift kiosk there, with the corrugated metal roof and front, in the alley?

He looks puzzled, but his eyes are alert. He's listening. Taking it all in. And with those words, *alcove, makeshift, corrugated*, she's pulling him back to consciousness, hauling him up from the deep.

Where the kite store is, she says. Where you caught the bus from karate class. Do you remember the kite store? You saved up your money for a kite, and you bought the dragon one. The most extravagant and complicated one they had.

Kite, he says. I lost the kite.

He had lost the kite, the first time he had flown it. It had flown beautifully, breathtakingly. And then it had wavered and plunged into the high top of a tree near the perimeter of the park, the only tall tree around, and had stuck there, immune to any coaxing or tugging.

Hauling him up into pain and frustration, into awareness of his own limitations and loss, possibly. Hauling him back not only to consciousness, but to suffering.

She says: There was something funny this morning in the kiosk next to the kite store. You remember that the metal front doesn't go all of the way to the pavement? You and Aidan always wanted to peer under it. This morning, I glanced at it and saw dozens of pairs of bare legs. Men's legs, women's legs. All crowded together, behind the corrugated front.

A grin. He's following, catching the image.

It was only after a moment or so, she says, that I realized it was a bunch of mannequins being stored.

Owen lets out a huff of laughter. He meets her eye. Too much, he says.

Too much.

I know, she says. But what can you do?

34

CLEO SAYS: I talk to everyone in the company. I start with the people with the least say. I talk to the cleaners. I take notes. I take video of people working and moving. I'll take video of you during meetings and at your computers, as you enter and leave the building, go to the restroom, eat lunch, talk in the hallways.

Doesn't that take a lot of time, the bearded one – Zack – asks. The other, Lucas, asks: Wouldn't that create privacy issues? The two men she's talking to are scarcely older than Olivia, she thinks. They had an idea for a software app, in university. They designed it. They've built a tech start-up around it, which grew, and now they have outgrown their premises. They are still figuring out how to run a business.

The program that the two young men created allows specialty food shops and restaurants to source and order food from local producers. It's called Connect-40, the number standing for the tradition of the "back forty," they'd explained, and also for the 40-kilometre radius inside which their clients mostly source the food products. The start-up has grown wildly, the partners tell her. There are now forty employees. They onboard every other week, one partner says. The employees are almost all under thirty. A woman of around Cleo's age turns out to be one of the partner's moms, called in to train the HR department, which has been hired in one go.

Cleo explains that she has software that blurs faces. She doesn't record sound, only sound levels. She tells them she can do her filming in a day. She'll come back if there's a day in the week in which their pattern shifts dramatically. She's learned that Fridays, in these tech start-ups, often involve different routines – group brainstorming sessions, lunch brought in, games.

She explains that she builds the space around the way people function in the business.

I build well-functioning biomes, she says. Not monuments.

That's her byline. She'll sometimes say *stages*, instead of biomes. Or, occasionally, *machines*. She likes the word *machine*, for its alliteration, but most clients don't respond well to it. The exceptions are high-powered professional couples with lots of kids. Blended families. They like the word *machine*. They get it: a house that works, like a well-functioning machine, actually frees everyone. There's more creative time, more leisure time. More time to be human, she pitches it.

The thing is, the bearded man, Zack says, it's going to be temporary. We're still growing. We'll likely need a bigger space in a couple of years.

It's a common story, with the tech start-ups. They've rapidly outgrown their original premises, and, like hermit crabs, are looking to trade up. There isn't the cash flow, yet, to lease a really large space. They are cautious, these young entrepreneurs. They're old enough to have seen the recession of '08; young enough not to have seen the ones of '90 and '83. They do not see things as cyclical; they do not yet believe that even if they lose all of their money, they will soon retrieve it, and then some. Cleo likes that prudency. She approves of it.

She says: I work with your budget. Whatever you can afford. She has to keep reminding herself to use the present tense, rather than the future, to convey the idea that she is already engaged in the work.

No monuments, Lucas says.

THEY'RE WALKING AROUND the space that they are going to lease: a warehouse, built in the late eighties, far enough east that it will be affordable, but only a few blocks from the rapid transit, and with workable neighbours: a cidery, a flooring showroom. She has discussed, already, the drawbacks of noise and smells and transport traffic. The young men are sanguine. The Realtor, who has let them in, is professional: he hangs back, doesn't interject. He hasn't worked with Cleo before. He says little. The warehouse is a cavernous box, nearly windowless. It's not apparent how it could be turned, easily, into desirable office space.

So, you see, Zack says. It's not really an office space.

But we don't really want a conventional office space, Lucas says.

But we do want a place where people can work happily.

Cleo says: It's a blank canvas. That's what's good about it. We can make whatever we can dream up.

And in our budget? Zack asks.

In your budget.

We're interviewing a couple more designers, Luke says. He says it reluctantly, though — he's young enough that he hasn't learned yet to dissemble completely.

Cleo nods. She says: Can I book a date to make a visit to your current space, to film? And for a presentation? She knows that there is competition.

CLEO WORKS THROUGH THE PROTOCOL she has developed. *Who are we?* she asks the employees, individually and collectively, and then collates the responses into an upbeat, somewhat flattering statement. *We are a group of millennials with undergrad and graduate degrees. We are excellent problem solvers. We are good at data analysis and digital systems and their interfaces. We are global citizens. We are committed to social and environmental change.*

Cleo looks at the files of travel photos on her computer. She looks at grand spaces: famous railway stations, plazas, cathedrals.

She researches wiring and Wi-Fi options. She runs calculations on girder strength, on air currents, on the tensile properties of a variety of plastics and fabrics that can be produced in large sheets. She looks up floating floor systems and track systems.

She talks to Sam and Olivia, asks them what kind of office space they'd like to be working in. She is, of course, interviewing the whole cast of Connect-40, but she thinks her children will be more honest with her, and Sam is really a different generation than the millennials in the workplace now – a Zoomer, Olivia says. Sam's generation is the future.

Cleo wants to present the Connect-40 group with the future.

Olivia says: Everything will be paperless. And there are still too many cords and cables.

Sam says: There won't be offices. We will work from home.

She draws up plans on her AutoCAD. A raised floor, supported by steel joists, of prefab sheets of a new product made locally of recycled tires. It's a breakthrough: she can run all of the wiring and HVAC under the floor, so fixed walls won't be necessary. The floor product is resilient and soundproof, and rigid enough to support vinyl plank flooring or linoleum.

Moveable walls; storage space that can be reconfigured; vintage, recycled chairs and work surfaces from Mogun's *Nordsøen* line. No monuments.

For the first time in as long as she can remember, she is taking on something that she has never done before, and she doesn't, at this moment, know how it will turn out. She is making it up as she goes along. She is undertaking something for which she has no interior maps, and she understands that it is the interior that is required here.

Everyone now has access to the same markets, the same images, the surface information. What she must create might not even be original, but perhaps it will be original enough.

SHE PASSES THE partners their headsets, slides the hand controls into their hands. She checks the system, presses start. A lightly-accented woman's voice says: *Hi, Zack; hi, Lucas. Welcome to the new workspace of Connect-40.*

From the warehouse girders are suspended translucent sails, each about ten square metres, each sprayed with transparent inks in representations of pearly Rococo clouds and blue sky. Among the sails, which form a kind of fragmented, articulated dome, hang pendant lights, warm LED, of course, placed so that there is neither harsh glare nor dim corners. The sails are baffles, softening the sound and light issues of the warehouse space. The effect of the diffused lighting is a softer, slightly warmer version of the light of the natural world, on, say, a sunny April day.

A large central reception space and concourse. A few curving banquettes in the greys and teals and oranges of the *Nordsøen* series. Folding chairs padded with materials in the same colours, easy to set up for larger meetings. Through this space the staff will move, in curving pathways delineated by the banquettes and the reception pulpit, as they perform their tasks, congregate, address their bodily needs.

Individual work pods open at the perimeters of the great domed space: made of interchangeable, interlocking panels, and each possessing a door that can be transparent or translucent at the touch of a button, each with a customizable desk top, computer space, and ergonomic chairs. Everything is on lockable wheels. Chairs and small laptop tables can be moved.

Then a common work area with large tables and a giant HD screen. A second common area, this one with floor mats, zafu cushions, lighting on a dimmer, a table with built-in power stations and coffee holders, both. The table is stored in, and rises, at the touch of a button, from a hatch beneath the floor; can be paused at knee level, suitable for the zafu cushions, or raised to normal table height. (The second common room is the only really fancy part of the design, except maybe for the individually programmable HD screens. Cleo has had one programmed to show cat photos; another has rock-climbing shots.)

A lunch room Mogun-style, with counter space and bistro tables separated by planter boxes and small wall fountains. Non-gendered washrooms.

The work spaces and individual pods are like clusters of stars, arranged in a spiral from the central concourse. And over all, the dome, with its panoply of cloud formations, like the domes of Chartres, of St. Paul's, but displaying not dreams of heaven or the drama of myth, but rather, the infinite and ineffable sky, with its nurturing, life-giving light. The sky, which is time, not fractured into the fragments of human memory, but limitless, contiguous, containing every possibility, every connection, all of the matter and energy that is or may be.

And every item in the plan recyclable and reusable.

She doesn't need to make monuments. Perhaps the world, at this point of time, does not need any more monuments, which is to say assertions of power, of greatness, of dominion. Perhaps right now the world needs for each of its seven billion inhabitants to live and work in comfort and dignity and circumspection, in spaces that welcome all, that respect both inhabitants and the natural environment, that lift the spirit in ways that do not trample others.

No monuments, but space, and light, and a shining, transitory passage through the world that is.

35

THEY WILL GO TO BED TONIGHT, Mandalay thinks.

Duane has taken to dropping by, on a couple of hours' notice, with the makings of dinner. Gourmet dinner, of course. Fresh pasta; chanterelles; duck confit; cave-aged Gruyère; seven-dollar baguettes, intense little cherry pastries. He sharpens her kitchen knives. He brings with him an enamelled cast-iron Dutch oven, a saucier, an omelette pan, and leaves them at her place.

When he arrives, Mandalay generally puts away whatever she's been working on and makes herself into Duane's sous-chef. Duane roots around in her cupboards and fridge, asks her to chop fennel and shallots, to separate an egg, to uncork the wine. She performs these minor chores, or she sits on a stool at the counter and drinks wine while he cooks up a meal that is always, always perfect.

He is doing this for his own pleasure, she understands. Something in him needs to prepare and eat an exceptional meal with someone. He needs to focus tightly on something physical, something creative.

And perhaps something in him needs to perform cooking rites in this kitchen, this house. It is half his house, of course, though he has never lived in it. But he has always disputed the ownership, always wanted to profit more from it, always wanted Mandalay to cooperate in making money from it, from the home in which she has raised their children. It's as if by cooking these meals, taking over the kitchen, he is exercising his owner's rights.

He is colonizing the house or the kitchen, perhaps. The house or herself. She wonders if on principle she should decline, but she finds she does not mind. Ten years ago, she would have minded; she would not have wanted to give Duane this space. But her sense of space has shifted cataclysmically. Walls that had seemed necessary, indispensable, have been torn open, crumbled to nothing.

And now she is sleeping with Duane, again, occasionally, after nearly twenty years.

She can tell if they are going to have sex fairly soon after he has arrived. Some signal passes between them, even as Duane is slipping off his shoes, hanging up his jacket on the row of knobs in the hallway. Something she knows from the way he moves, perhaps. Something she can read in the set of his shoulders or the angle of his head, even before he glances at her. And that then is confirmed by a look in his eye – a look that is a question, but more than that, something between a request and an offering. Whatever the look is – and it is both complex and fleeting – it does something to her, flips a switch in her brain, so that she's thinking *Yes? Yes,* all through dinner, gradually warming up, her synapses lining up and firing, fueling themselves on stored pleasure-memories, accelerating their activity just slightly over the course of the meal, so that a mild awareness heightens her senses and her attention.

Yes, she thinks, as Duane enters her kitchen, carrying his reusable shopping bag, a bottle of French wine; yes, they will have sex, later.

She rationalizes that she enjoys the little bump in social activity at the end of the week, the surprise and sensory pleasure of the food. She does not go out much, these days. She avoids the parties and other socializing with students and colleagues. It is too much effort, and at some level, it seems irrelevant. The truth is, she can hardly bear to be with anyone else right now. She doesn't want to talk about whether the department should order another enlarger or a large-scale printer with this year's capital expenditures budget. She doesn't want to go out for drinks with the visiting artist. She doesn't want to go to the visiting artist's lecture and slide show, either, though she does out of professional duty. She particularly doesn't want to listen to her colleague Celine giving her lunchroom updates on her step-children's latest outrages. She doesn't care. She cannot care. She can't bear to make small talk, or to allow herself to be distracted, or to interest herself in anyone else's life. She can't bear to be with anyone for whom Owen's accident hasn't been the ultimate, defining event of the past few months.

Only Duane, it seems, shares her grief. Aidan too, of course, but he is far away, at university, now: Mandalay and Duane have agreed (uncharacteristically) on this, that Aidan must pursue his studies, his life, and not be at home living in the shadow of Owen's accident. Only Duane now hangs on the day-by-day visits, has his day made hopeful or dismal by the reports on Owen. By Owen's ability to sit, unsupported, for two and a half minutes, to clench a fist, to bring a spoon to his own mouth. Only Duane can say, on the bad days: But think about how much progress he has made in the last six weeks, Mandalay. Or on the good days. Look at that. That's such a milestone.

Duane has become better at remembering where things are in her kitchen, and she has become better at collaborating with him. Don't get too used to this, she reminds herself. But her caution is purely in her head. She has begun to listen for Duane's Friday or Saturday afternoon texts, to remember to buy things like garlic and butter and flat-leaf parsley.

She has been almost waiting for him, this late afternoon. After working she has washed her floors and showered, and spent the last couple of hours in the bay window seat, with the sun slanting in obliquely, drying her hair, reading a book on new figurative painting, drinking licorice tea. Now he is in her kitchen, emptying a bag of littleneck clams into the sink, unloading a box of linguini, the sound of maracas, onto the countertop. He has brought bread. Does she have lemons? Is there a little of the Pernod left?

They consult. It is pleasant, like bathing in a warm pool. It's pleasant to be fed.

If it happened more than once a week, she would likely get quite fat.

Duane's groceries for one of these meals likely cost more than she spends on groceries in a week.

It can't last, can it? Does she hope that it will last? She must not get attached to it.

While she sits in the papasan chair, stroking Clytemnestra, Duane scrubs the clams with a brush he has brought for the purpose. He pours a bottle of white wine into the big pot. (There's twenty-five dollars, Mandalay thinks.) He crushes garlic cloves with the weight of his fist on a flat knife blade and slips the toes from their papery skins. He drops the clams into the simmering liquid in the pot, plop plop, and Mandalay remembers that the clams are animals, about to be cooked alive, and winces. She knows this is craven hypocrisy. She loves to eat clams.

And you like clams too, don't you? she murmurs to Clytemnestra, who has become so attached to her, who follows her everywhere, as she moves around the house, who watches her with an unblinking yellow gaze that is so kindly, so benevolent (for a cat) that she half wonders if, in fact, it is possible that Belinda's soul had chosen that vessel, on its flight.

Not really. If any soul were able to resist the beckoning of the doorway to rebirth, to instead escape the cycle of samsara, of endless rebirth and suffering, it would be Belinda's.

And Clytemnestra is appreciating Mandalay's excessive kindness and attentiveness, that is all.

Did you see Owen today? Duane asks, and she says that yes, she had visited him in the morning. Owen had not been doing particularly well. He had been surly, unwilling to get up, to undertake the morning rituals of washing and eating. He had let porridge drool from his mouth. He had pushed away the graphic novel she had brought him. And then when she had to go, he had clung to her hand and cried, had looked at her with frustration and pain, and underneath, his old self, his full consciousness, the full intelligence and awareness he'd had before the accident. He had been *there*, fully there, her son, Owen, and he had clung to her hands and cried.

She doesn't tell Duane all of this: she just says that Owen had been low energy, struggling.

She sets the table, moving off stacks of papers, wiping down the burnished maple, putting out placemats. She places bowls and plates, mismatched but beautiful, ones she has collected over the years from craft fairs. She polishes the wineglasses on a clean towel.

Owen had not been doing well, this morning. But Duane says: It's not linear. There are going to be lots of rough days. But look how far he has come.

Duane carries the bowl of linguini and clams to the table, pours more wine, turns off the overhead fixture. They sit. The candlelight gives a patina of comfort to the table.

Mandalay's niece Olivia takes pictures of dinners she has made or eaten, of beautifully set and laden tables, and posts them online. That fad is the height of something – Mandalay does not know what. But some occasions do deserve to be recorded, she will concede.

This is nice, Duane says.

Duane has visited Owen today, as well. He had caught Owen at a better time than Mandalay had. He'd been able to take Owen for a wheelchair stroll around the ward. Owen had had some conversations. He had so many friends, in the hospital. Everyone seemed to know him. Duane had been able to talk to the physiotherapist, who showed him a graph of Owen's gripping strength over the past six weeks. The therapist had been very encouraging. He said Owen was tracking with his gaze almost normally, and could remember a simple sequence of directions.

What do you talk about with Owen? Mandalay asks.

Duane looks uncomfortable. Well, he says. It might sound strange, but it's all that he's interested in. Hockey.

Duane! No.

He likes me to read him the scores. Who played, the night before. The goals, the assists, the plays. I've got TSN on my phone.

Duane.

He lights up, Duane says. Mandalay, he lights up.

It's ridiculous. Hockey. After what happened.

She hasn't yet seen Owen excited about anything.

He says: I was able to talk to Owen's orthopedic surgeon, while I was at the hospital. Did you see her?

No, Mandalay had been too early.

I think she will be calling you. But briefly, she mentioned that she wants to have a discussion about discharging Owen. She says his progress is very good. Her words: very good.

Very good news can be shocking, as well. Mandalay's breath stops; her heart stumbles. Her eyes sting.

He can leave the hospital? He can come home?

He can leave the hospital, Duane says.

It's such good news, she can hardly take it in.

Duane says, Hey, no crying, and reaches across to touch the corner of the dish towel to her cheek. It smells of onions.

She says: It's just…

I know, I know, he says. He turns his gaze to his plate. Why don't you pour some wine? he says.

Oh, Duane, she thinks. How diligently he had worked, in those months that they were dating, and in the years since, worked to avoid emotional intimacy. How meticulously he had set up walls, how thoroughly he had plucked out every ingrowth, plastered over every crack that might weaken his fortress.

He had been an assiduous lover, in their short time as a couple:

attentive, adept. He had always paid for their entertainments, and had taken her out for marvellous dinners, concerts, trips. He had shown her a good time, had taken care of her. But he had always made it clear that he was not interested in anything long term or committed or domestic.

She had not thought he would be involved with the twins. He had bought the house, retaining half interest, for her to live in with the boys – his lifetime contribution, he had made it clear. But then he had become involved. He'd become interested in the boys, when they were still quite small – around four or five. He'd wanted to direct their lives.

She should have resisted more. But he had offered the boys things she couldn't – better schools, trips, lessons. They had *liked* Duane. They had liked his gifts.

He had lowered his walls with them, she thinks. Just a little. Not so much as to be vulnerable, until, of course, this last year.

And with her? He still retains a certain distance. He makes her elaborate dinners, and eats with her, and then, usually, goes home. He does not let himself be vulnerable. Even in bed: physically and emotionally intimate, but not vulnerable.

They linger over the dinner and wine in the new way they have, and then Duane takes their empty dishes to the kitchen and puts them in the sink to soak and then finds her, takes her hands, kisses her.

She should resist; how can she continue to do this? But she wants the comfort of sex, of Duane's familiar body holding her in her bed. Wants it so much that she can't say no, can't stand on pride or dignity or even disapproval. She gives herself into his arms; she opens to him; she leads him to her bed.

They undress without hurry, but with intent, holding each other's gaze, as they have always done. Duane curls into the bed; she slides in beside him; he pulls her closer and lifts her legs over his.

Duane touches her as if her body were his own, she realizes. Not with ownership but with focus and responsiveness, as if his pleasure came from revisiting the shape and texture of hers, and from her responses to his touch. As if her body's lines and surfaces and responses themselves were the source of his pleasure, rather than the stimulation of his own body. He is the only one of her lovers, of the various men she has been with in her life, who has given her this sense.

She likes their lovemaking, which is both familiar and unfamiliar, and above all, intense, focussed, all-consuming. They are connected, deeply, for a moment; they are transported from ordinary life. It feels like a refuge. It feels like an altered state.

They cling to each other, in bed, as if they have been in danger of drowning. As if they can only save themselves by saving each other.

She has been waiting all of these years for him to speak his heart, but here it is. It has always been here.

36

CLIFF'S FRIEND KEN settles himself in his usual chair at the café table and laces his fingers together under his belly, as if cradling a sleeping sheepdog on his lap. He reminds Cliff of his foster father, Mr. Giesbrecht, a little. And also of his late stepfather, Darrell. There is a kind of expectant silence around the table. Ken nods, then speaks.

The leaders of the world, he says, have hidden motivations.

There are nods all around the table: nods that begin at the gut; forward inclinations of the whole upper body; slow thoughtful wags of jaws; minimalist torques of the neck.

The leaders of the world, Ken says again, have hidden motivations.

That is likely true, Cliff thinks, although he's not sure what Ken means. Motivations for what? Hidden from whom? But the others do not ask Ken to explain, and Cliff thinks it's too early for him to put his oar in. Better to listen and learn, at first.

He notices Ken's gaze on him, though, a somewhat quizzical look and nods his own head slightly, so as not to draw attention to himself. This seems to satisfy Ken.

The working man, Ken says, does not dream of what goes on in the halls of power. We are sheep. Blind sheep. We are complicit in our own blindness.

There's something about Ken's voice. Well, it's a nice deep voice, with that sort of rumble, that chest rumble, that you can hear in the voices of singers and radio announcers sometimes. But more than that, his words have a kind of rhythm to them, like he is reading the Bible or some old poetry.

The working man, like us, Ken continues.

Cliff guesses he means working man in a different way than the obvious, because none of the guys around the table at the café are actually working. The rest haven't said, but he knows that Lyle and Gord are on disability, same as Cliff himself, and Ernie and Pete have been laid off and are on EI. But obviously, it's ten in the morning and they are sitting around a table in the Wooden Spoon.

The working man is powerless to know, Ken says, what they've agreed upon amongst themselves.

More nods. We're all puppets, Ernie says.

We never see the strings, Ken says. We swallow what we're told. They've held the reins for all our working lives.

A silent parliament, Ken says. A stranglehold on truth. A masterpiece of lies.

His sonorous voice rolls on.

Amen, Gord says.

They're selling out our culture. Making it a shame to be a traditional family, or white. A shame to stay married or have kids. Make it easier for everyone to get paid to stay home, Ernie says.

Yep, Pete says. Nobody having kids no more. Just the coloured races. They're all having seven, eight kids. White Canadians averaging point five. Young people are too lazy or selfish these days. Only the Asians, the Africans are reproducing. If you understand mathematics, you see that in one generation, two, they will have multiplied hundreds of times; they will have taken over. And what does the government do? Lets them into the country, gives them jobs. White man can't get a government job anymore, and that's a fact.

How's your business doing? Gord asks Cliff. Them Pakis still running it into the ground?

Cliff feels a pang. He shouldn't have told the group what he did, that his business had been sold, or seventy-five percent interest in it, to the Punjabi brothers. It's not like it matters, who they are, as far as he can see. They have kept the business going, now, longer than he had. They have been very accommodating to him, too, about his disability.

It's not Paki, he says. They're from India.

Gord makes a noise in his throat like someone hawking up, and Ken says: It's all one nation, Clifford, united under the Allah.

Cliff is pretty sure that's not correct, but he doesn't want to draw the scorn of the men around the table, as he has in the past, for his ignorance of historical or political facts.

He has known these guys for years, from the café. They would do anything for him. They helped him move, after Veronika moved out and he had to sell the townhouse.

Ken had come over and fixed some things around the apartment. He'd got some double-faced tape and stuck down the gaping carpet seam, where the wheelchair got stuck, replaced a fuse in the old range and some burned-out bulbs, got some drapes from someone's garage sale and hung them up. He drops by often to see if there is anything he can do for Cliff.

Anyway, the guys at the coffee shop just like to talk. They are smarter than Cliff; they know more than him. Once or twice he'd questioned them about things that didn't make sense or sound right, but they are always able to point out facts he didn't know.

They point out things for him to read on the internet.

I tell you what, Pete says. The coloured races, they are always inferior to the white. It's scientific fact. They are lower on the evolutionary scale.

Evolution! Ernie says. That's another damned liberal lie. I read that it's all bunk. Someone found a leaf wedge in a piece of rock that supposedly had layers dating back billions of years. One leaf, cutting through all of those layers! Now doesn't that disprove it?

Are you saying you don't believe in evolution? Cliff asks, forgetting to lie low.

He hasn't really listened before. He has not thought about the rift between what the guys have been saying and what the world is like to him, Cliff. If there's one thing Cliff knows, it's how the earth formed and grew, how the billions of creatures on it have come to be. He hasn't just read every book he could find and watched every nature documentary made. He has *felt* it, in his observation of growing plants, in the way leaves uncurl and flow into being; in the way the earth tilts and wobbles and creates time and climate; in the way the soil holds a megacity of microbes all interacting with one another and the fungi and nematodes and earthworms and the roots of the plants that it anchors.

He thinks of Maria and Delores, the Filipina women who look after his mom, Crystal. They're sisters; they share a house in Powell River and look after each other's kids and take turns driving or bussing the long route into Butterfly Lake. He's watched them with Crystal, seen how they treat her. They care.

And then suddenly he has had enough. Enough for one day. He can't listen to their talk anymore. It has soured his stomach; it has soured the day.

Maybe more than the day. He wonders why he keeps meeting with them. There is something wrong with their talk, he can see that. It's sour. It's like sour soil: nothing can live or thrive in it.

They are souring the world, these men, with their ugly talk.

He starts to push to his feet.

You ready to go? Ken says. Wait, I'll come with you.

No, Cliff says; no, I'm okay. He has parked his truck a little way down the plaza lot, but he can make it now, going slowly.

Ken gets up and stands by Cliff's chair, as if to give him a hand. Then he takes off his hat, suddenly places it on Cliff's head.

Cliff gets up, using his knees, as the physiotherapist has been nagging him to do. He straightens his back. Oof. Oof. The cramping pain shooting from his back muscles throughout his body. The wrench of nausea in his gut. He breathes through it. He grips the table and breathes.

When he's on his feet he lifts off the hat and holds it politely toward Ken. No point in not being polite, is there? Then he turns, carefully, and begins the walk away from the table.

THE MOUNTIES HAD GIVEN HIM the name of a forestry consultant based in Powell River, and he calls her to come in, assess the damage, make suggestions. When she arrives, he sees that she's a woman of about his age. She says that she grew up just outside Powell River, that she has two children, in their teens, that she has recently moved back to the Sunshine Coast. She and Cliff talk for a long time, in the raw clearing of Cliff's forest. Elise, her name is. She's tall, a little taller than Cliff, with a long heavy braid of hair, nut-brown threaded with some silver. Her face is free of makeup; she's wearing real jeans, not the skin-tight kind, and boots, and a grey-green T-shirt that matches her eyes, with a plaid flannel shirt over it.

She says: I think you can let it become meadow. That will be a sort of natural progression. You'll get some Ribes moving in – that's currants and gooseberry – and some hazel. And then some alder and fir. The cedar will come back, but not for a few years.

She stands by the bier of toppled yellow cedars and seems to mourn them, as he does.

She says: You need nurse logs, but not five of them. You might as well sell them on. Or donate them, if you like. There's a project building houses, on Musqueam land.

He thinks he would like to donate the trees, yes.

She says: There's some damage you should mediate, so you don't get a monoculture of fireweed. You'll want to go in with a hand shovel, break up the soil where the heavy equipment has compressed it. Take out the cedar chips and trimmings, as they'll inhibit your growth. If you have the time and patience, you could transplant some native species individually from more abundant spots, dig them in.

He thinks he might have the time and patience.

She says: This is a sweet piece of forest. It would be so good to leave it as it is. Home to a complex ecosystem, a web of trees and other plants, of fungi and animals from the microscopic to the large and charismatic. She says it's a connective piece between two much larger forested areas – a channel so that animals can move from one place to the other.

Cliff feels, talking to her, that something long asleep in him is awakening. He thinks of the nature documentaries he used to watch; of the small pieces of land he had always tried to protect, when he had his own landscaping business. Of the small perfect forest that he had tended on a client's land, noting the wildflowers and shrubs, the mosses and ferns, that grew and receded and grew again.

He needs to be healthy again, to find a way to get back to work, to persuade the Singh brothers that he can do something useful. His affinity for plants is rising in his veins; it's sending tendrils through his arms; pushing at his fingertips. He wants to be working again. No, he wants his own business, in which he can do something different. No lawn mowing; no hedge-trimming, but rather, gardening solely with indigenous plants. Restoring ecosystems in yards large and small, all over the city. Inviting back the rainforest that once covered that western point of land.

37

THE FIRST THING OLIVIA SAYS IS: I'm not staying.

What?

I'm only here for a week, to help you get the house ready to stage. Then I'm going back to Toronto.

Have you got a job?

It takes *ages*, Olivia says, to get a job in environmental economics.

So what are you going to do?

I'll find a job. Retail or whatever. For the time being.

Okay, Cleo says. But you could do that here. And in Toronto you'll have to pay rent.

Yes, but I wouldn't be living with you, in your apartment, would I? Olivia says. So, I'd have to rent anyway. And it's my decision.

Have you got a place to move into? I thought you were shipping things back?

You don't need to worry about it, Olivia says. You don't need to make a big deal of it.

Am I making a big deal? Cleo asks.

Olivia says, Yes, you are.

They are in Olivia's big downstairs bedroom. Cleo has provided a number of large containers — big plastic tubs, packing boxes — as well as packing tape and labels and big black garbage bags for Olivia to use to sort her belongings. She has helped Olivia pull her stuff out of cupboards and closets, and now Olivia sits on a step stool surrounded by it all — the material stuff of her childhood. Storage tubs spill out spangled dance costumes, mounds of stuffed toys, childhood books, dolls and puppets and building toys, sheaves of notebooks and birthday cards and journals and scrapbooks and artwork.

The evidence of a privileged, enriched childhood.

She has asked Olivia to sort out her things, because there is quite a lot, more than they probably want to store, and because it seems respectful to let Olivia do it herself. But now her daughter sits there, scrolling through her phone, texting, and not making any headway. They have had a little nostalgia-fest, looking at Olivia's tiny dance costumes, starting from her preschool years – the neon Lycra jumpsuits, the tulle and ribbon roses and marabou-decorated velvet. Olivia has pulled some rather battered stuffies from a tub and held them up critically. But now she is stalled.

Do you need help? Cleo asks. She herself works best alone, especially when doing things like sorting, but she knows Olivia works best collaboratively. She likes company, interaction when she has a chore to do – even one that would seem to require a lot of concentration, like essay-writing.

No, Olivia says.

It's a surprise, Cleo says, trying to keep her voice light, casual. You told me you were planning to move back to Vancouver after you defended your thesis.

Maybe you just assumed that?

I don't think so, Cleo says. I think we had several conversations about the summer, and specifically, a month ago, you asked me to transfer money to your account to pay for your plane ticket and shipping your things back.

A *month* ago, yeah, maybe, Olivia says. Anyway, it was the same price basically for the round trip, so I got that instead. I'll pay you back when I get a job, if the money is important to you.

I doubt you'll have anything left after paying rent from a minimum wage job, Cleo says.

I'll manage, Olivia says.

There's something in the way Olivia says the word *manage*. A slight hesitation, an infinitesimal catch.

Olivia's pronunciation of that one word would have told her something was up, if she hadn't already been alerted by the gratuitous rudeness.

But Olivia won't tell her the truth at this point. The aggression and defensiveness tell her that.

She says: You might have let me know. I thought you would be here for the fall, and looking for a job here, and I made plans around that.

I never asked you to.

Cleo is pretty sure that the conversations had been clearly based on the premise that Olivia would be moving in with Cleo for a while, until she had a job, was able to get a shared place, at least. Even an entry-level professional job wouldn't pay well enough to cover Vancouver rents, but they had talked about Olivia finding work, probably in the investment arm of a bank, and then looking around for a roommate with whom to share. In the meantime, Cleo had said, Olivia could have her spare bedroom in her new condo. The condo she will buy, once she has sold her house. She has already rented a large storage unit, so that Olivia can have the space.

She has explained all of this. They have discussed it.

I don't think you listen very well, Olivia says, now.

Cleo holds herself still for a moment, does not answer. It is true, perhaps. Not in the way Olivia means it, but true that she is not good at hearing what Olivia is saying, behind her hostile back-talk, her anxiety-driven accusations.

She says, only, I wish you were staying for more than a week. I miss you. I've hardly seen you, these past six years.

I made *so* many trips back here, Olivia says.

Very short ones, Cleo thinks, but she says, only: I miss you.

You are always busy, anyway, Olivia says.

Is that what this is about? Is Olivia angry because she feels Cleo is pushing her out? Pushing her away? But Olivia is always the first to take her leave. If Cleo books time off, clears her agenda in anticipation of Olivia's visits, she's left with blank time while Olivia goes out with friends.

She feels she must correct Olivia's statements. She has not been an absent or distant mother. That is one thing she has not been, and it's unfair to be accused of it, as well as disturbing to think that Olivia has that misconception. But if she contradicts what Olivia says, their argument will just escalate. She will not do it, this time. She will not participate in letting the conversation escalate to a full-blown argument. She will not.

They are too fragile, both of them; the moment is too fraught. Something might break, irreparably.

She averts her face, blinks back tears.

I need to go out soon, Olivia says, abruptly.

But we need to get the sorting done, Cleo says. You're only here for a few days, you say. And the Realtor is coming next week.

Olivia says, abruptly: Throw it all out. I don't want any of it.

Cleo sighs. Of course they aren't going to throw it out. All of Olivia's keepsakes, her childhood treasures.

I'm serious, Olivia says. I don't want any of it. I'm not taking it back with me. I'll never have enough space for it.

I said I would store some of it, Cleo says. A reasonable amount. That's what parents do. I just won't have space for a dozen big boxes.

I don't want any of it, do you understand? Just throw it all out.

No, Cleo says. No. We can't do that. You'll want some of these things. You'll value some of these things, when you're older.

I have nowhere to put it, Olivia says. I'm not carting it around, when I'm basically homeless.

Oh, for goodness' sake, Cleo thinks.

And here's Sam, now, coming home from his job, slinging off his backpack as he starts across the room. She'll have to get Sam to pack up, too, but there's still time.

And Sam will be easy, as he always is. He'd been a difficult child: over-sensitive, clingy, fearful, until his teens, and then had become the dream son. He is practical, considerate, reasonable. He does not make her guess what he wants.

She and Sam can say anything to each other, and not be misunderstood. And he never asks for what is not possible to give.

Sam picks up one of the scruffy plush toys from the overflowing tub. Hey, it's Georgie, he says.

The past floods the room: Georgie, the stuffed otter without which, for many years, nothing happened, neither sleep nor car trips nor daily routines.

Olivia snatches it from him. Don't touch that!

Sam holds his hands up, palms out. I know, I know. He's laughing, and then Olivia laughs, too.

Cleo smiles. Olivia, she is about to say: Olivia, you're not going to toss Georgie away, are you? But she doesn't say it. She holds her tongue. It is not necessary to say it.

She says, instead: Who's hungry? Should we get some takeout, tonight? Should we do that? A big load of dishes from Sula?

She doesn't get up or bustle for her phone or the menu, when she says it: she sits where she is, on the small stool she has carried downstairs for the purpose of sitting and sorting items. She remains where she is, on the little stool, looking up at her tall grown children. Should we order in a feast? she asks.

And they look at her, and say yes, Mom, let's do that. Yes. And between them they decide on the food; they order it themselves; they pay for it themselves; they drive to the restaurant to pick it up.

They will survive, she thinks, while they are gone. They are grown, now: almost twenty-five and almost twenty-two. In spite of their reluctance to take on certain adult behaviours that she would expect, they are grown.

She remembers, now, Olivia's birth: how Olivia had fought against the contractions that would expel her into the world. How in the middle of one fierce contraction Cleo had looked down at her own naked swollen belly and had seen the outline of Olivia's back pushing up against the taut skin. And then how Olivia's pulse and oxygenation levels had dropped, dangerously, and how the nitrous oxide that was supposed to carry Cleo through the crushing pain of back labour could not help her; how she dropped to the bed and cried that she could not do it anymore. How Olivia had fought being born. And yet, they have photos taken minutes after her birth, in which she is gazing up at Trent, who held her first, and smiling placidly.

It's like there is something sticky, web-like, enveloping her and Olivia. Something that needs to be cleared away before Olivia can see her as just another human being. She can sense that Olivia feels that too — is fighting something she's not completely aware of. That Olivia's hostility is both a rude cry of her anxiety, of her fears of being unwanted, and at the same time the noise of her trying to break free of her role as daughter, as child.

Cleo wonders when Olivia will reach that magical age at which daughters are supposed to achieve emotional separation — are supposed to stop projecting all of their unhappiness onto their mothers, and move toward a friendly, adult relationship with them. It doesn't seem close to happening.

She wonders if there is something she has forgotten to do.

She hears the car in the driveway, the door opening, her children's voices. She climbs the stairs up to the living level, where her children have brought the food into the kitchen, the cartons and foil pans redolent with ancient spices, with bread and herbs, rice and pulses and meats. She moves, smiling, to the table, and waits as they hand around the placemats, the plates, the utensils, the warm steam-filled vessels of food.

Maybe it's something about the containers of richly sauced, spicy Indian food, the plenitude and comfort of it. Or maybe the beers they are all sharing, or the music that Sam has put on: eighties pop, which she had played for her children, danced to with them, when they were very young. Most of her music collection had been acquired in the 80s, when she was in her teens. The three of them sprawl now on the oversized orange sectional sofa, Olivia's feet in Sam's lap, her head on Cleo's lap, listening to (singing along with) Bonnie Tyler and Wham! and the Pointer Sisters. It's silly: none of them, Cleo suspects, would be caught dead doing this outside of this room, this circle of the three of them. Maybe it's that feeling of mutual silliness, mutual safety.

What is it that Olivia wants? she asks herself again, and this time there is an answer. Olivia had counted on moving home, on living in the house with Cleo and Sam, while she looked for a job in Vancouver. That is it. And being Olivia, she cannot say that: she cannot ask for what she most wants, if it requires someone else's generosity to gain it. She will never make herself vulnerable. She must deny that she ever wanted to move back, because Cleo has decided to sell the house and move into a small apartment where there is really not room for Olivia. A space that won't be Olivia's *home*, only a sufferance.

It is difficult for Cleo to imagine what Olivia is thinking: it has always been. Olivia is more like Trent, emotionally, as Sam is like Cleo.

Cleo says: If I kept the house, would you want to stay here? I'd need you to pay rent, of course. But it would be nice for me, not to have to sell the house.

She means that. She loves her house, has always loved it. It's just been a tight couple of years for her since she and Trent split, and she makes considerably less with her new business than she did working for Aeolus.

She gazes out, through the wide opening in the wall of glass sliders, at the trees and bushes that both shelter and are sheltered by the house. The tall Douglas firs, their branches a marbling of shadow and light, their trunks flickering with pine siskins. The pale swoop and call of one of a pair of grey jays that nest in the tops every summer. The reddening maple, the red berries of the mountain ash that will harbour waxwings through the winter. The sliver of ocean, blue and silver, in the distance.

It is a kind of labour, perhaps. If she can do it right, which is to say if she can wait it through with fortitude, wait out the pain, a new Olivia will be born, a young woman who has all of Olivia's best traits, her sweetness, her funniness, her agile mind — and who will also be amiable, who will be able to see Cleo as simply another human being, another woman, who is related, of her tribe, who is deserving of respect and affection and slack-cutting.

Or, not a new Olivia, but a new Cleo-and-Olivia. For it is the in-between that must be given birth to, the new web that will connect them.

What safety, what sense of security, does she still need to give her daughter, for them to reach that point? How does she need to change, herself?

How much more income would she need to be able to afford to keep the house on her own? It's not that much, actually. She would be house-poor, to borrow a term from her foster mother, Mrs. Giesbrecht, meaning people who spent all they had, more than they could afford, on a fancy house, and couldn't afford other things. She'd be house-poor. But she could afford it.

She might like to stay here, in her beautiful mid-century house, rather than move into a condo.

But more importantly, she wants another chance with Olivia. She wants a chance to repair and rebuild what was broken or unfinished, between them.

Olivia says: Of course I would pay rent. How much would you want?

Sam says: Wait. Are you going to stay here? I would want to stay also, then.

Cleo says: I thought you were looking forward to sharing a house with your friends?

Sam shrugs. If you're moving into a little apartment.

She can't think. Is this an option? Has she been about to make the wrong decision? Should she stay in the house, at least for a couple more years?

She says: I don't want to cook and clean for people. You'd have to pull your own weight, you two.

Olivia says: There will be three of us. My boyfriend Christian too.

So like Olivia to drop a last-minute bombshell.

Cleo sits up late with Olivia. They must discuss this person, how long he has been in Olivia's life (three years); what he is like, what he does. He is Dutch, Olivia says. He works in international aid. It doesn't matter where he lives, as long as it is near an international airport.

It is the boy Cleo intuited, when Olivia had wanted to leave school: she had wanted to go travelling with him. And Olivia had guessed, correctly, that she would lose him, if they were separated. Twenty-two is young for a relationship to survive separation, new friends, new adventures. But they have reunited; Olivia has found him again and won him back.

No thanks to Cleo and Trent, of course, that it has worked out, for it very nearly didn't, Olivia says. She very nearly lost him, the love of her life. He had gone travelling with somebody else. It is only chance that they got together again.

Cleo doesn't say: You should have told me. She does not know that she would have responded differently to Olivia's request to be funded for travel, three years ago. She doesn't know if she believes in the love of a life. And what kind of self-esteem did Olivia have,

Cleo would have asked, that she would pursue a man who could be satisfied with convenience, who would prefer her, but take up with another woman if she weren't available?

She doesn't say any of this. She sees, now, that in this web that will be built between herself and Olivia, certain things must not be said or asked, while other things must be voiced.

She says, you're welcome here, the two of you. You'll have to pay extra rent for him.

So she will not sell.

Outside, in the Douglas firs, a barred owl calls *Who cooks for you, who?*

What will I tell the real estate agent? she asks.

Mom, Olivia says, reprovingly. Have you signed a contract?

She has not, yet, no.

38

THE MEETING HAPPENS IN A hospital boardroom, a small room with a large table, a scuffed floor, a whiteboard, and surprisingly dusty windows through which the feeble January sun is not quite penetrating. There are six of them around a large table: Owen's therapists, a hospital administrator, Duane, Mandalay, Owen himself, his wheelchair positioned between her chair and Duane's.

The news is that Owen is ready to be discharged.

Oh, they are discharging him from the hospital too quickly. Why are they in such a rush? He has been doing well on the orthopedic ward. In spite of the humiliations and inconveniences of being a patient, he is doing well. He is healing. The best of neurosurgeons and orthopedic surgeons and therapists are available. She is able to come by the hospital every day; it's accessible from her house and the campus. She had thought he would stay here until he was walking, dressing himself, speaking. Owen's head bobs a little, above the neck brace; he has trouble swallowing his saliva; he can't get his tongue and lips and larynx to cooperate in forming sounds.

But they need the bed, they say. Owen is ready to move into something long term.

The hospital administrator asks Owen now if he is following the conversation. By BC law, Owen is still a minor. He's not yet nineteen. It's her decision; she's his custodial parent, for another few months. But it's good they are asking. She takes his hand, squeezes it. He squeezes back. His grip has improved a lot, the past week.

Owen nods jerkily, says yeah, and it's more of a word than a grunt today. He is getting so much better, where he is, where she can visit every day for a couple of hours. But he will be happy to go home. She knows that.

The neurological therapist, kitty-corner from her at the table, says now that he thinks Owen's speech difficulties, his lack of control over swallowing and head movement, is not the result of high spinal cord damage or brain damage after all, but of local impact from the fall, from bruising and interior bleeding and nerve damage in Owen's neck and throat area. They are going to try a new direction, in his therapy.

That is good news, right? she asks. If it's local damage? And he can have the therapist visit, right?

Good news, generally, the therapist had said, cautiously.

She thinks it is good news. Anything that is not spinal cord paralysis or brain damage is good news, right?

They want to move Owen to a different hospital, a rehabilitation hospital.

But I have a house, Mandalay says. It's in a great location. There's lots of room.

It's quite feasible, Mandalay says. We can easily bring in a hospital bed and all of the therapy equipment. I'll get a ramp made. There are only a few steps to the front door. I'll get a walk-in tub put in.

She looks sideways to Duane for confirmation. It will be easy to convert her house. He knows that. She has been awake for several nights, thinking it out. The logistics. Though she hadn't expected it to happen so soon. She's looked up online to see everything they would need, made itemized lists, priced out equipment and home care visits, researched grant money available.

The hospital rep, Lisa, says, Owen still needs twenty-four-hour care, at this point. We understand that you work...

Yes, Mandalay says, but I've interviewed four care aide businesses.

There's a lot of support available, through the Vancouver Health system. I've checked...

Duane says, Mandalay, I don't know if I agree that this is the way to go.

Of course it's the way to go. Owen should be at home. He should be at home, where he grew up, with her there to give him security, support. That is clear.

She knows she's talking too quickly. The meeting slot is so short, for a decision like this. And she's had too little sleep and too much coffee, and too much is at stake for her. For Owen.

Have you thought about what you would like? the hospital administrative rep, Lisa, asks. She has a good manner; she talks to Owen as to a fully-abled adult. But perhaps she asks too many questions of him, too quickly. Have you thought about the pros and cons? And do you have a preference?

Mandalay squeezes her son's hand again. Give him strength to follow the topic, she thinks. To articulate his preference. She knows he will want to be home, out of an institution. She will fight for him. It's just that his speech is not there yet.

She says: Owen, it's going to be a hospital full of elderly people who have just had hip replacements. It's too far out of the city. I won't be able to visit very often.

Duane says: What I'm thinking is this private rehabilitation facility. It's set up to do everything Owen needs.

He has brochures. He produces them from his briefcase.

Lisa says: That is a very good place. It's expensive, of course, but it's probably the best, for sports rehabilitation.

We can pay for it, Duane says, firmly.

I'm happy to go with public health, Mandalay says, equally firmly. It's done fine so far.

Mandalay, Duane says.

And she knows; she knows. He has gone over this more than once.

How it is the private therapists that Duane has paid for who have helped Owen most, in the hospital. How the best cervical spine specialist in North America was flown in to do the surgery, and that's why it was successful. (Max Gibbons had paid for that.) How right from the beginning, it was Duane's promptness in kneeling on the ice and doing CPR on Owen that had saved him from permanent, irreversible brain damage, because it took so damned long for the medical attendants in the arena to respond.

But it's still an institution. Owen needs to be at home, with his own things around him, with his family. The facility is just another hospital. Owen will be surrounded by strangers, staff and other patients. And the facility isn't close, for her, either. It's three bus rides.

Mandalay, Duane says. You can't take it on. And the house isn't set up for a wheelchair. The doorways won't be wide enough. The bathroom... I can't even start.

She can't believe that Duane isn't on board with this. That he is not supporting her. That he is siding with the institution, trying to put a barrier between her and her son.

Old resentments flare up now into her heart and throat. She is the one who *knows* Owen, who knows what nurtures him, what helps him thrive. She is the one who has been there with him the past eighteen years, or most of them, until Duane encouraged the hockey. She burns now: Duane has ever been her adversary, trying to usurp the boys on pretext of the logical, the mainstream, the authority of institutions.

The neurological therapist says, now, in a voice absurdly neutral, inhumanly matter-of-fact, that Owen himself has a preference, has a right to input.

She knows this is true. And she thinks she knows what Owen wants, but he isn't really able to articulate it, yet. The speech is not coming along as fast as she hoped.

Owen says, his head swaying slightly, his jaw working as if he has a big morsel of tough steak in his mouth: Rehab.

He says it very clearly. He must have rehearsed the syllables. Re-hab.

You'd prefer to go to a rehabilitative hospital? Lisa asks.

Owen nods. Yeah. He squeezes Mandalay's hand, doesn't look at her.

The physiotherapist says: The facility your dad is thinking of is a good one, Owen. It has a physio centre right in it, with a spa and pool and a hoist and exercise rooms. Individual rooms, twenty-four-hour on-call care.

Owen nods. He nods emphatically, clearly aware that he has to distinguish intentional from his involuntary movement.

This is what you want, Owen? Duane asks.

Yeah, Dad, Owen says.

MANDALAY WORKS FOR HOURS, driven by a furious compulsion to clean out her house: she piles boxes and bags of the boys' things, outgrown clothing, books, toys, on her front walk to be taken away by a charity pickup service. She scrubs; she polishes. Duane, visiting for one of his now infrequent dinners says that the house is looking rejuvenated. He seems tired, of late; he cooks less often, brings prepared delicacies, instead.

Then she dreams she is in one of the Asian grocery/pharmacies on East Broadway, and an elderly Chinese man in the dress of an earlier century is giving her a small celadon jar sealed with a cork and red wax. Smoke is travelling from the jar, but it is also cold to touch. She understands that the jar contains a medicated ointment for her hands. It's a good counter-irritant, the elderly Chinese man, who is a doctor, tells her. But don't eat it! Very poisonous!

She dreams that she uses the ointment, and discovers that she is no longer angry. Just like that. The anger has left, somehow, been swept away, with no residue. She feels calm hopeful even. Equanimous. When she really wakes up, she has to wonder if the anger has really left her. It's a mystery.

WHAT'S THIS? Mandalay asks.

It's a deed of gift. Duane says. For my half of the house.

What do you mean?

It's all yours now.

She can't make sense of what he's saying. Why? she asks.

He shrugs. I don't need it. You do. I've realized… there are things I should take care of now.

She feels suspicion bloom in her. She's known Duane a long time, now. They've been in this uncertain partnership for twenty years. They've been together longer than most married couples.

Okay, she says. And it's in trust for the boys, or something?

No, Mandalay. It's yours. You own it outright. You'll have to pay the taxes. But you can do anything with it you like.

She still can't process it.

Thank you, she says, finally. It doesn't seem enough of a response, but she has been caught unawares, and she just knows there is something behind Duane's sudden benevolence that she is not seeing.

You won't have a large pension, he says. Seeing as you started your career so late. But this will help you manage, if you don't do anything stupid.

Duane has such an empathetic way of putting things.

I've got funds set up for the boys, he says. For their education and so on. Not trust funds. They'll have to work. But there will be funds to help them buy their first condos. They'll need it, in this city.

She literally doesn't know what to say. That's very generous, Duane, she manages. She's conscious of strange emotions: confusion perhaps is the most noticeable. She understands neither Duane's gesture nor her own reaction.

Duane grins, his old ironic grin, his expression too amused, too self-satisfied to be truly malevolent, but too cold to be friendly. She looks at him, the breadth of him in his leather jacket, which is kind of a carapace; the creased heavy skin of his cheeks and neck;

the shining bald head. He looks like a Bond villain, as much as anything.

Old walrus, old villain.

But she also imagines, involuntarily, his body holding hers.

Demon lover. He will always use his ramparts of money to wall her in, to wall her out. He loves what she loves: the beauty of the world, of the senses. But he also loves, in his not-so-secret heart, to have her in his debt.

And perhaps she is not adverse to that. Perhaps she likes it, in her secret self.

She can afford to like it; she has the luxury of liking it, because she is free. In herself, she is free.

SHE TELLS AIDAN, on the phone.

Yeah, Aidan says. Dad likes doing things for people.

Is there a note of criticism in his voice? Toward Duane, or toward herself?

She tells Owen, visiting him in the rehab hospital.

Damn, he says. I was going to buy you a house. With the royalties to my biopic.

I know, Owen, she says. (Don't show pity. Don't show in any way that she thinks he is damaged, lesser.) But as I have a house, now, she says, maybe you can buy me a car.

You'll have to get your licence.

I'm planning to do that.

Really? You want me to teach you how to drive?

Do you think I don't know how to drive? Owen, I've been driving since I was fourteen.

Yeah, he says. Well. You still might need to learn some things.

No doubt, she says.

Are you going to quit your job?

Quit? she says. And do what?

Do your art full time.

It hasn't occurred to her that she could do that. I still need to live, she says. Groceries, taxes, all of that. But maybe she could.

She could have a studio in the basement. A real studio. Give classes, sell her work. Her long-term basement tenants are leaving, having completed their degrees. They're heading to grad school. They have become a true couple, these two young persons who have made their home in her basement suite for the past few years. They are moving into their adult lives. She could turn the suite into a studio.

Or she could keep it as a suite for one of the boys. Owen, maybe. It has outside access. Owen could manage it. He's close to leaving the rehabilitation hospital, now, though still not completely able on stairs. He could move into the suite.

Or Aidan could live with her, pay rent. Aidan is coming back to the city; he is transferring schools, programs. He doesn't want to do pre-law, he says, or law. He doesn't want to live back east. He has proven that he can, and now he doesn't want to. He had arranged a phone call with both her and Duane, at the same time, and Duane had not reacted at all to his news. Mandalay could tell that Aidan was as surprised as she was. She could hear that Aidan was bracing himself for Duane's angry reaction, which never came. Duane had just said, That's fine, that's fine, Aidan, and gone on to make suggestions about booking a flight back to Vancouver.

Aidan could live in the basement suite, and have privacy. And Owen could live with her upstairs. She could have a ramp built to the back door. A temporary ramp. Owen is getting stronger and stronger.

YOU SHOULD SELL, Cleo says. There's going to be a rezoning application and a mass offer. The block has already been half bought up, haven't you noticed? It's not public knowledge yet. A developer is going to buy up the whole block, and put up a big complex. Aeolus is designing it. You'll be getting an offer soon, on your place. But I could start looking for a condo for you now. Do you want to stay in the same general neighbourhood?

Mandalay has noticed the houses changing owners, renters moving in. The lawns getting weedy, the paint on stairs and porch railings starting to peel, the roof shingles curling, wood rotting in the perennial rain. And on her square block, at least three houses boarded up.

She feels the tug of her richly-layered, lived-in, almost organic house. She thinks about the way the light refracts greenly through the foliage outside her windows. How the shadows of the maple leaves splash purple-grey over the wide moldings of her fireplace wall, at a particular point in the afternoon. How she wakens to birdsong. The patina of the floors, the bubbles of air in the glass fanlight, the sense that her house is rooted deep, deep into the earth, and she by extension rooted also.

What if I don't want to sell?

Why wouldn't you sell? You'll get market value. You'll be able to buy a really nice unit.

I like having a yard. I like this neighbourhood.

It's all going to be built up in high-rises. And you don't garden.

I might.

These old houses aren't energy or space efficient. They're an environmental nightmare, really.

Mandalay knows this; she's not uninformed. It's just the idea that she could be forced. I was thinking of having a new entrance built, she says, and an accessible suite for Owen.

I wouldn't put any more money in, Cleo says, darkly. Anyway, you could have all of that in a condo. There are new condos, built for accessibility. And with gyms and pools and spas and so on.

But Cleo is keeping *her* house, Mandalay thinks, a little bitterly.

But I don't think a developer should be able to force me to sell my house, Mandalay says.

It won't be a developer, Cleo says. It'll be construction noise and zoning changes and mandated repairs and taxes. And your neighbours. The developers have already bought up half the houses on the block. They'll just rent them out, fill them with the kind of renters who don't mow the grass or pick up garbage, who have loud parties and deal drugs. The developers will just sit there until you get tired. But I get it. It's the principle of the thing, right?

Yeah, Mandalay says.

You could scale down, Cleo says. Buy something smaller, out of the city. Invest the difference, live off the interest.

Would that be feasible? She doesn't know enough about it.

Anyway, Cleo says. Smart move on Duane's part. His income is so high, he'll lose half of what he makes on the sale of the house to taxes. But for you, it's a primary residence, so you won't have to pay that.

She hadn't thought about it that way.

She could just sell the house. The boys are ready to live on their own. She could get rid of all of her possessions and travel for months at a time. On her own, this time, rather than as the luggage of a boyfriend. She could travel, see the best art collections of the world, be inspired by new cities and landscapes. She could go anywhere she wanted.

CLEO SEES HIM IN THE stream of passengers coming out of Arrivals. It's an hour since his flight landed, but he would have to have gone through customs and collected his bags, and she has been sanguine, waiting. She sees him now, a man in a grey jacket and glasses, a little over average height, neither lean nor chubby, neither ugly nor handsome. For a second or two she is able to see him like that, in a purely objective way, and then he slides into the familiar, and that is that.

He has an awful lot of luggage. It's a good thing, Cleo thinks, that she has brought her suv. He'd never have managed all of that on the airport connector and the Skytrain. She watches him; he looks relaxed, calm, is scanning the crowd. She sees the instant that he notices her: the change of something in his expression. Something subtle; a focussing of attention. Only she would notice it.

He moves through the concourse at the same pace as the crowd, glancing away from her to mark his position, the space his bags and trolley are taking up amid the crowd.

When he gets near, he says, simply: Cleo.

Karsten, she says.

CLEO AND KARSTEN are at a corner table in a restaurant. They have consumed food of some sort. There is lighting. There is décor. There are wait staff and other customers. These are all peripheral, barely registered. They make frequent, protracted eye contact. They smile. They touch hands, intentionally.

This is sexual tension, Cleo recognizes. Also more, perhaps. Yes, more. She feels that she is standing in a river; she has waded into this river. It is a warm river, energetic that will carry her delightfully for some time – possibly, even, for the rest of her life. She has only to wade in further, to plunge in, and she will have given herself over to the river. She can feel the current pulling at her now; it is insistent, but she has not yet given herself over to it. It is not inevitable that she will do so. But once she gives herself to it, it will feel inevitable; it will feel as though she has lost control to it. She will have been swept away.

She is not in it yet; she is on the brink, merely, feeling the tug of the current. She still has a choice. She recognizes that. At this stage, she still may choose. She must choose to let go. She will not be swept away until she chooses, but once she does, it will feel as though she has no more choice. The energy of the river will carry her along. For better or worse, she will no longer be as free as she is at this moment to choose.

She thinks: How do men and women come together in our fifties, when we are so guarded, when we have so much to lose, when we can foresee every bad outcome, and know full well that there are yet things that we do not imagine? When we have spent our adult lives removing drama and obstacles to a peaceful existence, when we have finally begun to know ourselves well enough to have fine-tuned our control over the detail of our lives, how do we venture to open ourselves to another person?

She holds eye contact with Karsten; she lets her hand rest in his; she curls her fingers into his, responding to the message of his hand.

He is a stranger, of course. She has known him for several years, but spent only a matter of weeks with him, and she suspects what she knows is mostly superficial. It is as if he is a building that she has been standing outside for a little while. She has walked around him, taken his measure, peeped through some windows, but she has not ventured inside. Likewise, she is a building that Karsten is approaching – with curiosity, with good intentions, with something like tenderness, even, but still, only approaching.

The surest thing that she knows about him is that when others say *We shouldn't*, he thinks: *We should*.

There are practical concerns. The plan is that Karsten will spend six weeks with her this fall, and then in the spring of the new year, maybe in March 2020, she will go live with him in Denmark for six weeks. Or so they have planned.

She may still decide. The current is pulling at her; her brain chemistry and her conditioning and even her hormones – she must still have hormones? – are all pulling at her, inviting her into the river, which, they are telling her, is one of deep delight, of transcendent pleasure. But it is still her decision. She is not yet in the current.

KARSTEN COMES IN with a newspaper and a bag from the bakery. It's a Saturday. Olivia is sleeping in; Sam and Christian have gone out for a bike ride. Cleo at her laptop hears Karsten's key in the lock, his shoes being removed, the paper rustling. His keys jingling onto the hook by the door. The rustle of his jacket, the closet door, the swing of the hanger, closet door again. He walks into the kitchen, presses his lips to the top of her head. She feels the rise of adrenaline and endorphins through her diaphragm, her throat: after so many weeks, she can still feel this.

Coffee? Karsten asks, and moves to the espresso machine that takes up a little too much of the countertop. He washes his hands; he decants and grinds beans; he measures, tap, tap; clicks the little cup into its place. *Globe* or *Province* first? he asks. Apricot or sour cherry pastry, or do you want to split both? He doesn't call them Danish, and finds it hilarious that Canadians do. He's addicted to Canadian newspapers, and buys print copies on the weekend, though he reads his Danish newspapers online, as he continues to work for his company online.

Cleo looks up from her laptop. The rise of pleasure. She feels her face softening. He is an ordinary-looking man, neither especially handsome or repulsive, she knows. She knows that it is her own brain that is conditioned to feel pleasure at his appearance. (She cannot get past how handsome he is.)

Two more minutes, she says. Just need to send this email.

It's a little more than two minutes, of course. Karsten puts the coffee mug beside her, gently, one of a set of little white espresso mugs that they bought together on West Fourth. He touches her shoulder, moves away.

She closes her laptop. It can wait. Work can wait. She takes Karsten's hand and holds it, even while he is taking his seat at the counter next to her.

She feels such intense complete nourishing joy swell in her that she thinks she will suffocate on it and die.

She had not thought. She had not thought.

She had not thought that such happiness in another human being would come her way again.

She had worried about what he would do here, in Vancouver, for six weeks. He has his work, of course. He's been making contacts, here: he's interested in a new type of building material, a laminated wood that is strong enough that high-rises may be built from it. It's an old idea become new, a renewable resource, a carbon sink, an alternative to concrete, which is problematic in many ways.

But how would it be for him living here? she had worried.

He has made himself at home, and she sees that it is one of his gifts to find a comfortable connection with his environment. He has bought them both e-bikes, and with her and on his own, he has been exploring the city. She has shown him her favourite spots, the sea wall and the park with its lush rainforest; the Asian markets, the museum on campus, the beaches. He is in love with the Pacific Ocean. He is in love with Asian and South Asian food and paddleboards and galleries and buildings old and new. He is in love with the quality of light, with coffee at an outside café in December. He reads the newspapers to find things to talk about and things to do. He has gone to a meeting to discuss the housing crisis.

And he is in love with Cleo's house. He understands her house. He treats it adoringly, running his hands over its wood surfaces, ordering Danish oils online, bringing in flowers.

He lies on the large sheepskin rug at the foot of the granite fireplace and plays music. For her. For the house.

So she can rationalize her union with Karsten, the felicity of it. But what she feels, even now, is not something that can be rationalized. It is something else.

She wonders if she can trust it; she admits to herself that she hasn't had to test it. Her relationship with Karsten is of a sort that she had not had to weigh emotion against rationality: that is the felicity. She recognizes that she has thoughts that are not rational – mostly a self-congratulatory thought that she has deserved this happiness, earned it, through making wise choices.

She has learned from her mistakes; she has made better decisions; she has found herself now with Karsten, whose demands on or expectations of her, whose habits and opinions and general modus operandi do not impinge on her comfort or sense of propriety, her desires, her other relationships, her sense of self. She vacillates between feeling that she has deserved it and worrying that she has not deserved it.

He understands and wants what she is, what she has to offer. It is miraculous. She has found a partner who wants what she has to give, and gives what she wants and needs. He does not feel compelled to cross her or mock her or demand of her what she is not suited to give.

It is like a new infant, this happiness. She is aware of it, constantly. She marvels that it has come into being. She worries about its nurture and preservation. She is conscious that she must not suffocate it or thwart its growth with too much attention.

Karsten's visit is nearly over. He'll return home to Denmark in a few days, and she won't see him until March. *March 2020*, she thinks. They are going to try this thing, this intercontinental romance.

But today she will be aware of the moment, the actual moment, that she is in: all of its forces and balances, what it contains. The pure existence of this moment that has been both constructed and happened upon, which is perfect, complete, in its entirety, lacking nothing, requiring nothing of her but to apprehend it, in the present, with her whole being.

KARSTEN IS WONDERING, now, if she would like to go see an open house on the North Shore. It is by an architect they both find interesting, challenging. They could take their e-bikes; they could have lunch somewhere, make a day trip of it.

Yes, she says. Yes, she would like that. She had not thought of it before now, but she would like it. It is precisely what she would like to do.

Karsten offers her the newspaper and takes a seat beside her. She lets her hand rest on his, for a moment, before she opens the paper. She will look at the political news, both domestic and global, and the economic news, and she will look at the news of arts and letters. She will take all of these things in.

But first, she will close her eyes. She will draw a deep breath. She will feel the place that she is in; she will focus on this day, its shared pleasure.

40

WE SHOULD COOK ONE LAST BIG DINNER before we have to pack up the kitchen, Mandalay says.

Yes, yes, Owen says. Great idea. We'll do it.

Aidan looks at her quizzically. This is a new expression, for Aidan. There's a reserve; that's how she would have to describe it. A holding back of a part of his thoughts and feelings that did not used to be in his repertoire. You sure, Mom? You really want to do that?

She is sure. It will hold up the packing and cleaning out for a few more hours, that is all.

We need to say goodbye properly to the house, she says.

The boys both nod. Neither seems to be having much of a reaction to the clearing out, to the fact that in a few days the house in which they grew up will be empty and ready for demolition. They don't seem to be having any pangs of nostalgia, at all. Both of them, though, have been solicitous of her, behaving as though she must be fragile, disoriented, full of regrets.

We should invite your dad, as well, she says.

They both look pleased.

Owen says: I'll go pick him up. Save him the drive.

Aidan says: He likes to drive. He doesn't like to be driven.

They are solicitous of Duane, too — but are more careful not to let it show, Mandalay thinks.

Aidan looks at her, as ever, for arbitration.

Just ask him, she says.

Owen says: I'll go for supplies, then. Give me a list.

He has a car, an electric car with modified controls that compensate for his two weak areas, his inability to turn his head quickly, and a left leg prone to what he calls charley horse. He's had the car two weeks, and he's happy for any excuse to drive it. It had been an extravagance of Duane's, of course, but the promise of it had sped up Owen's recovery, his motivation to do his therapy work, considerably. Even the small glitch that he had to wait a year after his last seizure – he had so many seizures, early in his recovery – to get his licence back had hardly discouraged him.

I'll make a list, Aidan says. Or god knows what you'll bring back. Mom? What do you want to cook?

She wants to cook something spectacular, messy, smelly. And not clean the kitchen after. And she wants to cook some old familiar favourite of the boys' childhoods.

She says: You choose.

But they can't choose.

She says, why don't you run down to the market, see what fresh seafood there is?

Will she spring for crab?

She will. She gets her wallet, presses cash on Owen, who, surprisingly, is the more careful with money. This might be the last time, she thinks, that I might give my sons money to go buy groceries.

They are off, in Owen's car, Owen finding it somehow necessary to squeal the tires a little pulling out from the curb.

Mandalay goes back to her packing. It is almost done, except for what they need to use until the last day. The house, stripped of artwork and books, seems smaller, scruffier. It has already withdrawn from her, she thinks. It does not feel like home.

Boxes fill the rooms. Aidan had the idea to colour-mark them – a quintessential Aidan idea. Green for everything Mandalay is keeping;

orange for Owen's things; violet for Aidan's. Fluorescent pink tape for the boxes and bags still to be donated.

What a house accumulates – what a woman and two boys accumulate, over less than twenty years in a house! And none of the three of them will have the space to simply store *stuff*. She feels that they have pared down painfully, jettisoning mementoes, scrapbooks, collections. But the boys do not want to take these things. They have already relinquished them. And though she can almost not bear to throw out their second-grade artwork, she has had to let go. (She has kept some things, though. She has some tubs.)

So it is a kind of purge that is happening, though there are so many boxes, still, of belongings to be moved.

The furniture will mostly go to a charity store – what the store will accept. (There's a certain kind of humiliation, when a charity store turns down your furniture donations.) Owen and Aidan, who are moving into an apartment with accessibility enhancements near the university, don't want any of it. They've bought new things, ultra modern. Disposable things, Mandalay thinks, but doesn't say.

The twins will live together, mutually supporting each other, Mandalay hopes.

Mandalay herself is moving out of the city. She has bought a piece of land. It is too far to commute, and she has taken a year's leave from her job while she works out what she wants to do about that. But she believes she will come back. (You can rent from us, Aidan and Owen say. You can rent a room from us during the week, when you are in town teaching.)

She has bought a piece of land far from the city, with a small house on it – a very small, old house, which she will probably have to rebuild, because it is leaky and drafty and not fire safe enough to get insurance. A small house, though, where she can live. Where, in fact an elderly couple lived, until recently, and where, reportedly, they raised four children, so in theory, it should be enough for Mandalay.

The property comes with a big insulated and wired garage, which is in considerably better condition than the house, and which will make a grand studio. She has bought a truck, belonging to the couple, as well: she will need to get her driver's licence. She has got her "N" already, passing the written test without difficulty. And Owen says he will buy her a dog, a big dog, to protect her in her retreat from civilization. (She says that she doesn't need a dog; she has Clytemnestra.)

It is not so far from civilization, though. It is perhaps twenty kilometers from a town, the town where Mandalay went to high school, in fact. And not too far from the house in which she grew up, where Cliff is going to live, now, with their mother. Next door, in fact, in rural terms.

In her new home, she will be alone. This will be something to get used to. She will get to know people; perhaps buyers will come to see her prints. She will give classes.

First, she will do her retreat in Baton Rouge, or rather on a bayou near the city. In spring of 2020, she'll finally go to Baton Rouge. She'll travel.

And after that, she'll live alone. She will have to develop her own resources, to find in herself her own consolation, her own encouragement, her own will to create and *be*.

The world has changed for her, she realizes, suddenly. She feels grounded, full of good will and optimism, but the world has shifted. It has rotated, has adjusted itself, clicked into a new track. It's not just the gift of the house. It's the fact of the gift, that Duane would do this for her.

It is a little difficult, still, to understand that.

Things will change for all of them, in the new year.

Her sons return, in not too long a space, with the provisions they have bought, and also with their father, who has, after all, accepted a ride. Now he sits, Duane, her lover, her enemy, her partner, wrinkled, a little shrunken, in a chair, directing the cooking of the crab, the making of the wilted lettuce salad and the rolls. In this house in which he has never lived, Duane watches, not always benevolently, as his sons attempt to follow his directions.

Duane is at the doorway to old age, she thinks. (Aidan has told her that Duane has pain, acute joint pain. That Duane does not like to speak of it.) He moves a little stiffly. He is quieter, less vigorous, in his interactions. He does not have the same zest for violent expostulation.

These changes come to all of us.

She and Duane are joined for life, now, in their shared sons. They have tried to exclude and contain each other, but their lives will always be connected, and in the recognition of this, she thinks, they both have at last learned to live with peace between them.

Duane has bought the boys an apartment, or more precisely, an apartment for them to live in. (No sense them renting from someone else, he says; they can pay him rent.) It is not a nominal rent. She is not sure she supports the arrangement, but it is not her business anymore. The building and the apartment have good disability access. The apartment has been specially built for a wheelchair, with wider doors and hallways and lower countertops, with a special shower. She had not known places like that existed. They will live together there, at least for the next few years. Owen will continue to work on his recovery, and re-take some courses. He hopes to become a physiotherapist. Aidan has decided to transfer from the university back east, and to change directions. He wants to become an architect; he will take a fine arts degree first.

Duane had not even blinked at that announcement.

It is good that Aidan and Owen will live together. Aidan will be challenged; he will have to learn to draw lines around his own desires, to protect his own interests. And Owen will learn to nurture, rather than simply fight. She hopes.

They have each a long road ahead, her sons. She hopes they will love the journey. At least it is being made as easy as possible for them. She has come to believe that it is not wrong, to try to purchase ease.

She sits at the table across from Duane, watching him while he calls into being this last supper. She feels tender toward Duane. A sort of gentle, friendly compassion. A well-wishing. She feels that she can see him in his entirety, see him whole and accept him, without anger or fear or longing. He has, in the end, given her what he had to give. What more can she ask? It is enough, enough.

41

CLIFF'S BODY HAS STIFFENED, even in the first couple of hours of driving, and the first few steps onto the beach are excruciating. The hinges of his knees are locked, his feet solid unresponsive blocks, his hip joints wobbly in their sockets, his spine compressed into something the size and rigidity of an umbrella shaft.

He stops out of necessity, flexes his knees, bends over at the waist to let his torso hang down. His arms dangle; his hands tingle with returning circulation. His fingers reach for the earth. He imagines someone holding him up by his heels, as if he were a newborn: his bones extending, his joints claiming space, his lungs expanding.

He can just hang out here for a moment.

At his feet, the beach stones take on definition: shiny black, quartz white, speckled, greenish, reddish, yellow-brown. They've been ground and polished to flattish ovals, mostly, ranging in size from the length of the top joint of his thumb down to the size of quail's eggs. They slide over each other easily, lie loose and responsive to whatever passes over them. His hands are lightly cupped: they look as if they're waiting to be filled with rain. He can feel his chest expand against his thighs, and relax, and expand again. His head is a pendulum, a tetherball, a fat jug of wine on a string.

Light crunching on the gravel: the boy draws near, shadow, feet. He bends over, mimicking Cliff's position. What are you doing? Oscar asks.

Stretching out my joints, Cliff says.

The boy laughs and bends over and effortlessly puts the palms of his hands flat on the stones. Cliff feels, within his stiff frame, the ghost of his own child-body, the lightness, the fluidity.

He straightens up, palms to thighs, engaging his core muscles. He has to use his arms as counterweights to swing himself up. His vertebrae find their places, stack themselves, more comfortably than before. There.

Hey, Oscar, he says to the boy. Let's explore, eh?

The boy is off like a pup, running back and forth, running circles around Cliff, stopping to peer and prod and turn objects over in his hands. They progress at the same pace, Cliff lumbering along, feeling his way, the flat oval stones sliding over each other. Each footstep has to be initiated with caution. He is a giant, a mountain troll. Crunch, crunch. The boy runs circles, stops to crouch and peer, doubles back. Cliff lumbers after him.

Cliff's knees protest at the uneven ground. They send up signals of self-doubt: they do not know if they can hold him up. His body is like a log balanced on two stumps.

If I were a car, Cliff thinks, I'd tow myself to the wreckers.

They walk back along the beach a little and Cliff sits, lowering himself onto the gravel, where there's a driftwood log to lean against. He won't be able to sit for long. The stones are hard, and there's damp below the surface. The log isn't high enough to support his back, and the beach is sloped, his legs not able to prop him.

Oscar crouches a little distance away, squatting, his stick arms and legs folded like a paper clip, his centre of gravity balanced over the feet in his tan sandals.

The boy says nothing. He pokes at the rocks, withdraws his fingers when he sees the wet undersides, begins turning them over.

Do you want to wade? Cliff asks. We could look for starfish.

The boy shakes his head.

Okay, Cliff says. That's okay.

After a minute the boy gets up. Cliff watches him out of the corner of his eye. He can't tell: is Oscar young enough to fall into the water and drown? He looks old enough to have the common sense not to. But Cliff can't be sure, can he?

The boy runs in a little circle, looks back at Cliff. He picks up a stick. He drags the stick along the water's edge. He squats there, jumping back a little as the waves brush his toes. He looks back at Cliff.

Cliff nods, doesn't make a move.

He keeps the boy in his peripheral vision, lies down on the stones. His back protests and then relaxes. It would be great if he could invert himself, lie with his head pointing down toward the waves, his feet higher, but assuming he could get himself into that position in the first place, he has no idea how he would get up again. Besides, if he lies down, he'll fall asleep.

But he must have dozed, because suddenly the boy is bending over him, in his face.

Do you have a bag? he asks.

What for?

My rock collection.

He has filled the front of his T-shirt with polished oval stones.

Cliff takes off his cap and the boy pours his collection in, a small avalanche, the satisfying clicking sound.

HE HAD NOT PLANNED to bring the boy along.

He'd planned to leave the day before, in fact. He'd wrapped up his business with the lawyers and the bank, packed everything he owned, except for the few big pieces – his bed, his recliner, his desk, which he'd shipped – in the back of his pickup truck. His apartment empty, ready for him to leave.

It had taken him half a year to come to that decision, and then only a couple of weeks to wrap things up.

The first thing was Cleo and Mandalay giving him the house, the property, at Butterfly Lake. He hadn't understood it, but when Cleo went to the lawyers, after Ben had gone and cut down those trees, she had found out that it had been theirs all along — that their father had set up some sort of trust, likely because of Crystal's mental illness, Cleo had said. So: it belonged to Cleo and Mandalay and him, not Crystal. And not Ben, because of the adoption. He and Mandalay had thought that Ben should be included, morally, even if not legally, but Cleo had said that Ben's adoptive parents were far wealthier than they, and Ben would never be in need.

And then Cleo had said — they had all been sitting around Mandalay's old battered dining table — Cleo had said, I don't need my share. Cliff, I'm giving it to you. And Mandalay had nodded, which made it clear that the two of them had already discussed it. They had discussed it and fixed it up between them, as they always did, those sisters of his, before they talked to him.

Mandalay had made them all dinner — some curry and lentil thing, which was typical fare you got at Mandalay's, unless her boyfriend Duane did the cooking, but it was good. Her cooking was always good. They'd sat at the table, just the three of them, the late sun slanting through those bubbled single-glass panes, making the old wood trim and table and floors glow, even through the ingrained dirt. He hadn't seen either of them for a few months, at that point, and now he saw that Cleo was thinner than before, and had lines around her eyes and lips that he could see in the slanting sunlight, and some white in her carefully streaked and styled hair, and Mandalay looked ten years older, her long hair threaded liberally with silver, her eyes pouched, her middle thickening. It had unnerved him, his sisters showing age.

It'll be yours, Cleo had said. On the condition that you promise to live there and take care of Crystal.

He had balked, at first. At moving out of the city. He'd said, first: I can't. My business is here.

Are you working much? Cleo had asked, and he'd been angry, then. He'd gone home angry, saying he wouldn't take it; he wouldn't be pushed into it. Angry at the thought of his two sisters conniving, plotting his life out, as usual.

Then, when he'd got home, let himself into his dingy place, he'd reconsidered. He'd thought again. He'd thought of the place at Butterfly Lake, how peaceful it was there. The trees.

And then he had realized: he could sell his share in his business, now. He did not need it, now, to feel like he was somebody.

He had called the Singh brothers, and they'd sat down with him, and they'd all together come up with a sum that seemed reasonable to him, and he'd taken it. Maybe he should have had a lawyer, but he'd thought it was reasonable, and he'd taken it, and it would give him a little nest egg, and without the rent on his apartment, he figured, he could manage on his disability. And maybe even pick up some work around Butterfly Lake, he'd thought. Something casual. Something that gave him a few hundred extra a month. If his back held out, he could pick up some landscaping work.

He would move back up there, he had decided. He had given the city his best shot but he was done with it now. He'd go back to Butterfly Lake, live in the house, fix it up. He'd keep Crystal with him as long as he could. With Maria and Delores to help.

He had sold his share in the business, had packed and shipped his stuff. At the last minute he had called Tammy, Oscar's grandmother, to let her know he was moving away, and to make sure he could stay in touch with Oscar.

Tammy had sounded pissed off. Who's going to look after Oscar when I go on my holidays?

He wasn't sure what she meant. Did she think they had an arrangement? Through her grumbling, he'd managed to put together some kind of a story. Ben was supposed to take Oscar for a couple of weeks, but had bailed. She'd phoned Cleo and Mandalay, but one was not answering, the other too busy.

Who looks after me? Tammy had demanded.

She's losing her marbles, he had thought.

I guess I'll call social services to take him for a break, she said. Though I am not sure if I'll get him back. They don't like you to take holidays. It's like you're expected to work twenty-four-seven. Everybody else is allowed to have a holiday.

Cliff had said, not believing she'd take him up on it, that he could look after Oscar. Do you have a spare suitcase? he'd asked. Can you pack up some toys and clothes? Not believing she was serious.

So he had waited one more day, and had gone to pick up Oscar. Tammy had not only packed a suitcase, but wanted him to take toys and blankets and other stuff. She had put Oscar's things in some big green trash bags, which seemed disrespectful. He took everything, because he didn't know what the boy would need, what he was attached to.

Or maybe because he, Cliff, knew he wasn't going to bring Oscar back.

Cliff had asked Tammy to give him Oscar's ID. He didn't know what kind of ID a little kid has, but there must be something, he thought.

Just in case, he had said.

He must have known.

Oscar himself seemed resigned, not upset, at the prospect of going away with Cliff. Cliff had been careful to ask him if he was willing to go, but Tammy had spoken for him. Of course he is. Of course he recognizes his uncle Cliff. The boy had said nothing, but had climbed into Cliff's truck willingly.

The first thing Cliff had realized was that he hadn't thought about some lunch for the boy. Cliff had some hard rye bread and cheese along, a couple of non-alcoholic beers, a few apples — all that he had in his fridge when he cleared out that morning. He doubted Oscar would be able to eat it, the dry tough bread, the cheese with its caraway seeds. Cliff had not liked it, when he had been given it, at the same age, at his foster parents', though he enjoys it now. The boy said he wasn't hungry, or more accurately, shook his head when Cliff asked if he was, but Cliff had spent time with him before, and also with his sisters' children, and he knew that a child's hunger can arrive full-blown, in an instant. Likewise a full bladder.

After the first ferry, he had pulled into a gas station, loaded up on the healthiest things he could find that could be eaten on the road, cheese strings and fruit cups and juice boxes. Puddings. They had macaroni and cheese in Styrofoam cups but he has no way to heat it. He had told Oscar to use the restroom, then realized he needed to let him in. The door was too heavy. He had stood outside listening: the sound of peeing, the flush. He had said: Wash your hands.

They had time, then, before the next ferry, and he had remembered the beach.

OSCAR RUNS AND CLIFF LUMBERS after him, his spine and hips and knees getting a workout on the uneven ground.

The sky and sea meet, cream and grey and wrinkled slate blue, a distance offshore. The distance can't be judged. The detail of waves is blurred. There's no perspective on which the brain may pin an estimate of distance. Closer in, the glistening amber-coloured bulbs of the bull kelp bob; the long kelp stipes and blades dampen the waves, and the surface is smoother, calmer, inside their floating band.

The beach curves in a mosaic of greys. Above the beach, the towering dark green of cedars. The smell is salt and kelp and resin. And rot, but a clean rot. He can hear the click and hiss of the gravel shifting under the waves, the pulse of it. Somewhere, a raven rolling out one of its seventeen varieties of calls. Glaucous-backed and herring gulls mewl in different pitches. Over top, a shrill peeping.

Ahead on the beach a flock of finch-sized sandpipers are stabbing short fine bills at a tangle of kelp the sea has disgorged. In his mind's eye Cliff sees the swarming mass of crustaceans on which they must be feeding. The sandpipers are camouflaged-printed in sand and darker sand colouring, and move in a sort of wave, disorienting the eye. Now Oscar has spotted them and runs toward them with a shout, waving his arms. The sandpipers lift off and wheel as one. Land a few metres ahead. Oscar runs toward them again, and they lift and settle again, a few metres ahead, again.

Why don't they just circle back to their feast? Or fly further, put more distance between themselves and the child?

Again.

It's as if they are luring the boy down the beach.

Ahead is a tongue of basalt outcropping. If Oscar tops that, Cliff will lose sight of him. He calls to him. Oscar turns, runs back. The sandpipers rise again like a wave and settle again to their feasting.

They squat at the edge of a pool in the rocky outcropping. The names of things come back to Cliff, either from his own childhood or from the nature shows he watched obsessively through his twenties: eel grass, bladderwrack, sculpin, limpet. Mussel, periwinkle, anemone, whelk. A snail moving more quickly than the others, and Cliff puts his hand into the pool, snatches it up, opens the fist to show the boy. A pair of claws, one larger than the other, and a face with stalked eyes emerge. The creature scuttles across Cliff's palm, and the boy squeals in surprise.

A crab, Cliff says, who has decided to live in a snail's shell.

The boy makes pincers with thumb and forefinger, begins to tug. Oh, no, no, no, Cliff says. He's hooked in there good. You'll tear out his innards.

The boy's face.

It's okay, Cliff says. We'll get a net on a handle. We'll explore more. We'll go to the beach lots.

He remembers now the patio set from his old townhouse, which is still in storage. He will rebuild the deck, at Butterfly Lake, and everyone who visits can enjoy it, sitting out on summer evenings with the bats. He'll invite Elise, the forestry person, to come by for a meal. She seems the kind of woman who has a good grip on the earth. He thinks of her boots rooted in the forest floor, her strong, beautifully formed hands, her hair, her eyes when she said the names of indigenous plants.

On the Earl's Cove ferry, they get out of the truck and stand at the railing. Cliff points out the fjords, a floatplane, a bald eagle. Oscar squints into the wind and take's Cliff's hand. An older woman smiles at them.

What is he doing? He is too old, too crippled up. The property at Butterfly Lake is too wild, too rough, for a small child. The house is falling apart. There are bears and cougars in the woods. Crystal is too addled. He tries to imagine Crystal through Oscar's eyes. And what will Maria and Delores think about a small boy underfoot? He can't afford to upset the women who care for Crystal.

But nothing to be done now.

It occurs to him that he might have done something very dubious, even illegal, in taking Oscar. He gets out his phone, calls his sister Cleo.

She says: Oh, Cliff. Then: It's probably for the best. I'll let Marlene know.

Marlene is Ben's adoptive mother, Cliff remembers.

Then Cleo says: You'll probably have to take on Ben, too, you know.

Yeah. He'll have to take on Ben. That's the cost of saving Oscar.

There's a laugh in her voice. And that is it. Something is different about Cleo, lately: as if she's younger, freer.

So is it okay, what he has done?

It'll be okay, Cleo says.

The ferry ploughs on through the sea, its white paint sparkling in the sun. Oscar asks if the ferry is an ocean liner. He points out to Cliff the lifeboats on swings, the gleaming rails, the seagulls and riveted windows. Where is this boat going? he asks.

It's carrying us up the channel, Cliff says. When we get off, we will be in a different place.

In the truck again, only half an hour left of their journey, Oscar falls asleep, wrapped in Cliff's jacket, and for a few moments Cliff forgets him. The highway rises; the trees grow taller, the forest thicker. A strange large bird wheels overhead, so high that Cliff can't identify it.

He'd have been about Oscar's age when he left Butterfly Lake, against his own will, against his mother's will. He's coming back now, not without trepidation. What will he do, in this dark lonely place? Who will he be? A deep primeval fear of the woods, of the dark, of lonely places, fills him.

He'll fix up the house. He'll take care of Crystal and Oscar.

He has given the city his best shot. He sees now that he can leave it and he will not become nothing. He will still know who he was. He will still be connected. It is inside of him, the gleaming, thriving, fast-moving city. It had tried to chew him up and spit him out, but he has it inside of him, the force and pride of it.

There in his house, on his wooded lot, he will now grow into himself. He'll put down his roots; he'll become shelter. He'll grow old and craggy, and wise. Wiser, anyway. He'll give himself to the small and vulnerable, so much as he is, in his cracked and feeble way, able.

The boy stirs and makes a small noise in his sleep.

Everything will be on Cliff's shoulders. He will make mistakes. He'll have nowhere to hide when he does. He'll have to keep his wits about him. He'll have to make better decisions. He'll have to take better care of himself. He will have to ask for help.

He will fight to keep Oscar. If the boy seems happy. He'll probably have to share him, but he thinks there's something that can be done. He'll talk to Ben's adoptive parents. He knows them, from when he used to spend time with Ben, when he and Ben were friends. He has visited them, recently, in their large house near the ocean. He thinks that they like him, that they'll trust him. He'll talk to Cleo.

Maybe Oscar will want to go to the school in Butterfly Lake, the little school that Cliff went to. Cliff imagines the school being friendlier, having softer edges. The parents all knowing each other; the teachers from the community, as well. Maybe Oscar will want to have skates and Cliff will drive him to the rink in Powell River. Maybe Oscar will want to do hockey.

But maybe he won't. Maybe he will just want to mooch around, watching things on the ground, on the forest floor.

He'll have to warn him about the bears and the cougars in the woods.

The thing will be to let him be who he is. To pay attention to him, but not try to make him into something with that attention. To be attentive: to watch and listen. To let him discover on his own. To be a soft place for him to land.

He continues to drive up the road, his hands resting lightly on the steering wheel. The last stretch to home.

Oscar stirs, opens his eyes. Where are we? he asks.

We're home, Cliff says. And they are: they are now passing the sign that says Welcome to Butterfly Lake. They are passing the little subdivision of newer houses. Around the next curve will be the driveway.

This is home? Oscar asks. He has his face pressed against the side window. The trees at the roadside, alder, mostly, flutter their leaves, a million green and silver flags.

This is home, Cliff says. One of your homes, anyway.

That's what it is.

ACKNOWLEDGMENTS

Much gratitude to friends and family for whatever insights turn up in my writing, and for encouragement and conversations, dinners, walks, and cat- and dog-sitting.

Thanks to Carolyn, who read the manuscript and gave good feedback, as always.

Thanks to Anne Nothof and Meredith Thompson at NeWest for encouragement and sharp, sensitive editing.

KAREN HOFMANN grew up in the Okanagan and taught English and creative writing at Thompson Rivers University. She now lives in Victoria, BC. A collection of poetry, *Water Strider*, was published by Frontenac House in 2008 and shortlisted for the Dorothy Livesay prize. Her first novel, *After Alice*, was published by NeWest Press in 2014, and a second novel, *What is Going to Happen Next*, the first book in the Lund sibling trilogy, in 2017. A short fiction collection, *Echolocation*, was released by NeWest in 2019, and third novel, *A Brief View from the Coastal Suite*, the second book in the Lund sibling trilogy, in 2021.